Table of Contents

Bang! Bang! BOOM! [NEW YORK!]

-VOLUME 2-

By Melanie Schoen
Cover art by Del Borovic

Copyright @2020
ISBN: 978-1-7327010-2-1
All rights reserved
Printing by Ingramspark

Bang! Bang! BOOM! [New York] is a prequel novel to BBBOOM the comic, beginning ten years prior. It was originally published on Tapas.io as a free-to-read series along with Del's illustrations. For more information please visit www.bangbangboomcomic.com.

MELANIE SCHOEN AKA CROIK

Melanie has been writing as a hobbyist for over twenty years, though more recently has been publishing original novels independantly as part of the Bang! Bang! BOOM! series and outside it. When she's not writing Melanie enjoys horror films, video games, and spending time with her sister and adorable dogs.

DEL BOROVIC

Del is a professional freelance illustrator and comic artist with over a decade of experience. She graduated from SCAD with a degree in Sequential Art and her work has appeared in multiple publications and anthologies. Comics is her true love, especially emotional, character-driven works. When not drawing her arm off, Del enjoys video games, cosplay, and traveling. She loves orange.

A Foot in the Door

Cheshire Bloom was all grins as he dressed in his brand new suit coat: a handsome, double-breasted Fiscella with side vents, fresh from the tailor. The wool was a deep and earthy burnt orange with the slightest hint of a pattern, perfectly matched to the season, elevated further by a chocolate brown silk necktie and wingtips. With his hair braided back and a broad-brimmed top hat perched on his crown he was, undoubtedly, an unmissable sight.

Cheshire hummed a cheerful tune as he bounded down the stairs of his apartment building, alight with excitement for the evening ahead. By the time he reached the street his heart had begun to pound, and he took a deep breath, reminding himself there was no reason to get *that* worked up. They hadn't even started yet.

But when he came up on Jakub leaning against the car, there was no reasoning away the anxious flutter behind his ribs. They hadn't seen much of each other the past two weeks, as per the boss' orders Jakub had spent most of it recovering, and Cheshire planning his next job. The circumstance of opportunity, privacy, and courage hadn't overlapped enough yet for them to have a *real* conversation about their unexpected "encounter" following Jakub's surgery, and it was starting to put Cheshire on edge. Sooner or later they would actually have to...talk. About it. Right?

Even so, Cheshire kept up his carefree grin as he approached. When Jakub spotted him his eyebrows raised ever so slightly, but his face gave away no more than that. Cheshire tried to read a few lines from even just that much, but he had so little confidence left in his instinct. How many years had he gone without any inkling what lay beneath Jakub's surface? So instead, he relied on his usual playbook. "How do I look?"

Jakub took a breath off his cigarette, keeping Cheshire in suspense. His face didn't change. "You always look good."

Cheshire blushed; he never would have expected to get a seemingly honest compliment out of Jakub, without some excuse or stipulation, let alone could have predicted the childish thrill it gave him. "You, too," he said, finally taking in the rest of him. He straightened. "Is that a new coat?"

Jakub took another drag. His gaze had taken on a certain intensity that definitely meant *something*. "Do you like it?"

"Yes!" Without thinking Cheshire tugged at Jakub's lapel even though it was already well pressed. The wool was sturdy, rich charcoal in color with a black button-down underneath—a far cry from the drab browns and tans he usually sported. "Yes, wow, this is Fiscella's fall cut! It really suits you. I hope my friend gave you a good deal."

He fussed with the seams a moment longer, only to realize that Jakub had gone very still. Blushing darker, Cheshire withdrew a step to give him some space. "Sorry. Just, it looks really good on you."

Jakub's cheeks were also a little red as he pushed away from the car. "Miklos helped me pick it out before he went back to Jersey."

"Oh! Good man." Cheshire watched, still a little out of sorts, as Jakub moved around the hood toward the driver's side. "We're going to have to do this a lot more often so you can get the most out of it."

"Only if it works," Jakub replied.

Cheshire was about to rush to reassure him when he was interrupted by the door opening behind him, and a thick Irish accent declared, "Bloody hell, Bloom, ye're really wearing *that*?"

Cheshire spun about, but his defense died in his throat at the sight of Edward Burke walking up. Burke was also dressed in a new suit for the occasion, but tweed, olive green, with narrow blue and red striping. It might have been forgivable if not for the plain brown pants he'd paired it with. Cheshire couldn't help but wince. "*You're* one to talk."

"What?" Burke brushed past him to climb into the back seat. "You don't like it do you?"

"It doesn't even—"

"Get in the car, Bloom, or we're gonna be late."

By then Jakub was already behind the wheel, so with a roll of his eyes Cheshire took off his hat and climbed in next to him. "Are we not waiting for Hannah? I thought she was riding with us."

"Change of plans," said Burke as Jakub started the car. "She already left for the hospital—Wanda's in labor."

"Really!" Cheshire whistled and elbowed Jakub. "Sure you shouldn't be there, too?"

"Barney's already named Hannah the Godmother," said Jakub, indifferent. "I'll visit after the job."

"She's got her whole family there with her," added Burke. "They're fine. We, on the other hand, have only one shot at this."

"You don't have to tell me," retorted Cheshire. "It was *my* idea to begin with."

"It'll be fine," assured Jakub. "Your plans always manage to work out."

Cheshire glanced at him, startled by yet another rare compliment, but then his eye caught on the steering wheel. Jakub was driving mostly with his right hand, with just the thumb of his prosthetic hooked around it. Even after everything, the gleam of metal gave him a start whenever he was reminded. Still, he reassembled his charm quickly enough. "Damn right they do. And this one won't be any different."

They took the bridge into Manhattan. By the time they made their way to Midtown the afternoon was passing into evening, and the city street-goers had transitioned. Though not to the extent that they would have been in better economic times, the Manhattan sidewalks were crowded with diners and thrill-seekers, tourists and socialites. Jakub parked a few blocks down and the three of them walked the rest of the way to the immense corner building with a brilliant, glittering signboard that read: The Calypso theater.

Heads turned as they entered. After all, they were an

eye-catching trio: Cheshire brilliantly overdressed for an evening cinema; Jakub, handsome but sour-faced; Burke, a clashy disaster, chin jutting forward. Cheshire was sure he heard his name at least twice as they made their way past the box office. He smiled and laughed and shook hands with a few curious men and women along the way. As they were passing the concessions he even handed out quarters to a few men and women waiting in line. By the time they'd reached the auditorium most everyone had noticed them, and they'd even attracted a pair of familiar faces: they were met before the door by Grace Overgaard and Thea Hallorran, fabulously dressed, arm in arm.

"Same old Cheshire," Grace teased, grinning. "I had a feeling I'd see you here."

"How could I miss the world premiere when the film's practically about *us*?" replied Cheshire. He flashed Hallorran a smile. "Besides, Jakub and I promised your date we'd make the papers."

"If anything tonight is making the papers, it's definitely that hat," said Grace, noticeably declining to correct Cheshire's assumption.

"I love it," Hallorran declared. "And I want one."

"I'll introduce you to my tailor sometime."

"I'll hold you to that." Hallorran turned her attention to his companions. "Mr. Burke," she greeted before settling more decidedly on Jakub. "Mr. Danowicz. How is everything?"

"Good," said Jakub. "I'm still getting the hang of it, but..." He lifted his left hand and used it to undo the button on his suit coat. "...I'm learning."

Hallorran beamed happily. "Excellent! Very impressive for so soon. I knew you'd have it figured out in no time."

Burke cleared his throat. "Begging yer pardon, but we should be getting to our seats, yes?"

The stream of people heading into the theater was growing steadier, and making them an even more obvious obstruction. "I guess that's our cue," said Cheshire. "Enjoy the show, ladies."

"Stay out of trouble," said Grace, the slant of her eyebrows a little too knowing. She and Hallorran showed themselves inside, and Cheshire and the rest followed, picking a seat relatively close to the exit.

"The paper said the first reel starts exactly at six

o'clock," said Cheshire as he reclined, Burke and Jakub on either side. He pulled a pocket watch from the interior of his coat and checked the time. "Then it's one hour to intermission, which will be fifteen minutes give or take."

"That's a small window," said Burke, scrunching his nose up.

"It's a fine window. As long as the truck is on time, we'll be fine."

"And if it's not?"

"Then we abort," said Jakub, comparing his watch to Cheshire's. "You'll finish the movie like nothing was supposed to happen." Satisfied, each tucked their watches back into their coats. "Do you see him?"

Cheshire took off his top hat and leaned forward, scanning the room. He had never met the mysterious "Lucky," self-proclaimed boss of all Manhattan's organized gangs, but he was armed with Burke's description: tall, lanky, thick dark hair, fancy. It wasn't much help in such a large theater and he couldn't see any pockets of attendees that were drawing more than their fair share of attention.

Cheshire admitted defeat. "Eggy?"

"I don't see him," Burke said, leaning into his palm. "But he's got to be here somewhere. No way he's missing an event like this, see?"

Cheshire smirked to himself. "Well, if he does, no way he's missing the next one." He reached into the inside lining of his hat and pulled out a small bag of peanuts. He handed one to Jakub. "You're sure you're ready for this, right?"

"Of course I am." Jakub tucked the peanut into his shirt pocket, and as the theater lights began to dim, he stood. "Good luck," he said, and he slipped out of the theater before the doors were closed.

Cheshire watched him go, allowing himself a moment for worry. He had felt a great deal more blind confidence for his plan when it originated with Hannah at the lead. There was no doubting Jakub's efficiency and composure, but his current dexterity...

Burke eyed him for a while before giving him an elbow. "You can call't off anytime," he said.

"It'll be fine," Cheshire said, being careful not to make a mess as he cracked open a peanut shell. "If he says he's ready, he's ready." He settled into his chair just as the title, *Chicago Smoke*, came up on the big screen.

***

Jakub took his time making his way down 50th Street. He took in the sidewalk crowds, the amount of traffic on the streets, the number of shops still open. If Cheshire had made his plan with an audience in mind, he wouldn't be disappointed.

Jakub lit a cigarette and crossed the street to where a black and white patrol car was parked along the sidewalk. After tapping on the passenger side window three times he let himself in.

Gertie was behind the wheel, already dressed in a blue jacket and slacks. It wouldn't have passed for a standard Manhattan police uniform under close scrutiny, but at a glance it was definitely convincing. Jakub held his cigarette between his teeth as he shrugged out of his jacket to change into a "uniform" of his own. "Is everything set?"

"The girls are in position," said Gertie. "We last heard from Leon half an hour ago—the car stopped for a dinner break right on schedule."

"Leon?" Jakub frowned thoughtfully as he struggled a little getting his mechanical hand through the uniform sleeve. "Shouldn't he be with his sister? The baby's coming."

"Really?" Gertie shrugged. "Well, no way to let him know now. What good would he be to her anyway? He gonna help her push?" She gave Jakub's sleeve a tug to help him straighten it out in the small space. "Better that he's here. He keeps saying he's got to prove himself again, after..."

She cast Jakub a sideways look he didn't return. "If it's what the boss wants, fine," he said. Finally dressed, he rolled down his window just enough to flick the ash from his cigarette. "He doesn't have anything to prove to me."

"If you say so."

They settled in to wait. Jakub passed the time with his left hand on his knee, practicing different movements: clenching his fist, pointing, waving, twisting a latch. He pulled a pair of gloves out of his jacket pocket, put them on and tried again. Over and over, for the next hour. Gertie wasn't much for conversation anyway and he wanted to be ready.

When the time drew closer, Gertie leaned forward against the wheel with a pair of binoculars. By then Jakub's cigarette had long since been smoked down and he was eager for things to get underway. The moment she straightened up, his heart gave a thud.

"I see it," said Gertie, passing the binoculars to Jakub so she could start the car. "Let's hope Bloom knows what he's doing."

Jakub looked for himself, and he could barely make out past the intersection the tall, domed roof of the armored car that was heading straight for 50th and 9th. He tossed the binoculars into the back as Gertie pulled into traffic. "It'll be fine," he said, and as they neared the theater he glanced to the upper windows. "Bloom always makes it work somehow."

***

Chicago Smoke wasn't, by Cheshire's estimation, a very accurate depiction of the thrilling bootlegger lifestyle, but it sure was entertaining. He laughed along with the rest of the audience through every sharp-witted argument between its clever protagonists, oohed and ahhed over their busty shared love interest, leaned forward with excitement through the gunfight that punctuated the end of the first act. It was overblown and melodramatic but it reminded Cheshire so much of the adventure serials and radio dramas he had been addicted to as a boy. It heightened his curiosity a hundred fold for what Chicago's leading families were really like, and how closely they matched their depiction.

As soon as the lights raised for intermission, Cheshire popped out of his seat. "Incredible!" he declared. He tossed his hat into Burke's lap. "Hold onto that for me—I need to go powder my nose."

"Don't take too long, okay?" said Burke, doing an admirable impression of casual.

Cheshire left the theater and headed toward the bathrooms, diverting at the last moment to instead slip down a side hall. Having surveyed the interior the week before, he had no trouble finding the employee stairwell and making his way up two steps at a time to the third floor. From there it was a right, a left, and another left to take him to an unused storage room overlooking the nearby intersection.

Cheshire slipped off one of his gloves and palmed the last of his shelled peanuts. He rolled it against his fingers, concentrating on the weight and the shape. "Heavy headed west," he mumbled to himself as he crouched down and opened a window for a better view. "Jake from the east. The girls blocking traffic." Already he could tell that the number of cars heading through the intersection had thinned, without anyone on the street having taken particular notice yet. He leaned just far enough out to get a better look westward and grinned at the sight of the armored car driving along, as oblivious as could be.

It was a golden opportunity, and all thanks to Burke's recent efforts selling the Kozlow name throughout Manhattan. It hadn't taken much effort at all to coax from one of the smaller gangs in Lucky's orbit that First National's armored cars were making more and more pickups in broad daylight, trying to discourage the rise of robberies in the tough economy. Only a little effort past that to learn which restaurant the drivers always chose for their dinner break, always at the same time. And when it just so happened that they would be passing the largest theater in town during one of the largest premieres of the year...nothing could have stopped Cheshire from taking the risk.

He watched the armored car approach the intersection—and the passably-painted Model A Jakub would be in approaching from the opposite side. Cheshire scanned the area one more time and then took a deep breath. Focusing. He sure hoped Lucky really was in the theater somewhere. Certainly Manhattan's premiere thug would hate to miss the real show.

The red on all four traffic lights blew out at once. Cheshire tried to keep it restrained, so as to maybe pass as some kind of electrical failure, but the one furthest got away from him a little—the casing split with a thunderous *crack* and shot the glass like a bullet through the awning of a nearby shop. A *serious* electrical failure, then. Cheshire ducked lower to be sure he wouldn't be seen, smiling to himself. "You're up, Jake."

***

Even though he was expecting it, Jakub flinched just as much as Gertie at the blast. All the surrounding cars stopped in alarm as smoke poured from the corner lights, one of them half cocked from the force. Jakub stared. As accustomed as he had become to the results of Cheshire's magic, it was the first time he'd seen it in action since the accident that claimed his arm. He hated that the familiar, tangy smell of the magic gave him goosebumps. Luckily he didn't have time to dwell on it, though, as Gertie was already stopping the car in the intersection, and it was time to go to work.

The heavy had halted partially through the intersection thanks to its less than ideal brakes. After some confusion the driver attempted to keep going, only to realize that the cop car was blocking their route, other startled drivers clogging the other lanes. As Jakub and Gertie disembarked, a security guard hopped out of the cab to meet them.

"Everything all right?" called Gertie before he could get too close, hands on her hips. She had clearly been practicing.

"We're fine," the man replied, casting mystified glances up at the traffic lights. "Mind clearing the road so we can pull through?"

"Sure, sure. Mind if I ask what you're carrying?"

Jakub veered off, circling to get a look at the back of the truck. "What does it matter?" the guard was asking, but he ignored him, resisting the urge to look up at the theater. *So far, so good*, he thought, spotting Leon running up the line of stopped cars. *As long as we're quick...*

Leon was red in the face, probably terrified, but he threw himself on the back of the armored car anyway. Pedestrians who had already stopped to watch the commotion began to shout and point. *Hannah would have been better at this than me*, Jakub thought, already a little embarrassed at the prospect of so many eyes on him. But it was too late to worry about that, so he screwed his fake police cap on tighter and picked up his pace. "Hey!" he shouted in his best American accent. "What do you think you're doing!"

Leon continued to pull furiously at the back of the car, making a good show of it. As Jakub wrestled him down the driver stepped down from the cab as well, increasing the drama of the unfolding commotion. "Did you really think that would work?" the driver chided as he gave Leon a sharp slap across the face. "That we'd just leave it unlocked for you?"

"Please, I just—I need the money," Leon blubbered, not

putting up a fight. "My family—"

Gertie and the other guard were headed their way, and as Leon continued to plead, Jakub turned back toward the steel-plated door sealing up the goods. There were two slots for keys and a Hallorran emblem etched alongside. *I hope she doesn't take it personally*, Jakub thought, and he wedged Cheshire's peanut into the handle.

"Looks secure," he called.

"Of course it's secure," scoffed the driver. "It's Hallorran made. Even *we* can't open it." He grabbed Leon by the scruff of the neck and started marching him toward the front of the car again. "Idiot. I take it you're going to arrest him?"

"Of course." Jakub took Leon's elbow, easing him away from the driver as they headed away from the rear. "Come along, now."

"B-But my family," Leon babbled. Jakub might not have been holding a grudge against him, but he couldn't help but wonder if Cheshire was, to have assigned him this role in the diversion. "They'll starve without me!"

"Tell it to the judge," Jakub grumbled, maybe going a little too far, judging by the strange look Gertie cast him. He cleared his throat. "Hurry up—we've held up traffic too long already."

Twenty... he thought, bracing himself for the next blast. *Nineteen...eighteen...*

***

"Seventeen..." Cheshire said under his breath as he bounded down the stairs back toward the lobby. "Sixteen... fifteen..."

He stopped right before the staff door, taking only a second to catch his breath and straighten his suit. With one hand in his pocket—still gripping the peanut—he strode into the lobby where many of the movie-goers had gathered during the intermission. Spotting a group of women he had treated to popcorn at the start, he headed toward them.

Visualize, he thought, running his thumb back and forth against the dimpled shell in his pocket as he pictured one just like it tucked into the latch of a steel Hallorran door. He outlined the shape of it in his mind and imagined a fire burning on the inside. *Three...two...*

"Ladies!" he greeted, and the trio grinned and welcomed him. "What did I miss?"

The explosion from outside was enough to startle everyone in the lobby. More than a few people shouted in alarm and everyone looked to each other in confusion. Cheshire jumped with them, pretending not to notice that Burke was heading his way. "What was that?" he declared, and he faked a nervous laugh. "Did the movie start without us?"

"That sounded like outside," said one of the women, pale-faced.

"Let's go see!" said her friend, and soon dozens of them were doing the same, everyone hurrying to the exits to get a glimpse of the source.

The intersection was in chaos. Though he had a very good picture in his mind Cheshire was sorry to have missed seeing the explosion, as he was sure it ranked among his best. The door of the armored car was swinging loose, smoke in the air, drivers out of their cars and fleeing into nearby shops. In no time there would be police everywhere, but for the moment there were only two—a very tall woman and a very handsome freckled officer, who were ushering the heavy's guards away from the detonation.

"It's a robbery!" Jakub shouted, bless his heart. "We have to get the car out of here!"

Gertie shoved Leon into the "police" car. "Go, I'll follow you!"

"Wait," said the driver, but by then Jakub had snatched the keys off his belt and was climbing behind the wheel. He tried for the passenger door but couldn't get it open before Jakub had started to pull away. He tried for the police car but Gertie was already racing after the heavy. The two security guards gaped at each other, speechless. And thus, right in front of the eyes of at least fifty baffled New Yorkers, the Kozlow Gang made off with five thousand First National dollars.

"What just happened?" asked one of the women next to Cheshire.

"It kind of looked like the cops just stole an armored car," said another, everyone watching as the security guards began to argue and curse.

"It kind of did," agreed Cheshire. "These are hard times

for everyone, I guess."

"Cheshire Bloom!" Grace stormed up to him, her eyes wide and incredulous, though she also seemed to be trying to look cross with him. "Tell me," she said, but then she paused, casting glances at the many people nearby. "*Cheshire.*"

"What?" Cheshire snuck his glove back on as he gave a helpless shrug. "I hope they let us finish the movie before the cops insist on questioning everyone. It was really getting good."

Grace glared at him, but Cheshire was over the moon, and his excitement was infectious. She gave up her exasperation and surrendered a helpless grin. "Yeah, it was," she said. When Cheshire glanced past her, he could see Hallorran hanging back, grinning as well.

The cops *did* come—the *real* cops, full of questions and outrage. Cheshire stuck close to the trio of women and was relieved to see that Burke had latched onto some fellows of his own, each of them firm in their alibis. "Would I still be here if I had anything to do with it?" he asked of more than one officer. A few were familiar enough with his reputation to find it infuriating.

He wasn't the only popular guest. When Cheshire was given a breather to take in the room, he noticed a peculiar number of officers gathered around a pair that had watched the heist unfold only a few feet away from him: a very large, pale man with a terrible haircut; and a curvaceous woman with a dark complexion draped in a very thick and very expensive-looking fur. He couldn't remember if he had taken notice of them in the theater, despite being a striking pair. As he crept a bit closer, trying to overhear the officers' questions, the woman looked in his direction.

Her recognition of him was obvious, but he couldn't quite define the strange mix of interest and irritation she was fixing him with. When their eyes met, she quickly turned up the collar of her fur and looked away, shoulders inching up as if shy. It drew the attention of her barrel-chested companion, who also glanced Cheshire's way. *His* expression was no less challenging: he grinned and gave Cheshire a wave as if they were old friends, even though Cheshire was confident he would have remembered that dull, straight haircut.

Cheshire followed his lead with a grin and a wave but was careful to divert his attention back to the various other movie-goers around him by the time the cops looked over.

Burke at last jogged over to him and returned his top hat. "Who's that ye're waving at?"

"Hm?" Cheshire thumped his hat back on. "No idea. You know'm?"

Burke very slyly cast an eye at the pair. "No. They know you?"

"Sure seems like it." Cheshire didn't want to get caught paying *too* much attention when the mystery pair was surrounded by so many cops, so he deliberately turned his back and looked to the crowd. "They gonna let us finish the movie or what?"

***

Jakub took the truck straight to the river. With the smoking back end and Gertie in the black and white they were able to blow through most intersections, and they made good time to a small pier closed in the hard times. Gertie's sisters met them there, and they quickly divided up the money bags between the two cars. Jakub took the wheel of one with Leon, Edith's daughters the other, and they split up to take different routes across Manhattan back to the bridge.

"It worked," Leon said, still a little breathless and afraid to celebrate too much. "I can't believe that worked."

"You did fine." When they stopped at a red light, Jakub tossed his cap and jacket in the back below the seat. In truth he still felt a little light-headed himself and was anxious to get back to Brooklyn as quickly as possible. He wanted to see Cheshire's face when the loot was counted and the celebrations began—with his handsome grin and his silver laugh and his fancy new suit. It made his face feel hot thinking of it, and he prayed Leon didn't notice.

"We should go to the hospital first," he said once they were on the bridge and headed home. "Your sister was in labor last I heard."

"Really?" Leon straightened in his chair, but then he frowned. "We're not going to drop the take off first?"

"Why? The cops aren't going to check a hospital parking lot for their thousands of dollars." He looked through the rearview mirror and could see police cars gathering at the entrance to the bridge, setting up a roadblock. He sped up. "It'll be safer there than home."

"Oh, right. Sure." Leon nodded a few times too many. "Wow. I still can't believe it worked."

They reached the other side, where the Brooklyn police were gathering as well. "I'll talk," said Jakub as Leon went pale. "Don't say anything, don't smile. Just keep looking nervous."

"No problem there," Leon replied weakly.

Jakub slowed to a halt next to one of the cop cars, even though they hadn't quite finished setting up an organized sieve for the cars exiting the bridge. As confident as he was, he kept his left arm out of sight after rolling down his driver's side window. One of the officers giving orders took notice and approached: an older gentleman Jakub had seen on duty many times. "Good evening, sir," he said. "May we pass?"

The officer leaned down, glancing between the two of them. "Where you boys coming from?" he asked. "And where are you headed to?"

Jakub didn't have to work hard to keep any incriminating emotion out of his face. "We're headed to the hospital—his sister's having a baby."

The officer considered that a moment and asked, "Boy or girl?"

Leon tensed as if working up an answer, but Jakub beat him to it. "We won't know until it's out," he said plainly. "But his sister's a girl."

The officer smirked, and after a quick glance toward the back seat—Jakub managed not to hold his breath—he straightened up again. There was a knowing look in his eye that didn't prevent him from waving them on. "Good luck to her," he said, and Jakub nodded his thanks and drove them on.

Leon let his breath out in a rush. "Shit, I thought he'd made us. Do you think the others will be okay?"

"Gertie can handle herself," Jakub reassured him. "They'll be fine."

He made a left turn after getting away from the bridge, but as he went to straighten the wheel out, he realized with a start—and a jolt of the car—that his left hand was clamped tight around it. He ground his teeth and tried to force the fingers to loosen, but he suddenly couldn't remember which muscles to flex or relax to make it work. With a muttered curse he pulled to the side of the road.

Leon watched, unspeaking, as Jakub gave the mounting plate above his elbow a sharp twist. The apparatus separated, and immediately the fingers relaxed into their default state, letting the arm drop into its support brace. Jakub glared at it for a while, frustration getting the better of him. "Fuck."

Leon gulped. "You okay?"

Jakub took a deep breath and reconnected the arm with a snap. "I'm fine," he muttered. After giving each of the fingers a wiggle to make sure nothing mechanical had seized up, he put the car back into drive and continued on.

"Jakub," Leon said carefully. "Listen, I—"

"What happened wasn't your fault," Jakub interrupted, though he then did his best to gentle his tone. "I don't blame you. So you don't need to say you're sorry again. I don't want any more apologies, from anyone."

"Sor...okay." Leon sank deeper into his seat. "I understand."

They continued on to the hospital mostly in silence. Jakub wished he could have said something more to reassure him, but he was too busy being grateful that Cheshire wasn't there to see the arm come loose.

By the time they arrived at the hospital it was nearing ten o'clock. It took some coaxing of the staff, but eventually one of the nurses led them back to where the Kozlow party was waiting: Barney, Hannah, and Wanda's parents were there, all of them laughing and hugging each other. It was one of the more bizarre sights Jakub had ever witnessed, at least to him personally. He had no idea how to respond when Barney ran over and grabbed him in a tight hug.

"It's a boy!" Barney declared. He leaned back, face aglow—Jakub could only stare. "It's a boy, and he's healthy, and he's *huge*. I wish I could show you but he's with Wanda in the ward—we're not allowed in."

"Congratulations," said Jakub, mystified to see Barney beaming so openly.

"We're going to name him Kasper, after my father," Barney prattled on excitedly. "Kasper Kozlow II. And then the next one will be after *her* father, and after that, maybe after a saint or something. You know?"

"He's not 'the second' if it skipped you," Hannah told

him, as if it wasn't the first time she'd had to remind him. But she was also smiling, which baffled Jakub just as much.

"So what? He's my son, I'll name him what I want." Barney clapped Jakub's shoulder a few times. "He's gonna be taller than either of us, they can tell already."

"That's...congratulations," Jakub said again. "How's Wanda?"

"Oh, she's fine. She was a champ. They said I'll get to see her in an hour, I guess." He glanced past Jakub and finally took notice of Leon, who was talking happily with his parents. "Leon!" He stepped past Jakub to repeat his enthusiastic greeting. "Leon, it's a boy!"

As the pair of them chatted, Hannah moved to take Barney's place with Jakub. "It's something, isn't it?" she said, her smile crooked. "Barney of all people, a father."

"Yeah," Jakub replied awkwardly. Seeing everyone so excited and cheery was having the opposite effect on him, and he didn't know what was expected of him. "It is. Good for him."

Hannah lowered her voice to keep from disrupting the celebrations. "What about the job? Did it work?"

"Perfectly," Jakub said, immeasurably glad to be talking about something else. "It went off just like Bloom said it would. Half the take is in the car outside."

"You brought it *here*?" Hannah gave a short, incredulous laugh. "Hell, of course you did. You'd better get it home, though. Between the baby and Bloom I'm worried about the boss' blood pressure."

Jakub was fairly certain that social niceties obligated him to at least offer to stay, but he couldn't bring himself to do so. "I'll give all the boys the good news," he offered instead. "We'll get the take stored away before anyone comes looking."

"Good." Hannah also gave him a hearty clap on the back. "Good work." What she meant was *I'm glad you're back,* but she didn't have to say it.

Jakub bid Barney goodnight, promising to visit once Wanda was released from the hospital and could take guests. Barney's spirits were too high for either of them to risk talking about the job considering who would get the credit for it, and he gave Jakub one more hug before seeing him off. With Leon staying behind for his sister, Jakub returned to the car alone, and once behind the wheel he let out a sigh. What a strange night it had been already, and he still had too much to look forward to.

The Kozlow building was alive with celebration when Jakub arrived. They greeted him with laughter and handshakes none of them would have dared a week ago. It was overwhelming, but at least it was better than, *How are you today?* Jakub endured, and though most of them had started drinking already, he managed to organize them well enough to move the loot to the cellar and into waiting crates. Gertie and her sisters arrived soon after, with tales of narrow escapes from over-eager local coppers, but they seemed more exhilarated by their ordeal than concerned. Soon everything was listed and stored, and Jakub made his report to Boss Kozlow.

Kasper was already partway through a bottle of whiskey when he received Jakub in his suite. "Good," he said, echoing Hannah's sentiments from earlier. "Good work. Though if they're so easy to fool, I wonder if we need Bloom next time at all."

Jakub felt his left hand start to seize up again, and he shoved it into his pocket. "We couldn't have opened the back of the truck at all without him. It was Hallorran made."

"He calls too much attention to himself," Kasper continued to grumble as if he hadn't heard. "Everyone will know this was us."

Normally Jakub would have kept quiet, let Kasper speak his mind and let his silence serve as his loyalty. He remembered Cheshire straightening the seams of his jacket and couldn't. "Sir, that was the point. We want the Manhattan gangs to see us as equals. With Bloom there it lets everyone know it was us without giving the police any evidence against him. It wasn't just about showing off—it's a smart plan."

Kasper didn't reply for a while, his gaze still focused elsewhere. After a lengthy delay he said, "Good to have you back, Jakub. Good work."

"Thank you, sir," said Jakub, and he kept his hand in his pocket as he showed himself out.

There, Jakub hesitated. Most of the building was still awake, and as he made his way slowly down the stairwell he could hear people moving about in several rooms, playing music and laughing raucously. The drinking had most likely resumed and it smelled like some were even preparing another round of supper. Rejoining them was as much an exhausting prospect as a welcome one, and Jakub leaned his back against the stair wall a moment, massaging the tense muscles above his prosthetic to get them to loosen. He might have abandoned everyone for well-earned sleep if not for a great cheer from the third floor, followed by very familiar, very welcome laughter.

Jakub rushed into the hall and there found the majority of Kozlow's loyalists who had wisely camped out in front of Cheshire's door. Cheshire himself was among them, one arm slung jovially around Burke's neck as he tried to unlock his apartment while laughing uproariously. He was every bit as flamboyantly dazzling as he had been earlier, and more so—his grin couldn't have been wider, every white tooth on display.

"They didn't even let us finish the movie!" he lamented, still laughing. "For my next heist, I'll be stealing the reels, so we can project it against the side of the building!"

He finally got the door open, and he tugged Burke inside amidst a chorus of cheers. Jakub hurried to follow. Once everyone settled there might not be any moving them until morning. Sure enough, as soon as they entered, Cheshire's entourage each began claiming space on the table, the chairs, even the open window sill and floors. Two ambitious new recruits took to the head and foot of the bed to have the best seats for the tall tale Cheshire was sure to regale them with. Jakub hung in the doorway, chest tight and out of sorts, until Cheshire spotted him just as he was opening a bottle of whiskey.

"Jakub!" Cheshire passed the bottle to Burke and headed straight for him. "You made it!"

He snatched Jakub up in a firm hug that had him seeing stars. He was warm and he smelled like fresh wool—Jakub went red and was too mortified to move, convinced that as soon as Cheshire let him go everyone would see the truth in his face. But then Cheshire pulled him toward the bed, shooing one of the newcomers out of the way so he could drag Jakub into a seat next to him on the mattress.

"Have a drink," Cheshire insisted, waving for Burke to give back the bottle. "We have to hear your side of the story, too! I hope you didn't lose the uniform—you were such a convincing cop."

"If you say so," replied Jakub, and relief had never felt so much like panic as he relaxed into Cheshire's side, a warm

arm over his shoulders. "I do still have the uniform."

"Perfect! You'll be a hit at Halloween." Cheshire pushed the bottle into his hand. "Drink! And tell us everything."

He was too handsome to refuse. Jakub took a long gulp and then quickly passed the bottle on before he could be goaded into more. He told a brief, stiff version of the events and was grateful when Gertie's sisters enthusiastically filled in the blanks. Cheshire listened with rapt attention, laughing and commenting along the way. He kept Jakub close at his side and refused several prompts to give his version of the events until Jakub was finished. But when he did cough up his story, it was with unmatched excitement, and Jakub listened just as attentively.

It was a bewildering experience. Over the past seven years he had spent dozens if not hundreds of nights just like this: tucked under Cheshire's arm, drinking until the early hours while everyone basked in Cheshire's merriment. It felt as much like home as anywhere could, and he should have been plenty used to it, enough to not make a fool of himself in front of everyone. But this time, when Cheshire's arm rubbed against his shoulders, he remembered its strength at his back, drawing him close. When Cheshire flashed him a winning smile, he knew what those lips tasted like. Whenever Cheshire took a breath, it reminded him of a quiet chuckle in a dark room.

And he couldn't stop thinking, *Maybe.* When the bottle came back around, he took another long drink. *Maybe, just one more time.*

***

Normally, by the time the booze and the stories ran out, Cheshire would find himself winding down and ready for a long night's sleep. For once, as the night dragged on he only wound tighter, growing more and more conscious of Jakub leaning into his side.

And he couldn't stop thinking, *He's glaring at me. That's a good sign, right?* His chest thrummed with energy every time Jakub shifted. *Can't you all just leave so I can find out?*

"Well, we drank all the liquor," Cheshire declared once the opportunity arose. "So you might as well all go home."

Everyone grumbled and laughed, and one by one they began to pick themselves up. Cheshire bounded to his feet and immediately felt a chill without the heat of Jakub's body under his arm. "Busy day tomorrow," he prattled as he shook hands with everyone making their way out. "Lots of money for us to spend, right? And newspapers to read."

"Hell of a plan," Gertie congratulated him at the door, and she gave him a punch to the arm that had him wincing. "But it won't work a second time."

"Then I'll come up with a new one," Cheshire assured her, and though she shook her head she was smiling as she left with her sisters.

There were still a few stragglers when Jakub stood up and said, "There's something in the take I wanted to show you."

Cheshire gulped. He turned around to find Jakub fixing him with that same heavy, dangerous look, and his skin prickled all over. "Sure!" he chirped, and he motioned for Jakub to head out ahead of him. "Just close the door when you leave, Burke?"

"Sure." Burke slumped his chin into his palm, eyes lidded, deeply sloshed. "Sure, sure thing, okay."

Jakub strode from the apartment, and Cheshire followed, nervously chatting all the way up the stairs. "All that practice with the peanut really paid off," he said. "Say that a few times fast, huh? It pays to practice your peanut when pilfering a pretty penny from police. Er, *as* police?" He chuckled. "You really were great, you know. Maybe the next premiere should have *you* as its star."

"I didn't do that much," said Jakub as they stepped out into his hallway.

"What do you mean? You did *everything*." Cheshire leaned against the wall while Jakub opened the door to his apartment. He licked his lips. "I'm really glad you were up to it. Hannah thought it might be too soon, but everything goes so much smoother when you're around."

"It would have worked just as well with Hannah."

Jakub let them in, and Cheshire closed the door behind him. *We're alone.* He gulped again as he glanced around the apartment. He had started to become accustomed to finding Miklos in the kitchen or on the sofa, and the absence made their sudden isolation even more palpable. They hadn't been alone in Jakub's apartment together since...

"I have another whiskey," said Jakub, "if you wanted to drink more."

"Sure, unless..." Cheshire shivered as he faced down Jakub's stoic expression, but he did manage a grin. "Did you really have something to show me? Or did you bring me up here to fool around?"

Jakub's already red cheeks flushed darker, and he hurried closer. Cheshire held his breath; Jakub collided with him with such eager insistence that he stumbled back, the door rattling behind his shoulders. Then Jakub's mouth was on his, just as heavy and confident as his glare had been, and he murmured happily in relief. *Oh thank God, I wasn't imagining it.*

Jakub drew him away from the door. His kisses were urgent and he tasted like the whiskey. Cheshire let himself be tugged into the bedroom step by step, his heart fluttering. It still surprised him just how aggressive Jakub was, and he had to struggle to keep up—he kept having to squash the incredulous little giggle that threatened to bubble out of him.

Cheshire tossed his hat on the nightstand. "You're sure you're not just drunk?" he teased, though he was harboring some concern that this would look like a mistake come morning.

"I *am* drunk," said Jakub as he started unbuttoning Cheshire's jacket. "But I've wanted to take this suit off you since you came out in it."

"Wow," said Cheshire before he could stop himself. He slipped his fingers under Jakub's shirt. "I didn't think you even knew how to talk like that."

Jakub made an embarrassed face and fumbled with the buttons. "Just...help," he grumbled, focusing instead on taking his shirt off. Before Cheshire had finished with his he was leaning in again, demanding another kiss. It was dizzying and wonderful.

At last Cheshire was out of his jacket, shirt, and tie. He tugged Jakub closer and flinched at the press of cool metal against his ribs. The reminder only managed to dull his spirits for a moment, though, as then Jakub backed him up against the bed. His pulse stammered all over again and he climbed eagerly onto the mattress. "You really did look good in the uniform," he said, charmed as Jakub untied his shoes for him. "I'd let you arrest me."

Jakub flashed him a look so inviting his cock twitched.

Maybe next time, he thought, grinning, as he finished kicking his shoes off and Jakub his. Then went pants and finally Jakub was crawling into Cheshire's lap, already hard and breath heavy. They wrapped each other up, their kisses beginning to bite. It still felt so impossible, and Cheshire could only follow Jakub's lead, letting the momentum sweep him up.

Jakub gave him one more, heart-melting kiss before pulling back to reach for the bedside drawer. He passed Cheshire a condom and a small bottle of oil. Cheshire smiled to himself as he unwrapped the condom. *I guess he was expecting we'd be back here after all*, he thought, but he didn't get the chance to say as much, as Jakub was already at his lips again. He went to slide the condom on Jakub, and was surprised when Jakub instead guided it to him.

Expected...and planned? Cheshire wondered, hissing quietly as Jakub slicked his cock with the oil. *I didn't think he'd be the type to—* Then his shoulders were forced back against the headboard, and it made more sense; Jakub was just as much in charge as their first time. It suited Cheshire fine. He welcomed Jakub into his lap and onto his cock, groaning in appreciation.

"Not too loud," Jakub warned him, though his voice was just as rough.

"Sorry," said Cheshire. He watched with fascination as Jakub caught his breath—drank in the furrow of his eyebrows, the red of his lip between his teeth. When Jakub began to move he had to clamp his own jaws shut to keep from letting out another throaty groan at the faster-than-expected pace. Clearly Jakub wasn't interested in wasting any time; he took Cheshire by the shoulders and rode him hard, not nearly as cautious about the headboard hitting the wall as he was their voices. Cheshire gripped his hips but it felt more like grasping a lifeline than helping him along.

"Jakub," Cheshire panted, trying to keep his wits about him. "You're really...okay with this?"

Jakub scoffed loudly. "You're still asking *now*?"

He screwed down hard, and both of them shuddered, not quite successfully stifling their moans. It was blissful up until Jakub's left hand clamped like a vice on Cheshire's shoulder.

"Ahh—" Cheshire hissed, gritting his teeth. His hand went instinctively to Jakub's to try to loosen it, though he immediately felt guilty. "Easy, easy."

Jakub hummed as if acknowledging, but his grip didn't let up. Instead he slowed his pace, rocking nearly off of Cheshire's cock and then back down. Though shivering with restraint he kept steady, and suddenly the tone changed: his expression softened, lips slack and eyelashes fluttering; his breath whispered and sighed with every pulse. He looked vulnerable in a way he had never shown before, and it was so thrilling Cheshire forgot that his shoulder was throbbing. When they kissed it was fuller and deeper, and Cheshire was in awe.

How did we not figure this out sooner? Cheshire wondered, overwhelmed by sentiment. He shifted so he could lean more deeply into the headboard and lowered one hand to Jakub's cock, just so that he could see his face with the first squeeze. Watching Jakub bite his lip against a groan was a beautiful reward; Jakub's heavy-lidded stare just before he leaned in for another kiss even more so. *No one's ever looked at me like this...*

Jakub hummed against Cheshire's mouth and began to speed up once more. Cheshire welcomed it, stroking him in time, letting passion and pressure mount between them until it overflowed in a fiery climax. Jakub followed a moment later, and the two of them smothered their voices against each other's mouth until they were panting and spent.

"I'm really okay with this," said Jakub, and Cheshire laughed and kissed him again.

That's as good as talking about it, right? Cheshire thought as they stretched out on the bed together, sharing a few more tired kisses. *This is good.*

"There really is more whiskey," Jakub offered. "If you want another drink."

"Mmm, I'm—" Jakub's hand finally came off Cheshire's shoulder, and he managed somehow to keep a flash of pain out of his face. "I'm parched! Why don't you get cleaned up—I'll grab the bottle."

"All right." Jakub frowned slightly, but he didn't seem to see through him; he kissed Cheshire again and climbed off the bed. "It's under the sink."

Cheshire waited until Jakub was in the bathroom with the water running before moving. "Shit..." He gave his shoulder a rub and could already tell he would soon have a dark, thumb-shaped bruise against his collar bone. He threw the condom out and tugged on his shirt on his way to the kitchen. The last thing Jakub needed was to see bruises.

Cheshire only took a few sips of the whiskey before Jakub returned. He handed over the bottle, but before he could take his turn in the bathroom, Jakub held up a cigarette. "Got a light?"

Cheshire lit it without thinking, but when Jakub took a long drag, savoring, he sensed some greater meaning behind the action he couldn't pin down. "Everything okay?"

"Yeah." Jakub waved toward the bathroom. "Go ahead."

Mystified, Cheshire took some time to clean up. When he returned he dropped into the bed and stretched out, making himself at home in the hopes that Jakub would find it too hard to ask him to leave. "We have to think that Lucky and his crew will have something to say about tonight," he said. "They've never come across the river before but that could change now, depending on whether he has a sense of humor."

"His boys were giving restaurant reviews to newspaper reporters," replied Jakub, dropping onto his back next to Cheshire. "He has a sense of humor."

Cheshire smiled and took a chance, draping his arm across Jakub's stomach as he wriggled closer. "Yeah, that's true." He watched Jakub's profile for a while as if seeing him for the first time, and he couldn't help but chuckle. "You have so many freckles."

Jakub cast him a strange look, but then he relaxed. He took one last drag off his cigarette and snuffed it out in an ashtray on the nightstand. "Do you wanna stay the night?"

Cheshire shrugged and then had to smile wide to hide his wince. "I'm too tired to move," he said, hooking his glasses over the headboard. "So unless you wanna carry me...?"

Jakub turned away, and Cheshire couldn't see what he was up to until he heard a shift and a *clink* of metal. It was with a pang of guilt that Cheshire realized he'd removed his prosthetic to set aside. But before he could dwell on it, Jakub backed up again, settling against his chest.

"You're too heavy for me to carry," Jakub mumbled.

"That's it, then." Cheshire pressed a tender kiss to Jakub's shoulder and relaxed against him. "You really were handsome in your new coat tonight."

"You, too," said Jakub, and soon both of them were fast

asleep.

***

Jakub woke up for the second time in Cheshire's arms, and it was no less emotional than the first. He turned his face into his pillow and prayed Cheshire wouldn't wake up until he had composed himself. *He's still here.* With a deep breath Jakub turned to see Cheshire's face, letting his sleepy calm reassure him. *This is real.* He couldn't even judge the reality against his imagining of it, because he'd never honestly believed it was possible, had never dared let fantasy go that far. But Cheshire was wriggling into him, smiling even in his sleep, and as Jakub kissed him he felt something fierce and defiant solidify in his chest.

Cheshire hummed and stirred. "'Morning," he mumbled. He peeled one eye open only to immediately wince against the light streaming through the windows. "Mm. Coffee."

"Coffee," Jakub agreed, and once his arm was reattached he helped Cheshire out of bed.

They got dressed, and after a quick peek in the hallway to make sure it was empty, they took the elevator to the ground floor. Jakub was sure to retrieve his suit jacket from Gertie's car on the way, looking to enjoy more compliments on his newfound good taste. As they settled in the diner for coffee and breakfast Cheshire was animated as always, recounting a more precise version of their heist and full of ideas for future ones. Everything was starting to feel like a brilliant version of normal when Burke burst into the diner brandishing a newspaper.

"Bloom! Danowicz!" He raced to their booth and all but threw himself in the seat next to Cheshire. "Lucky's *dead.*"

"*What?*" Cheshire snatched up the newspaper and began to read as Jakub leaned forward. "'Alonzo Lecce, better known by his alias Lucky Lecce, was found dead in his Manhattan residence late yesterday evening. Police are not releasing any details other than it is believed to be homicide.'"

"Explains why he didn't make the picture, don't it?" said Burke. "Christ."

"Hell, he really missed both shows, didn't he?" Cheshire said glumly. "Can you believe that timing?" He gave a shrug. "At least we have an alibi for it, I guess."

Jakub tugged the paper over to read for himself, but the article was more speculation than fact, full of reminders of the "alleged" criminal empire Lucky was leaving behind. "If Lucky is dead, who was his lieutenant?" he asked. "Who takes charge of the Manhattan gangs?"

"Fuck if I know," said Burke. "Lucky rounded them up from all over the city. Napoliello, his fixer? The west bankers? Any one of them could be bidding for power now."

Cheshire considered that for a long moment, and Jakub kept his eyes on him. He could see the gears behind Cheshire's eyes twirling to life and felt them grinding in his chest with anticipation. Whatever faith he'd had in his partner before, it had hardened tenfold, and in that moment he would have happily gone to war for him. He just had to say the word.

"Any one of them," Cheshire repeated, mischief curling his lips. "And after last night, I'd say our hat is in the ring." He smirked at them both but then focused on Jakub, beaming and devious and as handsome as ever. "This is going to be even more interesting than we planned for."

He clinked Jakub's mug in a toast, and the scheming resumed.

Moving On Up

Cheshire paced around the safe a few times, not that he needed to; he was playing for show now, cracking his knuckles, holding his fingers up to judge the distance like a Hollywood director. The room was near silent as he stepped back a dozen paces and stretched his shoulders. With a flick of his wrist, the door of the six foot tall safe exploded off its hinges in a fireball, crashing into the steel reinforced walls of the lab.

Jakub let his breath out, magic on his tongue.

Hallorran and the small collection of engineers that had come to watch reacted with mixed cheers and boos. A few passed dollar bills back and forth from bets won and lost. As Cheshire turned to his audience with a bow, Hallorran herself shook her head and then offered begrudging applause.

"All right, you did it," she admitted. She waved to her workers, who began rolling the next safe—a darker, squatter hunk of soon to be exploded metal—into the arena. "But *this* one might give you a challenge."

"I'm telling you, it's *really* magic," said Cheshire with a charming smile. "There's nothing you can put in front of me that I can't make *boom*."

"We'll see," said Hallorran, and her engineers began whispering again.

Cheshire shrugged and headed over to his newest test. Jakub chewed his lip as he watched, anxious for a cigarette.

It hadn't seemed like such a bad idea at the time, accepting Hallorran's invitation to see more of her operation. How it had turned into a demonstration and dare, Jakub wasn't entirely sure. He glanced to the surrounding engineers and technicians, wary of so many eyes watching Cheshire employ his magic so casually. Years of dominance in Brooklyn had safeguarded them from snitches, but there was still no way of knowing what that reputation was worth across the river.

Of course, Cheshire didn't seem to give that any thought. He spun the dial on the safe's front and looked to Hallorran with an appreciative smirk. "Why, I couldn't hear a thing!" he declared.

Hallorran folded her arms and watched him expectantly. "Well?"

Cheshire stepped back. Once again he made good sport of it all, rubbing his chin and leaning back and forth to take it all in. The engineers squirmed in anticipation. Then he backed off and clapped his hand over his eyes.

The door once again split open. Rather than target the mechanism he blew the hinges and handle at once. Jakub wondered if any of them were sharp enough to notice the difference.

Another mixed round of celebration and disappointment roused the gathering, and Hallorran dropped her arms with a muttered curse in Mandarin.

Someone at the rear clapped loudly as Cheshire made his bows, and Jakub glanced back. It was the stout, bob-haired technician that had assisted him through his operation months before.

While Cheshire consoled Hallorran and accepted the admiration of her employees, Jakub headed over to greet the tech. She offered her hand—her *left* hand—and Jakub took it, hesitating just a moment to be sure of his control. His handshake was firm, but friendly, and she grinned.

"Good to see you, Danowicz," she said. "Sure looks like you're doing well."

"I am," Jakub replied, only to falter. "Sorry, I don't think I..."

The woman smirked. "It's Tully," she introduced herself at last. "Tully Paris. S'okay, you spent most of our time together unconscious. You're taking good care of my boy there, I trust?"

"Of course." Jakub glanced behind him, to where Hallorran was clucking over the safe while Cheshire tried not to grin. "Actually, since I'm here, maybe you can help me with something."

"Sure. Doesn't seem like any real work is getting done around here today." She jutted her chin at the commotion and then took a step back. "Come up to the lab."

Jakub followed her out, casting one look back at the group. He managed to catch Cheshire's eye and gave a short wave, which he seemed to interpret well enough. *Just let him have his fun*, he thought as he rode the elevator with Tully up to her lab. *It'll be fine, and...he looks good when he's happy.* He scrunched his cheeks as they stepped off on the fourth floor.

Tully sat him down at one of the work tables, and he felt strangely at home among the many strewn tools and half-finished products. "It still locks up on me sometimes," he explained as he stretched his prosthetic across the table between them. "Especially when I'm...tense."

Tully dragged her tools closer, using a narrow hook to pop open the length of casing along the inside of his forearm. He flinched; for as much as he had adjusted to the limb, he still sometimes expected it to hurt. "There's not much I can do about that, mechanically," she admitted as she tucked a magnifier into her eye. "Your muscles just have to figure that part out." She tapped on the exposed pulleys and gears; Jakub watched very carefully, trying to make sense of every adjustment. "Move your middle finger," she said.

Jakub did so, watching with a kind of morbid fascination as the metal shifted back and forth, just like a tendon. "It does look a little stiff," said Tully. "It could use some grease."

She raised an eyebrow at him, and Jakub frowned uncomfortably. He remembered all her lessons and instructions well, but it was difficult to admit to her that he still found it disturbing, breaking himself open in such a way. When he didn't reply, Tully's expression softened and she stretched across the table for a grease gun.

"We'll take care of it," she said. "And then I can show you a few more tricks. I know it looks intimidating, but all of this can be adjusted pretty easily." She met his gaze seriously. "It'll get easier."

Jakub nodded, grateful and attentive as she talked

him through a few small modifications. She even put tools in his hand and encouraged him to poke around himself. It was eerie at first, but as the different mechanisms began to make more sense, the knot in his stomach finally unraveled. With everything fine-tuned and his confidence restored, Jakub sealed the forearm panel back in place.

"Thank you," he said.

Tully harrumphed. "Next time, I charge you."

She began not to clean up, but to shove her tools and supplies to various corners of the table. Jakub allowed himself the chance to look around the lab with greater attention, spotting several more prosthetics that were in progress, what looked like a miniature car engine...and the long stock and barrel of a rifle. It was sleeker than any he had seen before, but with a belt-feeder that looked overly large for a weapon of its size.

Jakub nodded toward it. "What's that?"

"Hm? Oh, my *other* boy." Tully flashed him a mischievous look. "Want a peek?"

***

"I promise," said Cheshire, not for the first time, as he handed his suit coat to the nearest engineer. "I did *not* smuggle anything in here."

Hallorran wasn't convinced, so he let her unbutton his cuffs and check his pockets to be sure. "You did *something*," she continued to accuse as she dug through his coat while the engineer held it up for her. "There's no such thing as *magic*."

Cheshire heaved a dramatic sigh. "You're right. It's a trick." When Hallorran whipped toward him, he shrugged. "But I'm not telling."

Hallorran glared at him, but slowly the humor crept back into her pinched eyes, and she wagged her finger at him. "You," she said. "Oh, you. I'm going to *get* you."

Cheshire laughed, but he did have to squash a sudden prick of apprehension to do so.

After a few more rounds of questions and teasing, Jakub returned, and he and Cheshire bid Hallorran and her workers farewell. They drove away from the headquarters beneath a dreary December afternoon, snow melting along the sidewalks. Cheshire was very pleased with himself.

"Hallorran is a powerful ally to have," he said, hoping it didn't sound too much like he was desperately heading off any admonishment from his partner. "And I think she realizes the same about us, yeah? We already know she doesn't have any problem keeping things off the books. She could be the leg up in Manhattan we need."

"That's insensitive," said Jakub, and Cheshire winced, only to realize that the very slight tilt of Jakub's eyebrows meant he was probably joking. Wonders never ceased. "You shouldn't have shown them so much of your magic, though."

Cheshire shrugged. "She's not going to rat me out. What good would that do her? There isn't even an award on my head yet."

"Yet?" Jakub repeated frowning.

"Yeah—we're famous outlaws, after all." Cheshire gave Jakub an elbow, hoping to coax some reaction from him to translate. He was eager for the practice. "You're gonna start seeing our faces on posters like the wild west."

"Yours, maybe," said Jakub, but there was no interpreting approval or disapproval from the thoughtful tilt of his head.

They stopped at a café for lunch close to Times Square, watching people move up and down the streets, carrying on their busy lives. All in all everything looked extremely normal. It made Cheshire squirm.

Jakub waited until the waitress had delivered their soups to broach the subject. "Burke still doesn't have anything, does he?"

"Not for lack of trying," Cheshire said with confidence. "Whoever has taken over Lucky's operations, they're being *extremely* careful about it, and quieter than a mouse. Every few weeks another lieutenant disappears, *poof*." He dropped a cracker into his soup, letting it bob and nearly spill. "Either it's every man for himself and there's no one person to point at, or it's *one* person, and everyone else is too scared witless to talk."

Jakub frowned thoughtfully. "I didn't think there was anyone *that* high up in the Manhattan gangs that could do that."

"Neither did I," Cheshire admitted, and he gulped down a few mouthfuls of soup. "They haven't even tried to retaliate for that truly inspired hit of ours. I guess we just have to wait until Burke's ear catches something for us."

After lunch Jakub insisted they do some prowling of their own, so they took to the city. They visited a few shops that were well known to be under Lucky's protection, wandered down to the wharf just to be seen. Cheshire couldn't help but be deeply pleased by the amount of recognition paid to him, but it didn't result in any new information. At last the pair headed back across the river, empty-handed but not yet discouraged. Whoever was pulling the strings, it wasn't as if they didn't know where to find the competition, after all.

As Jakub drove them back to their building, Cheshire leaned back in his seat. "You know, I've been thinking," he said. "Maybe I should get a new apartment, closer to the water."

"Why?" Jakub asked immediately, and with a sharpness that seemed to embarrass him right after. He rubbed his nose. "It won't look good to the boss. He likes having everyone close by."

"Yeah, but it's not so smart, is it?" replied Cheshire. "If Manhattan's boys come looking for us and we're all in one place. And you have to admit I'm the flashiest target."

"That's your own fault."

Cheshire smirked. "I wouldn't have it any other way," he bragged, but then he swallowed, and he lowered his tone. "Besides, I sure wouldn't mind being able to invite you over for a drink without worrying about how thin the walls are."

Jakub's cheeks went rosey, which was exactly the reaction Cheshire had been looking for. "I'll bring it up to Hannah," Jakub volunteered. "She's more likely to give the okay if it's my idea."

"Perfect," said Cheshire, and once they'd turned onto their street, he reached down to skate his fingertips along Jakub's thigh. Jakub looked to him with such intensity that Cheshire considered the merits of renting a hotel room to tide them over, but then his eye caught on the sidewalk outside their building, and the group of police officers there. "Uh-oh."

Jakub saw and immediately slowed. "Shit."

"It's all right." Cheshire leaned forward, counting at least five officers in uniform, as well as a woman in a blue suit arguing with some of Kozlow's men. "Let's go see what they want."

"You're sure?" asked Jakub warily, though then the woman looked their way, her eyes narrowing. There was no mistaking that she had spotted them. Making a run for it didn't seem like an option with police cars already lined up along the street, their drivers so close by.

"It's all right," Cheshire said again, and with a sigh Jakub parked along the curb. "We haven't even done anything lately."

They disembarked and headed toward the building, as easy as you please, Cheshire's face a picture of innocent curiosity, and Jakub's...same as usual. The woman squared her shoulders to them, expression tense as she waited. She was tall and her posture was strict, the lines of her eyebrows and the slope of her nose almost architectural, her suit and tie well pressed. Cheshire could *see* the title of "inspector" or "agent" written all over her. Even her hair, brown curls wound tightly off her shoulders, proclaimed discipline. She was barely saved from total Federal homogeneity by her hat, at least: a simple but elegant slouch hat with a lavender flower pinned to the side.

Cheshire reached the first of the officers and stepped around him. "Excuse me," he said, making like he was going to head into the building without anything more than a friendly smile. He didn't get past a second step.

"Cheshire Bloom," said the woman.

Cheshire turned, grinning curiously as if noticing her for the first time. "Yes? Can I help you?"

"U.S. Marshal Hazel Adalet," the woman introduced herself. "I need you to come with me."

"Marshal?" Cheshire repeated, ignoring the second part. "Then I was close—I had you pegged as 'Agent' for sure."

The officers and gang members around them shifted their weight, watching closely as if witnessing a stand-off. Hazel continued to stare back at Cheshire, unimpressed. "All the same," she said, "you're coming with me."

Cheshire faced her properly then, stuffing one hand into his pocket, which she eyed critically. "If you're here to confiscate my whiskey, you're a little late," he said jovially. He mimed raising a bottle with his other hand. "All gone."

"I'm not here about prohibition," said Hazel, irritation showing more pronouncedly on her face. "Get in the car, *now*."

Cheshire regarded her for a moment, still smiling easily. Kozlow's boys were still watching, tense as if waiting for a word from him that would turn this meeting into a confrontation or worse. Jakub was practically humming at his side, taut like a spring. But despite his bravado Cheshire *did* know better than to declare war on the entire U.S. Marshal's office. There was nothing to do but shrug, take a step closer, and say, "I'd be delighted."

Hazel gestured to the car impatiently, and Cheshire flashed the Kozlow boys an easy smile as he made his way over. But then she cleared her throat, added, "And you, Mr. Danowicz," and Cheshire froze.

That didn't bode well. But when Cheshire glanced back, he found that Jakub didn't look any different. Still tense, certainly—still ready for one signal from Cheshire to send him to action. But his face was as neutral as ever as he followed Cheshire across the sidewalk, and without a word he moved around to the car's far back door.

Hazel eyed him, waiting until both men were climbing inside to slide into the front passenger seat. One of the officers took the wheel while the others returned to their own cars, and soon the procession was underway.

Cheshire settled into the back seat. He wasn't terribly concerned, not yet—they had faced plenty of run-ins with authorities of all kinds over the years, even U.S. Marshals, and come away more or less unscathed every time. *It must be about the heavy,* he thought, unable to keep his lip from turning up. *She's got nothing she can hold us on.* But then his humor quickly died with the sudden realization...she had asked for Jakub by name, too.

Jakub stared straight ahead impassively. He chewed his lip in want of a cigarette but otherwise didn't seem concerned, either. If Hazel had the armored car's driver, there was a possibility of him recognizing Jakub, and that ought to be taken seriously. But there wasn't much left to do but play their parts well, so Cheshire took a deep breath.

"You're going to tell us what this is about at some point, aren't you, Madam Adalet?" he called to the front.

He was right behind Hazel's seat, so even seeing her head turn, he had to rely on his imagination for her unamused glare. "'Marshal' will suffice, Mr. Bloom."

"Oh, sorry. I'm not sure what the etiquette is for these situations." Cheshire smoothed down his necktie and fussed with his cuffs. "Usually when I'm arrested I have an inkling of what it's for, and can be better prepared."

"You know what it's for," Hazel retorted.

Cheshire clicked his tongue. "I honestly don't. Maybe we can play twenty-questions for it?"

Hazel turned further, shifting in her seat so that *this time* Cheshire would be sure to see the hooked slant of her brow. "I'm not here to play word games with you."

"Neither am I," Cheshire said cheerily, glad to have that better view. He wanted *her* to see just how calm he was. "This is my attempt to interrogate you. How am I doing?" When Hazel didn't answer other than to intensify her glower, he added, "I know I'm no federal agent, but maybe you can give me some pointers."

"Shut up," Hazel snapped, and she turned forward again so sharply that her curls bounced against her ears. "Save it for the station."

The station, as it turned out, was one Cheshire knew especially well: Precinct 49. It held only one mark of distinction for him, which spurred his heart over a few stumbled beats as they pulled in. He made sure none of that apprehension made it to his face, even though he could feel Jakub watching him.

They climbed the front steps and headed inside to be greeted by a slew of anxious and curious eyes. The normal bustle of the police at work went quiet as Hazel and a pair of officers led their captives toward the far end of the room. Cheshire paid them no mind, at least outwardly. He kept his smile in place, hands in his pockets, Jakub silent and intimidating by his side. The cautious attention being paid them was gratifying, certainly—*this* was the notoriety he had dreamed of as a boy— but as they moved closer to a desk near the rear, his hair stood on end. He wasn't sure he'd know how to react.

But Detective Daniel Alice wasn't at his desk, despite the coat draped over the back of his chair, the open folders laid out. It took Cheshire a moment to locate him—standing at the back of the office, next to a hall that led even further into the building. His arms were folded over his chest and his eyes heavy with mistrust. Cheshire managed not to gulp, smile nailed in place, as they passed.

"Detective," he greeted.

"Bloom," Alice replied coldly.

And that was it, seemingly. He allowed the group to

pass, and though Cheshire should have left well enough alone, he couldn't stand not knowing what they were really up against. He paused and turned back, feigning innocent curiosity. "You're not joining us?"

To his surprise, Hazel turned back as well, watching Alice just as expectantly. But the detective shook his head. "Marshal, you have use of the rooms," he told her, ignoring Cheshire. "And you have your deputies. That's as far as I'm required to cooperate."

"Suit yourself," said Hazel, displeased but not pressing the issue. She continued on. "Let's go, Bloom."

He followed, though only a few steps later she motioned for him to enter one of the hall's side rooms. As he did so, one of the deputies tapped Jakub and gestured to a different door across from it. After a moment of angry stalling, Jakub begrudgingly complied. He cast Cheshire one more hard look that probably translated to *Keep your mouth shut* before the door closed him in.

The separation caused Cheshire's confidence to falter, but only slightly. It wasn't as if they had complicated stories to keep straight, and now that the threat of Alice had passed, he was convinced he had nothing to fear from a newer, younger challenger. The room they entered had only a bare table with two chairs on one side, one on the other. Cheshire helped himself to the two-chair side, just to watch Hazel's deputy flounder a moment. Eventually the poor man decided on the less embarrassing option of standing behind Hazel's chair as she took her seat opposite.

"Well, you got me," said Cheshire, reclining as best he could in the small, uncomfortable chair, hands folded in his lap. "But I still don't know what this is about."

Hazel, meanwhile, folded her hands on the table, leaning forward. "Where were you October Twenty-fifth?"

"The twenty-fifth?" *So it's the heavy after all,* Cheshire thought, which was relieving for him, but for Jakub it was another matter. He squinted and pursed his lips as he gave the matter deep thought. "What day was that? A Tuesday?"

"Saturday," Hazel said crisply, watching him closely and offering nothing more.

"Oh! *That* Saturday?" Cheshire nodded sagely. "That was the cinema premiere! You should have just said that."

"And you were at the premiere?" Hazel pressed.

"I mean..." Cheshire shrugged. "You know I was, right? It'd be pretty anti-climatic if you brought me out here to ask about an event I didn't attend. So I assume *someone* told you they saw me there."

He made a show of glancing around the room, as if such a witness were already there with them. The room didn't have any windows for spying—a positive ID of him at the scene would have only hurt their case rather than helped, anyway. When he drew his attention back, Hazel was glaring at him, still as stone.

"You were spotted there by dozens of eye witnesses," she said. "Before, during, and after the theft." She raised an eyebrow at him. "You're not going to deny noticing the armed robbery just outside the theater, are you?"

"Not at all—it was thrilling. Better than the picture."

Hazel looked to the deputy, and he unbuttoned the front of his coat, pulling from inside a file folder. He handed it to Hazel, who set it down on the table without opening it. Cheshire contained his curiosity. "There were five thousand dollars stolen from that car," Hazel resumed, interlocking her fingers over the folder this time, as if taunting him. "The car itself was badly damaged. The locking mechanism was destroyed by some kind of explosion."

"Fascinating," Cheshire said dryly. "What's that got to do with me?"

"You're a well known arsonist and thief," Hazel retorted. "It has *everything* to do with you."

Cheshire shrugged in return. "If you say so."

"You started small time," said Hazel, not yet losing her patience, but Cheshire could already see she didn't have the stamina to outlast him. "Home invasions, safecracking. Graduating to warehouses, a steel plant, an auto repair shop..." She fixed her eye on him. "And now armored cars."

"You've obviously been talking to Danny," said Cheshire. "But I've never been charged with a crime, let alone anything as serious as all that. So you must be thinking of someone else."

Hazel opened her file and began to page through it. "It's you," she said confidently. "Whether or not the locals are interested in going after you has nothing to do with me. And where I come from, we recognize the work of magic." She stopped paging through her file to fix him with a knowing look. "You *reek* of it."

"Thanks," said Cheshire.

He hadn't been trying to be clever or difficult—he was, internally, half reeling from the thought that the federal government had agents well-versed in the supernatural to throw at him, which should have occurred to him long before then. Still, it worked enough to cause Hazel some pause. She glared at him until it was painfully obvious he had no intention of giving her anything else.

"The lock on that armored car was broken open in a matter of moments," Hazel tried again. "Only magic could have done that."

Seeing her slightly off kilter set Cheshire straight once more. "Okay," he said.

Hazel's eye twitched. "You've been spotted at every relevant scene in the past several years."

"If you say so."

"You've mutilated and *murdered* people with this magic," Hazel persisted. "And that's all you have to say?"

Cheshire squashed a tiny pang of guilt and gave another shrug. "I'm sorry, but I don't know what you *want* me to say. I don't have any magic and I've never hurt anyone." He winked. "Except a few broken hearts."

Hazel clenched her fist against the table.

***

Jakub sat across from a pair of marshal's deputies, but his attention wasn't on them; he saved his glare for the mirror on the far wall, which bore a frame to try and hide the fact it was sunken into the wall. Whoever was watching from the other side Jakub wanted them to know *he* knew they were there.

"Jakub Danowicz," said the elder of the two deputies. "You're one of Kozlow's best boys, aren't you?"

"What of it?" Jakub asked impatiently.

The deputy looked surprised, as if having expected a denial. "You've been pulled in half a dozen times since entering the country," he continued. "Suspected of theft, transportation of illegal liquor, arson and assault. You've seen and done it all, haven't you?"

"Do you mind if I smoke?" asked Jakub.

The deputy frowned, and he and his partner exchanged a look, but then he relented. "Go ahead."

With his right hand, Jakub reached into the pocket of his coat. He flicked open the box of cigarettes with his thumb and pulled one out with his teeth. The deputies watched, taking note of every action, as they were meant to. Only once Jakub had lit and was enjoying his first drag did he speak up again. "So? Are you going to ask me if we're responsible for Lucky?"

The deputy raised an eyebrow. "You know something about Alonzo Lecce's death?"

"Isn't that why you're here?" Jakub cast another glance at the mirror and finally settled on the pair in front of him. "Kozlow's crew shows up in Manhattan the night he dies. We control most territory east of the river, now. Why *not* try for Manhattan?" He breathed a wreath of smoke. "If you're hoping for a cut of his territory you'll have to wait, though. Lucky wasn't us and it'll take a while to bring all the gangs together again."

"They're already—" the younger deputy started, but the first quickly hushed her quiet.

"The bureau is looking after the Lecce murder," he resumed. "We're with the U.S. Marshal's office investigating the armored car robbery on October twenty-fifth." He flipped open a small notebook. "You were identified as being at the scene and we'd like to take your statement."

Jakub took another drag. "I already gave my statement to the police at the cinema."

"No, you didn't. There's no statement from you on record."

"It wasn't much of a statement."

"Then you won't mind giving it to us again now," said the woman, a bit too eager for her own good.

Jakub gave them a few moments of silence. "I went with Bloom and Burke to the cinema for the premiere," he said eventually. "I didn't care for it, but Bloom seemed to like it. Melodrama."

"We're not asking for—" said the man, but the woman leaned forward suddenly.

"What were the two protagonists fighting over in the first act?" she asked, eyes gleaming.

"A woman," Jakub answered precisely.

"And what did Georgie give her at the New Year's ball?" she pressed.

Jakub blinked. Who would have guessed that Cheshire's many recountings of the night would come in handy weeks later? "A derringer pistol. For her garter."

"And who did she end up with?"

"I don't know. They didn't let us finish the picture."

The deputy leaned back, satisfied with his answers. Her superior gave her a look and then continued his questioning. "How much of the robbery did you see?"

"No more than anyone else," said Jakub impassively. "I went out with the others when I heard the explosion. We saw the armored car drive away. I thought the police were handling it—I didn't know it was a 'robbery' until the papers started talking the next day."

The deputies considered that for a while, and Jakub got the distinct impression they were suppressing the urge to glance over their shoulders. *They have the driver*, he thought, resisting the same urge to look to the window. *They're trying to get him to identify me.* He continued to wait patiently while the pair mulled over their possible questions.

"The robbery was carried out by a man and a woman," the head deputy continued at last. "A slight man with dark hair and a poor complexion, and a very tall woman with short hair."

"Slight?" Jakub repeated, offended, and both shifted slightly. "You're implying that's me?"

"You were seen entering the cinema but the police didn't see you leave with the rest of the guests," the deputy argued.

"I blend in," said Jakub, and he imagined Cheshire smirking next to him. "I hope you're not thinking I set off an explosion and drove an armored car through busy streets in my condition."

"Your condition?" the woman echoed curiously, just like he had hoped.

Jakub lifted his left arm to the table, letting it fall an inch so that it rattled loudly. Both deputies jumped and then stared. He was careful not to move at all with them looking at the limb so closely, their expressions shifting from surprise to confusion. They exchanged another long stare.

And while they were dumbfounded, Jakub took the

opportunity to glare at the mirror again. *If you're really back there*, he thought, willing the message to show in his face, *you had better reconsider.*

***

"You really expect me to believe this was all coincidence?" Hazel demanded. A shrillness was creeping into her tone, and she slapped her fancy hat down onto the table next to her files. "The front man of Brooklyn's leading crime family shows up in Manhattan on the night of a high profile murder *and* the robbery of an armored car, and you have *nothing* to do with either?"

"Nothing, sadly," Cheshire replied, calmer than ever. "If I could take credit, I sure might, because it sounds *really* impressive."

Hazel seethed, though she fought herself down from whatever her first retort would have been. "We have the driver of the car," she said. "He's going to identify your friend as one of the robbers. So how sure are you that don't want to talk to me?"

"I'm sure," Cheshire said, trying not to let himself dwell on the possibility Hazel was putting forth. Jakub could take care of himself and had never failed to talk his way out of suspicion, despite his social shortcomings. Even so, Cheshire's nerves suddenly got the better of him. "In fact, I think I'm done talking to you entirely."

He stood, his chair scraping back. Hazel immediately pushed to her feet as well but was a step too short to intercept him before he could reach the exit. "I didn't say you could leave," she said. "We're not finished here."

"Am I under arrest?" Cheshire asked, his hand on the door. When Hazel ground her teeth but couldn't answer, he smirked. "If not, there's nothing stopping me from walking out this door."

He opened the door and stepped into the hall, and he nearly ran straight into Jakub leaving the opposite room. After a moment of surprise, he grinned openly. "You all finished?" he asked.

"Yeah," said Jakub coolly, and though he was holding his left arm in an awkward manner, he headed back the way

- 41 -

they had come without further explanation or a glance back. Cheshire was happy to follow.

"Bloom!" Hazel protested as she chased them to the mouth of the corridor. "You're not fooling me!"

She reached for his arm, but before she could take his sleeve, Detective Alice intercepted. "Marshal," he said patiently. "If they're not under arrest they're free to go. And I can't let you arrest them without evidence."

"Evidence?" Hazel repeated, exasperated. "It's *magic*. What evidence do you expect to find?"

The pair of them continued to argue as Cheshire and Jakub moved on. But Cheshire couldn't help himself. When he glanced back and saw the marshal so agitated, it put a smile on his face, and he wanted her to know it. "Marshal!" he called.

Hazel whipped around, anger written all over her, and Cheshire offered her a wink. "Better luck next time," he said.

"Son of a—" Hazel took a step toward them, but again Alice drew her back. The cold distrust in his eyes dampened Cheshire's triumphant spirit, but not enough to prevent him from chuckling as he and Jakub showed themselves out of the station.

"Phew!" said Cheshire once the pair of them were out on the sidewalk again. He stretched his neck and shoulders as if they had been detained for hours. "Well, that was certainly educational, wouldn't you say?"

Jakub was staring at him. His brows were drawn in and his eyes intense, and Cheshire thought, *Ahh, he's making that face.* Cheshire straightened his tie. "I don't know what you told them," he said, smirking. "But I'm sure it was brilliant."

He leaned in for a kiss, but before their lips could touch, Jakub flinched back, saying, "What?"

Cheshire froze awkwardly. "What?"

"What are you doing?"

"I'm just..." Cheshire straightened up, his cheeks red. "You were making that..." he started to explain, but then he looked again, and the words withered in his mouth. Jakub continued to glare at him, as usual, but... *Oh, no,* Cheshire realized. *No, that's actually him angry this time.*

"Sorry!" he chirped, and then he cleared his throat, struggling to recover a jovial tone. "Sorry, misread that one. Let's, um...get a cab." He started walking to get them away from the station. "Really rude of them not to offer us a ride back, don't you think?"

"What did you tell them?" Jakub asked as they walked. He scrubbed his hand across his cheeks self-consciously; the subtle blush he was trying to hide only made Cheshire's attempts to interpret more complicated. "That marshal looked ready to throttle you."

Don't worry about any of that now, Cheshire counseled himself. "She sure did, didn't she? Can't imagine why; I barely said a word."

Jakub snorted with disbelief. "This isn't like the local police," he scolded. "Even if you manage to scare her off, the feds will send someone else. We need to be more careful."

"She's got nothing on us," said Cheshire confidently. "You can't prove magic in court."

"She can with a witness." Once they were far enough away from the station Jakub gave his left arm a shake, wiggling his fingers. "You shouldn't have been showing off this morning."

Cheshire pulled a face, and luckily he spotted an approaching taxi. He moved closer to the street to wave it down. "You were all for it when we went in."

"I was not," Jakub retorted crossly. He dropped his cigarette and snuffed it out against the curb. "I warned you."

"Hallorran is not going to turn me in," Cheshire tried again. "She likes me—she said so."

"She said so." Jakub narrowed his eyes on him. "In those words?"

"Well...not in exactly those kinds of words, but in words that could be implied, yes."

The taxi stopped, and Cheshire held the door open so Jakub could enter first. He did so, stoically, and Cheshire couldn't help but gulp as he took the seat next to him. But a car ride in silence was not one of the options on Cheshire's menu, and once they'd pulled away from the curb he barreled onward.

"In any case, I'll be more careful from now on," Cheshire promised. "Keeping it under wraps. There are plenty of other ways for me to make a fool of myself in public."

He glanced to Jakub, hoping for some sign of amusement, but Jakub was glaring out the window instead. "And in private," Cheshire added, a little sullen. "But, at least that will be further away from the boss soon. Should save him some embarrassment."

"Not until I okay it with them," Jakub reminded him. "It'll take some convincing."

"Sure, sure." Cheshire sighed with semi-forced enthusiasm. "Just think of the new closets I'll have to fill."

Cheshire chatted idly about the wishes for his new living space for the rest of the drive, since that was an easy enough topic for the cabbie to overhear. Only once they were headed into their building did Jakub speak up more than to snort to move the conversation along. "The deputies let something slip when they questioned me," he said. "Someone *has* pulled the Manhattan gangs together already. I assume the feds know who."

"Damn, I should have pressed the marshal about it." Cheshire hummed thoughtfully as they made their way up to his floor. "What else did they say?"

"That's it. If only we had better contacts inside..."

"Most of the precincts are in our pocket by now—might as well get in on the feds," Cheshire agreed. "I'll mention it to Burke, see if he has any new leads." He stopped in the stairwell at his floor, hesitating. "I really will be more careful, okay? No more showing off the magic."

Jakub stared back at him, and Cheshire braced himself for a stern talking to. But then Jakub moved closer, took his face in both hands, and rose up on his toes for a kiss. Cheshire was too caught off guard to make much of it—by the time he reached for him, Jakub was already pulling back.

"Good," said Jakub, and he slipped past Cheshire to continue up the stairs without looking back.

Cheshire watched him go, leaning back against the door frame. *How am I ever going to get the hang of this?* he wondered, but he smiled to himself as he stepped out into the hall in search of Burke. He wasn't one to back down from a challenge.

***

"Bloom says he didn't give them anything, and I believe him," Jakub reported. "All he has to do is deny, and the feds don't have a case. I convinced the others that a credible witness wouldn't have missed the fact his assailant was missing an arm.

They seemed to buy it."

Kasper listened intently from behind his desk, his fingers steepled atop it. He didn't appear cross or concerned, to Jakub's relief. He had never taken the threat of the law very seriously in any case. Hannah, on the other hand, was leaning against the nearby bookshelf. Her folded arms didn't bode well.

"Good," Kasper murmured after a considerable pause. "Good work. Tell Bloom to keep his head down for a while—whatever the next big job is, leave him out of it. The marshals have plenty to keep themselves busy with. They'll lose interest in him."

"I agree." Jakub looked to Hannah, waiting for her to offer her thoughts. When she didn't, he took breath and continued. "Even so, I think we should take...certain precautions."

"Precautions," Kasper echoed. "What do you mean?"

"Now that the permits have gone through, those new buildings by the river are going to start construction," said Jakub, reciting the logic he had hastily assembled before this meeting. "It's a big project, and one of ours should be nearby. Bloom is visible enough on his own that having him around will send a message."

"You want to put him in charge?" Hannah asked doubtfully.

"I want to put him next door." Jakub spared her only a glance before focusing on Kasper. "I'm sure there's an empty apartment close by he can rent. Something nicer than he has now will keep him happy and give him something to do there while we wait for the heat to cool off."

Hannah shifted her weight. "Bloom gets carried away easily. We don't want him getting it into his head that he's the boss around there."

"I'll make sure he doesn't," Jakub replied, just coldly enough that it came off extremely convincing. Even Kasper nodded.

"I see your reasoning," said Kasper. "But he *is* something of a loose canon. I like having him where I can see him."

Jakub hesitated to say more. Even if Cheshire wasn't there—and Hannah would never share anything said in this office with him—it made his stomach turn anyway. "Of course," he said carefully. "He stands out wherever he goes. But...that just makes him a bigger target." Kasper straightened up, and Jakub could feel Hannah's stare growing harder, but he continued. "We still expect Manhattan to come down on us eventually. If they or the marshals come for him...better he's not *here* when they do."

Kasper spent another long, thoughtful pause on those words, mulling them over as if chewing through them. He looked to Hannah, and though Jakub chose not to check for himself, whatever was in her face must have convinced him. At great length, he nodded. "Yes. I agree." He leaned back in his chair with a sigh. "Hannah will make the arrangements. Nothing too gaudy—just enough to keep him happy. We'll pick a few more of the boys to move, too, so it doesn't look like he's being singled out."

Jakub nodded. "All right." A shiver ran under his skin. "Do you want *me* to—"

"No," Kasper said predictably. "No, you stay right here." He waved vaguely. "Hannah will make the arrangements."

"Yes, sir," said Jakub, and seeing it was best not to push his luck, he headed out of the apartment.

Hannah came right behind him. "Are you sure this is a good idea?" she asked. "The last thing we need is for Bloom to get a big head."

Jakub stopped in the hallway to face her, a pulse of honest frustration behind his ribs. "He's been with us for years, and he's always been loyal."

"He has," Hannah conceded. "But things change." She fixed him with a searching gaze. "Was this really your idea? Or was it his?"

"Mine," said Jakub, wondering if he would regret later how easy it was to lie to her. "Barney will be glad for it. Now he can bring his family to visit the boss without having Bloom underfoot."

Hannah sighed, making a face that spoke of too much time spent listening to Barney's complaints on that topic. "True enough," she said, and together they headed down to their floor. "At least Gertie is out that way, too. She can keep an eye on him."

"He'll be fine. This will be good for everyone."

When Jakub reached his apartment, he went straight to his bed and threw himself on it. There was plenty of daylight left, but he was already exhausted, praying for the clouds to darken so he could get some sleep. As he curled up, chilled but not wanting to move to reach for a blanket, he marveled at how quiet the building suddenly was.

There would be no more coming home late to the sound of merriment from Cheshire's apartment. No outrageous stories through the night as Kozlow's little soldiers jostled for a drink and a good seat. No waking up with a hangover only to be soothed by Cheshire's laughter making its way through the halls. He should have been more concerned about encroaching gangs and federal agents, but those worries couldn't reach him. The move hadn't even happened yet and already he missed Cheshire. It hurt more than he thought it should have.

It'll be better, for everyone, Jakub told himself as he burrowed his face into his pillow. *More privacy. Less distractions. Less Hannah around.* He grumbled as he kicked his shoes off and tried to work beneath the covers while moving as little as possible. *And once we know more about Manhattan we'll be working together every day anyway. It won't change. I'll see plenty of him.*

Jakub gave up on the bedding and just twisted into the most comfortable position he could manage. *He suggested it because he wants us to have more time together, not apart*, he continued to rationalize. *He said so himself. He's not running away. He went for that kiss, didn't he?*

His cheeks flushed, and he smothered his entire head beneath the pillow. *I'm so stupid.*

***

Ten days later, Cheshire had a charming new apartment on Kent Avenue.

The boss had ordered most of his available hands to the move of Cheshire and three others. They made light work of the essentials, as the apartments were already decently furnished. The bulk of the effort went to Cheshire's wardrobe.

"Look at this closet!" Cheshire declared as he sorted and resorted his jackets on the racks. "I have room for at least... six more ensembles." He laughed to the sound of everyone groaning. "And even more in the hall! What do you think?"

He looked to Jakub, who was plugging in a bedside lamp. Cheshire had talked at him an awful lot through the day without much response, and the silence was getting under his skin. When Jakub returned his latest with a disinterested hum, he tried not to let it dampen his spirits. "One thing I just can't figure out," he said as he finally settled the garments to his liking. "Whatever happened to that fantastic Christmas jacket I had made a few years ago?"

Jakub fumbled with the lamp, which Cheshire made an effort not to notice. He was still sensitive about his dexterity, after all. "What about it?" he asked without looking back.

"I can't remember the last time I saw it." Cheshire checked through the garment bags one more time to be sure. "I was hoping we'd find it in the move... You haven't seen it?"

"No." Jakub finished what he was up to and straightened. "I assumed it got ruined that night with the Foleys."

"Right..." Cheshire chewed his lip a moment. He didn't remember all that much from that night at the plant, between the drinking and the injury... He gave the scar on his cheek a rub. "Yeah, that's probably it." He turned away to survey the space.

Jakub had moved to the door and was waiting for him there. His expression was hopelessly blank, but Cheshire couldn't shake the feeling that there was more to it than that, something he was meant to puzzle out. "What do you think?" he asked, his real question, *What are you thinking?* struggling behind it. "Hannah picked a good one."

"She did," said Jakub.

He was staring, maybe even waiting for something. Cheshire glanced back into the apartment's living room—how new for him, to have separate rooms at all—but there were still several people milling about, helping to stock his kitchen. "It's going to be strange, huh?" he said distractedly. "We've been under the same roof for so long."

"Yeah," said Jakub.

Cheshire edged a bit closer. "I'm gonna miss not having you around all the time."

"Yeah," Jakub said again, but then he looked away, making Cheshire feel as if he'd misstepped.

"But you're welcome any time, of course," Cheshire tried to recover. "In fact, we're probably going to celebrate a *lot* tonight. You'll stay, won't you?"

"Sure," said Jakub, and he started to walk out.

It didn't feel right to leave it that way. Cheshire grabbed Jakub before he could get too far—twisted his arm across Jakub's front, drawing him back by his shoulder. He turned Jakub to face the bedroom while closing the door with his other hand—not enough for the close of the lock to alert anyone outside. Feeling Jakub go tense against his chest made his heart pound, nervous and hopeful at once.

"In fact, I'm going to get another key made for you," Cheshire said quietly, close to Jakub's ear. "That way you can come in and out anytime you want." He licked his lips, praying that this time, he wasn't misinterpreting Jakub's slow intake of breath. "You can just...slip in, without anyone knowing. Anytime."

Jakub leaned into him, still tense. Cheshire could feel his eyelashes flutter. "You'd like that?" he said, bordering on sarcasm.

But Cheshire was determined to take it seriously. "I would," he replied, sincerity making his voice rougher. He swallowed and felt Jakub do the same. "Anytime—all the time." He chuckled quietly. "It's a much bigger bed than I'm used to. I'll be lonely by myself."

He didn't really think Jakub would fall for a line like that, but it sure seemed to get to him after all; Jakub grabbed Cheshire's arm and twisted, angling for a kiss. Cheshire happily obliged, humming with renewed confidence and nervous exhilaration—the rest of their crew was only a few feet away. In fact, he could hear footsteps approaching. He held Jakub's lips as long as he dared and urged him back just as someone pushed against the door, thumping him in the back with it.

"Sorry," said Hannah, and Cheshire was embarrassed to abandon Jakub to her for a moment, but there was no way he could keep a panicked grin off his face then. He went to check on the lamp Jakub had just positioned while Hannah asked, "You two all right?"

"Fine," said Jakub, his voice as level as ever. "Let's finish up—I'm hungry. Coming, Chesh?"

"Yes!" Cheshire bobbled the lamp shade, fixed it, and then turned back to them with a very casual, very inconspicuous smile. "Yes, let's break in this place properly!"

In the kitchen, one of the boys had already opened a bottle of whiskey, and they were setting out every available glass, bowl, and saucer capable of holding a few sips to share it with. They laughed and toasted to Cheshire's newfound freedom as if he were a graduating schoolboy. And just as the conversation turned toward a real meal, the phone rang.

Cheshire didn't think anything of answering. He still had a teacup with whiskey in one hand, laughing, as he brought the receiver to his ear. "Brand new Bloom residence," he greeted cheerily.

"Well howdy, Bloom," said an equally jovial but completely unfamiliar voice. "Sure is swell seeing you again."

Cheshire laughed, glancing into the bedroom to see if one of the boys had picked up the second receiver. It sat in its cradle. "Ah, well," he said. "I wish I could say the same, but this is a *telephone*. And sadly I can't see you through the line, friend."

The stranger on the other end laughed with him. "That *is* a shame. Because I'm sure that Fiscella you're wearing is even more impressive up close."

Cheshire's stomach turned over as he again made a sweep of the room—everyone was accounted for, none of them paying any attention. "You like it, do you?" he said, stretching the phone cord as far as he could as he looked to the apartment entrance, and finally the windows. All the curtains had been thrown open for the sake of better lighting during the move, giving him a view of the cleared construction site across the street, and the river beyond. He squinted into the afternoon light. "I'll introduce you to my tailor."

"Oh, I think our time together would be better spent introducing you to *my* tailor," the man replied, so affable it barely registered as condescension. "You come on over the river any time, Bloom. We'll have a gas."

"Chesh?"

Cheshire jumped, startled to find Jakub right beside him. He motioned for quiet, but by then the line was dead. He waited a moment to be sure before hanging up. "Did you hear that?" he asked.

Jakub frowned at him. "Who was it?"

Cheshire moved to the west-facing windows and peered out. He was starting to draw everyone's attention, but he ignored their questions for a while, scanning the immediate view for any glint of light off binoculars. It had to be someone at the construction site—across the river was too far. No spyglass was good enough to spot him from Manhattan, and yet...

"Cheshire," Jakub insisted. "Who was on the phone?"

"It was..." Cheshire caught himself grinning, and he threw his arm around Jakub's shoulders. "I'll tell you later," he whispered, and he turned both of them toward his other guests. "Greetings from my new neighbors!" he explained, tugging Jakub back toward the phone so he could retrieve his teacup. "Now let's get back to finding something to eat."

LUCKY

Barney gathered his troops in the basement of his new building in Maspeth. It was out of the way for most of them, but Jakub could only assume he had something to prove. He had spread a map of New Jersey across a work table and encouraged Jakub and Hannah to look over the route he'd highlighted with marker. It followed the rail tracks.

"You want to rob a train?" Jakub asked incredulously.

"This is the route the postal trains take," said Barney, drawing a line with his finger. "Goes right through North Bergen, then up over the state line. There are a few freight stations it hits that would be easy to ambush, and they're not taking as many passengers." He snorted. "After Bloom's stunt last October fewer businesses want to use a heavy to transport their shit. It could be a good haul."

Hannah eyed the map critically. "Are you just assuming? Or do you have some intel?"

"I'm not making it up," Barney snapped, but then he puffed himself up and drew his temper back. "Postal trains are always carrying bearer bonds and payroll checks and sensitive documents. They get hit down south all the time. And if we pull this off in Jersey then the Manhattan gang will have to finally acknowledge us as a rival."

Jakub frowned but didn't have a chance to answer—the basement door banged open, and Cheshire's familiar laughter echoed down to them. Barney scowled at the stairway, which hopefully kept him from noticing Jakub's equally intense but much more anticipatory stare. Though since the move they hadn't seen much less of each other than usual, Jakub's stomach still flipped whenever Cheshire entered a room. How ridiculous it seemed to him, that after finally getting what he'd wanted for so long, that same anxious and eager reaction had only gotten worse.

"You didn't start without us, did you?" Cheshire asked as he hopped down the last two steps into the basement. Burke was close at his side, Gertie, her sisters, and the other Kozlow boys from his building close behind. Though Cheshire was grinning there was a strange moment of tension in the room as Barney's Maspeth boys sized them up. An observer might have thought it a meeting of rival gangs rather than an organization under one boss.

Barney pulled a face and looked to Burke. "Why'd you bring *him* here for this?"

"The hell would I not?" Burke retorted, with such easy, self-assured aggression that Barney visibly withered. "If y'really wanna hit the RPO, ye're gonna be needing yer biggest cannon, yeah? Bloody nonsense *not* to bring him."

Cheshire smirked, not bothering to throw in a word for himself. It set Barney's teeth gnashing, prompting Hannah to clear her throat. "The boss says he doesn't want Bloom in on this. He's supposed to still be lying low so the marshals don't pick back up on his tail."

"Horse shit," scoffed Burke, and Hannah and Barney both bristled.

"She's right," Jakub cut in. "The moment something explodes the feds will be looking for Bloom again. If they find a way to prove what he can do, that's the end of the big cannon." He met Cheshire's gaze. "But I have something else we can use."

Cheshire's smirk deepened, and then with a great big sigh and a helpless shrug he joined Jakub around the table. "If it's what the boss wants, nothing I can say," he declared. "But I at least want to know the score so I can give myself a very public alibi."

Jakub nodded, and as everyone began to settle down again, he looked to Barney. "What's the plan?"

Barney stiffened as all eyes turned to him, but then he shook himself up and returned to his earlier confidence. "We're gonna hit the RPO train as it heads through North Bergen," he said, pointing it out for the newcomers. "It has to stop at the freight yard to load the mail. A few of us can slip aboard there. The mail car will be at the rear so we can grab the workers without firing up the whole train. The rest will wait at the ferry stop in Ridgefield with the van. We load what we can and take off."

Cheshire hummed as he leaned over the map, and Barney eyed him as if expecting some critique. But it was Hannah who spoke up, and Jakub could tell she was doing her best to confidently support him. "What about security at the Ridgefield stop? If they're expecting the train there will be workers, even that late at night."

"Nothing we can't handle," Barney returned with a determined nod. "We'll round them up and shove them in a boxcar. Push comes to shove they eat lead."

Jakub's frown deepened, and Hannah must have seen, as she quickly said, "All right, but let's try to not let it come to that. The cops don't mind so much when we're killing each other, but civilian workers are something else."

"Sure, fine." Barney waved his hand dismissively. "That'll be up to you—I want you leading the landing point team. Jakub, Gertie and I will take two of the boys to board the train. Five of us will be plenty."

Jakub glanced to Cheshire, who was still smiling but offering nothing. For once whatever he was thinking didn't show in his face, which Jakub found irritating. He even had the fleeting sensation he was being deliberately opaque to throw Jakub off, as little sense as that made. "What if Hannah and the others have trouble at the yard?" he asked, trying to distract himself from it. "If there's more security than we're expecting, the rest of us would be pinned down in the mail car as soon as we get there."

"It'll be fine," Barney insisted, but then he shrugged beneath the weight of Jakub's stare and tried again. "Eighty-third street runs alongside the track. If there's trouble Hannah can send Burke down the road with some kind of signal."

Burke folded his arms. "Oh, you think ye're dragging

me into this?"

Barney leaned his palms against the edge of the table as he returned Burke's glare. "It's about time you got your hands dirty, isn't it?"

"Aren't I the one who got you the map?" Burke shot back, and the earlier tension returned to squeeze the room again. Cheshire only raised an eyebrow. "Aren't I the one who dug up the schedules and timed the damn train, all 'cause you asked so sweetly for it? Aren't I—"

"Enough," said Hannah. "Burke, it's not like you'll even need a gun."

"No—maybe he should," Barney interrupted, and even Jakub tensed. "He thinks we owe so much of this plan to him, maybe he should be right there on the damn train with us."

Burke leaned back, and in his face there was a momentary flash of honest fear before he could crush it beneath a scowl. "Oh, so *now* you think ye're getting me on that train? Well you better go ahead and line up another grand idea behind that one, 'cause I amn't about to take orders from the likes of you."

Barney bristled and straightened up as if meaning to round the table toward him. "You little—"

"Does the train have to stop?" asked Cheshire.

Barney and Burke were both so caught off guard that they stopped to stare at him, as did everyone else. Jakub held his breath, his left arm aching as he tried to catch Cheshire's eye. *Chesh please, don't make this worse!*

"What the hell does that even *mean?*" demanded Barney, though he was just as baffled as angry. "*Of course* it has to stop."

"Does it, though?" Cheshire leaned over the map, and though confused, everyone shifted a little closer. "The trip from the freight yard to the ferry is only fifteen minutes, if that. Before it even really has time to pick up speed, it goes around this curve." Cheshire walked his fingers along the railway. "If you uncouple the last car just before, it'll lose momentum and stall out. If Hannah and the rest of the crew follow along on Eighty-third like Barney suggested..." Cheshire followed the curve of the road with his other hand. "...You can practically roll the bags out the door and into the trucks."

"You can't uncouple a train in motion," said Gertie disapprovingly. "Not with it under load."

Cheshire leaned away with a shrug. "It'd be pretty easy for me," he replied, and he shoved his hands back into his pockets. "But then again, I'm not invited."

Barney's hackles went back up, but Jakub quickly stepped forward to defuse. "I can do it," he said, not that he cared for the number of eyes that turned his way. "I can blow the coupler."

"With what?" asked Hannah, eyeing him seriously. "Dynamite?"

"Something like that."

Barney scoffed. "The whole point was to *avoid* blowing things up."

"No," Jakub said quickly, overcome with the sudden determination that Cheshire's plan had to work. "No, the point is to avoid *Bloom* blowing things up." He could feel Cheshire's eyes on him but didn't dare look back, fearful of what a smile would do to his composure. "The more we rely on his power, the better the chance that the cops will catch on or find a snitch. If we can give him an alibi that's iron tight this time, they'll have to accept it's not just his magic, and they won't be able to link all our jobs together so easily. And that's better for everyone, not just Bloom."

Barney took a deep breath, but then he paused, glancing about the room. The energy had shifted again, and though Jakub had to fight not to shift uncomfortably beneath the attention, it was in his favor. Trying not to pull a face, Barney swept his hair beneath his cap. "All right. If you're *sure* you can cut the last car off, we'll do that." His expression tightened. "Burke can drive one of the trucks."

Burke tensed again, but then Cheshire put a hand on his shoulder and said, "He'll be great at it."

Barney carried on with the meeting, picking out the Szpilman boys that would be joining them on the train. Jakub left him to it, grateful that Cheshire and Burke stayed attentive and undisruptive throughout. It wasn't until Barney waved everyone out that he was able to give Cheshire a heavy look— which he then immediately regretted, because there were still a *lot* of people around, and the smile Cheshire flashed him twisted his stomach all over again.

"Don't take it out on Burke," Cheshire said, the man in question tucked under his arm, as the three of them huddled just outside the building. "Barney's never liked him anyway."

"Had it in for me," Burke agreed. "But I answer to the Boss, and as long as he's still breathing, that's *all* I answer to, you know?"

Jakub turned his collar up against the drizzle. "I know," he said. "But if you're gonna tell Barney that, don't do it in front of everyone."

"Ye're saying I should do it behind his back?" Burke retorted, though he was leaning back against Cheshire's arm, still not quite accustomed to Jakub's heavy stare on him. "Like everyone else?"

Jakub frowned, but before he could ask more, Cheshire laughed. "Don't worry," he said, "I'll keep a closer eye on our Eggy here." His eyes twinkled in the street light. "What about you? You coming by tonight?"

Jakub suppressed the flutter of butterflies in his stomach. "...It's late," he stalled. "And a long drive back."

"So? I'd give you a ride home."

Hannah came out of the building, dragging on her coat, and Jakub clenched his teeth. She was already watching them expectantly—if something was on her mind and she didn't have the chance to say it now, odds were she'd show up at Jakub's door first thing in the morning. He didn't want to have to explain to her why he'd spent the night at Cheshire's under the circumstances.

"Tomorrow," he said. "We can work out your alibi then."

"Sure." Cheshire grinned, and he relinquished Burke as Hannah approached. "Enjoy the long drive back," he said with a hint of sympathy, and then he turned, heading to his car where his building-mates awaited.

Hannah cast him a look but didn't comment. "Ready?" she asked.

It *was* a long drive back, and a quiet one. Whatever Hannah was mulling over, she didn't seem interested in sharing it with Burke. It wasn't until they split up at the Kozlow building that she tugged Jakub aside.

"Did Barney tell you about this train business before tonight?" she asked, shaking her coat out.

"No." Jakub slicked his hair out of his face. "He's just trying to get one up on Bloom. He can still do that with this plan, even if it was Bloom's idea. Maybe then he'll calm down."

Hannah sighed. "Yeah, probably," she said unconvincingly. "I just wish he'd come to us first. We could have talked it out and saved a scene." She met Jakub's eyes and relaxed a little. "Thanks for stepping in."

Jakub struggled not to frown at the misplaced sentiment. "Sure. I'll see if I can talk to him before the job."

"Thanks." Hannah nodded gratefully, and they wished each other good night.

Jakub returned to his room, but he knew immediately that he wouldn't sleep. He stripped out of his jacket and dropped onto the sofa, trying to think of something to keep him busy rather than staring at the bedroom wall the rest of the night. But it was no use. Even with the drizzle turning to rain outside, the building around him felt too quiet, too hollow. Too cold. He thought of Cheshire's laugh ringing down the basement stairwell and considered taking a shower instead, letting warm steam and his imagination supply distraction and release. He told himself he was still considering it even as he climbed to his feet and headed for the door.

"Stupid," he muttered, and he shoved his arms into his coat.

It was just nearing two in the morning when Jakub let himself into Cheshire's apartment with his spare key, and immediately he felt better. The sound of the rain was soothing instead of isolating, and the smell of Cheshire's cologne hung in the air. Though his first instinct was to head straight into the bedroom, he hesitated. Cheshire had certainly given his permission, and it wouldn't be the first time. But he struggled with a sudden reminder from his saner self that it was childish for him to have made the trip at all.

So instead he hung up his jacket and headed to the kitchen table, which for the past few weeks had been taken up by gun parts and tools. His visit to Tully's workshop at Hallorran had left him inspired enough to try a few things out for himself, which had finally begun to take true shape. He hadn't meant to take over Cheshire's brand new space with the project, at least not straight away, but it had seemed more convenient than not at the beginning—at least for him—and it was a perfect excuse now. Everything would have to come together in working order sooner than he'd planned, considering he'd just promised the weapon to Barney's heist.

The bedroom door opened. Jakub kept his nose in his work, pretending not to notice as Cheshire emerged, dressed in his pajamas. "I thought you said tomorrow," Cheshire said, smothering a yawn as he strolled up behind him.

"It *is* tomorrow," said Jakub, not looking up as he slid a freshly chiseled piece back into place. "Sorry I woke you, I just realized I need to have this finished and tested before next week."

"Oh, sure."

Cheshire leaned up against the back of Jakub's chair and watched him work for a few minutes. His presence made it increasingly difficult to continue, but it was a scintillating tension that Jakub savored. Over and over he reminded himself that these moments they spent together could lead to more, rather than just the hope for more. He didn't *have* to draw it out like this, but the relief of knowing that he could made him want to.

"You're really getting the hang of it, aren't you?" Cheshire said.

"I guess so." Jakub drew back the loading handle to cock the rifle with a loud *clack* and then pulled the trigger, watching the mechanisms spring into place. "It's my first time putting something together like this, but I learned a lot at Hallorran. The next one will be better."

"Oh...yeah, I'm sure it will," said Cheshire, and the momentary confusion in his tone drew Jakub's attention. His eyes had darted away and the tiny flash of guilt Jakub saw tightened his lungs. *Oh. He means the arm, doesn't he?* He curled his prosthetic fingers self-consciously, wondering how closely Cheshire had been watching them.

"Is it going to be a while?" Cheshire asked, back to his usual charm. "Should I make coffee?"

"No, don't worry about me." Jakub turned back to the table and began moving tools aimlessly around. "You can go back to sleep, if you want."

Cheshire hummed again, but then he moved around the chair to instead lean his hip against the table. A familiar sliver of mischief crept into his voice. "You know, I don't mind you borrowing the space," he said. "But it's not what I had in mind when I gave you my spare key."

Cheshire threaded his fingers through Jakub's damp hair and smoothed his bangs back. That was more like it. Jakub straightened up, the heat he had been seeking by coming here swelling in his belly. His tidying slowed. "What *did* you have in mind?"

Cheshire traced Jakub's cheek with the backs of his fingers, down to his jaw. Jakub allowed himself to be prodded, and when he tilted his chin up to meet Cheshire's eyes, a shiver went down his spine.

"I can *show* you," Cheshire said, sing-song. "But it's back in the bedroom."

Jakub gave up on any pretense of playing hard to get; he stood, turning to face Cheshire for the kiss he had been hoping for. But before he could reach for him, Cheshire captured both of his wrists. The unexpected display of strength sent Jakub's heart pounding.

"Ah, ah, ah," said Cheshire, smirking. He had already grown so much bolder and Jakub was embarrassed by how arousing he found it. "Let's clean you up first, so you don't get grease on my new—"

Jakub leaned into and kissed him. He pulled at his hands just enough to make Cheshire tighten his grip; how incredible it felt, having even that small portion of Cheshire's strength turned on him. But he *was* eager to take it to the bedroom, to indulge in the soft, springy mattress and naked sheets, and he pulled away from Cheshire's lips before they could get carried away. "Okay," he said breathlessly.

Cheshire grinned and let him go, only to snag Jakub by the hips and turn him around. As Jakub grabbed up a rag to clean the grease from his fingers, Cheshire pressed up behind him. He slipped his warm hands under Jakub's shirt to tickle his sides, kissed the nape of his neck and rubbed eagerly up against his ass. When Cheshire's broad palm kneaded into the small of his back, Jakub's knees felt weak, and without thinking he leaned forward. If only Cheshire had pushed a little harder, he could have had Jakub right then and there, fucking him over the kitchen table.

With a deep breath Jakub gathered his wits and turned around to show off his cleaned hands for inspection. "Good enough?"

Cheshire tugged Jakub's left hand closer and kissed the

inside of his palm. Jakub could have sworn he felt it. "Perfect."

They tugged each other into the bedroom, articles of clothing dropping along the way. In the dark, early hours they twisted together beneath silky sheets, blissful and electric, then fell asleep to the sound of the rain. When Jakub awoke a few hours later, the usual impact of incredulous and anxious emotion he usually experienced waking up in Cheshire's arms had dulled. Instead he felt awed...and safe. He fingered a lock of Cheshire's hair and watched him sleep for a while until dozing off until morning.

***

A week later, Jakub called Cheshire the evening of the heist. "We're just about to head out," he said, the phone tucked against his shoulder as he finished lacing up his boots. "Gertie's already at the yard and says the coast is clear. You're set on your end?"

"Reservations made," Cheshire confirmed. He heaved a deep sigh. "It's not going to be nearly as exciting as your night. I still wish I could be there."

"We'll be fine." Jakub wished he could, too, but he worried that saying so might put ideas in Cheshire's head. "You're just upset you won't be the one telling the story once we're done."

Cheshire laughed, giving Jakub all the confidence he needed. "Yeah, honestly? You're right. But I know you'll do great. Then *you'll* be the one bragging to the boys."

Jakub blushed at the thought. "I'd rather not."

Cheshire laughed some more, but then he quieted seriously. "There's a big ol' moon out tonight, Jake. Be careful."

"I will," Jakub promised.

Jakub grabbed up his suitcase and headed downstairs, sharing similar sentiments with Hannah before they split up. Barney was already waiting with the two Szpilmans; one of them moved to the back seat to allow Jakub a seat next to Barney. With his new rifle tucked in the trunk and Jakub reluctantly at Barney's side, they sped off.

"It's been a damn long time, hasn't it?" said Barney, drumming his fingers anxiously against the steering wheel. "Since the two of us were on a job without Bloom?" He snorted.

"Shit, I can't even remember."

"Me, neither," said Jakub. "It'll be fine, though. The plan makes sense."

Barney grumbled again, but Jakub wasn't interested in debating the plan or Cheshire's involvement in its creation. He leaned against the door, trying to catch a glimpse of the full moon through the buildings.

***

Cheshire arrived in Lower Manhattan precisely on schedule. The restaurant he had chosen for his alibi had been growing in popularity as the city's best Chinese, attracting customers from all over with its large, open floor and boisterous atmosphere. It was the perfect place to stand out without appearing suspicious. More to Cheshire's needs, it was one of the closest and most often visited restaurants to the South District offices of the US Marshals.

Grace met him at the entrance, and after greeting each other warmly, they followed the maître dᴘ to their table near the center of the floor. Already Cheshire spied a few customers glancing up from their meals, some of them dressed in the unmistakable plain-cut suits that government workers endured. If they were lucky, there would be a few courthouse clerks or maybe even a deputy dining that night.

"You look good," said Grace as they were seated. "But then, you always do, don't you?"

"So do you," Cheshire replied, and though both were teasing, there wasn't any arguing it was true: they had coordinated in complementary colors, Cheshire in a rich, plum three piece and Grace in a green Chiffon dress. Beneath the warm gold lighting they might as well have been royalty as far as he was concerned.

They chatted brightly over their drinks, dim sum carts whirling by. Cheshire dialed up the charm and humor to get Grace to laugh as much and as honestly as possible, and she played right along, by now well-accustomed to performing as decoy. But once he was satisfied with the amount of attention they'd drawn to their presence, he did take the opportunity to tease her on a more personal subject.

"So," he drawled, raising an eyebrow. "How are things

with Thea?"

"Oh," said Grace, which pretty much told him everything. She took a sip of wine. "She's fine. Well." Grace sighed and then fixed him with a caricature of a smile. "You're really going to make me say it?"

"What?" Cheshire tried not to cringe as he reached for his own glass. "I'm honestly asking—I haven't heard a thing."

Grace eyed him a moment longer, and judging him sincere she dropped her shoulders. "Thea and I are just friends," she surrendered. "Apparently that's all we ever were to begin with." She took another, longer drink as Cheshire winced sympathetically. "Not that I really *expected* more than that, you know? She's wrapped up in her business, and I've been trying to get musicians together for a band—a group of my own. It was only just some fun."

"Even so, I'm sorry," said Cheshire. "I know you were hoping for...more than that."

Grace waved away his clumsy attempts to make the conversation more awkward. "I'll find it," she said confidently. "In fact..." For a moment her expression grew wistful, but seeing that Cheshire was about to latch on and question that detail, she quickly cleared her throat. "Anyway, enough about me. What about *you*?" She smirked at him. "I figured that by now you'd have some molly lined up to participate in these escapades of yours."

Cheshire gulped. "Actually..." he said, but then he stopped, no idea how to finish that sentence. He tugged at his collar to relieve the heat stretching down from his ears. "I have... someone."

"Oh?" Grace lit up with curiosity. "Who? Why isn't she here?"

"I think," Cheshire amended.

"Think what?"

"I *think* I have someone."

Grace sagged with a withered look. "Chesh," she told him, "I'm sorry, but if you only *think* you do, you probably don't. That's the mistake *I* just made."

"No, I mean, I do," Cheshire said, struggling to recover. "He's just...a tough read. We've been sleeping together for a while, but I don't think it's for fun." He laughed awkwardly. "I mean, it's fun! But *he's* not...fun...?"

- 63 -

"Why are you so nervous?" Grace asked, leaning into her palm. "You didn't have a problem telling me about Leon, and that sounded *loads* more complicated."

"Oh, no, this is so much worse!" Cheshire said, laughing. Realizing he was starting to draw more attention than he cared for, he gulped down the rest of his wine and finished with a gasp. "It's Jakub."

Grace laughed. "No really, Chesh, you can tell me."

"No, I..." Cheshire forced himself to smile. "Really. It's Jakub."

All identifiable emotion drained from Grace's face, nearly taking her freckles with it. "What?"

***

Jakub rolled down his window a crack for a breath of fresh air. The night was bright and damp, moonlight illuminating even the drab metal containers of the train yard. Workers tugged their collars up as they rolled large bins full of canvas sacks up planks into the parked train. If any of them had taken notice of the Model A parked in the narrow service road a hundred feet away, they hadn't given any indication.

Barney drummed his fingers loudly against the steering wheel while waiting for the train to finish loading. He had been antsy from the very start of the job and his energy hadn't let up, amplifying the nerves of the two Szpilman boys he'd brought with them. It put Jakub on edge.

"You don't have to be so nervous," Jakub said, winding the mainspring of his prosthetic tight. "This is going to work."

"I'm not nervous," Barney muttered. He paused in his drumming to rub his eyes. "I didn't get enough sleep with all the *crying.*"

It took Jakub a few beats to realize what he meant. "Oh. How is he? Little Kasper?"

"He's great! He's incredible." Barney slapped himself in the face and shook his head. "Wonderful. Wanda can't wait for another."

The workers finished loading the last of the bins and began backing away from the platform. "That's it," said Jakub, and he tucked the winding key back into his jacket. "Let's go."

They all climbed out of the driver's side to avoid notice,

and Jakub moved to the trunk to retrieve his suitcase. He popped it open and lifted the recently-completed rifle out, taking only a few moments to make sure everything was in order. Confident, he slung it over his shoulder and followed Barney closer to the tracks.

The train blew its whistle to signal its readiness to depart, and the sound of it sent a chill down Jakub's spine. *It'll be fine*, he told himself as they stayed low, creeping through the grass. *We've practiced this.* He gave his metal fingers a few stretches to make sure they wouldn't lock up as the train slowly ground into motion. He breathed in. *You can tell Chesh all about it later.*

As the train began to pull away, Barney led the charge. Long before the engine could get up to full speed he leapt across the small ditch that separated the tracks from the service drive and then grabbed for one of the boarding handles. He hauled himself aboard the baggage car with only a slight stumble on the rain-slick metal. Stas went after him, depending on some help from Barney to climb on. By then the car was moving past, and Jakub ran alongside, waiting for the back end of the car. It approached faster than he'd expected and he jumped for it before he was ready; his left hand snapped around the handle tight but his right faltered. Luckily, Gertie had already boarded on the other side, and she grabbed his jacket to draw him in.

"Thanks," said Jakub, and the two of them helped the last of their group, Ian, onto the train.

"My sisters will come back for the cars," Gertie said as they huddled against the mail car door. "Did anyone see you?"

"I don't think so." Jakub leaned away from the car as far as he dared, but they had already moved far enough away from the yard that the workers were only specks. Any shout of alarm they might have raised would have been well drowned out by the clack of the spinning wheels. His stomach lurched abruptly at the motion and he drew himself back in. "Ready?"

There was a shout from the baggage car ahead of them, and Gertie and Ian both drew their pistols. A minute later the door twisted open, revealing Barney, Stas, and a train worker lying unconscious on the floor of the car behind them. Blood matted the man's hair, but Jakub couldn't tell if he'd been shot or bludgeoned, and the sway of the train made it impossible to see if he was breathing.

"Stas and I will secure the car," said Barney, resituating his cap on his sweaty forehead. "Watch our backs. As soon as the workers are tied up, Jakub blows the coupler."

Everyone nodded agreement, and they shifted positions in the small space to let Barney and Stas take the door. Jakub put his back to the baggage car, trying not to look at the scenery beginning to speed past them on either side. With rifle in hand, he took a deep breath as Barney twisted the door open.

***

"*Seriously?*" Grace gaped at Cheshire in astonishment, waving her chopstick erratically. "How is that even possible? He doesn't even *like* you."

Cheshire laughed nervously as he flagged down one of the passing dim sum carts. He wasn't sure he'd ever *stop* laughing nervously. "I know! I thought that, too!" He blushed at the waiter eyeing him curiously and began pointing to dishes at random, just to hurry the interaction along. "No one was more surprised than me, believe me."

"But he's always making that *face*," Grace carried on, and seeing the dumplings he'd selected, she dragged the basket to her side of the table. "I swear he looks at you sometimes like he's going to vomit."

"I know! But it's actually a good thing, see?" Cheshire grimaced at the face *she* made at him; it was hopeless to try to explain the very subtle nuances to Jakub's typical expressions he had been making such an effort to study. "He *can* make other faces, you know. Nice faces."

Grace shook her head emphatically. "I can't picture it. At all."

Cheshire wanted to reply that he hadn't been able to either, not until he'd seen for himself: Jakub's shy little smile in the diner the first morning after; Jakub's eyelashes fluttering and lips slack when caught in a moment of pleasure; Jakub's heavy, almost *needy* glare only a few nights ago when he'd snuck into Cheshire's apartment. He thought of Jakub glancing at him over his shoulder, leaning over the kitchen table, and his ears went hot.

"It's taking some getting used to," Cheshire admitted, waving the waiter on once he'd amassed entirely too many plates and a refill of wine. He chuckled at himself some more as he passed more to Grace. "But it's...really something. I don't really know how to describe it, honestly. After all this time to just... all of a sudden! But it seems to be working, you know?"

"I guess it would have to be," Grace said, pulling a face. "To risk the rest of the gang finding out."

At last Cheshire's good humor faltered. "Yeah." He swirled his rice noodles around with his chopsticks. "That's the kicker, I guess. I don't think it would go over well."

"If anyone believed it at all." Grace, too, frowned more deeply as she ate. "You've got a lot more to lose here than him, you know. You should be careful."

Cheshire forced another laugh. "What do you mean?"

"I mean, what if he's not looking at this the same way you are?" said Grace, and Cheshire quickly sobered again. "What if everyone finds out and he cuts you loose to save face? What if it goes badly and he takes it out on you somehow? I know I haven't been around as much, but I remember how Barney and Hannah were. One word from Jay and you'd be...?"

"...Mincemeat," Cheshire agreed, grimacing. "But he's not like that."

"Do you know that?" Grace pressed, true concern showing through her furrowed brow. "When have you ever seen Jakub going steady with *anyone*? Do you really know what he'll do if it goes south, if everyone finds out?"

Cheshire's stomach turned, and he reached for the wine. "Well, no, I guess not. But I'm sure it'll be okay. Barney's an asshole but he's not..."

Cheshire couldn't finish that sentence with confidence, and when Grace saw as much she gave a sigh. "Chesh, I'm sorry. I'm not trying to rain on your parade here, I'm just saying...be careful." She smiled wisely. "Maybe try to figure out what you really have before you go too far, okay? Just be honest with him, and maybe you'll get some honesty back."

Cheshire's lip turned up. He was fairly sure she wasn't making a deliberate jab at their own history, but it felt like one, and he quickly drowned any unadvised retort with a gulp of the wine. "Yeah, you're right. Thanks for looking out for me."

Grace reached across the table to give his wrist a squeeze, and then they both leaned back, each taking a deep breath to clear the air. "Tell me about your next big operation," Grace prodded, and it was back to easier topics as they continued the meal.

***

When Jakub first glanced into the mail car, he knew immediately that something was off, but he vastly underestimated just how much.

There was only one worker in the car: a very tall, very broad man dressed in a railway uniform that was clearly too small for him. He was seated on one of the mail sacks along the wall, arms folded on his stomach and round chin tipped forward in sleep. A small blue cap sat atop his straight, unattractive haircut.

Barney and Stas exchanged a look before proceeding carefully inside. There was no sign of any other workers, only bins of mail on either side, some sacks propped against the walls. They only left the station minutes ago—it didn't seem right. But without any explanation immediately visible Jakub didn't know how to begin warning his fellows, and he could only tighten his grip on the rifle as Barney approached the man on duty.

Barney clicked back the hammer of his revolver, and Jakub was paying close enough attention to see the man's eye flick open, then close again.

This is a setup. Jakub pushed away from the baggage car, ready to shout, but before he could get a breath out the worker jolted awake.

"Oh, God!" the man cried, startling back. He threw both hands up. "Don't shoot!"

Barney startled too and nearly pulled the trigger, not that he'd even had time to properly get the man in his sights. He scowled and gathered himself up. "Keep those hands up, big guy," he said, and he motioned with the gun for the stranger to stand up. "Cooperate and I won't have to kill you."

The man stood. He was just over six feet tall and nearly as wide as the car's narrow walkthrough, making maneuvering behind him impossible. "Yes, whatever you say," he said, hands raised as he took a step toward the rear. "I don't need any trouble."

"See if you can get some of those sacks into the bins,"

said Barney as he walked the worker to the rear of the car. "They'll be easier to load that way."

"Stealing mail is a federal offense," said the worker, and Barney scowled, shoving the muzzle of the revolver into his chin. The worker leaned further back. "No trouble!"

Jakub stepped into the car, but he didn't make any move to help as Gertie and the two Szpilmans began hoisting any loose sacks they found into the bins. He kept his gaze on the stranger: the man was complying but much too calmly, watching them work with interest rather than fear. "Boss," he said. "There's rope."

He motioned to a loose rope tied around one of the sacks to keep it close to the wall, which Gertie began to unwind. Though he didn't seem to share Jakub's caution, Barney nodded. "Turn around," he ordered, motioning again with the revolver. "Put your hands behind your back."

"I'm not great at that," the man replied, but he turned in the cramped space and lowered his hands. "But do what you gotta do, friend, I'm not here to judge."

Gertie advanced with the rope, but before she could begin tying, the man turned over his shoulder again. "Just one question," he said, and he arched a narrow eyebrow at her. "How're you gonna uncouple the car without Bloom here?"

Gertie straightened. "Wha—"

The stranger's fist crashed into her jaw before she saw it coming. Moving faster than his size dictated he felled her with a single blow, then reached for Barney's revolver. His hand palming the cylinder was huge, preventing it from firing, and Barney barely had time to curse before he was dragged into a fierce headbutt. His back hit the ground with a loud thud.

Jakub's pulse thundered as he watched the stranger take Barney's gun in hand—too close to his allies to risk firing the rifle. He reached for the revolver in his belt but by then bullets were flying. The stranger took two to the chest from Barney's boys but he barely flinched, his aim unwavering as he shot Ian straight through the eye. Stas leapt for cover behind one of the bins, but the stranger didn't relent, a powerful kick thrusting the bin up against the one behind it. Stas screamed as his arm was trapped between the metal rims with a crack of bone.

Jakub reeled back. The revolver flashed and he felt a sharp, shuddering impact along the length of his metal forearm as the bullet struck. As he threw himself back out through the door he almost lost his balance, and he had to let go of the handgun to catch himself against the boarding rail. In a matter of seconds he was the only one left, and the stranger was already storming down the car toward him. He wished that Cheshire was there.

"Hey!" the man shouted, his foot falls heavy enough for Jakub to trace even above the clack of the train. "Show me that big gun you've got!"

Jakub spun back through the doorway, slamming the butt of the rifle into the man's sternum. Rather than a soft diaphragm the stock clanged against something metal beneath his shirt, dulling the blow from what he'd hoped for. It was only enough to stagger him for a moment, but Jakub took as much of the advantage as he could—he struck again, popping the man under his chin and then throwing his full weight forward. It bought him a few steps, enough for him to turn and jerk the rifle to his shoulder.

Hannah and the rest will be waiting, he thought. *If we can outnumber him in the open—* He pulled the trigger.

The coupler exploded in a fireball of splintering metal. The blast rocked the car on the track, and for a moment Jakub's stomach turned nauseatingly at the thought of them derailing, just as they entered into the curve. That concern was cut off by the man pouncing on him from behind. Arms like iron bars twisted around his stomach, pinning his arms and crushing his ribs. Without enough breath even to curse, he could only struggle weakly as he was lifted off his feet.

"Not bad," the stranger huffed. "Not bad at—"

Jakub threw his head back and felt his skull knock against teeth; the man yelped and sputtered. "Ow, fuck! Stop squirming, God bless ya."

The man squeezed tighter, and Jakub fought harder to weaker results. The pressure forced all the air out of his lungs, and he writhed, the veins in his temples pounding. But the train was slowing—he still stood a chance if only he could get free, just for a moment. Out of options, he scraped to get a grip on his metal arm and gave it a sharp twist.

The lock disengaged, and Jakub wrenched his bare elbow free of the man's suffocating bear hug. He jammed the steel mounting plate as hard as he could into his attacker's face and nearly fainted from relief when the arms around him went slack. Gasping and shuddering, Jakub clawed for escape. As soon as his feet touched the ground he ran for the door.

The train hadn't stopped but Jakub didn't wait—he leapt clear, the impact rattling his knees as he landed and rolled. He was still skidding down the embankment when he heard the brakes engage, and gradually the mail car squealed to a halt.

"Hannah?" Jakub called. He drew a switchblade from his boot as he staggered upright along the side of the road. The gleam of approaching headlights from a pair of trucks helped calm his hammering pulse, and he turned back to face the train car, already trying to think of how he could lure his enemy out. *Aim for the head*, he thought, ready to pass the instructions on as soon as the rest of Kozlow was there to assist.

The trucks braked behind him, and Jakub could hear people getting out of the cabs. He glanced over his shoulder, eager for Hannah at his side, only to find himself on the other end of a shotgun. An older woman he had never seen before with dark skin and silvery hair motioned at him with the gun. "Drop the knife."

Jakub stared, slow to comprehend. As he watched, more unfamiliar figures climbed out of the trucks, each brandishing a firearm. By the time it became clear he was surrounded, there was nothing to do but as he was told. He dropped the knife; the woman kicked it away.

"Are you all right?" she called, and Jakub turned to see the stranger climbing down from the train. He had the Hallorran prosthetic in one hand and was wiping his face with the other.

"Bit my fucking lip," the man said, smearing blood across his palm. He rubbed it on his shirt front, and in the moonlight Jakub saw glints of metal beneath the bullet holes. "You?"

"Fine. Like clockwork."

Jakub glanced between them, his confusion giving way to caution. A dozen armed thugs were moving with purpose, climbing the small hill to the train. They passed orders to each other not unlike Barney had done earlier—they were taking the bins.

"Who are you?" Jakub asked, eyeing the stranger. "Who tipped you off?"

"I was really hoping to meet Bloom on this one," the

stranger said, gazing up at the train. "Even though that *was* a real nice explosion." He glanced to Jakub. "Has it always been you? All that magic talk wasn't just for show, was it? Fucking disappointment, that would be."

Jakub clenched his fist until it ached; he could feel his muscles clenching against the mounting plate on his left arm in turn. "Who are you?" he demanded again. "What the hell is this?"

"There'll be time for that later." The stranger turned to face him and stepped closer, looming into his space. His lips twisted into a smirk. "Right now I wanna know how you're gonna help me meet Cheshire Bloom."

***

As soon as the guest of honor made her appearance, Cheshire could sense the arrival, and he smiled to himself. *Only our second meeting and I can smell her,* he thought smugly. *And to think Jakub was worried.*

He leaned back in his chair as he dabbed his mouth with a napkin, taking the opportunity to survey the restaurant floor. Sure enough, US Marshal Hazel Adalet was prowling among the tables. She was dressed in a similar if not the same blue suit he had seen her in before, likely having been drawn directly from her office at the courthouse down the street. As soon as she spotted Cheshire her face grew dark and she marched over toward their table.

"We're up," said Cheshire, and Grace's eyes flashed. She still enjoyed this part.

"Mr. Bloom," Hazel greeted tersely. "You're awfully far from home this evening."

"Not at all, Marshal," Cheshire replied, flashing her a winning smile. "I happen to love the Lower East; it's my home away from home." He gestured across the table. "Allow me to introduce you to Grace Overgaard, lead performer at the Olivier Hotel." He smiled at Grace. "Grace, this is US Marshal Adalet."

"Pleased to meet you," said Grace.

Hazel narrowed her eyes on her. "Same." She latched back on to Cheshire. "Should I be keeping my eyes open for an explosion?"

Cheshire shrugged. "The food isn't *that* spicy."

"I know you've been laying low on purpose for a while now," Hazel carried on, hands on her hips. "But sooner or later you won't be able to help yourself. I *will* catch you."

"I'm right here," Cheshire replied. "You've got me."

He could have spent all evening teasing the poor woman, but then something in Grace's face changed; she looked toward the door and then back to Cheshire, staring hard, as if there was something he was meant to notice. But Hazel was rambling about the constraints of the law or some such, and he didn't think it safe to turn his head and draw her attention as well. Thankfully he didn't have to wait long to understand, as then Burke crossed the dining room toward the rest rooms. He cast Cheshire a quick, hard look, just enough for Cheshire to see the bruise darkening at his temple, before he slipped into the men's room.

Cheshire's heart gave a thud. *What's he doing here? Did something go wrong?*

"The locals may be too scared to stare you down, but I'm not," Hazel finished. "Remember that."

"Yes, I sure will," said Cheshire, even though he'd barely heard. He forced himself to meet Hazel's glare with a smile. "But does it have to be *now*? I've got my eye on the dessert cart heading this way."

Hazel continued to glare, but lo and behold a cart was heading over, and she was forced to take a few steps back to put herself out of its way. Once it had passed she couldn't resist one final, "Next time, Bloom," before she turned back toward the entrance.

Cheshire lifted his glass as if to take a drink. "What's she doing?"

Grace took a casual look. "Talking to the maître d⊡. It looks like she's getting a table."

"Great," Cheshire muttered. He waited a little, sipping his wine to appear unconcerned, before his nerves got the better of him. "Keep an eye on her for me," he said as he stood.

"Good luck," said Grace, and she worried her lip between her teeth as he headed toward the bathroom.

Burke was waiting in the men's room, pacing back and forth in front of the mirrors. He spun around as soon as Cheshire entered and all but pounced on him. "Bloom!" He grabbed Cheshire's arms and shook him. "Bloom, we gotta go.

They got them—they got everyone, we have to get over there."

"What? Who?" Cheshire took him by the elbows to steady him. "Slow down and tell me what happened." He gulped. "Where's Jakub?"

"Manhattan has them!" Burke took a deep breath and pawed at his face a moment, trying to regain his composure. "They jumped us on the road—outnumbered us two to one. I don't know how they knew 'bout the job but they were waiting! Waiting on us to show. Marched everyone into the trucks and sent me here to get you."

"Shit." Cheshire's mind spun with too many questions, though only one made it to his mouth. "What about Jakub? The ones on the train—are they all right?"

"I dunno," Burke admitted. "I don't know fuckin' anything right now, except I'm supposed to take you to some hotel." Cheshire reached for Burke's face, but his hand was brushed aside. "I'm fine. Can't we please get the hell out of here?"

"Okay, okay." Cheshire took a deep breath and herded him out the door. "Tell me the rest on the way."

Back at the table, Grace looked up from her dessert with concern. "You all right?"

"Don't know yet," Cheshire said, and he pulled a few bills from his wallet. "I'm sorry, but do you mind taking a cab home? This should cover the bill and the fare."

"It's fine," Grace assured, and the worry creasing her brow reminded him of their conversation earlier. "Go on."

Cheshire left the cash with her and bid her goodnight. As he and Burke finally made their way out of the restaurant he couldn't help but cast a glance in Hazel's direction. She was being shown to a table, but now there was an officer with her, talking close and quiet to her ear. Cheshire ducked behind a potted tree to avoid her gaze as he retreated.

Burke drove them to the Four Thrones hotel just off of Battery Park—an old building renovated many times over the years, modern trimmings on old red brick. Cheshire's heart was in his throat as he followed Burke inside. Whatever had happened, whatever Manhattan wanted, he could talk their way out of it somehow. Their two sides hadn't been toeing around each other all these months just for a blood bath. If he could figure out right away what they were after, he could negotiate.

Or if not...I can still kill them, Cheshire thought, clenching his teeth. *If Jakub's all right and it comes down to that...*

The hotel lobby was warmly lit, with plenty of patrons milling about. Many of them glanced over as Cheshire and Burke entered, taking note of the latter's bruised face. Cheshire straightened his back and tried to project only easy confidence, even as his imagination warned him everyone there was against them.

A tall, middle-aged woman in a heavy jacket beckoned them to the elevators. "You must be Bloom," she greeted stiffly, motioning for them to get inside. "The Boss is waiting."

"If I'd known I had an appointment, I would have been here sooner," Cheshire replied, hands in his pockets as they rode the elevator up to the top floor. "Your boss has my number, doesn't he?"

The woman didn't respond. Normally Cheshire would have attempted some other angle, but his palms were hot and itchy, and he was determined to stay focused.

The elevator opened with a chime at the penthouse, and Cheshire's stomach dropped. The room had been cleared out, furniture pushed to the walls to make room for the nearly three dozen men and women crammed inside. Though the majority seemed to be Manhattan gang members, Cheshire's attention was drawn first to their captives: Jakub, Hannah, Barney, and the rest had been crowded into a corner on their knees, arms tied behind them, held at gunpoint. Though several sported bruises and bloody noses, and one of Barney's men was pale and shaking with pain, Jakub at least didn't seem injured. Their eyes met, and Cheshire swallowed, a shiver running through him at Jakub's concerned expression. Cheshire offered a quick smile as reassurance and faced his hosts.

He recognized the pair immediately, which came as a surprise, though he would later think that it shouldn't have: it was the man and woman from the theater who had reacted to him with such familiarity. They sat together on a broad lounge, the heavy-set man reclining easily, the woman at his side eying him critically over the collar of her thick fur coat. There was very little to draw from their varied expressions of curiosity and distrust. Cheshire took a deep breath.

"Cheshire Bloom, at your service," he greeted. "I'm

sorry to have kept you waiting."

"Take your hands out of your pockets," said the woman in a thick Puerto Rican accent.

Cheshire did so, showing off his gloves. "I'm not armed."

"You wouldn't need to be, would you?" replied the man with a tiny smirk. "So say the rumors."

Cheshire was already looking forward to the aftermath of this encounter, when he would let Jakub say "I told you so" as many times as he wanted. "I can't imagine what you mean," he said. "But I'm just here to talk, Mr...?"

"Masterson." The man hopped to his feet and came forward with hand outstretched; Cheshire betrayed no worry as he accepted the overly-firm handshake. "Herbert Masterson, friends call me Herb."

"Glad to hear we're friends already, Herb," said Cheshire, taking note of the bullet holes in Herb's white button down. He glanced past it to the woman watching them. "Do you mind introducing me?"

"My pleasure." Herb chuckled and slapped Cheshire on the back as he turned. "Cheshire, meet Camila Reynoso." He smirked. "But to you, Lucky."

Cheshire blinked in surprise. "Lucky?" he repeated, and Camila sat up straighter, adjusting her glasses. "She looks incredible for a dead man."

Herb gave his shoulder a squeeze, and Cheshire winced, accepting the warning. "Lecce's yesterday's news," said Herb. "Done, forgotten. Who's that? No one I know." He relaxed his grip and patted Cheshire instead. "Our Lady Lucky is all there is now. And she's all New York needs. You understand, don't you?"

Cheshire glanced back to Jakub, who was watching almost unblinkingly. Hannah was subtly shaking her head. Cheshire wasn't sure what either was trying to communicate, and Burke's grim frown wasn't any more help. *Well shit, here goes nothing*, he thought. "Oh yes, I understand. But I don't think I agree."

"Oh?" Herb, one hand still on his shoulder, leaned in closer. "With which part?"

"The 'New York doesn't need *us*' part you're implying."

"Bloom," said Hannah, warning.

"Go ahead," said Camila, nestling into her fur once

more. "Explain."

Cheshire licked his lips. Between Camila's unfaltering stare, and Herb continuing to impress himself on his space, he wasn't sure which deserved his attention more. "What I mean, is, New York is pretty big," he began, carefully, but with as much affable charm as he could muster given the situation. "And Kozlow has been doing just fine in Brooklyn for years now. It wasn't your predecessor who chased out the Foleys, solidified the waterfront and united with Queens. That was *us*."

"And you think that means something to us?" challenged Herb, though he still sounded as if he was enjoying himself immensely. "A few piers in Brooklyln and a new building?"

"I sure do." Cheshire cast him a sideways glance. "I think someone who spent just as long pulling all the Manhattan gangs into one operation knows *exactly* what that's worth."

"Then you *do* agree," said Herb. "'Cause the next logical step up is 'one operation' for *everyone*, right?"

Cheshire hesitated, and in that pause Barney rose up on his knees. "Bloom doesn't speak for us," he said. "If we're negotiating, then untie my fucking—"

The man behind Barney kicked him between the shoulder blades, sending him sprawling onto his face. Two steps forward and he shoved the muzzle of his shotgun into the base of Barney's skull. Hannah jolted and leaned forward as Barney went stiff. "Wait," she said. "Please, don't!"

"Who's that?" asked Herb, jerking his thumb.

"Boss's son," Cheshire replied in a *you know how it is* tone, and Herb nodded, sympathetic. "Go easy on him?"

"Sure, sure." Herb signaled to his man, who stepped back but didn't move to help Barney onto his knees. "*Should* I be negotiating with him instead of you?"

Cheshire was sure Hannah's eyes were digging into him, but he didn't dare look. He could only trust his instincts. "Herb, please. This situation is fraught enough for me as it is—do you really have to put me on the spot like that?"

The room tensed, but without missing a beat Herb burst out laughing, and he slapped Cheshire on the back a few times—almost enough to make him stumble. "Sorry, sorry," he said, still chuckling, as he finally left Cheshire's side. He thumped down on the lounge next to Camila and then leaned toward her with a secretive smile. "I told you, didn't I?"

"He's all right," said Camila, mouth hidden behind her fur. "Tell him."

"She says you're all right," relayed Herb gladly. "And this is how it's gonna be." He leaned forward, looking as if he might vault to his feet again at any moment. "You? All of you?" He twirled his finger at the captive Kozlows. "You work for us, now. You don't pull a job like tonight without our say-so, and we take forty-five percent off the take when you do. Thirty percent of whatever you've got cooking right now, including that new building." He clapped his hands together. "Let's shake on it."

"A counter offer," Cheshire said before Herb could stand. "You take whatever came off that mail car and we call it a night."

"No, no, that's not how you do this." Herb wagged his finger at him. "You're supposed to come back with a lower percent and we haggle, yes?"

"One hundred percent of the mail car," Cheshire replied easily. "Zero percent of everything else. But I'll send a signed telegram informing you of the next one." He shrugged. "Unless you'd rather go by whatever spies you have on my building? I assume that's how you found out about the train?"

"Thank your friend." Herb waved, and the woman from before shoved Burke forward with the muzzle of a revolver. Burke kept his jaw tightly shut but there was panic in his eyes as he looked to Cheshire. "He's in and out of your place all the time," Herb went on. "So I had someone keep an eye on him—caught him up and down Eighty-Third, timing that train. Wasn't so hard to figure out after that."

Burke grimaced guiltily, and Cheshire smiled back, mouthing, *It's okay.* "That's awful nosey of you," he told Herb. "Here I thought we were being considerate by taking our business to Jersey this time."

"No, you were being *cheeky.*" Herb sighed and shook his head. "I gotta say, I'm a little disappointed, Chesh. I had high hopes you would *get it*, but you don't, so let's try again." He gestured as he spoke, ticking his fingers off. "Forty percent of your future takes—there, see? I lowered a little. Twenty-five percent off the building. And my friend here won't blow off *your* friend's head right now, how about that?"

The woman cocked the revolver loudly, and Burke went

so pale Cheshire was worried he might faint. Without thinking Cheshire swept his eyes over the woman, sizing her up, planting her outline in his mind. He could kill her before she pulled the trigger, he knew that much. *But could I kill the rest of them?* he thought, looking to the rest of Camila's forces. Sweat slicked his palms as he hesitantly caught Jakub's eye again. *What if there's too many? Even if I could get them all at once, would that be too many?* He could feel heat coiling in his chest in preparation. *Would Bunny come back for me?*

Cheshire drew his gaze back to the woman behind Burke—if he had to destroy her, that might at least buy enough distraction to get enough of the rest. "I know she won't, whatever percent you're asking for," he said, not taking his eyes off her trigger finger. "That's not really sweetening the pot for me."

Herb was quiet a moment, at last, and the woman glanced between him and Cheshire. As cryptic as his words were she seemed to come to some comprehension of the danger she was in, and she slid her trigger finger further down the grip. "What are you gonna do?" Herb asked after a few beats, his tone lowered. "Use your magic? I sure would like to see that."

"I'm sure you would." Cheshire committed as much of the woman to memory as he could before transferring his attention to Herb. "But, you wouldn't. See it, I mean."

"Oh!" Herb straightened, grinning. "That's more like it. A threat for a threat, huh? But—"

"Herb," said Camila, and he immediately quieted. She slipped one finger out of her fur to beckon him closer. He leaned in, and this time her whispers were too quiet to make out as the stalemate waited, tense and teetering, for them to finish.

Herb nodded, looking vaguely disappointed at first, but obedient. He turned back to Cheshire with a calmer smile. "Okay, Chesh. Let's be honest here—you haven't been pulling our pigtails all this time for nothing. You wanted our attention and you have it, so what's your final offer?"

"A partnership," Cheshire answered immediately, and taking a chance, he turned his full attention on Camila. "We keep to our side of the river, you keep to yours. We'll give you a good price on liquor and a safe pier for imports when you need it, if you can spare some muscle from time to time." He took in a deep breath. "And when a good score comes up, like this?

We work together: equal risk, equal payout. There's a lot you can do with talent like ours if you have the imagination to put it to work."

"The freckly one is the only one with talent so far," said Herb, eyebrows raised. "I'm still waiting to see your magic."

"Herb, it's all right," said Camila, and again Herb deferred to her. She tugged her collar down to face Cheshire properly. "I have a pretty good imagination."

"Then, you accept?" Cheshire asked, sure not to let too much of his relief show even as the woman behind Burke lowered her gun.

Camila took Herb's hand, using it to push to her feet. "Twenty percent off the price of your liquor," she said. "Use of the pier when I ask for it. You can keep half from tonight's job and all your heads." She offered her gloved hand. "And you don't try anything outside Brooklyn without my permission and my men. Fifty-fifty."

"Fifty-fifty," Cheshire agreed, and he lifted her hand to kiss her knuckles.

Camila motioned to her troops, and they began holstering their weapons and untying their captives. Burke swayed on his feet, and Cheshire took him by the elbow to steady him, but no more than that, as they weren't quite finished; as Camila retook her seat, Herb stood again, and crossed to Cheshire for a handshake of his own. "Chesh, come on," he said. "Fifty percent is *more* than forty-five. Have you never done this before?"

Cheshire laughed, squeezing Herb's large hand as tight as he dared. "Herb, buddy, that building is my *baby*. I'll give up five percent of any heist to keep your hands off it."

Herb laughed, too, and finally had to slip his hand free. "Fair enough, fair enough," he said. "Oh, and don't forget." He snapped his fingers at one of the men. "Give Freckles his thingy back."

A man stepped forward holding Jakub's prosthetic arm; Cheshire bristled as he watched Jakub stoically accept and replace the damaged limb. For Herb's sake, he managed a smile. "Thanks."

Herb gave his shoulder another clap. "Looking forward to doing business with you," he said. "But scram, okay?" Laughing, he shooed them off. "Your trucks are just outside. Nicole will get you set up with your half of the take."

"A pleasure," said Cheshire, and he kept hold of Burke as they turned back toward the elevators.

It wasn't until they were in the vestibule, waiting for the elevator to come up, that Burke started to come into his senses, and he tried to pull away from Cheshire. "The bloody fuck is the matter with you?" he hissed, shaking all over. "They almost killed me!"

"Shh, I know." Cheshire didn't let him get away, fearful of making too much of a scene. "Calm down, Eggy, it's over now."

"Don't you 'Eggy' me," Burke retorted. "Were you the one with a gun to yer head?" He tried to exhale more anger, but his eyes were already red, his breath choking. "Fuck, I thought—"

"I know, I'm sorry." Cheshire reeled him in, and was relieved when Burke allowed it. He wrapped his arm around Burke's quaking shoulders. "You're okay, though. I wasn't going to let them hurt you, I promise."

"Fuck," Burke said again, but then he gave up, covering his face with both hands. Cheshire accepted his weight against his chest and kept him steady. He turned as best he could to see the rest of the group huddling closer, but he managed only a glimpse of Jakub before Barney shoved his way forward.

"Bloom, that was real fucking stupid," Barney admonished, though he had sense enough to keep his voice down. "You could have gotten *all* of us killed!"

"Yeah, well, I didn't, did I?" Cheshire's knees weren't doing so great, either, and he was eager to get something solid against his back, or at least a few seconds to breathe. "We can hash this out later."

"No—you do *not* speak for Kozlow, period," Barney insisted. "Guns to our heads and you're making threats? For this little weasel?"

"Fuck you," Burke spat from between his fingers. "That was my neck out there!"

"You little—"

Barney reached for him, but Cheshire pushed him back, tightening his arm on Burke's shoulders. "Lay off him—it's been a rough night."

The elevator doors opened with a chime, and the older woman from before stepped past all of them to enter first. "This

- 81 -

isn't over," Barney snarled, and he boarded, though keeping as much distance between him and the woman as possible.

Hannah went next, helping along Stas, who was cradling what appeared to be a broken arm. "You did fine, Bloom," she said quietly. "But we *will* have to talk to the boss about this."

"Yeah, I know." Cheshire waved her on. "We'll meet you back there."

They managed to fit a few more in, and as the rest waited for their turn, Cheshire finally spotted Jakub. As soon as he moved closer, Cheshire latched onto his shoulder; he needed to feel him, solid and unharmed, beneath his hand. "Jakub—you're okay?" he asked urgently. "You're not hurt?"

"I'm okay," Jakub said, and he looked like it. Then he reached up to cover Cheshire's hand on his shoulder, and he suddenly seemed less okay after all. "It's over."

Cheshire tried not to grimace. He was overwhelmed suddenly with the impulse to draw Jakub closer, too, hold him tight and kiss him, so much so it took his breath away. But he didn't dare. "Good," he said instead, and he gave the back of Jakub's neck a squeeze, still fighting his instincts. "Fuck, I'm glad. I was worried about you."

Jakub nodded, and his hand tightened against Cheshire's wrist as if he were fighting the same. Then the second elevator chimed, and with twin breaths they let each other go.

Would it really be so bad if everyone knew? Cheshire thought, ill with frustration as the rest of them piled into the elevator. He cast a quick glance back at Camila and Herb, who were leaning close together, watching them as they whispered to each other. The thought that they might have spotted and seen through him, however unlikely, sent his heart racing again, and he flashed them an innocent grin before stepping out of view. As much as he hated it, he resisted the urge to draw Jakub close again, choosing instead to offer Burke more words of encouragement on the way out.

***

Jakub kept quiet most of the drive back to Brooklyn. He sat in the rear and let Burke and Gertie explain to Cheshire what had happened, as much as they knew. Cheshire was full of awe and sympathy for their ordeal, and afterward told them about seeing Hazel at the restaurant. At least some part of the ordeal had been a success.

Back home, Gertie took Stas to the hospital to have his arm checked over, while Jakub, Cheshire, Burke, Hannah, and Barney made their way to the penthouse to relay everything to the boss. Hannah did the explaining, while Kasper listened stoically, as per usual. Jakub held his breath when she came to the negotiations at the hotel, fearful of how she might spin Cheshire's performance. Hannah herself seemed to wrestle with the prospect, as she took her time before getting to it.

"Bloom was able to strike a deal," she said neutrally. "We sell them liquor at eighty percent cost, allow them use of the docks. In exchange we keep our autonomy, as long as we consult with them on whatever jobs we want to pull off in Manhattan."

"We have always *had* autonomy," Kasper replied, leaning back in his armchair. "That shouldn't have been up for trade."

"They were asking for much worse," Burke spoke up. Though he had regained his composure his eyes were still red, and he rubbed at them self-consciously. "They wanted a cut of everything we do from now on—they would *own us* if not for Bloom."

"It shouldn't have been up to him," snapped Barney. "Cheshire Bloom doesn't make decisions for this gang."

Cheshire, who had spent the conversation leaning against the arm of a sofa, gave a shrug. "Masterson asked for *me*, specifically. If you wanted to negotiate I would have thought you'd done it before I got there."

Barney glared at him. "I was *tied up!*"

"We're not fighting about this," Hannah interrupted. "It was a shit situation and Bloom did the best he could. We're all lucky to be alive." She lowered her eyes. "Luckier than Ian."

Barney cursed under his breath, and Jakub lowered his eyes. Luck had everything to do with them surviving the train, he knew that much, but as far as he was concerned it was Cheshire who had saved them from the new Lucky. "She's right," he said. "It's done now so we just have to figure out what comes next."

Kasper mulled that over for a while. "Well. The liquor ban is ending, so cheap booze isn't going to help them for much longer anyway. And keeping the pier manned for them is not an issue." He stroked his beard thoughtfully. "If we do come across something profitable in Manhattan, it's not as if we couldn't do it quietly. They wouldn't have to know."

"I'm not in favor of trying to pull one over on them," said Cheshire. "They'd know."

"Only because of your little rat friend here," said Barney, and he gestured to Burke.

Burke puffed himself up. "I was only doing as *you* asked me to!"

Kasper grunted impatiently. "Enough, We'll worry about that later." He looked to Hannah. "In the morning, get everyone on that mail. Open everything, burn whatever's useless." He sighed and rubbed his eyes. "There had better be *something* useful come out of this."

"Yes, Boss," said Hannah, and taking that as a cue, she stood and urged everyone else to do the same. "I'll come up tomorrow as soon as we know."

"Yes, fine. Good night."

They left the penthouse, and Jakub immediately tugged Cheshire aside, trusting Hannah to do the same for Barney—emotions were still too high for more confrontation. "We already put someone in your old apartment," he told Cheshire as he tugged him toward the stairs. "But you can sleep on my couch, if you don't want to head across town this late."

"Y-Yeah," said Cheshire, struggling for a casual tone. "Yeah, that'd be great, thanks. I want to be here bright and early for mail call."

They headed down the stairs, and thankfully Hannah stalled Barney long enough to fully separate them all. As they reached the next floor, Burke abruptly took in a deep breath and turned to face Cheshire. "Sorry," he said matter-of-factly. "For yelling at you."

Cheshire smiled with such warm relief that Jakub felt a twinge of jealousy. "Don't worry about it," he said, and he dragged Burke forward, giving him a tight, one-armed hug and a thump on the back. "You're all right?"

"Yeah, I'm a'right." Burke shrugged him off self-consciously. "But I ain't going out in the field again, remember that."

"I won't ask you to," Cheshire assured, and they bid

each other good night.

At last Jakub was able to let them into his apartment. Cheshire took a look around and whistled. "It hasn't really been that long, but it feels like it," he said, closing the door behind him.

Jakub turned toward him, and seeing Cheshire back in his space wore down the rest of his composure; he threw his arms around Cheshire's middle like he had wanted to do back in the hotel. Cheshire swayed just slightly with the weight, caught off guard, before embracing him back. "Hell, Jakub," Cheshire murmured, and Jakub sank into him gratefully. "When Burke said they had you... I was worried."

Jakub turned his nose against Cheshire's collar, breathing him in. The swift panic of the train and torturous tension of the hotel melted away, and all he wanted was to be closer, warmer. "I don't care what the boss says," he muttered. "You don't get to sit out again."

Cheshire chuckled, and the gentle rumble of his voice put Jakub deeply at ease. "Damn right. It'll take more than Barney on a bad day to keep me out of the next one."

"Good." Jakub leaned back, and he was tempted to go for a kiss, but something in Cheshire's face held him back. It was the concern, he thought. Cheshire was still smiling but his eyes were somehow haunted, his mouth hesitating over some words. Jakub had no idea what might come out of him then, and he shivered, unprepared.

"Listen, Jakub," Cheshire said, and he licked his lips. Jakub held very still. But then Cheshire's expression twitched, and whatever he had been about to say was swallowed up by his same easy smile. "I'm really glad you're okay."

Jakub blinked at him, not sure what to think. He couldn't force enough strength out of his chest to ask what Cheshire had meant to say. "You, too," he said, embarrassed by the close stare and the blush it was drawing into his ears. He took a step back. "You don't really have to sleep on the sofa."

"I'd hope not," Cheshire replied, and he allowed Jakub to lead him into the bedroom. Though both were too exhausted to do more than sleep, it was enough.

fiLL In

It was a bright and sunny summer morning when Cheshire Bloom and his companion strolled into the Union City branch of First National Bank.

There was no mistaking him, with his honey-blonde hair, impeccably-tailored plaid waistcoat, and sing-song salutations. His reputation had been stretching across the river for months, with all manner of civil and civilian employees put on their guard. The man alongside him, though not instantly recognizable, was no less impressive: massively built, with broad shoulders and a barrel chest, a look of smug mischief in his face. They took a sweep of the office and zeroed in on a young clerk, who was making the mistake of staring openly at them.

"Good morning!" Cheshire Bloom extended his hand across the desk, and the clerk shook it without thinking. "I'm sure you can help me, though you'll hate to do it. I'm here to close my account."

The clerk gaped back at him. "You're Cheshire Bloom."

"Ha! I get that a lot." He looked to his companion with a smirk. "Do you think it's the hat?"

"Must be," the man replied. "Because I sure want to arrest you for wearing it."

They laughed, the clerk looking on in bewilderment, before carrying on. "No, really, I'm Sam Quaid," said Cheshire Bloom. He pulled a crisp, folded collection of papers out of the inside of his waistcoat. "Here's my employee card, and my most recent account statement. That should be plenty for identification, don't you think?"

The clerk accepted both documents and looked them over. He could feel sweat trickle down the back of his neck as the tellers cast glances in their direction. Nothing about either document appeared out of place, with proper signatures and letterheads intact. The clerk studied them anyway, then their owner, praying that if he stalled long enough the bank manager would become suspicious and come to his rescue. He'd read the papers after all—he knew a man like this was far out of his league, and dangerous to cross.

"You said you'd like to...close your account?" the clerk stammered.

"Yes, that's what I said. I have investments to make with that money." Cheshire Bloom gave him a few moments longer, still smiling pleasantly. "Do you need to call my employer to verify?"

The big man smirked as if looking forward to it. With his manager still at the other end of the office, pretending not to notice, the clerk had no choice but to take a deep breath and say, "No, Mr. Quaid, I'll have that for you in just a moment."

Cheshire and Herb managed to keep the bulk of their humor in check until after they had left the bank, a fat envelope tucked under Cheshire's arm. "You sly piece of shit," Herb said once they were out on the sidewalk, and they laughed all the way to Cheshire's car.

"It's really not as hard as you'd think," Cheshire said as they sped back toward Manhattan with the windows down. "No one wants to rock the boat. If you're confident and prepared, you can get *anything*." He cast Herb a sidelong smirk. "Don't tell me you haven't done it yourself."

"My smile doesn't work as well," replied Herb, digging into his pockets. "The knuckle crack, on the other hand, never fails."

Cheshire gave a short bark of laughter. "Oh really? Didn't work on me."

"Those pearly whites of yours didn't work on me, either," Herb shot back. He pulled a cigarette out of its case. "Guess that makes us each other's weakness. Got a light?"

"You know I do."

They stopped in traffic waiting for the bridge, and Cheshire turned toward Herb. With a flick of his wrist...he pulled a matchbook out of the band around his hat and tossed it over.

"Fucking tease," Herb scolded, shaking his head. He lit his cigarette and then threw the rest of the matches out the window out of spite. "You're a goddamned disappointment, Chesh. To me and your ancestors." He laughed, and Cheshire did, too, despite his impulse to cringe.

After a lengthy drive full of similar humor, the pair of them pulled up to a handsome, red-bricked building in Greenpoint. With construction complete only a few lines of fencing remained of the endeavor, in the process of being removed even as they strolled up. Herb whistled as he snuffed his cigarette out on the sidewalk, admiring the large windows and broad foyer.

"We only just started taking offers at the first of the month," Cheshire said as he led Herb to the elevators, "and we're already eighty-five percent full! Some of that is our own people, granted, but for the most part it's regular folks. Reputable, even."

"For the most part," Herb repeated skeptically. "It's a very pretty little building, I'll give you that. What'd they end up naming it? Something Downs?"

They entered the elevator, and Cheshire pressed the button for the top floor. "What's on the deed doesn't matter. Who wants to live in a building called 'downs'? *Heights*, that's the ticket." Cheshire waggled his finger, letting his fervor that had been wasted on Kasper slip free. "*Moreton Heights*, now doesn't that sound sophisticated? Makes a fella feel like he's moving *up* in the world."

"Sure, Chesh, sure," said Herb, humoring him. "Moreton Heights in my heart." He crossed his finger over his chest.

They stepped out of the elevator into the penthouse floor, one long hallway stretching out with only a single door on either side. "Saved the best for ourselves, of course," Cheshire continued to tour-guide, leading Herb to the door on the left. "This is where the *real* magic is happening."

He let them into a broad, open apartment, hardwood floors and floor-to-ceiling windows on the river-facing side. It made for a pretty view, but the water wasn't what demanded immediate attention: though fully furnished as an upscale dwelling, Kozlow's workers were treating every inch as a workspace. Papers and envelopes covered every available table, sorted into clearly divided piles. Gertie and her sisters were hard at work in the dining room, sorting and labeling, reading off names and addresses to each other. Another group had set up around a coffee table, asking each other for bank stationary as if playing at cards. Everyone offered Cheshire a smile and a nod as he and his guest passed. In a far corner of the living space, great big mail sacks lay sagging and nearly empty.

"It's taken a long time to go through it all," Cheshire admitted as he continued to lead an amused and, he hoped, impressed Herb through the apartment. "But we were methodical, that's for sure. Most of it we forwarded on to keep people none the wise—after opening it up, of course. Gertie there found a way to reseal the envelopes that you can't hardly tell."

Herb whistled again. "So, what did you end up with? More than Mr. Quaid's banking records."

"Names, addresses, bank records," Cheshire replied, ticking them off on his fingers. "Bills, invoices, bearer bonds, employee cards, licenses. Even a will or two. Still working on how to get a payoff on *those*."

He opened the door to the bedroom, where even more workers were tapping away at typewriters overlooking the balcony. "A name and an address is all you need, really," Cheshire said, accepting a finished paper from one of them. "It was Burke's idea."

Herb read the letter, nodding along. Cheshire no longer had to only hope he was impressed. "Patty Iglet's Police Charity," he said. "Are you for real?"

"Doesn't it look real?"

"It does." Herb laughed and slapped him on the back so hard he might have tumbled over if he hadn't braced himself. It didn't take knowing Herb long to learn to prepare for that. "Really damn real, in fact. You're seriously getting people to just send you their money, huh? To help coppers catch *you*?"

"It's poetic," Cheshire insisted. "Ironic."

"It's psychotic, and I love it." Herb handed the letter back to the worker. "What else you got?"

The last stop was the study. Cheshire opened the door

to a curt, "I'm busy!" from Burke seated behind the desk, surrounded by even more papers and envelopes. His sleeves were bunched around his elbows and he had a pencil and a pen poised in either ear. He startled when he finally glanced up and saw who had entered. "Mr. Masterson?" His expression contorted through a few hesitant options before settling on mostly forced casualness. "Hold on, I've got it here," he said as he began moving papers around.

"Burke's been doing a bang-up job," Cheshire said cheerily to cover up the time. He tossed the envelope from the bank onto one of Burke's already tilting piles. "We've got a few fake charities in the works, so we can switch them out before the coppers catch wind to any of them. And now that we've got a system, there are plenty of other ways for us to get lists of names and addresses that aren't as flashy as robbing a mail car." He sighed. "Though to be honest I wish I could take a stab at one myself this time."

Burke at last offered up an envelope, which Herb happily accepted. His eyes widened as he peeked inside and saw the numbers on the check. "For me?"

"It's your fifty percent," said Cheshire, managing to stay on the more pleasant side of smug. "Like I promised."

Herb considered that a moment and then once again burst out laughing. He snatched up Burke's hand and pumped it vigorously before doing the same for Cheshire. "Chesh, you're really something," he said as they stepped back outside the office. "Your ancestors may still think you're a failure, but mine are coming around. This is good! Real good."

"Glad you think so, Herb." Cheshire leaned back, hoping Herb would read only easy confidence, and not the deep relief. "It's been a lot of work, but you have to agree, it's worth it."

"I have to, I have to." Herb tucked the envelope with the check into his shirt pocket and frowned abruptly. "The little guy in there ain't still scared of me, is he?"

Cheshire raised an eyebrow. Hoping it was the right move, he replied, "Well Herb, you did threaten to blow his head off a while back. Kid's got a good memory."

Herb pursed his lips, and after a thoughtful moment he turned back toward the office. Cheshire's heart skipped but there wasn't time to stop him, if stopping him was even the smartest option. By the time he could regret saying something,

Herb had already twisted the door open and was leaning in.

"Hey," he said. "It's Eggy, right? We're on the same side now, so lighten up."

Burke blinked at him owlishly. "What?"

"*Lighten up*," Herb repeated. "No more being scared of me, got it?"

Burke turned red and straightened up behind his desk. "Who the hell says I am?" he snapped back.

"Better!" said Herb, and he leaned back out of the office, closing the door behind him.

Cheshire relaxed. "Well done," he teased. "I'm sure that did the trick."

A wicked smirk flashed across Herb's face. "I couldn't help myself," he admitted, and he pushed on Cheshire's shoulder to turn them back the way they'd come. "Is that it, then?"

Cheshire allowed himself to be prodded. "One last thing."

He let them into the second of the top floor apartments—just as lavishly decorated as its twin, though lacking in bustling workers and mail fraud. No expense had been spared on the hand-crafted furniture and white crown moulding, the expansive dining table and liquor cabinet. Herb took it all in again with a keen and interested eye, and as they finished on the balcony overlooking the river, he abruptly said, "Perfect. We'll do it here."

"Hm?" Cheshire leaned his elbows against the rail, smiling to himself. Herb was a lot to handle even for him, but it couldn't staunch the pride he held for what they'd accomplished on what was supposed to be a simple pet project. "Do what?"

"Lucky's going to be entertaining some guests," said Herb, and Cheshire's ears perked. "Local and less so. Some of them don't like the idea of meeting at the Thrones, so I've been looking for a more neutral venue."

"Well, gee," said Cheshire, his lip quirking. "I can't imagine why."

"What, you're holding a grudge, too?" Herb scoffed loudly. "Christ, you Europeans are sensitive."

Cheshire chuckled but didn't bother trying to correct him. "Herb, friend, of course you can borrow the penthouse. I'll make it shine like The Olivier." He straightened up again, ready to set his mind to business once more. "When'll it be?"

"Tonight," said Herb, and he watched for Cheshire's reaction.

To his credit, Cheshire remained outwardly very calm. "Tonight?" He chuckled some more. "It's already eleven, how can I even hire a caterer in that time?"

"Everything's already lined up," said Herb, and Cheshire's pulse kicked up as he realized that he was truly serious. "I'll just throw our staff in the back of a van. You've got two full kitchens here and plenty of help. Dinner at eight. Easy as pie."

"Booze?" Cheshire asked, his mind starting to reel. "Entertainment?"

"I'm sure you can handle it." Herb continued to watch him closely, something sharp in his expression. "You *can* handle it, right, Cheshire Bloom?"

Cheshire managed not to squirm despite his discomfort. He'd dealt with plenty of big personalities in his time at Kozlow, but generally they weren't clever or patient enough to administer *tests*. Even if there was only one right answer he hated the invisible pressure of all of Manhattan against his back. He flashed Herb a bright smile. "And then some."

"Perfect! Then I'll just borrow a phone and—"

"But I'll need a favor back," Cheshire interrupted. "You're gonna owe me for this."

"Ha! Nice try." Herb wagged his finger at him. "This is a favor all right, from *me* to *you*. You want to be on the nice with these people, believe me. You'll be thanking *me* tomorrow."

Cheshire made a face, not willing to give up that easily. "Yeah, all right. But I'll still be sending you an invoice. Fifty-fifty of everything, like we agreed."

"You're not cute," said Herb. "You know that, right?" But he relented, and they shook on it.

Cheshire gave him use of one of the upper rooms and then hurried to begin the preparations. Telling Burke came first, and once he got the profanity out of the way he took it like a champ, springing to action. "I can get us the liquor," he said. "And round up the troops to at least make sure the place is clean enough. The rest is you."

"I'm on it," Cheshire assured him. "I'm going to run back to my apartment and make some calls, then I'll be back."

"I know ye're just going back for the jacket that

matches that vest, then," Burke called after him. "I'll be here working while you do!"

Cheshire all but skipped down the sidewalk and across the street to his own building. He had no idea what manner of guests Camila would be hosting and how best to entertain them, whether it be music, gambling, something more audacious? Herb was enough of a mystery himself, let alone his nearly silent partner. He flicked through the different options and even climbed the stairs to his floor just because the movement made it easier to think. As he let himself into his apartment he was already planning which numbers to dial first—after retrieving his matching jacket—only to be halted in his tracks.

The balcony door was open, and beyond it, Jakub leaned against the rail, looking out toward the river. He glanced over his shoulder at Cheshire's entry and looked like a bona fide piece of art: the slope of his spine; the gleam of summer sunlight on his profile; the easy, almost inviting tilt of his eyebrows. Jakub had snuck into the apartment plenty of times, but coming home to him waiting was still a new enough occurance to put butterflies in Cheshire's stomach. It somehow felt ridiculous but also *right* at the same time.

Cheshire grinned openly as he crossed the room, and seeing his intentions, Jakub hurried away from the balcony. What there was to be embarrassed about several stories up, Cheshire couldn't fathom, but he slowed his pace enough that they were safely within the apartment by the time they came together in a kiss. Cheshire cupped his cheeks and Jakub melted into him, warm and eager.

A year ago, it would have seemed impossible. Even six months ago he would have expected a bit more resistance, had even practiced at suaving his way through the layers. Jakub's upturned face made him squirm, and a funny little impulse bubbled up. "Hey, Jake. Do you think I'm cute?"

Jakub blushed and his brow creased. That was more familiar. "You don't need me to tell you."

"No, but, you *could*." Cheshire brushed his thumbs against Jakub's high cheekbones. "I think *you're* cute."

Jakub ducked away shyly, which was adorable, and he eased Cheshire's hands off him, which was less good, despite being exactly his intention. With a little more distance between them it was easier to breathe. "Don't be stupid," Jakub muttered, sweeping his hair back with his left hand.

The light from the balcony caught on Jakub's prosthetic, and Cheshire noticed a shadow in the outside of his forearm. He frowned and considered leaving it be, but then found himself commenting anyway. "Is that the same spot from the train...?"

"Oh." Jakub looked down at his arm as if only just remembering: the metal plate was still dented from the botched train robbery. Jakub had never fessed up entirely to how it had happened, and the thought that it had been a bullet had kept Cheshire up the night afterward. "Yeah. It's not hurting anything. I can hammer it straight once I get around to taking the plate off." The subtle twitch at the corner of his eye suggested he wasn't keen on the idea, but he didn't give Cheshire time to pry. "How did it go with Masterson?"

Cheshire leaned back. He still felt silly and a little anxious for some reason, and he shoved his hands in his pockets to keep from fidgeting. "It went fine! Almost eight hundred dollars in that account. And Herb—" He paled suddenly, everything rushing back. "Shit, I gotta get a move on!"

"What?" Jakub followed a few paces behind as Cheshire hurried into the bedroom in search of his suit coat. "What's the matter?"

"Herb laid a real whopper on me," Cheshire explained as he pawed through his closet. "He wants to host Lucky and some of her big shots at the Morey, *tonight*. He said he's sending over their chefs but who knows if we can trust him!" He finally located the champagne suit coat to match his ensemble, though was then off again to hunt out an appropriate pocket square. "Burke is handling the booze, but hors d'oeuvres, music, company? If I'm lucky Grace and her band will bail me out this once..."

Jakub watched him scamper around the room. "What do you need me to do?"

"Oh? Oh!" Cheshire finished fussing with his attire and turned back. "Come back across the street with me. I can handle making the calls, but Burke will probably need help rallying the troops." He smirked. "They're a lot more productive with you around."

Jakub folded his arms, making Cheshire's point for him beautifully. "If you say so."

Cheshire grabbed up his book of phone numbers,

and the two of them left the building together. It really was a beautiful day, bright sun and a cool breeze, with a night that promised to be full of energy if nothing else. As they stepped out onto the sidewalk, Cheshire again felt a foolish instinct flutter up through his chest. "Hey, Jakub," he said before he could stop himself. "We're, like...going steady. Right?"

Jakub straightened up, tense and staring forward. "What do you mean?"

"You know, it means..." Cheshire shrugged. Why was he suddenly so nervous? He shoved his hands into his pockets again. "Means we're not sleeping around, with other people. You know?"

"Why, do you have someone in mind?"

Uh-oh. Cheshire glanced to him and gulped; Jakub's expression hadn't changed, exactly, but his eyes were hard and he still stared straight ahead. "No," Cheshire said quickly. "Of course not." He chuckled, nerves getting the better of him. "You're over so much, how would I even find the time? Let alone the stamina."

"I'll give you your key back," Jakub replied coldly, "if that's what you're getting at."

"What?" Cheshire began to sweat through his new ensemble. "No, I'm not—hell, Jakub." They were getting close to the building, and he knew there would be no getting another word out of Jakub once there were other people around. In desperation he took Jakub's elbow to tug him to a halt. "Hold on, that's not what I—"

Jakub pulled free, but he did stop, and he stared back at Cheshire hard and unblinking, so unnaturally still that Cheshire regretted having said anything at all. They stood awkwardly for a moment as Cheshire struggled, determined to put every word in the right order this time. "There's no one else," he said. "And I'm...I'm happy with that. If you are." He cringed as new doubt squirmed through him. "Unless you—"

"No," Jakub said, his face red. "There's...I'm fine. With how things are, I mean. Just us."

"Okay." Cheshire let out a long breath and then shook himself, chuckling to dispel the tension. "Sure, okay. Sorry, just figured I'd ask."

Jakub continued to stare back at him, making him feel all over again like a cornered mouse. "Okay." He looked away suddenly, posture growing tense again. "I'll still give you the key back, if you—"

"No, no, please." Though it didn't feel like the wisest decision, Cheshire threw his arm around Jakub's shoulders and began leading them back on their path to the building. "I *want* you to have it. I like coming home and finding you there."

Jakub's shoulders remained stiff beneath Cheshire's arm. "You're sure?"

"Of course!" Cheshire continued to laugh, so eager to be rid of the anxiety he'd caused he felt nauseated. "This is going to be a long night, so you better stay over when it's done. I'll need your help scraping Burke off the floor by morning."

"Okay," said Jakub, and finally, thank goodness, he began to relax. "If you say so."

***

They split up from the elevator, Cheshire stepping off at a lower floor to check on Herb while Jakub continued to the penthouses. As soon as the doors closed behind Cheshire's grin, Jakub sank against the elevator wall, his knees nearly jelly. Lucky, that Cheshire had insisted on the elevator having a handrail to lean against.

Why would he ask that now? Jakub thought, over and over, as he arranged and rearranged his hair as if that would make him more presentable somehow. *Who's going to be here tonight?* Once a few breaths had calmed him down enough to focus, he started the elevator up toward the top floor. *Has he been thinking about it that much? There has to be a reason.*

The elevator reached its destination, but Jakub didn't exit right away. He replayed the entire exchange in his head, trying to remember every exact word and tone and expression on Cheshire's face. There was so much to question and wonder about that it left him dizzy, and his heart wouldn't stop pounding. But above it all...Cheshire hadn't called it off.

They'd been at it for almost a year, after all—the longest Jakub had known Cheshire to court anyone. He had been expecting and dreading it all to come to an end eventually. Why wouldn't it? But he took a deep breath, reminding himself of the most important part.

He said he likes having me there. Jakub smothered a

tiny smile against the inside of his palm and then forced himself to at last abandon the safety of the elevator. *He wants me to come over tonight.*

Jakub sought out Burke, who was zipping between the two penthouses organizing the preparation efforts. He was only too happy to follow Burke's marching orders and pass tasks on as necessary. Cheshire had been right—it was going to be a long night, even more so with the promise of Cheshire's apartment waiting afterward, and he wanted to be through with all of it as quickly as possible. His fervor did wonders for their efficiency.

He said there's no one else, Jakub thought, his intensity scaring off some of Gertie's younger helpers as he put fresh polish to the dining room table in vigorous circles. *He just wants me.* His cheeks burned happily all afternoon.

The Manhattan chefs arrived, along with a slew of Camila's workers. They were serious and efficient, particularly the silver-haired Nicole that had once held a gun to his head. The two of them shared a silent nod of understanding to put it behind them.

Grace showed up later with her bandmates in tow. She made a big deal of the favor she was doing as Cheshire led her around the penthouse by the elbow, showing off the venue. "I honestly don't know who's coming," he told her, Jakub listening in as he transferred his energy into rearranging the chairs more times than necessary. "So start with the quieter, classy stuff and we'll feel them out, go from there."

"I've done this a time or two, you know," Grace retorted playfully. "I'm sure I can handle it."

She turned away as Cheshire continued to speculate about their guests and spotted Jakub. Their eyes met, and she squinted at him for a moment, curiously. Jakub went back to his chairs, his ears hot—she had never paid him much attention in the past, and him her, and he didn't want her to catch him staring. But as she and Cheshire crossed back across the apartment, she steered them into the dining room and offered him a smile.

"Hi, Jakub," she said pleasantly enough. "It's been a while."

"Hello, Grace." Jakub straightened up awkwardly. Cheshire was giving off a panicked grin and it put him on his guard. "Thanks for agreeing to help us out on such short notice."

"A paying gig is never an imposition," Grace replied. "Let me know if you have any requests tonight—I'll sneak one in."

"...Sure." Jakub glanced between her and Cheshire—she was too polite and his entire face was crooked. "I will."

She knows, Jakub thought suddenly, the mismatch in their demeanors clicking into place. His gaze hardened on Cheshire, who flinched beneath the unspoken accusation in confirmation.

"She's a real sport!" Cheshire declared, tightening his arm around Grace's elbow. "Isn't she? C'mon, let's get the rest of the band settled."

He started to turn away, but Jakub was already too keyed up from the conversation earlier to let him get away that easily. "When you're done, I need you here," he said.

Cheshire gulped and was thwarted in his escape when Grace slid free from him. "You can have him now," she told Jakub cheerily. "I can handle my own crew." She cast a smile between them. "I'll see you tonight."

"O-Oh, okay!" Cheshire watched her go as if she were a life preserver being carried away on rolling waves, and once she was out of range he turned to Jakub with an apologetic wince. "She's not going to tell anyone."

"Cheshire," Jakub said crossly. His face was hot but there were so many people still moving about the apartment— some theirs, some strangers—and he couldn't trust himself to say more than that without drawing attention.

"It's fine," Cheshire assured him. His hands lifted and then hesitated; Jakub's shoulders hitched, both wanting and dreading that instinctual contact Cheshire always seemed to go for. The two of them shifted awkwardly. "Really, who would she tell? Barney?" He scoffed. "He wouldn't believe her even if she did. Everything's fine."

"Okay." Jakub let his breath out. "Sorry."

"No, sorry, I..." Cheshire laughed, making everything even more normal. "Gosh, are we something today? I need a drink."

"Me, too," Jakub agreed. He was already exhausted, but his attempts to let the anxiety drain off just weren't landing— he could still hear Grace moving about the apartment, directing her peers into the space. Even though he believed she could be trusted, the thought of *anyone* knowing the secret he'd clung to for years clenched his stomach against his ribs. "There'd better be whiskey at the end of this."

"I've got a bottle stashed at my place," Cheshire promised, winking. "You're doing great work—I'll see you later!"

He hurried off again, and Jakub sighed. *Just keep at it,* he told himself, arranging the chairs one final time. *It'll be over soon enough, and then you'll go back together and fool around and fall asleep. And everything will be back to normal by morning.*

His fingers fumbled around the back of the chair, and one side hit the ground with a thump. Jakub took a moment to work his prosthetic and get his coordination back, and he couldn't help but glance to the dent in his forearm.

If the bullet had damaged any of the mechanisms, it would have caused much more noticeable problems in the last several weeks. It was only a cosmetic flaw, and he could hammer it out at any time. He was just nervous. There was no reason to open it up. It was the nerves.

Jakub tugged the winding key out of his back pocket and gave it a few twists in his wrist just to make sure he had enough tension to last the evening, and afterward he snuck into the kitchen. Gertie was setting out bottles of booze. She'd cracked open one of the vodkas herself already, and the two of them each stole a shot, just to settle down. Then he plowed on again, seeking out Burke for more orders.

Camila herself arrived just before six. Despite the warm summer she was dressed head to toe, her blouse buttoned to her neck, her skirt reaching her toes. Her dark hair was piled high in meticulous curls. She made a full sweep of the apartment without saying a word and then seated herself in the living room as if claiming territory. Herb brought her a drink without being prompted.

"It's cozy," she said, which seemed to Jakub the best praise they could have hoped for.

Everyone not well-dressed enough to serve dinner was herded into the next apartment. Despite the papers and sacks strewn about, everyone managed to find a place to sit or stand, speculating over the guests for the evening and whether they'd be allowed to pick over the leftovers and booze. Jakub took it upon himself to stand at the door, holding at bay the looky-loos and dragging inside any wayward goons that hadn't gotten the hint.

More importantly, it gave him an unobstructed view of the elevator. The first of Camila's guests to arrive, guided by an exuberant Cheshire, was a man Jakub did not recognize: a tall, ashy-haired gentleman, with full lips and a handsome smile. Three men with strong builds accompanied him, though only one was allowed into the penthouse. Hired muscle, apparently. Jakub caught the remaining pair's attention and waved them over.

"You can wait with us here until they're finished," he offered, and luckily Gertie was nearby to offer them a less stoney-faced invitation. Jakub heard her ask where they were from as they found sitting room with some of the older Kozlow boys near the fireplace.

"Chicago," said one proudly. "South side." They immediately became the center of attention.

A Chicago gang? Jakub thought, wracking his brain for what small scraps of news he'd picked up from the national papers. When Cheshire passed by again, heading toward the elevator to ferry the next guest, Jakub caught his arm. "Chicago?" he said, eyebrows raised.

"I know!" Cheshire grinned excitedly. "I need to have a word with that Herb—he was holding out on me." Laughing, he hurried on.

The rest of the guests filtered in, depositing "the help" along the way—some also from Chicago, some from Manhattan, Union City, and Boston. Jakub was starting to worry if they'd have room for much more when the elevator opened one last time, and out stepped much more familiar arrivals: Kasper, Barney, and Hannah, Cheshire making a face alongside.

Jakub froze. He had been so caught up with getting everything ready for Cheshire's sake, it hadn't occurred to him that their boss ought to be made aware of the impromptu event, and his first instinct was to expect a scolding. By the time he realized they were there as guests, Kasper had stopped in front of him.

"There you are," he said, and he motioned Jakub out of the doorway. He eyed Jakub's crinkled button-down. "You're not really dressed for this, are you."

"I didn't know I should be," Jakub admitted.

"I'd lend you something," Cheshire offered, and the thought threatened to make Jakub blush again, "but I don't know how much it would help."

"He's fine," said Barney. He was more dressed up than usual himself, in a dark suit coat and a brimmed hat instead of his cap. "Let's go, Jakub, before the Jersey boys drink everything."

Jakub stepped forward, baffled—even more so when he realized Hannah was taking his position at the door. "How long have you known about this? I didn't hear until this morning."

"We'll discuss that later," said Kasper. He depended heavily on his cane as he led the way into the penthouse. "Just keep your ears open."

Barney followed after, then Jakub. The interior already looked very differently than it had during the preparations, with candles lit, windows shaded from the evening sun, Grace's band plucking away at a slow jazz number. Camila and her guests were milling about in spatters of conversation and drinks. Jakub smoothed his shirt as best he could and looked to Cheshire. "Do you know what's really going on?" he asked.

"Not exactly, but I have a few guesses." Cheshire smirked with mischief, but then Kasper stopped and turned toward them.

"Not you," he said.

Cheshire halted. Jakub wasn't sure he even understood what Kasper had said until he saw the smile drain completely out of Cheshire's face, and a sick feeling clenched in his stomach. "Sir?" he said, hoping they'd misheard or misinterpreted.

"Jakub stays," said Kasper, continuing to stare at Cheshire with cold disdain. "We'll call for you if you're needed."

For a beat, Cheshire was completely blank, though Jakub could see his gloved hands curl to fists. A few faces from deeper in the apartment looked toward them, including Burke near the bar and a curious Herb. Jakub burned as he tried to think of some way to interject. Then Cheshire took a breath and the grin snapped back into place. "Right, of course," he said brightly. "I'll be right across the hall."

"Wait," said Jakub, his chest tight. He looked to Kasper, but seeing that he and Barney were already moving away, he turned back to Cheshire. "Chesh, don't—"

"It's okay," Cheshire reassured him with a smile that

didn't quite reach into his eyes. "You can tell me all about it later." He gave Jakub a clap on the shoulder and showed himself out.

Jakub clenched his jaws. It took him a moment to convince himself to continue inside, and by then Herb was at his shoulder, startling him.

"What's up with Bloom?" Herb asked, jerking his thumb at the door. "Stagefright?"

"Uninvited," said Jakub, struggling to sound neutral.

The dry twist of Herb's lip suggested he already figured as much. He clapped Jakub on the back, harder and much less welcome than Cheshire, and steered Jakub deeper into the room. "I'll save him a lambchop," he said. "Come on, Freckles—I'll introduce you around." Jakub grimaced but couldn't refuse.

***

Cheshire closed the door behind him and then leaned back against it. He could have sworn the room hummed against his shoulder blades, and for a moment it put a tremble in his knees. He felt heavy and too warm in the champagne-gold suit, and the weight pulsed behind his throat. He didn't even know at first what name to put to the emotion.

"Bloom," said Hannah, watching him from the opposite doorway. "Don't take it personally."

Cheshire huffed out a laugh. "Oh, don't worry," he said, letting that indescribable burn harden into a much easier to dissect frustration. "I'm not."

He crossed the hall, and though reluctant, Hannah stepped further inside to make way for him. Cheshire moved to the center of the apartment and whistled loudly to gather everyone's attention. Curious eyes turned his way—low-rung gangsters of different genders, sizes, and temperaments, but all with one thing in common.

"All right all'a ya," called Cheshire, grin plastered across his face. "We all know this isn't the prettier of the two rooms, but I'll be damned if we don't have the better time while we're stuck in it. Booze and chow are on the way, and I *know* one of you can bang something half decent out on that fancy piano. So have at it!"

The room cheered approval, and with a whoop of his

own Cheshire moved to the liquor cabinet. It wasn't the best stock, but once dinner across the hall was underway he'd be sure to swipe a few of the fancier labels from their bar.

"Bloom," Hannah said under her breath as she leaned in beside him. "What are you doing?"

"I'm entertaining our guests!" He pulled out a few bottles to place in the nearest outstretched hands. "Look at the muscle in here—we're one 'my boss can beat up your boss' away from a brawl. So let's just keep them happy."

"Alcohol is not going to help that," Hannah protested.

"Sure it will." Cheshire passed her a bottle of whiskey. "Have a drink, Hannah, lighten up. We've both earned it."

Hannah made a face, but then with a deep breath she uncorked the bottle and took a swig. "I'm going to tell the boss this was your idea."

"Please do," Cheshire quipped, and he turned back to the crowd, determined to find some ears aching for a story.

***

Jakub had no clue what to do with himself. He allowed Herb to lead him around the room, introducing him to Camila's guests and their associates, just like Cheshire would have if he'd been there. As he *should have* been there to do. Jakub greeted each with as much civility as he could muster, given that his insides were still squirming with sympathetic fury for the unwarranted ejection. It wasn't until he was shaking hands with the tall blonde gentleman that had been first to arrive that he was finally able to pay attention.

"Angelo Passerini," the man introduced himself, the smooth baritone of his voice much deeper than Jakub had expected from his gentle appearance. "You're local here, isn't that right?"

"Yes, sir." He recognized the name—the Passerini were a powerful family in Chicago, and the largest and most organized bootleggers in the country. "I'm one of Kozlow's."

Angelo clearly had never heard of them, but he was gracious enough to smile charmingly as if he had. "Oh, yes. It's good to meet you—and thank you for helping to arrange this evening. It's very exciting, to put faces to all the names we've been reading about in the papers."

His gaze flickered about the room briefly, giving the distinct impression he was looking for one face in particular. "Someone I can help you find?" Herb asked, eyebrows raised.

"Well, there's a rumor I was hoping to confirm while I'm here," said Angelo, a smile playing at his lips that reminded Jakub of Cheshire. "That one of your New York friends might be a witch."

Jakub swallowed. He could just hear the fiendish curl in Cheshire's warm chuckle as he toyed with a reply to that. But it was Herb's biting laugh that answered, and Jakub couldn't keep himself from hating him for it.

"If you find a witch while you're here, you let me know," said Herb jovially. "Because other than the Kozlow whiskey—" he thumped Jakub hard on the back, "—I haven't seen one *spark* of magic around these parts."

Angelo chuckled, not believing him. "I certainly will. And in the meantime, I'll gladly try the whiskey."

Herb cast Jakub a look that rang distinctly of *hop to it.* Jakub felt gears in his arm twitch, reminding him of the subtle dent in his forearm. "I'll be right back," he said, listening to Herb sing the whiskey's praise as he headed swiftly back across the apartment to the kitchen.

Burke, despite his mismatched jacket and tie, had found himself in the role of bartender, and he muttered under his breath as he poured a glass for Jakub. "What's up the boss' arse anyway? Why keep Bloom outt'a this?"

"He's trying to save face after the mail train," Jakub supposed. He glanced back at the guests and spotted Kasper and Barney speaking to two men near the windows: a wiry, hard-angled older man with very pale skin, and a younger Latino man in glasses beside him. They all seemed to be nodding and agreeing with each other over something—Barney might have even grinned. "It would be hard for anyone to stand out with Cheshire around."

"You mean, hard for Barney not to make a fool'a himself if Bloom is heating his seat?" Burke sighed with disgust. He began scratching notes onto a pad of paper he'd set on a small table behind him. "Well, fine, then. If it forces the kid to man up an inch, that's good for us, yeah? Bloom gets it."

Jakub remembered the heart-wrenching blankness that had fallen over Cheshire's face when told he had to leave. He had to dig his thumb into the inside of his elbow to get his prosthetic fingers to loosen out of a fist. "Pour me something," he said.

Burke raised an eyebrow but didn't comment as he poured Jakub a glass as well. "Let me know if you hear any gossip," he said. "I'm keeping notes." He nodded toward Kasper and Barney with their companions. "That over there is Chicago's North End Boss, O'Shea, and his money-man, Efrain Granada. Got the boss excited about some race track they're after." He snorted. "Well we ain't about to be racing dogs in a Brooklyn basement, and if they think we're gonna be fighting them, either, best they have another think lined up behind that one. Dirtier business than I want a part of."

Jakub frowned as he watched the four men converse. Kasper had never warmed up to the idea of cooperating with other gangs and families, so he must have seen some extra appeal to be entertaining O'Shea at all. It made him nervous. "I'll keep an eye on them," he said distractedly.

"Please do," said Burke. "Let me know if you pick up any other morsels, a'right?"

"All right." *Chicago has heard about Cheshire's magic* wasn't something he wanted in writing, not if it was getting back to Kasper and Barney, so Jakub scooped up both glasses and headed back. His was empty by the time he handed Angelo the other.

Herb called the assembly to order soon after, and everyone found seats around the dining room table. Camila took the head, as was expected, Herb at her right. A stout, barrel-chested Italian man claimed the first seat on her left, and he and Herb glared smiles at each other in tense familiarity. As the rest of the table filled out, Kasper contented himself with the opposite end, Barney and Jakub on either side. The first course was served, and after Herb gave a short but enthusiastic toast the meal began. Only after everyone had finished their soup and polite small talk did he at last bring them all to business.

"Now that no one's starving, it's time to talk about why we're really here," he said, while gangsters in hastily pressed waistcoats traded out the empty bowls for plates dressed in lamb chops and vegetables. "We're all business people of a certain caliber. It took a lot of time and hard work to get here, sometimes at each other's expense." His gaze darted to the man across from him, who returned it with a grimace. "But it's about time we all worked a little *less* hard, don't you think?"

"You mean, how's about we all stay the hell outta your way?" said the man opposite him. "Or we end up like Lucky?" His mustache curled when he snarled, and Jakub suddenly remembered the man from one of Cheshire's "briefings": Gallo Napoliello, one of the late Lucce's top fixers.

Herb waved his hand dismissively. "We're not here to talk about the past. This is *future* business, here."

"We don't have future business with you," spoke up O'Shea. "Not unless you can answer the question."

A few others around the table nodded and muttered in agreement. Herb eyed them with disappointment. "We didn't call you all here to make threats, if that's what you're asking," he said. He laughed. "If that were the case we'd all be eating a cheaper cut, believe me."

"Then I think it's time you stated your point a bit more clearly, Mr. Masterson," said Angelo, folding his hands against the table. "Or better yet, let Ms. Reynoso speak for herself, since she is the one that invited us here."

Herb's brow hardened, but he didn't look irritated; there was a hint of protective instinct in the expression that Jakub felt he recognized. All eyes turned to "Lucky" Camila Reynoso. She had been calmly eating during the talk and did not look up right away, though she was clearly aware of their close scrutiny. At last she took a deep breath and lifted her head.

"I want us to be like politicians," she said, and mixed reactions circulated the table. Her shoulders crept up; she seemed honestly shy about their continued focus on her, and Jakub felt a pang of empathy. "Next year is an election year. Everyone will have favors to ask. Senators will ask governors, mayors will ask ministers. It's how the system works. I want us to have a system."

"Allies," Herb clarified for her, leaning forward against the table. "Like us and our Kozlow friends across the river. Independant, but when there's something we can help each other with, we do." He lifted his glass to Kozlow. "Like this dinner."

Jakub glanced to Kasper. If Cheshire had been there, he could have charmed them through the exchange with ease, negotiating just as he had when they were at their most desperate. But Kasper stared back at Herb with heavy-lidded disdain, Barney beside him too confident for anyone's good. He dreaded having no choice but to sit back and watch.

"If you're going to use us as an example, the rest of your guests might as well know how our partnership first came about," said Kasper. "With a gun to my son's head."

Eyebrows went up around the table, particularly from the out-of-towners. Napoliello grunted with righteous vindication. Herb's smile sharpened but he refused to abandon his humor as he gulped down his drink and then sighed loudly. "I think they'd be just as interested to know *why*," he replied. "But like I said, this isn't about the past."

"You 'spect anyone at this table to accept you as a partner after the shit you've pulled?" Napoliello insisted aggressively. "After what you did to Lucky?"

Before Herb could reply, the Harlem boss—known only as Big Mitts—cleared their throat. "He's right," they said, continuing to gnaw through the lamb chop. "We want to know what happened with the *real* Lucky."

"Well *all* do," agreed O'Shea, and everyone nodded and murmured along. Beside him, Efrain Granada adjusted his glasses and stared down into his lap. They were close enough that Jakub could see he was scribbling notes into a small, leatherbound journal, just like Burke.

"As if all of you wouldn't—or haven't—done the same," Herb retorted, but then Camila tugged on his elbow, and he quickly fell quiet.

Camila took another moment to compose herself before speaking up beneath the watchful eyes. "I killed him," she said, and then she paused to take in a deep breath. "I cut his throat with a razor, and then I cut as much of him as I could. Then Herbert helped me chop him into little pieces, and we went to the cinema." Her eyes flicked along the table as she dipped her chin, as if missing her furs. "I just wanted him to know I didn't belong to him anymore."

The table went silent. Big Mitts stopped eating and even Napoliello bit his lip. After a few beats Camila nudged her glass toward Herb, and without a word he filled it with whiskey. She sucked it down.

Then O'Shea, the Irishman from Chicago, cleared his throat and gruffly asked, "Did Kozlow's boy rough you up, too?"

Barney stiffened, his eyes bulging as everyone's attention swiveled. Jakub grimaced and looked at Kasper, but the boss didn't react. That didn't stop the rest of the table.

"O'Shea, please," said Angelo crossly.

"Whatever tryst she had with Lecce has nothing to do with the rest of us," O'Shea retorted impatiently. Efrain eyed him as he spoke, his pen stilled. "But that didn't stop her from interfering with Kozlow's business, and it won't stop her from interfering with ours if we go along with this 'politician' nonsense."

Big Mitts let their silverware hit the plate with a clatter. "You all wanted to know the score with Lucky, and now we know. It's not hard to understand."

"No, he's right." Napoliello regained all his steam as he sat up taller in his chair. "We're talking business, now. Who's to say all this fancy dinner crap isn't cheese in a trap. We've got no reason to cooperate with this woman."

Jakub sank deeper into his chair as the rest of the assembly fell to argument. Herb poured himself another drink, his expression easy as if unaffected by the commotion, but Jakub could see Camila's hand tight around his wrist. *Cheshire should be here*, he thought for perhaps the hundredth time, cringing as Barney joined in to agree with O'Shea. *He'd laugh and find a way to calm everyone down.* He looked to Kasper and found himself angry with how firm and unmoved the man was by the entire affair. *Does he really not understand that Barney is only alive because of Cheshire?*

"Sir," he said, rallying his courage. "We can't make an enemy out of Manhattan."

"We're not," Kasper assured, drumming his fingers against the table. He seemed satisfied with the tension he had caused. "She just needs to know we don't belong to her." He cast Jakub a sideways look. "Like she said."

Jakub clenched his teeth, but he didn't know how to express his disgust with so much consternation already sizzling around them. *I shouldn't have let him push Cheshire out.* The fingers of his left hand clicked against his knee. *Everything about this was a mistake.*

Herb put both hands to the table and stood, with such force that a few of the dishes closest to him rattled. "Fair enough!" he declared, tempered frustration in the grin he flashed them all. "Fair enough—you have your...concerns. But you're missing the bigger picture, here." He gestured as he spoke, and for a moment his eyes went to Jakub, giving him the distinct impression that *he* had been hoping for Cheshire's attendance, too. "Prohibition is ending, folks. When the country goes wet again, our profits are going dry. To the pigs this is their last chance to collar us—we've already got feds sniffing around."

He shot a look to each of the guests in turn. "Pretty soon you're not going to have to worry about me cutting you up into little pieces, 'cause the flat foots'll be the ones hacking your bits off, I guarantee it."

"Begging your pardon, Mr. Masterson," said Angelo with an almost fatherly patience, "but my wife has already secured the cooperation of our local and federal law enforcement back home. I can't speak for the room, but I suspect in all our cases you'll have to make a better offer than that."

A few of the smaller-town thugs pulled faces—not everyone was as well-connected as Chicago's South Side Passerini Mafia, and some appeared tempted by Herb's overtures even if they were loath to admit it. Even Gallo Napoliello chewed at his mustache a moment before his brow suddenly hardened.

"You can't do nothing 'bout the feds anyway," he accused, swinging the mood again. "Ye're all talk, and nobody knows it better'n me, Masterson."

Herb flexed his fist, the dull *crack* of his knuckles clearly audible through the room—Napoliello flinched back and braced himself. But then Herb was smiling again. "Fair enough!" he repeated, loudly, and he thumped back into his chair. He went straight back to eating, and the rest of the table looked on, confused.

"Is that it?" asked Big Mitts as Camila, too, resumed her meal.

"Got anything else to add?" said Herb. He wasn't quite as skilled at covering up his irritation with mirth as Cheshire, his knife cutting harder than necessary through the lamb.

"No." Mitts reached for their glass. "I guess not."

"I invited you all here to make an offer," said Camila without looking up. "If you don't accept, let's at least enjoy the rest of the dinner."

Napoliello regarded each of them cautiously as the meal

slowly resumed around them. "Fair enough," he said at last, and he helped himself to more drink.

The band started back up, and Jakub turned in his chair in time to see Burke whisper something in Grace's ear. She nodded, and once her cue came started into a slow-tempo ballad to help calm the room. Burke shared a nod as he passed back toward the bar, his eyes a little frazzled. Jakub felt the same.

"You see?" said Kasper, and Jakub reined his focus in. "Manhattan doesn't have as many teeth as they'd like us to think."

Jakub didn't know how to answer, only to realize a moment later that he wasn't expected to—Kasper was speaking to O'Shea and his partner. "I'm not surprised," O'Shea was saying. "This new generation doesn't understand how those 'systems' came to be in the first place: not just connections, but family."

"Family," Kasper agreed. He squeezed the back of Barney's neck, who puffed himself up, but his eyes were on Jakub. "Isn't that right, Jakub?"

Jakub imagined the weight of Kasper's hand against the back of his neck and his skin crawled. "Yes, sir."

Dinner continued, and with the band, the booze, and a lavish dessert the mood of the room gradually improved. Once Herb had recovered from his petulance he was back to the charming host, eager to regale their guests with more tales of their Manhattan lifestyle. When the meal was through, no one was eager to be the first to leave, instead relaxing about the table and the apartment, smoking and enjoying Grace's singing.

The tension didn't evaporate entirely, however. Jakub could still sense pockets of conversation about the room dancing around the subject, feeling each other out to try and determine who, if anyone, was interested in Camila's proposal. Who had favors to barter. Who had a throat that needed cutting. When Jakub had an opening to leave Kasper's side, he headed for Burke. He accepted another drink and longed for an arm draped across his shoulders.

"What do you think he'd'a done if he'd been here for that, then?" Burke asked, leaning his elbows against the bar. "Hard to imagine him convincing the ornery ones, but maybe..."

Jakub scanned the room. *What would Cheshire do if he came in now, knowing how it went?* His attention slipped to Herb, who was guffawing at something Angelo's muscle had said, slapping him heartily on the back. He made a face and instead focused on Camila near the balcony door, who was speaking with Efrain. *Maybe that's what he'd do*, he thought, and he downed his shot, letting the liquor give him courage.

Camila and Efrain were speaking in Spanish, not bothering to quiet as Jakub approached. Once they had finished they looked to him, and Jakub almost lost his nerve. But *someone* had to say it, and if Cheshire wasn't there to do it himself...

"Ms. Reynoso," said Jakub, "I just want you to know that despite the scene at dinner, we're not unhappy with our arrangement with you and Mr. Masterson."

Camila and Efrain shared a look that Jakub couldn't interpret at first. "The old men are very stubborn," said Camila, "and the young men come to apologize for them. It makes me hopeful for the future."

Jakub hadn't entirely meant it as an apology for Kasper, considering Barney really *had* been threatened at gunpoint, but he wasn't about to correct her. "Me, too," he said.

"There are ways we can cooperate without an all out alliance," added Efrain, adjusting his glasses. "We were hearing earlier about your efforts into a variety of mail fraud schemes that all sound promising."

Heat flared across the back of Jakub's neck, and his eyes darted to Kasper, then Herb. *Is one of them taking credit for Cheshire's idea?* "It's all thanks to Bloom," he said, probably too loudly. He still felt guilty about not saying more when Cheshire was being kicked out, and the drink made it easier for that frustration to spring forward. "He and Burke have done good work."

Camila ducked slightly into her shoulders. "And where is Bloom? Everyone wants to meet the witch."

She and Efrain looked to Jakub expectantly, but he had no idea how to respond, or how Cheshire would have wanted him to respond. To be coy and excite their curiosity? To deny outright to protect the secret? He wasn't skilled in either case and wanted only to be rid of their company—of the entire room, of Herb's obnoxious bleating and Kasper scheming with the too-similar O'Shea, of all the doublespeak and arrogance.

"I'm going to check on him," Jakub said, and without waiting one moment longer he turned and strode straight out of the penthouse.

It was easier to breathe in the hallway. Jakub slicked his hair back and found it sweaty, and he wished he was back on Cheshire's balcony that morning, full of anticipation and energy. Now his head was hot and spinning, and he didn't know if he could place more blame on the alcohol or the company. *Why can't this night just be over?* he thought, undoing the first few buttons of his shirt.

A muffled cheer echoed out of the next room, and Jakub's heart gave a thump. Then he was moving again, hurrying into the second penthouse.

The atmosphere could not have been more different. The various gangsters were moving from room to room, laughing and smoking, passing bottles to each other. In the kitchen some were taking turns trying to roll a lime across the table into a row of cups. In the parlor the coffee table had been overturned to serve as a catch for dice, and in the bedroom an inebriated blonde had captivated a group of suitors with lines of dirty poetry. A duo at the piano plucked out a jaunty, meandering duet. And in the sitting room just off the balcony Cheshire entertained the largest pocket of rambunctious guests: they were playing a round of poker, laughing and jostling all the while, betting not with dollar bills but envelopes full of other people's mail.

"No trying to read the addresses!" Cheshire scolded, slapping playfully at the hands of the man next to him as he tried turning an envelope over. "The mystery is half the fun!"

They laughed together drunkenly, and for nearly a full minute Jakub could only stare. Cheshire was fully in his element and all the more striking for it: hair mussed beneath his hat, jacket strewn behind him, tie loose and sleeves rolled. He sat at the head of their impromptu gambling circle, the center of attention, grinning ear to ear as if he hadn't stopped for hours and never would. When he looked up and spotted Jakub, his face lit up with excitement that had Jakub blushing down to his toes. No one but Cheshire had ever looked at him that way, and it was terrifying, and he hoped he never stopped.

"Jakub?" Hannah touched his elbow, tugging him toward her as if she'd been trying to get his attention for a while. "Is everything okay over there?"

"Everything's fine," Jakub reassured her, nodding, and then he slipped free so he could join Cheshire on the floor.

"Jakub!" Cheshire immediately threw his arm around Jakub's shoulders and drew him tight; the room was already so happily crowded that no one would have thought anything of it, allowing Jakub to relax deeply into Cheshire's side. All the frustration of the opposite room was sent fluttering away with one of Cheshire's familiar chuckles close to his ear. "I'm so glad you're here! I'm losing!" He pulled Jakub with him as he reached across the current pot for an opened bottle of bourbon. "Drink up and put on your poker face, your people need you!"

Jakub accepted the bottle, and despite a warning from his buzzing head—which felt suspiciously like Hannah's eyes on him—he took a long swig. The rest of the circle cheered him on. He finished with a gasp and turned on Cheshire, determined to enjoy the rest of the evening. "Deal."

"Yes, sir!" Still laughing, Cheshire shuffled the cards.

They spent an hour together in bubbly, joyful amusement. Despite the warm drink in his belly dulling his focus, Jakub won back almost all of the mail Cheshire had gambled off. Cheshire murmuring congratulations into his ear was the far greater reward. As the celebration around them grew lazier, sleepier, they reached the final hand of the night, and Cheshire and Jakub each pushed all the winnings they had left into the pot.

Cheshire eyed Jakub over his hand, eyebrows crinkling in serious contemplation. Jakub stared back, unmoved. Then Cheshire's lip quirked, and he lowered his cards. "You're bluffing," he declared.

Jakub's heart bounced and fluttered, and he lowered his hand. Just one pair to Cheshire's straight. Watching Cheshire celebrate his victory over the pot had him vibrating. He wished he had the courage to kiss him right there in front of everyone.

I should have told him when he asked me, he thought, licking his lips. *That he's cute—no, handsome—no, beautiful!* He hunched in on himself. *I should have stood up for him against the boss. He would have for me.*

Cheshire offered him the last sips from the bottle they'd been sharing, and Jakub finished it off without thinking. As they and their gambling partners dragged themselves upright, he realized that his left hand wasn't responding as it should have. He stared at it a moment, but his brain was swimming in too much booze and mirth for him to concentrate on the right muscles. *Oh well.* Ignoring it for the time being, he helped Cheshire one-handed in rounding up the other guests.

At long last, the festivities drew to a close. Camila's various guests collected their henchmen—some baffled, some amused, some annoyed by their various stages of inebriation. Jakub stayed back, helping Gertie and her sisters make a meager attempt at tidying up; Cheshire stayed by the door, smoothing over any irritations as an excuse to catch glimpses of the departing bigwigs, and to offer Grace another round of thanks as she and the band departed.

"Chesh, what the fuck is the matter with you!" declared Herb as he passed with Camila on his arm. "You were supposed to be in there backing me up."

Jakub turned to look. Cheshire rubbed the back of his neck, his grin scraped thin across his face. "Sorry, Herb, you know I wanted to." He hesitated, and Jakub noticed Hannah nearby, watching him. "But *someone* had to keep an eye on things in here," he finished diplomatically. "How'd we do? 'Cause I dunno about you, but *my* guests loved it."

Herb scoffed, an honest twist of irritation in his expression. "Sure, sure. Like clockwork. I'll tell you all about it over lunch someday."

"Good night, Mr. Bloom," said Camila, and they moved on, taking their workers with them.

Jakub started closer, thinking the night was finally over and they could escape, only to hear Barney's voice out in the hall. His instincts suggested a retreat toward the kitchen, but Hannah was already heading out, motioning to him to follow. He pressed his mouth in a thin line as he did so.

"You better not have let them drink through that whole liquor cabinet," Barney was saying. He seemed to be in a good mood—smirking at Cheshire without his usual contempt or apprehension. "Couldn't you have found some other way to keep them busy?"

"Herb asked me for a party," replied Cheshire, leaning against the door frame, arms folded. He shrugged. "I delivered."

Barney snorted. "Make sure everyone's back to work in the morning," he said, and he sauntered off. Kasper, already partway down the hall, didn't look back.

"Ready, Jakub?" asked Hannah, but Jakub was watching Cheshire.

"I'm staying," he said. "Help clean up."

Hannah frowned at him doubtfully. "You're drunk," she said, as if not quite believing it herself. "And you can't drive your car back. You can ride with me."

"I'm not drunk," Jakub insisted, and he feared that was the perfect time for his balance to give way, but he managed not to make a fool of himself. "I'm going to help clean up and take an empty room."

"...All right." Hannah wasn't convinced, but she didn't press any further. "Good night. We'll talk tomorrow." She clapped him on the shoulder and then offered Cheshire a nod on her way out.

"Good niiight," Cheshire sang after her. He reassured Gertie and the remaining Kozlows that they weren't *actually* going to attempt any further cleaning until the morning, and gratefully they headed downstairs to pick from the building's many empty rooms.

Finally. Jakub shifted from foot to foot as Cheshire closed the door and the room fell quiet. His head spun and his chest felt huge and hollow—as thrilled as he was for them to have achieved privacy, something in Cheshire's face as he looked over the apartment held him back. "You gonna be sick?" he asked.

"Who, me?" Cheshire draped his arms over Jakub's shoulders and drew him in with a quiet hum. "Mmm, thank you."

"Hm?" Jakub welcomed him close. It didn't seem like either of them were steady enough to make it across the street, so he took a step back and tugged Cheshire with him, in the direction of the bedroom. "What for?"

"You came," Cheshire mumbled, needing only a little prodding to follow Jakub across the penthouse step by step. "I was so lonely without you."

Jakub buried his nose in Cheshire's collar as he continued to clumsily lead the way. "No you weren't. You had everyone."

"Yeah but..." Cheshire sighed against Jakub's ear. "They didn't like me."

Jakub's shoulder clipped a corner, and he startled, fingers digging into Cheshire's back. "What? No—they did. You're..." Jakub fumbed them around the wall so they could continue on. How had Cheshire's mood soured so quickly? It reminded Jakub of that terrible blankness in his eyes when he was forced out of the dinner. *I should have said something before*, he thought, and he groped after the words to reassure him. "You're cute."

Cheshire sighed again, and for a moment Jakub was hopeful that he had successfully comforted him. They stumbled around a lamp and finally bumped into the open bedroom door frame.

"I worked really hard, you know," Cheshire carried on, sniffing pitifully. "I just wanted to meet everyone."

The awful, unproductive dinner smeared across Jakub's memory. "No, you didn't. You wouldn't like them."

They reached the bed, both so eager for rest that they thought nothing of scattering piles of papers in all directions as they tumbled onto it. As they stretched out together on the mattress Jakub looked to Cheshire's face and hated the distress he found there. It reminded him of tearful confessions years ago, and he tried to think back, remembering there was something he was supposed to have said then, too. He traced the scar on Cheshire's jaw up to his split ear as if it would jog his memory. When it took too long to recall, he clutched at the only words still close to him. "Don't be sad," he said firmly. "You're cute."

Maybe Cheshire simply hadn't heard the first time, because *this* time, the hard wrinkle of his brow loosened. "Yeah?"

"Yeah! You're cute." The brim of Cheshire's hat was crammed against the pillow, so Jakub knocked it off his head to keep it from creasing. He reached for his glasses, too, only to misjudge how stiff and unresponsive his mechanical hand had become in his drunkenness—his metal knuckles smacked into Cheshire's cheekbone with a quiet *thunk*.

"Ow," Cheshire mumbled, and though he didn't sound particularly injured, Jakub's throat clenched and he wanted to cry for having hurt him when he was already fragile.

"Sorry." Jakub took off Cheshire's glasses with his good hand and tossed them aside. "I'm sorry." It didn't seem enough, so he pulled Cheshire closer again, rubbing his cheek to get the sting out of it and stroking his hair. "I'm sorry I didn't... I should have..."

"What?" Confused, Cheshire started petting him, too. "Are you okay?"

- 116 -

Jakub grimaced. They weren't making sense—he couldn't comfort Cheshire the way he wanted to, when he needed him to. "You're cute," he said again, because he couldn't think of anything else and at least that had worked a little before. "So don't listen to anyone else."

"Okay," Cheshire mumbled, and he smiled, thank goodness. With eyes closed he relaxed into Jakub's arms. "Thanks."

He hummed sleepy nonsense for a while as he wriggled, bit by bit, closer up against Jakub's body. It didn't take long for him to fall asleep. Jakub tried to stay awake a while longer, as if he could watch over him even though he wasn't any clearer. He rubbed Cheshire's back and breathed in the smell of his hair until drifting off.

***

Jakub awoke to the sound of Cheshire's voice, and he smiled into the sheets, wishing it was closer. Then he heard someone answer.

He shot up and instantly regretted it; the penthouse bedroom splintered across his eyes, everything hazy and stabbing at once, and his stomach heaved. He clamped his hands over his mouth, and his metal knuckles banged clumsily against his jaw. *Bathroom!* His eyes watered as he stumbled off the bed and looked for the closest doorway. *Toilet!*

Sturdy hands took him by the arms, pushing and supporting him forward. Cheshire's voice was back, closer, trying to reassure him. But Jakub had only one concern at the moment, and he was barely able to make out the shape of the toilet before he dropped to his knees and threw up into it.

"Easy," said Cheshire, one hand rubbing gentle circles into his back. "Take it easy."

Jakub squeezed his eyes shut, taking deep breaths until he felt steady enough to lean back. Cheshire offered him a towel and he accepted to wipe his face. "Thanks," he muttered.

"That's a first, then," said Burke, and Jakub flinched, having forgotten already that Cheshire had been talking to *someone.* He glanced over his shoulder and found Burke standing in the doorway.

Burke leaned back. "Sorry. Just never seen you that far

hungover, 's all."

Jakub turned forward again, embarrassed. "I'm fine."

"Give us a minute, okay?" said Cheshire, still crouched at Jakub's side. "No one is *that* eager to get back to work."

"I'll start some coffee," Burke offered, and he headed back through the bedroom.

Jakub flushed the toilet and leaned back. His stomach still felt like a clenching fist and his head ached, made worse by even the dull light streaming through the small bathroom window. He couldn't remember the last time he'd had so much to drink and paid so badly for it. Thinking it would take too much effort to move just yet, he stayed still, rubbing his eyes as if that might get the sting out. He forgot about everything else until Cheshire touched his shoulder.

"Water?"

Cheshire offered a glass, and Jakub grimaced as he accepted. After spitting some in the toilet he took a slow, careful sip. "Thanks."

"A little too much for one night, huh?" Cheshire said, keeping his voice blessedly low. Gently he massaged the base of Jakub's skull with three fingers. "Sorry if I was egging you on."

"No, you..." Jakub closed his eyes, leaning into the touch. He wanted nothing more than to curl up against Cheshire in a warm bed again, in a dark and quiet room where he could groan in peace. "I shouldn't have..."

Jakub remembered suddenly where they were, and he tensed, twisting toward the door. There was only so much that could be explained away by a concerned friend and if Burke could see them—

The door was closed. Jakub tried to relax but was assaulted by a whole new round of concerns, and he turned to Cheshire with growing panic. "Burke, did he—"

"It's okay," Cheshire quickly reassured him. He drew his hand back. "It's just Eggy. He found us asleep, but he didn't think anything of it."

"But..." Jakub gulped, his nausea beginning to return as he thought back through the night's events. A blush burned all across his face. "I was so ridiculous," he murmured, trying to sink further away from Cheshire without moving too much. "Everyone must have seen how I..." He cringed, mortified. "What if they all know about us now?"

Cheshire leaned back on his hands to stare at Jakub in confusion. Then he laughed, and despite Jakub's tender ears, it didn't bother him at all. "You don't have to worry about that," Cheshire told him.

"But I..." Jakub scrubbed at his mouth self-consciously. "I wasn't making a weird face?"

Cheshire laughed some more, shaking his head. Jakub was amazed by how cheerful he was, despite the roughness in his voice and the red in his eyes from just as much drinking as his partner. "Not any weirder than always! Half the reason Burke came looking for us was because of Gertie—she told him you looked ready to murder someone last night, probably me." He flashed Jakub a smirk. "Not everyone is as used to it as I am."

He may have been aiming to reassure, but Jakub lowered his eyes, uncertain how to take that. As relieved as he was to know no one had caught on, he didn't much like the idea either of a room full of strangers assuming he had any malice for his charming lover. He squirmed, unable to effectively rally his wits with his head still heavy and spinning. Before he could come to any proper response, Cheshire spoke again.

"Would it really be that bad?" Cheshire asked, quieter. "If everyone knew?"

Would it? What few thoughts Jakub had managed to string together flitted away again as he met Cheshire's seeking eyes. He stared back, trapped. His heart began to pound and he had fleeting visions of moving to Cheshire's side against Kasper, glaring back at him in devotion and defiance. But the words he would have to say—the stabbing sensation of eyes from all sides glaring back at them, the questions and even accusations that would follow... He could just as easily envision Barney's hand shaking around a pistol.

Jakub's stomach lurched, and as much as he tried to fight it back, there was no winning; he leaned over the toilet again, throwing up the few sips of water he'd managed to get down along with the rest of his bile. Cheshire startled and hurried to support him, saying, "Sorry! Sorry—forget it. I know."

"It's not—" Jakub croaked, but then he had to stop again, coughing as carefully as he could to keep from gagging again. Only after he'd regained some breath did he try again. "Sorry. It's not that."

"No, I know." Cheshire refilled the glass with water from the sink while Jakub wiped his mouth. "It's complicated, right? I get it." He hesitated before laying a hand on Jakub's back. "Things are great like they are now—no reason to get everyone worked up over it."

Jakub accepted the glass again, rinsing his mouth out without risking another drink. His left hand shuddered in his lap. "I shouldn't have let the boss throw you out," he said, the words leaping out of him as if they had a mind of their own. "I'm sorry."

Cheshire blinked, caught off guard, but he always managed to compose himself so much faster than Jakub could; he smiled, both heartwarming and painful. "Hey, don't worry about that. That had nothing to do with you." Cheshire smoothed his mussed hair out of his face. "He's the boss."

Jakub wasn't satisfied with that, but he bit his lip. *What if I say the wrong thing again and make this worse?* he thought as he pushed away from the toilet and set the glass aside. *I was so hard on him yesterday. If he's fine with things now...isn't that enough?*

"I think...I'm done," he said, but he already didn't like the sound of that, and he hurried to add, "With puking."

"You're sure?" Cheshire seemed back to his tired but cheery self as he hooked one arm under Jakub's. "If I put you in the other penthouse, should I bring a bucket?"

"I'm okay." Jakub could have stood by himself, but he let Cheshire tug him to his feet anyway. Once there he was glad he had, as the bathroom spun a moment before straightening out again. "I don't need the penthouse, I'll just—"

"It's fine—you'll be out of the way, but I can still keep an eye on you." Cheshire slung his arm around Jakub's waist and herded him out of the bathroom. "Come on, when will you get a better excuse?"

"...All right."

Jakub allowed Cheshire to lead them through and out of the penthouse. He kept his head down as they passed the kitchen, where Burke and a few lazy Kozlow workers were half sprawled across the table waiting for coffee to bring them back to life. Though he couldn't make out any of their sleepy conversation, he couldn't help but fear he was the topic for some inexplicable reason. But Cheshire swept them past and out the door, chatting about the weather or something else equally mundane, to prevent anyone from trying to interrupt them.

"I want to hear all about it when you're feeling better," Cheshire said as he sat Jakub down on the bed in the second penthouse. He knelt to help Jakub out of his shoes. "Burke said he'd give me the low down, but I'm sure he exaggerates."

"I don't know how he could this time," said Jakub, fumbling with his shirt buttons. "It was pretty bad."

"Ha! Well, at least I can feel some vindication, then." Cheshire straightened up and took over the unbuttoning. "Herb thinks it's so easy to just throw a nice party, huh?" he said as he helped Jakub out of his shirt. "To make nice with people who have no reason to like you? Maybe he learned a thing or two."

A tiny thread of bitterness had crept into his tone that made Jakub's mouth taste sour all over again. "Next time, you don't get to sit out," he said. Then he frowned. "I *mean it* this time."

"Oh, don't worry about me." The shirt was helplessly rumpled but Cheshire folded it anyway before setting it aside. "Just get some rest and we'll plan our next scheme later."

He looked ready to leave, so Jakub snagged him by the sleeve before he could get too far. Trying not to wince, he lifted his left arm. Cheshire still smiled, but he took the duty seriously as he loosened the leather strap holding the prosthetic to Jakub's upper arm.

"It looked like it was giving you some trouble last night," he said quietly. "Are you sure it's not damaged?"

Jakub gave the arm a twist so that it separated into Cheshire's hands. "It's just hard to concentrate on moving the fingers," he replied. "Especially drunk."

"And you *were* pretty drunk." Cheshire set it within reach on the bedside table and turned back. "Do you need anything else?"

Stay. Jakub swallowed and shook his head. "No, I'm fine. Thanks." He blushed as he slid into bed. "For looking after me."

"I'll come check on you in a few hours," Cheshire promised. He seemed to take a little too much pleasure from tucking Jakub in and ruffled his hair fondly. "I'd give you a kiss, but not until you brush your teeth."

Jakub snorted quietly. Already the pillow beneath his

sore head did wonders, the next best thing to having Cheshire beside him. "I'll have to come back to your apartment," he said, eager for the excuse. "I have an extra there."

"Okay," said Cheshire, chuckling. "You owe me a night over anyway. But maybe the whiskey can wait."

He bent down to press a kiss to Jakub's temple. "Then you can tell me some more about how cute I am," he said into his hair.

Jakub flushed, mortified. "You remember that...?"

"I sure do." He chuckled as he moved to the curtains, making sure they were fully drawn before heading to the door. "Sleep tight," he said, and with a wink he showed himself out.

Jakub took a deep breath and burrowed into the plush mattress, letting the cool sheets soothe his burning cheeks. He was determined to sleep off the rest of his hangover as quickly as possible.

***

Outside the bedroom, Cheshire took a moment to catch his breath and clean his glasses. Then with a deep breath and a roll of his shoulders, he was off again.

That was a stupid thing to ask, he thought as he moved back through the penthouse, which had cleaned up well in the aftermath thanks to Camila's caterer. *Of course we can't let everyone know yet.* He gulped as he headed back toward the other apartment to rejoin Burke and the others. *If ever? We've been over this—Kozlow would never let it go. He made that much pretty clear.*

Cheshire sighed, hesitating in the doorway. *Grace was wrong—Jakub has just as much to lose as I do if anyone finds out. But it's fine, like this.* Once he was able to paste his smile back on, he propelled himself into the kitchen.

"Good morning, everyone!" he greeted boisterously, and he was met with a round of queasy groans. "That coffee ready yet?"

Conversation was bland and sparse. It wasn't until Gertie had herded everyone into the other rooms to resume operations that Burke tugged Cheshire to the balcony. With a breeze off the river clearing their heads, Burke finally relayed the events of the dinner. Cheshire listened, trying not to let concern for poor

Jakub stranded at the table ruin his focus.

When Burke had finished, he let out a long sigh and leaned against the rail. "Sorry, but it was a waste of time," he admitted, digging a cigarette out of his pocket. "Maybe worse. By throwing their weight around without landing, Manhattan made themselves look like chumps. It won't go well from here."

Cheshire lit the cigarette for him, and after Burke had taken the first drag, he motioned to get one of his own. "Masterson's not the type to lose gracefully, that's for sure," Cheshire agreed. "I wish I'd known from the start what they were up to. Maybe I could have talked them out of it."

"What use is there worrying now?" Burke gave a jagged shrug. "I don't think the boss came off all that great either, but he and O'Shea hit it off somehow. If we come out with one more ally than Manhattan did, bully for us."

Cheshire let out a long breath and passed the cigarette back. "That almost worries me *more*. But you're right—no use worrying about it. Let's just keep our ears wide open for what they do next, huh?"

"Are my ears ever closed?" Burke shot back. "The hell do you think I do?" They jostled each other playfully as they headed back inside, but once there Burke scratched the back of his neck. "You really did good though," he said. "No one can say you didn't bring up yer end, that's for sure."

"Thanks, Eggy." Cheshire smirked. "Do me a favor and tell that to everyone you see today."

Burke rolled his eyes. "I'll start with Danowicz," he said, and Cheshire felt his cheeks go rosey. "He gonna be all right? Never seen him that green."

"He's fine!" Cheshire chirped, and then he chuckled to cover himself. *If anyone's face is going to give us away, it's mine.* "He's not built for diplomacy, is all." He threw his arm around Burke's shoulders and steered him toward the office. "Let's get back to work. Sooner or later we'll land a score that even Boss Kozlow will have to be impressed by."

Burke agreed, and they carried on, eager to be out ahead of whatever came next.

LIKE STRIKING A MATCH

It didn't come as much of a surprise to anyone when, only three months after the dinner at the Morey, the body of Gallo Napoliello turned up with its throat cut.

"All things considered, I'm surprised Herb held out for as long as he did," said Cheshire. "He was never going to let one of the old Lucky's boys live, not if there was a chance of him getting support from out of state. And if the meeting went as badly as everyone said, *someone* had to pay for it. Are you sure you don't want a splash of color?"

Cheshire turned away from his closet and held a blue-violet necktie up to Jakub's collar. It probably wasn't fancy by Cheshire's standards, but Jakub still blushed at the thought of wearing something so eye-catching and...silk. He cleared his throat and genty urged Cheshire's hand back. "It's a funeral, Chesh. It's not really the time for fashion."

"Says you," said Cheshire, and he looped the tie around his own neck. Jakub paid close attention to him tying the knot. "It's not like we're going to pay respects anyway. Herb just wants us there to make a statement." He finished and smoothed his jacket down as he faced Jakub properly. "Well?"

At a glance, Cheshire was dressed in a normal, black suit, plenty appropriate for a funeral—it was only up close that someone would notice the delicate pinstriping and monogrammed cufflinks. Jakub was torn between wanting to roll his eyes, and wanting to roll the fresh wool under his palm. "It's a statement," he said. "But you don't need me to..." He frowned, swallowed, and started again. "It looks good on you."

Cheshire grinned, puffing his chest out. "You think so?" He smoothed down the lapels and then reached back into the closet. "Let's get you set up, too," he said as he offered up a new piece. "A very normal, classic black necktie just for you."

Jakub accepted it and drew it around his neck. "Do you really think this is a good idea?" he asked, trying to keep Cheshire's attention off his hands as he made his first attempt at the knot. "Getting all of Manhattan together again so soon could lead to... I don't want to know."

"Is it any better of an idea to refuse?" Cheshire replied. "If this is a power play and we don't show up, that's only going to make them more desperate to reestablish the hierarchy."

Jakub finished his knot after only restarting twice, and he faced Cheshire with his hands at his sides, eyebrows raised, daring him to comment. Cheshire pursed his lips and held out for as long as he could. It seemed to cause him physical pain. "Do you mind if I...?"

Jakub held his ground a moment longer; it made him blush to think that he had grown bold enough to tease. "Go ahead," he said at last.

Cheshire's shoulders sagged with relief, and he hurried to untie the sloppy knot. "You just need a little more practice," he said. "Let's hope Herb gets fed up with the lot of them, so we have lots more occasions to dress up for."

"That's not funny," Jakub muttered, but then Cheshire took him by the shoulders and turned him around. His cheeks darkened further as Cheshire reached around him to knot the necktie.

"I know you don't really care about this stuff, but it *does* look great on you," Cheshire said happily as he tightened the knot to Jakub's throat. "It'll be mostly Manhattan people there, so they won't think twice about seeing you in a tie."

Jakub swallowed, leaning back into his chest. "It's just a tie—it's not a big deal."

"Just trying to put you at ease. I know you hate being the center of attention."

He wrapped his arms across Jakub's chest and gave him a squeeze—Jakub took in a deep breath as if he could inhale and capture the sensation, so he could call on its memory later. "Thanks," he said, and, summoning his courage, he turned his face towards Cheshire's. "I, um. I appreciate you always looking after me."

Cheshire hummed against his cheek. "You do a lot more looking after *me*," he replied. "That's..." He chuckled, and Jakub's mood was dampened a bit with the realization of how nervous Cheshire sometimes was with him. "That's what you do, right? When you're steady with someone?"

"Yeah," Jakub hurried to reassure him, even though it made him squirm. "Of course it is."

"Good." Cheshire gave him one more tight squeeze and then let go so he could steer them toward the full length mirror next to the closet. "Take a look," he said cheerfully. "See? Tasteful and handsome."

Jakub took in his reflection and wasn't sure how to name the emotion that came over him. He hardly spent any time in front of mirrors—was fairly certain he didn't own one, other than a small, pocket mirror he had used a handful of times when working on his guns, or one of the boss's cars. It wasn't often he was faced with his own...face. He blushed again as he fingered the knot Cheshire had just tied for him and looked over the suit. Nothing about it seemed all that extraordinary to him: he was clean, sure, his hair combed, a noticeable lack of wrinkles in his jacket. It shouldn't have felt any different, let alone special. But Cheshire sure seemed delighted, so he tried to look more closely. He only gained more self-conscious embarrassment for the effort. What was so endearing about plain black and a faceful of freckles anyway?

"I like it," Jakub said, so determined to be supportive that Cheshire saw straight through him.

"You don't have to force it," Cheshire replied, and he chuckled as he straightened the lines of the jacket along Jakub's shoulders. He deadpanned his face to match Jakub's usual demeanor. "I'd be satisfied with 'it'll do.'" Jakub started to protest, flustered, but Cheshire continued. "But thank you for humoring me."

He kissed Jakub's cheek, which wasn't nearly enough; Jakub turned so he could meet Cheshire's lips for a proper kiss. "It's what you do, right?" he said, cheeks burning; Cheshire's grin, surprised and pleased, made it worth it.

They left the apartment together and met up with Burke in the lobby, who for once showed remarkable restraint in his attire. For the most part, anyway—he had accented his plain black jacket with a navy blue tie, with wreaths of orange making up a paisley pattern. Cheshire gestured sharply at him.

"Really, Burke?" he said, flabbergasted. "You're wearing *that*?"

"What?" Burke betrayed not one ounce of self-consciousness in the face of Cheshire's disdain. "Yours is blue, too."

Cheshire made to argue, but then he stopped himself, shaking his head. "Just make sure you stand next to Herb instead of me," he said as he led them out of the building. "Or I'm going down in the hole with Napoleon, I swear."

"Ye're a mental case," Burke retorted, and Jakub stayed out of it, content to be amused by their bickering all the way to the cemetery.

The church service had been held in Manhattan, a poorly kept secret meant only for close relatives and friends. Likely his remaining family were hoping to avoid any entanglements with Lucky and her crew, with tempers still so high and prides tarnished. So naturally, as soon as Herb had figured out that the burial would take place in Brooklyn's Woodside, he had spread the news as far and wide as possible. As the three of them parked and headed for the cemetery entrance, Jakub wasn't surprised to see Big Mitts and their crew already milling about, as well as a group of the Union City Boys who must have gotten up early for the trip.

"This is a bad idea," Jakub said again as they leaned against the stone wall a calculated distance from the rest of the "mourners."

"Bloody disrespectful on top'a that," agreed Burke. "Napoliello was a right prick, but they could wait for him to be in the ground before gunning down his relations."

Cheshire scoffed, though he didn't sound as sure as he usually did. "It's broad daylight, outside their normal turf. Herb isn't an idiot—they're not going to start a gunfight." He shrugged. "Not today, anyway."

Jakub eyed the Union City Boys as they passed a lit cigarette between them. At least two had pistols shoved down the backs of their trousers. They might have just been smart enough to come prepared—Jakub had his own revolver inside his jacket—but then again, maybe they knew something. He tugged a pack of cigarettes out of his coat. "I'm not so sure teaming up with Manhattan was a good idea from the start," he admitted. He then quickly shook his head. "Not that we had a choice at the time."

Cheshire shrugged again, and when Jakub held a cigarette out, he lit it with a snap of his fingers. "It's a little hairy," he admitted. "But the boss said he wanted us to expand, and there are only so many directions to head in. If we can make nice now, Barney's gonna thank me for it eventually." He laughed. "That'll be the day, huh?"

"Yeah, someday when you got pigs on your balcony 'stead of pigeons," said Burke. "But if ye're feeling lucky, you can try yer hand today."

He motioned to further down the curb, where another car had just pulled up, and Barney and Hannah climbed out. They were dressed for the occasion, Barney sporting his hat from the Morey dinner he was so proud of. Jakub frowned around his cigarette as he watched them approach. *This is going to be that terrible meeting all over again*, he thought, studying them for weapons. *If not worse.*

"Gentlemen," Barney greeted, a note of sarcasm to his voice. It was always off-putting to see him in a good mood. "Ready for round two of the Great Manhattan Shit-show?"

"Sure are," said Cheshire, smirking along. "Glad you could make it."

"Couldn't live up to the name without you," Burke added.

Barney shot him a glare, but he didn't get the chance to retort; Cheshire laughed and threw his arm around Burke's neck in a playful headlock. "Ha! Good one. He's funny, ain't he?"

Barney eyed them both and then snorted. "A riot."

"I don't see Reynoso," said Hannah. Jakub couldn't help but feel sorry for how tense and exhausted she looked already. "Or Masterson."

"They might have found a way into the ceremony," suggested Cheshire. "I'm sure they'll come across with the procession."

Barney snorted again and adjusted his hat, even though it didn't need it. "That Masterson is a piece of work. Takes some balls to go after your enemies at a funeral."

"You're here, too, you know," Cheshire reminded him.

"And so are you," Barney shot back. "Honestly, I'm surprised—you two been so chummy lately, I figured you'd come with him." He scoffed. "You could have ridden his dick all the way over from Manhattan."

Jakub tensed and pulled the cigarette from his mouth before he chewed straight through the filter. The subtle tug of hurt at the corner of Cheshire's mouth twisted his gut and forced the words straight out of him. "Barney, shut the fuck up."

Everyone turned to stare, bewildered, but Jakub went back to smoking, determined not to falter. *I should have stood up for him before*, he thought with heavy conviction as he stared back at Barney. *I'm not letting the chance go ever again.*

Burke gave a short back of laughter, breaking the momentary tension. "Funny," he said. "Ain't he?"

Barney glanced between the three of them, off kilter and at a loss. "Just stay sharp in there, all right?" he muttered, and he moved on toward the cemetery entrance. "Nice tie, Jake."

Hannah cast Jakub a questioning look, and only then did he feel uncertain of his outburst. She continued on without comment. Once the trio was more or less alone again Cheshire wrapped his other arm around Jakub's neck and drew him in. He pressed his lips close against Jakub's ear.

"God, I could kiss you right now," he whispered, and Jakub shivered, but then he let go of both his companions and laughed. "Sorry, Burke," he said. "Just pigeons for me this time."

"'Bout time someone said it," replied Burke. "Not that I can believe you just did."

Jakub exhaled a puff of smoke. "I just don't want him in there with a big head," he said, though he couldn't help a feeling of triumph.

Their humor was cut short moments later by the arrival of the hearse and its procession. Everyone looked on as members of Napoliello's family and gang filtered out of their cars, and the pallbearers took up their positions. Just as Cheshire had suggested, Camila, Herb, and a slew of their goons emerged at the tail end of the proceedings. Both were handsomely dressed in long fur coats that didn't seem necessary given the mild weather.

"Christ," muttered Burke, and he patted himself down for a cigarette. "A 'piece of work' is right."

Jakub tried to watch everything at once. Napoliello's relatives were stone faced as they bore the coffin into the cemetery, though he could see many of them shift, suppressing the urge to glance behind them. Camila and Herb followed arm in arm. Herb even cast a smirk at each of his guests, though his eyes were hard, taking stock of everyone who had chosen to accept his invitation.

"It's obvious what he's trying to do," Jakub said quietly as the three of them fell into step behind the other gangs. "But he's messy, and this is dangerous."

"First sign of trouble and we're gone," Cheshire promised.

They marched on. All things considered it was a very pleasant day for a funeral, with a bright, cloudless sky overhead and only a faint breeze rustling the grassy plots. Nearly as soon as they passed through the gates they were surrounded by rows of headstones on either side of the lane, names and dates stretching on into the distance. Jakub tried not to look at them, focusing instead on the different groups ahead. Barney and Hannah were conversing quietly, but everyone else was tense and stoic, their eyes on Herb, as if waiting for a signal they weren't certain would come at all.

"Think Herb dug a few extra ditches to prepare?" said Burke, chewing on his cigarette without lighting it. "Bang, bang, kick, thud, problem solved."

"That's not funny," Jakub scolded him. He looked to Cheshire, expecting to have to curb some quip from him as well, and was surprised to find Cheshire's expression dull and serious. It wasn't often he couldn't find even a trace of a curled lip on the man. "You okay, Chesh?"

"Hm?" Cheshire shook himself, and immediately the smile Jakub was used to snapped into place. "Oh, sure. It's been a long time since I was in a cemetery, that's all."

Jakub thrummed with curiosity. *His parents?* he wondered, eyeing Cheshire for clues. *He's never mentioned them, so maybe...* But Cheshire was watching Herb now, focused on the present, nothing to give him away.

"Same, then," said Burke. "Not much to miss, though,

is there? Bones in the ground. Like it makes any damn difference where you end up after ye're dead."

Parents, Jakub thought with greater confidence. He vaguely remembered Burke saying something about coming to America with his uncle as a child, and the clipped bitterness in his voice wasn't difficult to puzzle out. He frowned, taking a last breath of his cigarette before dropping it beneath his foot. It occurred to him that he had no idea if his own parents' bodies had ever been found or buried.

The group turned down another lane to the east, taking them to the waiting plot. Everyone fanned out around the open grave, and with the coffin lowered the priest began a few last rites. With the service already conducted at the church, and Napoliello's relations painfully aware of their many unwanted guests, it was bound to be a short ceremony. Camila and Herb stood close to Napoliello's cousins, their manners appropriately solemn compared to the tense irritation of the mourners. Everyone waited for what they assumed to be the inevitable conflict.

But Herb didn't signal for anything. He and his boss listened respectfully to the prayers of the old priest, and they remained still as the coffin was finally lowered into the earth. They didn't interfere with or try to participate in throwing earth over the grave. As the burial concluded, it slowly dawned on the different gangs that the fight they had all come dreading might not take place at all.

"I guess that's it?" mumbled Barney as the crowd dispersed. Herb and Camila, once again arm in arm, moved boldly to the front for the walk back toward the entrance with their entourage in tow. "They brought us all out here for nothing?"

"Not for nothing," replied Jakub. He watched as Big Mitts and the Union City Boys hung back long enough for the rest of the Napoliellos to fall into line behind Camila. Even after the disastrous dinner, everyone had heeded Manhattan's call— everyone had been prepared for a war they had no reason to fight. They had more than made their point.

And as soon as they reached the cemetery's main lane, Jakub saw it: the entrance had been blocked by a collection of familiar black and white police cars. A line of uniformed officers awaited the procession, each of them as prepared for violence as the gangs had been, and at the front of them, hands on her hips, stood US Marshal Hazel Adalet.

"Oh, Herb," Cheshire murmured, only loud enough for Jakub to hear. "What the hell are you up to?"

"Is this where we turn tail?" asked Burke, the same unlit cigarette dangling from his mouth.

"Stay calm," said Hannah. "Keep walking."

Camila and Herb didn't break stride, so the rest of them had no choice but to follow suit. It took an agonizing length of time to make the walk as anxiety wound everyone tight. Jakub stayed close at Cheshire's side. *We could just walk away,* he thought, casting a quick glance deeper into the cemetery. *Turn around and head to the wall, hop over and double back when the coast is clear.*

"Officer," Herb greeted once he had nearly reached the exit. "Can we help you?"

"Marshal," Hazel corrected him stiffly. She waved for him to continue on. "This doesn't concern you, Mr. Masterson." She looked past him to the rest of the approaching procession, and Jakub took in a deep breath in preparation as her eyes landed on them. "We're here to speak with Barney Kozlow."

What? Jakub looked to Barney, who stopped in his tracks. Hannah took his elbow, obviously baffled but desperate to keep him from saying anything stupid. Even Cheshire seemed thrown. But when Jakub returned his attention to Herb and saw the hint of a smile he was trying to hide, it made perfect sense. *Napoliello wasn't the only one that spoke out against Manhattan at that dinner*, he thought, sweating into his jacket. He looked to Burke and found the same conclusion there. *But how can he have leverage over the feds?*

"The rest of you need to move on," Hazel continued, motioning to the other gangs who were also a mix of confused and bitterly resigned. "Pardon our intrusion."

"Herb, what's the big deal?" asked Cheshire. "We all got the message already."

Herb gave an exaggerated shrug. "Like the lady said—doesn't concern me." He looked to Camila. "Ready?"

"Yes," she said, and the officers parted enough for them and their crew to continue on.

"Hey," said Cheshire, and before Jakub could stop him, he hurried after them. "Herb, wait up!"

Hazel shot him a glare, and Jakub held his breath as

the pair passed each other, but she didn't try to stop him; she was heading for Barney. Forced to split his focus between them, Jakub stayed at Barney's other side. The rest of the gathering was still shifting uncomfortably: Big Mitts and their crew moved tentatively toward the exit, while the Napoliellos and Union City boys hung back, too curious to know Kozlow's fate, and the cops tried to watch everyone at once. For his part, Barney didn't seem to know if he was furious or petrified, and he stared back at Hazel with harried eyes.

"I'm Barney Kozlow," he said roughly. "What do you want?"

"I have some questions for you," said Hazel, and to her credit she seemed unfazed by the electricity in the air around them. "But this isn't the place for it. You need to come with me."

"We have a right to know what this is about," said Hannah, still gripping Barney's arm.

"No, you don't." Hazel tapped the marshal's badge pinned to the lapel of her suit jacket. "We're not going to stand around here making more of a scene than necessary. Please come with me."

Burke crossed his arms and glared back at her. "He's not going anywhere unless ye've got a warrant on you."

Hazel cocked an eyebrow and then reached into her jacket. "All right."

Jakub cast a quick glance past her. Cheshire had managed to stop Herb and Camila just within the cemetery gate, a nervous smile in place as they talked. Mitts had paused nearby, and they and the rest refused to be ushered on by the increasingly anxious police officers. If the standoff carried on for much longer...

"I have a warrant for your arrest," said Hazel, flipping open a paper pulled from her jacket. "For the murder of Gallo Napoliello."

Barney paled, and Hannah kept a tight grip on his arm. "That's ridiculous," she said as everyone shifted and murmured. "We've never had anything to do with them."

Hazel quickly tucked the warrant back into her jacket. "All the same, he's coming with me."

"We all know who's responsible," spoke up one of the Napoliellos, pointing emphatically at Herb and Camila by the gate. Jakub took a step back as attention across the group shifted; his companions took notice and stealthily did the same. "That bitch and her attack dog murdered Gallo, and you're wasting time with these small time weasels? He's right fucking there!"

"Ma'am, you need to take you and your family home," said Hazel, losing patience. "Let us do our job."

"She does have a point," called Herb, his smugness drawing an incredulous look even from Cheshire beside him. "I really hated Gallo Napoliello. It makes a lot more sense."

"You son of a—" the woman began, but she was interrupted by the sound of a sudden gunshot, and the cemetery erupted.

Jakub had no idea where it had come from at first. The familiar *bang* of a .38 revolver sent his heart skipping, and everyone started moving at once. Barney, Hannah, and Burke fled for the east wall—the Union City boys toward the opposite. One of the boys had his gun in his hand already. As Jakub turned to run he caught only glimpses of Big Mitts and their crew diving for cover while the police drew their guns, and Cheshire dragging Herb by his fur coat around the stone wall out of the cemetery. Their eyes met for a brief moment but there was nothing either could do other than retreat in opposite directions.

"I'll kill him," Barney huffed as the four of them sprinted between rows of headstones toward the east wall. "I'll kill that fat bastard!"

"Just run!" said Hannah.

She had one hand twisted in Burke's coat and was practically dragging him along. Burke's eyes were round with fright as he struggled to keep up, while Jakub was too overcome with confusion to feel any concern for himself. *Of all of them, Jersey?* he thought, trying to make sense of it. *What the hell are they thinking?* He glanced behind them at the sound of more gunfire, but the parties had scattered, and it was impossible to pick out the various factions. He did, however, catch sight of two of the police officers following them. He drew his revolver.

They reached the edge of the cemetery, where the stone wall that started at the entrance ended in favor of iron rod fencing. Barney didn't hesitate; he threw himself at the fence, nearly reaching the top rung in a single leap. Hannah and Jakub rushed to help, and with each taking a foot, they boosted him over the top. He landed roughly, gripping the bars to keep from spilling to his knees.

"Hurry up!" he snapped. "Leon's place isn't far from here—we can make it."

Jakub and Hannah assisted Burke over the top next—he cursed the entire way over. But as Hannah made the climb with only minimal help from Jakub, the cops finally made it in range.

"Hold it!" shouted one as they both leveled pistols. "You're all—"

Jakub opened fire, each shot taking chunks out of headstones and monuments. The cops dove for cover. As Hannah dropped to the other side of the fence she peered through with concern. "Jakub—"

"I know," he reassured her as he shoved the gun back into its holster. *The last thing we need now is dead cops.*

He jumped, catching as high up as he could on the bars and bracing his feet for leverage. He stretched his left hand and felt his fingertips hook over an ornament, but when he tried to pull himself up, the metal digits twitched abruptly, and he couldn't keep his grip. The shift in weight would have dragged his feet back to the ground if not for Hannah and Burke reaching through the bars to support him.

"Back off, pigs!" Barney shouted, and he fired a few shots into the dirt to keep the police from trying anything. With Hannah and Burke's help Jakub was able to make another lunge for the top of the fence, and he dragged himself over and down the other side.

"What about Bloom?" Jakub asked as soon as his shoes touched the ground. "We can't just—"

"He can take care of himself," said Hannah, and she took hold of Burke again as she led the way across the street. The other side held small homes crammed close together, offering plenty of narrow lanes and backyards for them to lose the pursuing cops through. "We need to get off the streets and worry about him later."

"I hate this," muttered Burke, allowing Hannah to pull him on. "I really do."

Barney gave him a push. "Shut up and keep moving. They're still on us."

They weaved through the buildings, and gradually the

distant pop of gunfire ceased. Jakub glanced behind them and couldn't see any sign of the pursuing officers. But more than that he listened for *booms*, even breathed deeply through his nose as if he might be able to catch the smell of Cheshire's magic on the wind.

No, he knows better. Jakub swallowed and forced himself to keep pace with the others, further away from the melee. *Adalet didn't come for him—she's got nothing on him. He'll be fine.*

***

The first gunshot caught Cheshire completely off guard. He had been trying to keep eyes on Herb, on the Napoliellos, on Barney, on Hazel—that one of the Jersey boys would draw on them was the furthest thing from his mind. Apparently, even Herb hadn't considered it as a possibility; his expression went blank with surprise and he rocked with the report of the gun.

Is he hit? Cheshire thought. With the thick fur coat cloaking Herb's already broad frame no wound was visible, but there was no mistaking the paleness that came over his features. Cheshire grabbed him by his coat and turned, dragging him around the entranceway's stone column to get them both out of the line of fire.

He caught a glimpse of Jakub moving to flee and felt a flash of relief. *He'll be fine. He can get out of this, easy.*

Cheshire pushed Herb up against the stone wall just outside the entrance and only then realized that Camila was close at his side—all but clinging to him. "Are you shot?" he asked, though he already knew the answer; he could smell the blood, could even feel it slicking his black gloves.

"It's nothing," said Herb, even if his grin was mostly grimace. He reached for his left shoulder, and at last Cheshire could see blood seeping through the fur near his armpit. "Who the fuck shot me?"

Chunks of stone exploded off the walls, and Big Mitts and their crew retreated from the cemetery amidst more gunfire. Cheshire could hear the cops shouting orders and others swearing wildly, and there was no telling where the sides had been drawn or when it would spill into the streets.

"Come on," Cheshire said, and he drew Herb away from

- 136 -

the wall. "Let's get out of here."

Camila immediately moved to Herb's other side. "Start the car," she ordered one of their followers, who ran ahead down the sidewalk to obey. Thanks to the Napoliellos there were an awful lot of cars stretching behind the hearse to go past, and they didn't make it more than a few steps before Cheshire realized how unsteady Herb was. He tried to hurry them on, only to be interrupted by shouts from behind.

"Hold it right there!" yelled what sure sounded like cops, and when Cheshire turned to look back, he could only watch as two officers were gunned down by figures emerging from the cemetery. A pair of Napoliello's former goons rounded the gate, eyes wide with the panic of the shoot out, and they quickly spotted the retreating Manhattanites.

Cheshire dragged Herb down behind the bumper of the nearest car just as more gunshots rang out. He could have sworn he felt a bullet pass through the end of his ponytail. As the Manhattan gangsters traded shots with their attackers, Herb struggled to draw his gun, so Cheshire took it from him. He managed to get a few shots off but didn't accomplish anything, until Camila snatched the gun from him. She leaned out around the car and shot one of their attackers straight between the eyes. One of her men clipped the other and sent him diving back through the gate.

"You're *still* not going to show me your magic?" Herb asked incredulously.

"Not in front of cops." Cheshire yanked him upright once more, though it took a great deal of effort. *He's too pale*, he thought, and he was relieved when another of Herb's boys came to help support him. *He's losing a lot of blood.* The coat must have been absorbing a lot more than its dark color was letting on. Swallowing a curse, he looked to Camila. Her eyes were hard and her knuckles white around the gun. She could see it, too.

What happens if Herb dies? Cheshire thought, his head spinning as he helped drag Herb down the sidewalk to the waiting car. *Is Manhattan done for?* The sharpness in Camlia's demeanor said otherwise. *Jakub was right—this was one big mistake, but they're gonna make everyone else pay for it.*

He shoved Herb into the back of the car and climbed in after. Two pairs of broad shoulders made it extremely cramped but Cheshire was determined to know just how bad things were. As familiar left-hand Nicole took the wheel, Camila beside her, Cheshire finally yanked Herb's coat and jacket back to see the damage.

The bullet had caught him in the arm, between his shoulder and bicep. As soon as the wound was uncovered it pulsed with fresh blood, and Cheshire hurried to shove the full pressure of his palm against it. Herb jerked, swearing at him.

"Where's the closest doctor?" Nicole asked as she pulled away from the curb, scraping the bumper against the car in front of them.

"Elmhurst." Cheshire shook his head and forced himself not to say it. *He won't make it, not when he's losing blood like this.* But when he met Herb's gaze, the truth was there anyway, plain to see. Herb's lip curled.

"So who was it?" he asked, grimacing.

"I didn't see," said Cheshire. He resisted the temptation to look to Camila again. *Is there nothing I can do?* It suddenly didn't seem that long ago that he had contemplated unleashing his full magic on Herb and his entire roomful of Manhattan goons, and here he was, scrambling for a way to save him for fear of he didn't know what.

An idea came to him then, skating along his nerves in a chill. Without giving himself too long to think on it he stripped one glove off. *If this works, it might save his life,* he thought, and he tore Herb's shirt away from the gunshot so he could press his bare palm directly to the wound. *And if it doesn't, don't stop.* He took a deep breath and finally looked behind him to memorize the shapes of Nicole and Camila in the front seats. *If you kill him with this, you'll have to kill them, too.*

"Herb, take a breath," he said, and then he shoved his shed glove between the man's teeth to quiet his attempt to question. "Bite this." He took a deep breath of his own. "Please don't explode."

Cheshire concentrated on the torn flesh surrounding the deceptively small wound. *It's just like lighting a cigarette,* he told himself. He pictured the glowing butt of a lit cigarette, burning just like he had done for Jakub a hundred times. Biting his lip, he imagined putting that same fire into *just the surface* of Herb's shorn flesh. *Bunny please, don't blow him up.*

The magic surged, and with a small burst of light and

a puff of smoke, Herb's wounded arm burned and singed. He screamed into the glove, writhing and shoving; his thick fingers dug bruises into Cheshire's biceps. Cheshire did his best to keep him still, afraid to let go even though his palm ached with the heat. It wasn't until Herb had finally started to catch his breath that Cheshire realized Camila had turned in her seat and was holding the gun to his head.

"I'm helping!" Cheshire lifted both hands in surrender, and in doing so displayed the outcome of his work: Herb's inner arm was scorched, excruciating even to look at, but the bleeding had stopped. "If we get him to the hospital quick he can still..."

He turned his head, and abruptly Camila leaned back. Her expression shifted from murderous to shocked, and she lowered the gun. Cheshire caught a glimpse of his own face in the rear-view mirror, and finally he understood her reaction—bright lines of glowing red streaked from his forehead down to his chin, making up the same pattern branded on both his palms. It only lasted a few seconds, swiftly melting away to leave only his stunned expression staring back at him. But Camila had seen, and she leaned away from him, crossing herself.

"What the hell did you do?" demanded Nicole.

She didn't sound surprised or frightened enough to have seen the sigil; Cheshire quickly turned back to Herb just in case. "I cauterized the wound...I think." He pulled out his pocket square to cover the ghastly burn with. "It's not bleeding as badly. Just get us to the hospital as fast as you can!"

Herb groaned. He was drenched in sweat, eyes rolling back, but his grip on Cheshire was still strong. "Take it easy, Herb," Cheshire awkwardly consoled him. "You'll be all right."

Herb spat Cheshire's glove out and sagged deeper into the carseat. "It was one of the Jersey boys," he said through gritted teeth. "Wasn't it?"

Cheshire gulped. "We're almost there," he replied. "Just try not to move too much for now. You're gonna make it."

Herb sighed, and at last his grip began to relax. "Thanks," he muttered. His eyelids were heavy and pinched with fatigue but he met Cheshire's gaze. "You're my hero."

Cheshire felt his stomach turn, and he hoped Herb was in too much pain to see that queasiness in his face. "Don't mention it."

At the hospital, Cheshire stayed with Camila while Nicole organized the rest of their crew. His gloves were full of blood but he kept them on anyway, nervous about Camila seeing his brands. It was probably too late for that kind of caution, but he couldn't help it.

"Herb's the toughest son of a bitch I've ever met," he told her, not for the first time, as they waited for some word from the doctors. It wasn't the truth but he didn't think she'd question. "He'll be fine."

Camila didn't reply. She was nestled deep in her fur coat, staring straight ahead with a vacant, yet somehow still intense expression. He found it deeply unsettling and struggled to find something new to say.

"I know what you were both trying to do today," he began cautiously, watching her face for any reaction. "But if you keep trying to strong arm everyone into doing what you want, this is going to keep happening."

"It won't happen again," Camila said quietly, but with a certainty that chilled him. "I'll make sure of it."

"You can go after Union City, sure. Burn it to the ground if you want. That'll just make you more enemies."

Camila's gaze shifted toward him. "It worked for you and the Foleys," she said.

Cheshire gulped and rubbed the back of his neck, only to cringe at the dried blood he was smearing into his collar. "Well...I guess. But only for a while—we ran into plenty of trouble with other gangs after that." He thought briefly of the Townshead boys and the terrible cost they'd exacted from Kozlow encroaching on their perceived territory; it made his palms itch. "You can't keep throwing your weight around without blowback. You may have friends in the feds but that's going to run out eventually, too."

Camila sighed and straightened up from her thick collar. "You're wondering how we did it," she said. "Framed your boss' son. We paid off a witness—it was easy." At last she met Cheshire's eyes directly. "I'm not afraid of the feds."

"Can you..." Cheshire licked his lips. "Would you mind *un*paying your witness? How am I supposed to keep working with you if you put my boss in jail? Kozlow will go to war for this."

"Come to Manhattan," Camila said, as if it were obvious, and Cheshire froze. "Leave Kozlow."

Leave Kozlow? Cheshire stared back at her, speechless. He couldn't quite wrap his brain around the suggestion, as suddenly all he could think about was Jakub. *He made it out of the cemetery fine, I'm sure*, he thought, despite attempts to stay focused with Camila watching him so closely. *They probably found a way to Leon's...* "Um, what?"

"Come to Manhattan," Camila repeated, her voice so low and firm that he feared for a moment she might try to hypnotize him. "You saved my dear friend's life today, and I'll reward you for it. You don't need to stay loyal to Kozlow and his son after how they've treated you."

"How they...hold on." Cheshire shook his head, which unfortunately didn't help to clear it. "I can't do that. Kozlow is..." He faltered, suddenly feeling very small beneath Camila's unwavering attention. *Kozlow is where Jakub is. He'd never leave them. Would he?*

"Kozlow is the boss," he tried again. "What is everyone going to say if I hop the river right after you frame his son? They're gonna think I had something to do with it."

Camila blinked. "So?"

"*So?* So...come on, you know how that looks." Cheshire began to sweat but this time managed not to reach for his neck. "My reputation matters to me. I'm not a snitch and I'm not a turncoat, sorry."

Camila let out a sigh and sagged back into her nest of fur. "I'm disappointed in you."

Cheshire swallowed back a grimace. "You Manhattan people sure know how to hit below the belt," he said, hoping to take the sting out by making light. No such luck. "If this is what your idea of a 'reward' is I'll keep my magic to myself next time."

Camila gave a tiny shudder, and Cheshire froze again, fearing he'd overstepped. She slipped one gloved hand out of her coat. "Do you have a nickel?"

"Uh...sure."

Cheshire handed one over, and he watched, baffled, as Camila pushed to her feet and headed across the waiting room to a payphone. Her call lasted only a few minutes, and then she returned, settling down into her furs again like a wild animal in its nest. "The little Kozlow will go free," she said. "But he *will* learn his place." She fixed Cheshire with a serious eye. "I'm only doing what I have to, to survive."

"I know," Cheshire said quickly, his emotions tipping between relief and apprehension. "Please just...survive more quietly for a little while, maybe?" He smiled weakly. "Or at least, keep it to the other side of the river, so I can help calm this side down?"

"Agreed," said Camila, and once she had relaxed into her seat, Cheshire did, too.

***

Jakub and the others made their way across town one alley at a time, and at last they reached the Szpilman's hardware store in Maspeth. They hid out in the basement, Burke expressing his disbelief over the events again and again. Jakub took a seat on the piano bench with his back to the instrument so he could watch the door. Even if Marshal Adalet knew to check Barney's in-laws, the basement entrance was hidden well enough that they shouldn't have to worry about being found out, but that didn't stop his caution. He smoked down the rest of his cigarettes while they waited.

"It's not safe to go home," said Hannah, sitting next to Burke on the sofa while Barney paced back and forth in front of them. "It might not even be safe to call. The police came to the funeral because they knew it would be easier to catch you there than at your home. They'll probably have officers around the building to keep you from going back in."

"We can't just sit down here forever!" Barney gestured angrily as he continued to pace. "What if they go after Wanda? After my *son*? Lucky is out of her mind—I'll make her *pay* for this!"

"We need to find out what they used to frame you, and how we can turn it against them," insisted Hannah, keeping her tone even to try to calm him down. "If they've bought someone out we can pay more—if it's forged evidence, we can destroy it. We'll figure something out."

"Masterson's no fool," Burke added. "If he wanted to start a war wouldn't he have killed you, too? If it's a warning he's keen on delivering, there'll be a way out of it." He made a squeamish face. "Prob'ly not something you'll like, then."

Barney turned on him with a scowl. "What, you're a fan? You and Bloom both have been up his ass from the start! How do I know you—"

"Barney," said Jakub, and Barney flinched as if suddenly wary of being on the other end of Jakub's temper again. But he kept his voice low, following Hannah's example. "Bloom left with Masterson. He'll be able to get out of him what their real game is. There's no point getting worked up until we know what they want."

Barney scrubbed the back of hand across his mouth, and though at first it didn't seem as if he had any intention of backing down, with a deep breath he finally dropped into a chair. "I know what they want," he grumbled. "They're just pissed because of that stupid fucking dinner. Whatever their 'game' is, I'm not playing it! They're gonna learn they can't fuck with Kozlow."

"They will," Hannah assured him. "Once we handle the feds first."

They waited for another hour. Leon came down with an offer of booze—just a few swigs each to calm the nerves. He didn't have any news for them. Jakub tried not to worry, as Cheshire had gotten himself out of much worse scraps, but he still ached to see him. He just needed to be sure.

The phone rang. Hannah answered, and everyone held their breath, straining their ears. After listening for a while, anxious but quiet, Hannah shifted back and forth. "You're sure?" she asked. "We could just... All right. Yes, you're right. I understand." She hung up.

"Well?" Barney asked impatiently as he pushed to his feet again, ready to resume his pacing. "What's going on?"

"It was your father," said Hannah. Her face was grim. "The marshal is there, and...he wants us to come home."

Barney gulped. Despite all his temper and bravado there was fear in his eyes. "You're sure?"

"Yes." Hannah waved him forward. "Come on. I'm sure he has a plan."

Burke made a doubtful face, which luckily Barney didn't see as they all moved toward the exit. Without further speculation or conflict they piled into Leon's car and headed south across Brooklyn to the Kozlow's. As they expected, a herd of police cars awaited them, just like at the cemetery. Hazel stood on the sidewalk. Her hair was tousled and there were spots of blood across the front of her blue suit jacket, and her eyes locked onto their car the moment they turned the corner. Beside her, Kasper leaned heavily against his cane.

"He has a plan, right?" said Barney as they parked. "You're sure."

"I'm sure he does," replied Hannah, but she didn't say more than that as they disembarked.

"Barney Kozlow," Hazel called, as authoritative as ever, as if no interruption at the funeral had taken place. "These officers are going to handcuff you, and you're going to get into this car."

Barney eyed the approaching officers warily. "I didn't kill anyone."

Hazel glared back, unmoved. "I'm not going to ask again."

"Go on, Son," said Kasper, gesturing Barney on. "Answer her questions, and be respectful."

Jakub stood back, tense and uncertain what to do as he watched Barney put into handcuffs. *The boss must know what he's doing. But what if the feds have more on him than we know? What if he really does go away for this?* He looked to Kasper and found the man's expression unreadable. *Will he really go to war against Manhattan?*

Barney looked downright nauseated as he allowed the cuffs to be put on him. The officers ushered him into Hazel's car, while Hazel herself shared a few more quiet words with Kasper. He nodded and then waved Hannah over.

"Think this is really it?" Burke whispered. "We're fucked, ain't we?"

"I don't know," Jakub admitted, and his attention was drawn to the end of the street, where a cab had pulled to the curb. The back door opened and a head of honey-blonde hair poked out, only to duck back into the car a moment later. Jakub's heart began to pound, and he glanced at each of the officers—it seemed as though no one had noticed. He licked his lips. "But there's nothing else we can do right now."

Once Hannah finished with Kasper, she returned to Jakub and Burke. "I'm going to follow them to the station," she relayed. "This is how we find out what they have on him. Stay with the boss, okay? He needs to know everything that happened."

"Sure," said Jakub, forcing himself not to look again toward the cab. "Good luck."

Hazel sped off with her prisoner, and one by one the police cars followed, then Hannah. Kasper started heading inside even before the last one had pulled away. Though Burke followed immediately, Jakub hung back, and once the last car was gone he was rewarded with Cheshire climbing out of the cab.

Jakub's shoulders sagged with relief. "Cheshire."

"Jakub!" Cheshire jogged down the sidewalk to him with equal relief plastered across his smiling face. "Thank God, you're okay. Aren't you?"

"I'm fine." Jakub looked him over, and the hairs on his neck stood on end when he realized Cheshire's gloves and sleeves were covered in dried blood. "Are you?"

"Oh—yeah, I'm fine." He turned toward the building and motioned for Jakub to follow. "I'll tell you all about it."

The pair of them ducked inside, and after Cheshire had a moment to drop off his gloves and jacket in Jakub's apartment, they joined Kasper and Burke on the top floor to confer. Burke relayed their half of the morning's exhausting events and Cheshire his. Jakub couldn't help but frown deeply as Cheshire described the use of his magic.

Kasper, too, regarded him with a stern and troubled look from across his desk. "You saved Masterson's life?"

"I didn't have a choice," Cheshire insisted. "And it's going to work out for us—he and Reynoso agreed to call off the feds. Adalet will ask him some questions, the witness will say he made a mistake—it'll be all right."

"That doesn't change what they've done," said Kasper. "Manhattan does not control us, and we cannot allow them to continue thinking they do."

"Don't they?" said Burke, but when Jakub shot him a glare, he winced a little and hurried to explain himself better. "They've got us by the balls on this one, at least. We gotta wait until Barney is in the clear before we even think about retaliating."

Kasper's brow furrowed more deeply, so Cheshire tried

his hand again. "They're only showing off for pride's sake," he said. "If we let them think they won this round, they'll calm down for a while. And we've been doing good business with them—there's no reason to keep going back and forth until it's war."

"A war they started," Kasper said icily. "Which we're more than capable of finishing." He fixed Cheshire especially with a piercing look. "Like we did the Foleys."

Cheshire leaned back, and Jakub wasn't sure what to make of the clear hesitation in his face. "I'd rather it not come to that," he said, with more honest seriousness than he usually showed the boss. "We can coexist. It'll be better for everyone."

"If we are going to get paybacks, it doesn't have to be now," Jakub added, and Kasper immediately fixed his attention on him. "Once Barney is freed, we can let everything settle down and figure out where Harlem and Union City end up. We can bide our time and come up with a real plan. Or, we find a way to make them useful to us. If the other gangs are worried about surviving Reynoso, maybe we can play nice and let them wear each other thin before risking ourselves."

Kasper grumped thoughtfully, and he nodded. "Yes, you're right. If they're able to wield the US Marshal's office, we need to be able to, too. We need more ears in Manhattan and beyond. We need to get a step ahead of them."

Neither Cheshire or Burke looked convinced, so Jakub hurried to keep Kasper's attention away from them. "We will," he said. "If we're patient, we can beat them."

Kasper nodded again. Jakub led the three of them out of his office before any more could be said.

"What a fucking mess," Burke muttered as soon as they were out of the penthouse. He looked ready to launch into a screed, but then Cheshire cleared his throat.

"Can we go to your apartment, Jakub?" Cheshire asked. "There's...one more thing you should both know."

His demeanor was serious enough to put Jakub on edge, and he quickly agreed. The three of them retreated to his apartment and huddled around his small table to share cigarettes and a bottle of whiskey between them. And then Cheshire let the truth tumble out.

"Lucky asked me to leave Kozlow for them," he said, and Jakub almost choked on his cigarette smoke.

"Ye're fucking serious?" Burke exclaimed, though he then quickly hushed himself to a near whisper. "Seriously?"

"I'm serious!" Cheshire leaned his elbows against the table. "I told her no, of course. Today was exactly the 'shitshow' we all thought it would be. Why would I ever want to be a part of *that*?" He glanced to Jakub and flinched guiltily. "And! Of course, I wouldn't betray Kozlow anyway."

Jakub frowned. His stomach churned and he wasn't sure why. "Who else knows?"

"On our side, just the two of you." Cheshire loosened his tie nervously. "I don't know about on their side, though. She kind of hinted that part of the reason they went after Barney was because of me."

"Fucking hell," muttered Burke. He took another long swig from the bottle. "You'd better be keeping your lips sealed about that, then. Any Kozlow would shit kittens if they thought for a second you'd really jump ship." His gaze darted to Jakub. "Right? Bloom's solid so there's no reason to tell them."

"No, there's not," Jakub said, and seeing Burke's relief made him bristle. *Did he think I would say anything?* But then his severe expression made *Burke* grimace, and he tried to relax. "No one says a word: not to the boss, Barney, Hannah, or anyone else." He looked back to Cheshire. "And you *have* to make sure Lucky knows you're not interested. If she thinks there's a chance you'll change your mind, she might try something else that won't be as reversible as a witness's mind."

"No, no, I'm on it," Cheshire reassured him, emphasizing with gestures from his cigarette. "I was very clear—I'm no traitor." He took a quick drag. "Herb owes me and I'm gonna make real sure he remembers it, the next time he tries anything."

They stayed holed up in the building for most of the day. Everyone of Kozlow's was eager to hear the story of what had happened at the cemetery, which led to a lot of visitors over the hours. They listened to the radio for news, but it wasn't until Edith showed up in the evening with a heaping of supper that they had the full report: two police officers and three others killed, half a dozen more injured. Most of the Napoliellos had been arrested along with all but one of the Union City boys. But other than Herb himself, the Manhattan crews had escaped mostly unscathed, and the streets everywhere could only wonder who would act next.

At one point after supper, when Burke returned to his own apartment for a nap of exhaustion, Jakub finally had Cheshire to himself. He drew him into the bedroom, kissed him hard and then met his gaze seriously. "You're really all right?"

"I am if you are," Cheshire replied playfully, but then his grin sobered. "You don't have to worry about me, Jake. I meant it when I said I'm no traitor."

"I know." Jakub leaned into his chest, needing a few moments of Cheshire's arms around him. "Not that they deserve it. You've done more than enough for Barney after the way—"

"It's all right," Cheshire interrupted as he obliged him with a firm embrace. "Really. I just want things to go smoothly, however that has to happen."

Jakub sighed. "I know."

He tugged Cheshire into another kiss, and as sweet as it was, he couldn't stop from wondering. *Would he be happier, away from Kozlow?* He held Cheshire tighter. *Manhattan can't be trusted, either, but he deserves better than this.*

They left the bedroom just as the news came in: Barney was being released.

He made it home with Hannah just after sundown. By then Wanda had come down with Kasper Jr., and she with the rest of Kozlow's loyalists gave them a warm reception. Just as Cheshire had reassured them, Hazel's supposedly reliable witness had recanted their statement, and with all other evidence too weak on its own, no charges would be filed. Barney took great pleasure in recounting Marshal Adalet's frustration, as if he could claim any credit for it. But at the very least, he had been spooked enough that it didn't take as much to convince him of their patience strategy as it had his father. He had no intention of putting himself in the crosshairs again too soon.

And it worked, for a time. Cheshire and Jakub gave their well wishes to Herb when he was discharged from the hospital, arm in a sling but otherwise on the mend. They had his assurances that he had every intention of laying low for a while. Between booze and mail fraud business was good, and both sides of the river continued on in tense but peaceful coexistence. Even Manhattan itself relaxed back into its status quo.

But it didn't come as much of a surprise to anyone when the rest of the Union City Boys washed up on the river shores. No one had seen a thing.

A Normal Goddamn Date

Jakub put it off for as long as he could. He ignored the occasional twinge from his fingers, covering up any fumbles that occurred in front of others. It wasn't *that* bad, he would tell himself. Better than not having an arm at all.

But eventually it wore him down. He could pretend not to notice when Cheshire restrained a look of sympathy, but ironically, it was when Cheshire mastered not reacting at all to his lapses of dexterity that proved the last straw. Jakub invited Miklos to his apartment, and they spread newspaper over the small work table in his living room.

"You could just take it back to Hallorran," Miklos suggested as he pulled a lamp closer. "I'm sure they'd help you tune it up, especially if you pay them."

Jakub laid out his tools in easy reach and sat down on the floor. "I don't want Tully to see it like this," he said, and his face screwed up briefly. "She'd scold me."

Miklos smiled with understanding as he joined Jakub at the table. "Well, I'll help however I can. Just tell me what to do."

"I only need you to help me keep it steady," said Jakub. He disconnected his prosthetic and set it on the table, so that the dented plate on the forearm faced them.

"Sure."

Miklos slipped his hand into Jakub's, gripping it like he would if it were a flesh and blood hand, still attached to its owner. It gave Jakub a chill which he quickly tried to shake off. "Thanks," he mumbled, and with a deep breath he began unscrewing the metal plate that served as his skin.

"Jersey has been pretty quiet lately," Miklos chatted while Jakub worked. He must have sensed that the distraction was a welcome one. "But tense. I've seen more police on the streets at night. With the Union City Boys gone, I think everyone assumed that Lucky's crew would make a showing, but I haven't heard anything so far."

"They did promise Cheshire they would stay low for a while." Jakub placed the screws he'd removed on the table in an orderly line. "But Masterson will be healed up by now. I can't imagine he'll sit on his hands much longer."

Miklos hummed thoughtfully. "And how *is* Cheshire?" he prodded, a note of gentle teasing in his voice. "I haven't seen him in a long time."

Jakub removed the last of the screws. "He's fine," he said. Try as he might, he couldn't ignore the expectant look Miklos continued to fix on him, and his cheeks reddened. "*We're* fine."

Miklos' smile deepened as he helped Jakub slide the plate free. "I'm glad to hear it."

He placed the plate aside, and both of them quieted a moment with the inner workings of Jakub's prosthetic exposed. Rods and pistons replaced bone and muscle, grease smeared across the metal taking the place of sticky blood. Jakub swallowed hard, thoughtlessly reaching for his stump as a feeling of heat swarmed up the limb he no longer had. The last time he had seen his own arm it had looked like this: gruesomely laid open, surreal and unfamiliar to him. He could taste smoke in his throat.

Miklos rubbed his back through the thin cotton of his undershirt. "Take a breath," he said quietly, and Jakub did so, letting the stale air of the apartment take the place of unwanted memories.

"Thanks," said Jakub. After another moment to steel his nerves, he leaned over the opened arm. "I'm all right."

"It's okay if you're not," Miklos offered, but when Jakub shook his head, he took the hint. "The dent was around here," he said, pointing out the spot halfway down the forearm. "But this is the closest piston and it doesn't look damaged."

"Maybe the impact shook something out of place," Jakub mused. He tugged the lamp closer, and while Miklos held the arm steady he reached gingerly into the mechanisms. As eerie as it was, he forced himself to remember Tully's instructions, and the smooth, deft certainty of her hands. By following the piston down toward his wrist, he discovered one of the tension wires had slipped its track and was pinned behind an exposed screw head.

"There's your culprit," said Miklos. "How bad is it?"

Jakub drew a magnifying glass closer to be sure. "The wire itself isn't damaged," he said, and gradually the tension began to unwind from between his shoulders. "I think if I replace that screw, get the wire back in its track and tighten it up...it should be fine."

"Good." Miklos grinned and gave Jakub a gentle clap on the shoulder. "See? Not so bad. How long have you been putting this off?"

Jakub grimaced with embarrassment and began loosening the screw. "Too long," he admitted. "I should have done this right after, but..." He sighed and confessed the truth. "I didn't want to find out it was something I couldn't fix myself."

"Would it really be so bad?" said Miklos, but he didn't wait for an answer. As soon as the screw was high enough he twisted it free and compared it to Jakub's collection of spares. "I know how important your self-reliance is to you, Kuba. But you have people to lean on when you need it."

"I know," Jakub replied, meaning it. He threaded the wire back into its proper track and could have sworn he felt his left pinky twitch. "Thank you."

Jakub finished the repair and took the opportunity to apply fresh grease where necessary. Before they replaced the forearm plate, he guided Miklos through carefully tapping the dent out of it. As the last screw was tightened he even allowed himself to wonder if he could reinforce the metal with something stronger, or even possibly to embellish it...

Jakub shook his head. He wound the mainsprings tight and then connected the limb. After a few deep breaths he clenched his fist, and was relieved to see all five fingers respond. He stretched and even wiggled each digit to be sure. Nothing caught or fumbled.

"It looks pretty good," said Miklos, leaning back on his

hands. "How does it feel?"

"Better," Jakub admitted. "Much better." He relaxed and even smiled with relief as he waved to Miklos. "Thank you for your help."

"Of course."

The phone rang, and Miklos began tidying up their supplies while Jakub answered. There were only so many people who called his apartment, but his heart still skipped when Cheshire's voice sang through the receiver.

"Jakub! It's me." Cheshire laughed as if that itself was somehow amusing. "Sorry, this is short notice, but are you busy tonight?"

Jakub glanced to the clock—it was nearing five o'clock. A little late to be planning a job for the same night. "Why, what's going on?"

"Can you come for dinner tonight?" Cheshire asked, downright effervescent. "Herb held a table for us in the Olivier's VIP room, but it has to be *tonight*. Are you free?"

Jakub leaned back as his head spun. "Dinner with Masterson," he said slowly, "at the most expensive restaurant in town?"

Cheshire laughed some more. "Wild, huh? But not *with* Herb—Herb adjacent. It'll be us and Grace. Apparently he wants to sweet-talk her into performing at the Thrones, so it's a two-birds one-stone kinda thing. She's bringing her new girlfriend." Cheshire's voice lowered then to a near conspiratorial whisper. "It'll be like a double date."

"A date?" Jakub repeated dumbly, and he flushed when he noticed Miklos raising his head.

"Yeah. Are you in? I'll come pick you up, if you are." Jakub could easily imagine Cheshire's playful smirk as he spoke. "I won't even ask you to wear a tie, if you're that convinced it's bad luck. Just grab that black jacket and you'll be fine."

Jakub plucked at his grease-stained undershirt. "I'll have to...clean up."

"So, you're in?" Cheshire pressed. He chuckled, sounding so much younger than himself. "You'll come to dinner with me?"

"Y...Yeah." Jakub gulped. "Yeah, it's a date," he said, and in a fit of self-consciousness he hung up.

Miklos raised his eyebrows as Jakub turned toward

him. "Chesh?" he supposed.

"Yeah. Sorry, Miksa, I—" Jakub frowned suddenly, glancing to the phone and back. "I just hung up on him," he realized aloud. "Shit. Should I call him back?"

Miklos chuckled as he climbed to his feet. "You should take a shower," he said, and he steered Jakub toward the bathroom. "I'll finish cleaning up in here."

"Sorry. I was going to ask you to stay for drinks..."

"We can do that any time," Miklos reassured him. "I'll go bother your friend Eggy for booze if I get thirsty." He gave Jakub a gentle push. "Go get ready for your *date*."

Jakub's face burned all the way to the bathroom. He stripped out of his filthy clothes and set his prosthetic aside so he could step beneath the shower spray. He and Cheshire had shared plenty of meals before, even dinners—even dinners *alone*—but they'd never used that word before. *Date*. It made him feel silly and ridiculous for it as he scrubbed vigorously.

Dressing wasn't too difficult, as he only had a few items in his wardrobe that would have been appropriate for the Olivier's caliber anyway. He picked a black shirt that would disguise his lack of a necktie and a jacket to match, then dug around his room for a comb.

Miklos will have to help me here, he thought, taking it with him into the living room. There he stopped, only then realizing that Miklos wasn't the only one waiting for him.

Hannah was seated on the sofa next to Miklos, the two of them chatting about the same New Jersey news shared earlier. She glanced up at Jakub's entrance and looked surprised; Jakub could only depend on instinct to turn his expression to stone.

"Hannah," he greeted. "I didn't hear you come in."

"You look very handsome," said Hannah, though there was suspicion in her sincerity. "All this for Masterson?"

Miklos leaned forward against his knees. "I told her about the call," he said, and Jakub trusted him enough to relax. "When Manhattan says 'jump' there's not much else you can do, right?"

"I don't want to make waves," Jakub said. He waved the comb at Miklos. "Help?"

Miklos happily moved to assist. *Relax*, he mouthed as he accepted the comb, and Jakub managed a slight nod before holding still.

"I'm a little nervous about how quiet it's been," Hannah admitted as she watched. "Barney's been hoping to hear something we can move on, but there's no news on a job, and they haven't asked to use the pier for months." She frowned. "But you and Bloom are going to dinner with them?"

"We're just making nice," Jakub said. "Bloom saved Masterson's life—they're showing their appreciation."

"I know." Hannah sighed and folded her arms. "That's what worries me."

Something's on her mind, Jakub thought. *Did Burke say something to her?* He caught Miklos' eye, and Miklos seemed to understand at once; he handed Jakub back the comb.

"That's the best I can do for you," he teased, and then he straightened Jakub's collar. "I'll pop downstairs and see if Eggy has that drink for me after all."

"Sure," said Jakub. "Thanks for your help today."

"You said that already." Miklos nodded to Hannah as he stepped into his shoes by the door. "Nice to see you, Hannah."

"You, too," she replied, and Miklos showed himself out.

Now that they were alone, Jakub sat down on the arm of the sofa to better face Hannah seriously. "I know we're all nerved up over Lucky," he said, "but Bloom's just trying to keep the peace. It's just us, and them, and Harlem now, and Big Mitts is thrown in with Lucky. Peace is the best we can do."

"I know," Hannah said quickly. "And I agree. But hell, Jakub you know what Barney's like." She ran her fingers back through her hair; she seemed uncharacteristically anxious over it. "All he wants is to get even, and I can't blame him. And the more Bloom chummies up to Masterson, the worse it gets."

"Bloom is playing nice with Lucky's people *because* Barney keeps trying to rile them up," Jakub argued. "We can't go to war with them. They can hit harder than us, and if Barney goes after them without a plan, they'll do to him what they did to Napoliello."

"I know," Hannah said again, frustrated. "But he and the boss are set on doing *something*. A plan is what we need." She uncrossed her arms and turned to face him better. "Barney may not admit it, but you and I know we used to be able to count on Bloom for that."

"Used to?" Jakub repeated, and he hoped Hannah didn't think too hard on how sharply it came out.

If she did, she didn't show it. "He helped us undercut the Foleys at every turn," she carried on. "And this thing with Manhattan started the same way. I'm just..." She frowned down at the cushions a moment to collect her thoughts. "He seems more interested now in showing *off* to them than showing them *up*. I'm just worried."

Jakub ground his teeth. He was tempted to glance to the door, fearful that at any moment Cheshire would appear and blunder right into a conversation that required better preparation than either of them had done. "'If you can't beat them, join them,' you mean?"

"That's not an option for Kozlow, we both know that."

"Yeah." Jakub sighed, and with a day of tension already winding him tight, he found himself resorting to honesty. "But maybe Kozlow is *wrong*. Aren't you tired of trying to leash Barney? It's only going to get worse once his father is gone."

Hannah leaned back slightly, though her surprise twisted soon after into resignation. "I was hoping *being* a father would help," she admitted. "Maybe calm him down a little, but..."

Hannah sighed and pushed to her feet. "He's family," she said. "All I can do is try to protect him. That's all any of us can do until he learns for himself. Right?"

Jakub stared back at her. Her loyalty was as heartbreaking as it was admirable, and it exhausted him. "Right," he said, but only because he didn't know what else to say. "If I get the chance to talk to him...I'll try, too."

"Thanks, Jakub." Hannah fussed with her hair again, and Jakub offered her his comb. She smiled crookedly and accepted. "If you're going through with dinner, keep your ears open," she said as she brushed her long hair out. "Maybe Masterson will let something slip, if he's with Bloom. Something we can use."

"Sure." He accepted the comb back when Hannah finished, and before she could turn for the door, he stood. "Just so you know, what Bloom is doing is *also* protecting Barney," he said. "I know you can admit that even if Barney can't."

Hannah surrendered a long sigh. "I know. But what can I say to him? Whenever someone encourages him, he gets carried away." She fixed Jakub with a look that was playful, but unmistakably serious beneath it. "Even when it's you. We don't need that, either."

Jakub tucked the comb into his jacket as an excuse to break the unwanted eye contact. "I'll try to talk to him, too."

Hannah nodded, seemingly satisfied. "We'll find a way through this," she said. "We always have." She gave him a pat on the arm and then headed for the door. "Make sure you order a huge chunk of meat if Masterson is paying."

"I will," said Jakub, and as soon as she was out of the apartment, he hurried to find a cigarette.

***

Cheshire's day had gotten off to a slow start: waking up late to a thrumming headache and a scratchy throat, telltale signs of an incoming spring cold, only to be swamped by piles of paperwork from Burke. The call from Herb late in the afternoon turned everything around. By the time Cheshire arrived at the Kozlow building, he was sure he was glowing, all ailments and concerns long gone. He had settled on his champagne-gold suit for the occasion, determined to give it a good showing after having missed its intended audience at the Morey dinner. *He'll be in all black anyway,* he reasoned as he bounded up the steps. *So it'll be a good match.* He hummed a jaunty tune as he showed himself into the building, only to have the melody killed in his throat.

Miklos Horvay was waiting in the lobby—in fact, he was standing just beside the elevator, completely unavoidable in his lavender hair. Cheshire gulped. He had only seen Miklos in passing a handful of times since Jakub's accident, and more to the point, since he and Jakub had started sleeping together. In that time he had yet to develop a decent strategy for how to approach a reunion.

If he's waiting for Jakub, he won't be happy to see me, Cheshire thought as he faked a casual smile. *He and Jakub used to...* "Hey, Mik," he greeted. "Long time no see."

Miklos glanced over and smiled. He didn't look put out or even surprised to see Cheshire heading his way. "Hey, Chesh," he said. "How have you been?"

"Good! Super good." Cheshire pressed the button for the elevator, and immediately the doors opened. "You? You *look* good!"

Miklos arched an eyebrow and swept his gaze up and

down Cheshire's suit. "So do you."

"Thanks!"

Cheshire slipped into the elevator and gulped again when Miklos joined him. "Going up?" he said, and then he chuckled as he hit Jakub's floor. "I assume you're here for Jakub, but um, he and I..."

He hesitated, knowing how insensitive it would be to brag, when that was all he felt like doing given the monumental occasion. Miklos watched him curiously, and when he took too long to recover, he prodded, "You have plans?"

"Yes! Dinner plans." Cheshire rubbed the back of his neck. "I'd invite you to come with, but it's not my dime."

"Oh, I know," said Miklos.

"You...do?"

"Uh-huh."

Cheshire eyed him, unsure if he was meant to ask how. "Oh. Well, maybe next time, huh?"

The elevator stopped on Jakub's floor, but when Cheshire moved to the door, Miklos took his arm to prevent him. He stopped, breath held. Though he was prepared for it, he still sometimes got the shivers when their conflicting magics interacted through touch. "Yes?"

"Give it a minute," said Miklos, and just as he said so, Jakub's door opened. It was Hannah who emerged, and Cheshire ducked deeper into the elevator until she had passed by on her way to the stairs.

"She was in a serious mood," Miklos explained as Cheshire breathed a quiet sigh. "I figured you didn't want to be in the middle of that."

"Thanks." Cheshire flashed him a grateful smile, but then he paused. *The mature thing to do would be to say something,* he thought, and he cleared his throat. *He and Jakub are still good friends, after all.* "Hey, Miklos. Sorry if this is awkward, but I just wanted to say...well, sorry."

Miklos looked at him, puzzled, as they stepped out into the hall. "What for?"

"Because you and Jake..." Cheshire squirmed awkwardly and shoved his hands into his pockets. "You were a thing, right? Right up until, well, he and *I* were a thing." He gave a huge shrug. "I'm glad you guys worked it out but I didn't want you to think I'm, you know, some kind of ratfink for..."

He trailed off at the sound of Miklos laughing at him. "What?"

"He and I were never 'a thing'," Miklos said, and his hair almost seemed to glitter with good humor. "We're just friends, Chesh."

"But..." Cheshire frowned at him intensely; he could very clearly remember things he had heard through the walls, back when his and Jakub's apartments were side by side. He had even caught Miklos once or twice leaving Jakub's place early in the morning in those years before the accident, and the week he'd spent living with him immediately after. "But you *were*," he tried again, thinking Miklos hadn't caught his use of past tense.

That only made Miklos grin wider. "No, it really wasn't like that." He gestured past Cheshire with his chin. "Ask him yourself."

"Ask me what?"

Cheshire turned and was rendered speechless. He had seen Jakub well-dressed before, even recently, but there was definitely something different and striking about him—more than just that his hair was so neatly combed. He seemed... lighter, even eager, as if he might defy all expectations and break out in a smile at any moment. Cheshire couldn't bring himself to look away in case he might miss it.

It took him an awkward moment too long to realize that Jakub was holding up a cigarette. He lit it with a snap, and the tiny puff of smoke jolted him back to almost half his full senses. "Jakub! Wow, you look fantastic." He grinned and felt himself blushing as he reached into his jacket. "I brought you something—I promise it's not a necktie."

He tugged out a gold, silk handkerchief, delicately folded, to tuck into Jakub's jacket pocket. "You don't have to wear it," he said, even as he smoothed it into place. "I just thought it might...complete the look. You know?"

Jakub spared it only a glance before returning his gaze to Cheshire's face. His eyes pinched happily. "Thanks."

Oh, I want to kiss him so bad, Cheshire thought as he dragged his hands back. He knew just how Jakub would taste, of smoke and magic, and it made his fingertips tingle.

"You match now," Miklos noted slyly, and Cheshire and Jakub both blushed darker as they followed him back into the elevator.

"What were you going to ask me?" said Jakub as they began the descent toward the lobby.

Cheshire's grin twitched. "Oh, nothing! It's nothing. Just a misunderstanding."

Miklos glanced at him sideways; apparently he was in a mood for mischief. "Did you really think that all this time?" he asked with clearly fake innocence.

Cheshire began to sweat as Jakub frowned curiously between the two of them. "Well, yes! Of course I did!" He lifted his hat so he could smooth his hair back. "But if I was wrong and everything is fine now, great!"

"Oh, it's fine," Miklos assured him. "More than fine."

"Good!"

Jakub looked back and forth, his brow furrowing. "What are you talking about?"

"Nothing!" Cheshire laughed, and was saved by the elevator doors opening. "We'd better get going if we're going to make it in time. See you later, Mik!"

Miklos saw them off with a wave. "Enjoy your dinner!"

The pair of them climbed into Cheshire's car and they sped off, into the traffic headed for the Williamsburg Bridge. Cheshire drummed his fingers against the steering wheel in a swift, aimless rhythm. "Sorry this is such short notice," he said. The silence was too daunting *not* to fill. "I called you right after Herb called me. But it's just too good of a chance to pass up! Even with a woman on the inside I haven't been able to score the VIP room before now. He must have been saving up for this since the funeral, that prick."

Jakub rolled his window down so he could flick the ash off his cigarette. "He can't help but throw his weight around," he said. "He only does a favor if you have to rush to accept it. Just like the Morey dinner."

Cheshire surrendered a crooked grin. "Yeah, you're probably right. But how could I say no?"

"The fact you *can't* is the point," said Jakub, but then he lightened up again. "Still...thanks for inviting me."

"Of course! Just don't tell Burke, or I'll never hear the end of it. I'll make it up to him somehow." He chuckled, determined to reclaim the joyful momentum that had carried him to Jakub's building in the first place. "We'll make a night of it. Grace will be there—she has some new beau she wants to show off. Sounds like this one might be a keeper."

Jakub hummed to show he was listening, but he didn't offer more than that. After a brief silence had passed, which Cheshire spent with more anxious finger-drumming, he realized he couldn't contain his curiosity after all. "So, um." He aimed squarely for casual inquiry and fired. "Were you and Miklos ever a thing?"

Jakub snorted smoke through his nose. "What? What kind of thing?"

"You know, you were..." Cheshire caught his brow wrinkling; he wrangled an easy smile back in place. "I know for a fact you fooled around," he teased, and Jakub flushed red. "But Miklos said you were never steady."

"*That's* what you were talking about?" Jakub asked, exasperated. When Cheshire could only shrug, he took a long breath from his cigarette and let it out. "No, that was just...as friends. Miklos isn't interested in going steady with anyone."

"No? Oh." Cheshire frowned as the image unexpectedly tightened his stomach. The thought of Jakub that night of the wedding leaving with Miklos, the two of them slipping into bed together... He fidgeted. "I guess that makes sense," he said, and he laughed. "For a long time I couldn't imagine *you* going steady with anyone, either."

Jakub turned to look out the window and fell still. His silence prickled against Cheshire's skin with an almost nauseating suspense, and when he finally replied, it was so mumbled Cheshire couldn't make it out.

No possible way could he let that pass without knowing. "I'm sorry, what?"

"Me, either," said Jakub without looking back, though his red ears gave away his embarrassment. "I haven't...before now."

"Really?" Cheshire blurted out before he could stop himself. He quickly shook his head; it was suddenly hard to think, or even breathe, with the rush of giddy relief bubbling in his chest. "Well sorry, but you're pretty damn steady now, huh?" He laughed some more and couldn't stop grinning. "I may not be paying for dinner, but this is still a proper date, so I hope I can count on you for *dessert*."

His chuckling was cut short by Jakub's hand coming

to rest on his thigh. The firm pressure of metal digits sent his heart pumping and he was hard pressed to keep his eyes on the road.

"Miklos came over today to help me with this," he said, and Cheshire's mind buzzed with uncomprehending white until the subtle flex of Jakub's fingers made his meaning clear. "We tuned it up. It's a lot easier to work, now."

"Really?" Cheshire's grin softened, and he lowered his hand to cover Jakub's. "I'm glad," he said simply, though he hoped to convey that he understood what an effort that must have been for him.

Then Jakub's hand squirmed higher, dipping toward the inside of his thigh, and Cheshire's elation snapped back into simmering excitement. He tightened his grip on Jakub's hand to keep it from sneaking further. "If I pull over, we're not going to make the first course," he said breathlessly.

"Herb can wait," Jakub replied, and his steely insistence had Cheshire's toes curling. He stretched his pinky to press against Cheshire's groin.

Cheshire made a quick look of their surroundings; they had already moved into the bridge traffic and would soon be over water, with only the shoulder to pull off on. In broad daylight that was a bit too bold even for him; he pulled Jakub's hand from his thigh and kissed the back of his palm. "Save it for the hotel," he said, but he kept hold of Jakub as they continued on.

They chatted about business for the rest of the drive: safe, easy topics to keep Cheshire's mind off the heavy look Jakub was fixing him with. Several times he considered skipping dinner to instead drag Jakub into one of the hotel's lavish rooms. They arrived at the Olivier in good time and met Herb in the lobby, who was well dressed in a double-breasted jacket and red silk tie.

"Chesh!" Herb greeted. He gripped Cheshire's hand and pumped it mightily, as if he still had something to prove even if his arm was no longer confined to a sling. "I told you to bring a date, and you brought your bodyguard. What gives?"

Cheshire laughed to cover up his momentary falter. He sure wished he had mapped out a clever explanation ahead of time. "Well, Herb, quite frankly, you *scare* me," he said, continuing to shake Herb's hand. "And Eggy wasn't available—what's a poor fellow to do?"

Herb laughed back, and after a few more seconds, he was forced to extricate himself from Cheshire's grip first. "All right, all right, I'll allow it, since he cleans up so well. Good to see you, Freckles."

He thumped Jakub on the shoulder, who remained still and stony beneath the attention. "Thank you, Mr. Masterson."

"Mr. Masterson," Herb echoed, raising his eyebrows at Cheshire. "If only everyone at Kozlow was so respectful, eh?" He waved for them to follow him across the foyer. "Ms. Overgaard is already seated—let's not keep the ladies waiting."

Jakub cast Cheshire a look that he was, for once, at no loss to interpret: *Is he eating with us?* Cheshire gave a helpless shrug and felt his fatigue from earlier in the day creeping up on him. But he was determined to make the most of it, and just before they stepped into the elevator he gave Jakub's hand a reassuring squeeze, which Jakub returned.

The hotel's VIP lounge was on the tenth floor, and as soon as they stepped out of the elevator they were greeted with sweeping, tall-windowed views of the evening Manhattan skyline. The lighting was soft, warm, and intimate, wooden furniture and cream tablecloths, knock-offs of classical artists on the walls. The clientele was mostly older, and Cheshire thought he even recognized a face or two from the papers.

I guess this is what Manhattan gratitude really looks like, Cheshire thought with a smirk as they followed Herb toward a table near the windows. He was relieved even more so to see that it only seated four. Grace and Camila were already seated there, Grace in a shimmering blue dress and Camila wrapped in a mink stole. They leaned close together as they chatted like fond sisters.

The third woman at the table Cheshire had never seen before: an African American woman with a glossy white dress over her dark skin, thick hair fanned out in tight, natural curls. Her features were soft and elegant. But when she raised her gaze in their direction, her wide, brown eyes gave Cheshire a chill. Long before they were within each other's space he could feel goosebumps prickling up and down his neck, not unlike the electric warning of magic. Her eyes narrowed—she must have felt it, too.

She's a witch? Cheshire thought, and for some reason his throat grew tighter the closer they approached. He dug his fingertips into his itching palms. *It feels like Miklos, but...more than that. A lot more than that.*

"Cheshire," Grace said warmly once they had reached the table. She stood, and he snapped into instinct, greeting her with a peck on the cheek. "It's so good to see you! I want to introduce you." She gestured to her guest, who had also risen from her chair. "This is Emma Peabody."

"A pleasure to meet you," Cheshire said brightly. "I'm Cheshire Bloom." He braced himself and offered his hand; as expected, the moment they touched the backlash of magic skittered up the length of his arm. His heart skipped and his stomach clenched with nausea, so much stronger than anything he had encountered before.

Emma squeezed his hand, showing no flinch or surprise. "I'm happy to meet you," she said. "Grace has told me a lot about you."

"Oh, no," Cheshire lamented, prompting laughter from Grace and Herb. He nudged Jakub forward. "This is Jakub Danowicz, my...partner."

Jakub's shoulders crept up, but he shook Emma's hand with only his usual amount of social awkwardness. "Hello."

"Pleased to meet you, Jakub."

Herb clapped his hands together. "Well, everyone acquainted," he said jovially. "And you have your table—my work is done." He helped Camila out of her seat and then moved behind Emma to help her back into hers. "Enjoy your meal, everyone. And go easy on the wine?" He fixed Cheshire with a playfully stern look. "I mean *you*, mister."

"It's your tab," Cheshire teased back, and had to brace himself again as Herb thumped him on the back.

"Two-bit thug is what you are," Herb retorted. "Well, enjoy spending my money, then." He offered Camila his arm, and the two of them headed toward another table that awaited them. "You owe me."

Cheshire rolled his eyes as he held Grace's chair for her. "This is supposed to be making us even," he complained to the table. "I saved his life, you know."

"Oh? He didn't mention that." Grace sat down and filled her glass from a bottle of wine already on the table. "I thought you were here to help butter me up so I'll do another gig for him."

"Since when do you take *my* advice?" Cheshire moved to the next chair, and was a little disappointed to see Jakub had already seated himself. Even if it might have raised some eyebrows, he would have liked to offer him some gentlemanly courtesy. He cleared his throat and took a seat. "Butter can come later. I want to know how you two met!"

"Emma's the newest member of the band," Grace said proudly, and she reached across the table to take Emma's hand. "She plays the meanest saxophone I've ever heard! And she has a lovely voice, too, when I can convince her to sing."

Emma smiled shyly. "I'm not that good; she's just being kind."

"My ears know talent, believe me," Grace shot back. She was positively aglow when she smiled back at Emma; Cheshire imagined he knew just how she felt, and he wondered if his face gave as much away as hers did. "If we do perform at the Thrones it would be a good chance to try out a new set with a duet, so you'd better convince me to do it, Chesh."

"You should be careful about doing business with Masterson," said Jakub. "He has deep pockets but he has a funny idea of how favors work."

"It's not my first time dealing with career criminals," Grace reassured him, and she cast Cheshire a sly glance. He shrugged innocently. "At most it only has to be the once. And it'll put me in a good position to renegotiate my contract *here*." She tipped her wine glass in a salute.

"We'll be very careful," added Emma. "I wouldn't let her do anything reckless."

"Oh, I believe it," said Cheshire. He glanced between the two women, burning with curiosity. *Does Grace know she's a witch?* He poured glasses for Jakub and himself. *What could her magic be like?* "I can tell already, she's lucky to have you."

Emma returned his seeking look with a brief, tight-lipped frown. "That's very kind of you to say," she said.

Grace doesn't know, then, Cheshire took it to mean. *Is it really my place to say anything?* He glanced at Jakub, who was taking a ginger sip of his wine. *I haven't told him everything, either.* He gulped. "It's just the truth," he carried on. "I've known Grace for a long time, and I've never seen her light up as much as when she introduced you."

Grace blushed and gave his shoulder a push. "God,

- 164 -

you're so embarrassing," she scolded, but he was telling the truth: nothing could have squashed the happy gleam in her eyes. "But she *is* incredible."

Emma ducked slightly into her shoulders. "What about you two?" she changed the subject. "How did you two meet?"

Jakub tipped his head back in a gulp while Cheshire let out a nervous chuckle. *I guess she would be sharper than Herb.* "Oh, well, that's a *long* story," he said, caught between cheer and trepidation. "A long and *illegal* story. We were breaking into people's houses to steal money for booze."

Emma looked to Grace with surprise, who grinned and said, "See? I wasn't joking."

"Oh, my." Emma frowned dubiously despite her efforts to remain polite. "How...exciting."

"Are we going to order?" Jakub asked loudly, which raised a chuckle from all of them that left him deeply flushed.

"Yes, let's order," said Cheshire, and he caught the eye of one of the waiters. "Then I can tell you a few of our *tamer* adventures."

As promised, Cheshire filled the time waiting for their food with the mildest of their many criminal encounters: the impersonation trick he and Grace had pulled against the Foleys in Astoria, the inside peeks at Hallorran's headquarters, and most especially, the Robin Hooding of the Olivier delivery truck. Emma was a gracious audience, expressing interest and congratulations where appropriate. She even put a few questions to Jakub and coaxed answers out of him. Once or twice Cheshire caught Herb and Camila glancing their way, but they didn't make a repeat appearance. All in all, it was a very pleasant evening.

Even so, by the time dinner was finished, Cheshire found himself exhausted. He tried to blame it on the possible onset of a simple cold, but whenever his eyes met Emma's, he felt their heat pound between his temples. His palms by then were clammy inside his gloves and he couldn't shake the goose bumps. When the table began debating which expensive dessert to charge to Herb's tab, he finally pushed out of his chair.

"I'm going to find a washroom," Cheshire said. "I'll split whatever Jakub has." He cast Jakub a wink, who blushed and stumbled over a protest as he headed toward the far end of the dining room. *He's going to be mad I left him with them*, he thought with a wince. *But I just need a moment to clear my head.*

***

Jakub watched, dismayed, as Cheshire abandoned him at the table. He buried himself in the dessert menu. "Chocolate cake," he said, only because after a dinner of expensive dishes he'd enjoyed but couldn't pronounce, he was eager for something a bit more familiar. He peeked over the menu, hoping that Grace and Emma would entertain each other in Cheshire's absence without any effort from him, only to realize that Emma was also standing up from the table.

"I think I'll visit the powder room myself," she said. "Something light for me, please?"

"Oh—of course," said Grace, who looked half ready to follow her. But she settled again as Emma moved on, leaving the pair of them alone and facing each other.

Grace took in a deep breath. "So. Jakub."

"Grace," Jakub replied, placing the folded menu back on the table in resignation.

"You look very handsome tonight," Grace continued, and Jakub did his best not to shift self-consciously. "You know, when Cheshire first told me about you two, I could hardly believe it! But now that I'm really seeing you together, I think I understand."

Jakub frowned. *What the hell does that mean? Am I giving us away with my face after all?* That time he couldn't help scrubbing the back of his hand across his mouth. "Um. Thank you."

The waiter approached, and Jakub finished the wine in his glass as Grace related their dessert order. Once the waiter moved away both of them glanced longingly toward the restrooms, and in catching each other in the act, an awkward understanding calmed them both. Jakub picked up the mostly drained wine bottle, and Grace nodded, nudging her glass toward him.

I guess I've known her as long as Cheshire has, Jakub thought as he refilled each of them a modest portion. *Not...as well, though.* He swallowed his embarrassment when reminded of those nights when they were teenagers, and he could hear

Grace and Cheshire fooling around through the walls of their apartments. He had tried so hard then, to make himself forget about any hope of having Cheshire for himself. They had simply been too handsome of a couple, too well matched in looks and humor to think he could have ever competed.

This might be your only chance to ask, Jakub thought, and with another sip of drink to build his courage, he faced her. "Can I ask you something? Personal?"

"Oh, boy," said Grace, though she was smiling. "Here it comes. Go ahead, I'm ready."

Jakub frowned again in befuddlement and almost lost his nerve. "Um. Why did Cheshire break up with you?"

Grace gave a mighty snort. "Is that what he told you?" She rolled her eyes. "Let me tell you, then, don't believe whatever he said. *I* broke up with *him*."

Jakub's prosthetic tightened reflexively against the tablecloth. "Why?"

"Well, it was..." Faced with having to actually answer, Grace faltered uncomfortably. She took a sip of her wine to stall. "He's charming, and attentive, and generous—all those wonderful things. But the one thing he isn't is *honest*."

Jakub continued to tense defensively, though the distant hurt she was trying to banish from her expression quickly began to wear that down. "He's not..*dis*honest," he said. "He just exaggerates sometimes."

"And that's fine!" Grace said quickly. "Really, but it was *more* than just that." She scooted her chair closer so that she could lower her voice; the secretiveness didn't sit well with Jakub, but he did lean closer to hear. "You *have* to know what I'm talking about," Grace continued. "It's so hard to get him to admit to anything really *serious*." She began gesturing with her hands as she spoke. "He and I were steady for a year—I told him *everything*. But in all that time he never said one word about himself that was really *real*. Not about his family, his parents, why he came here, what he wants to *do* with himself. He wouldn't even tell me where he lived before Brooklyn, because he's not *from* here any more than either of us are."

Jakub listened, his brow furrowing. "He's from Albany," he said without thinking, remembering their first meeting on the steps of the Kozlow building.

Grace reared back and regarded him with as much

confused surprise as if he'd produced a live mouse from his jacket pocket. Then her shoulders drooped, and she laughed weakly. "There, see? You already know more than I ever did."

It was such a simple, trivial piece of information, but the thought that he was the only one to know it filled Jakub with an unseemly amount of pride. "He doesn't like to talk about the past," he admitted carefully, thinking of Cheshire's faraway expression from the cemetery. "But...neither do I, I guess."

Grace smiled crookedly. "Yeah, I guess so." She lowered her chin into her palm. "Maybe you're just that good for each other, then."

Jakub's chest swelled; the thought that someone would see him and Cheshire as as much of a match as he'd seen Cheshire and Grace was almost overwhelming. "Yeah," he said, eager for Cheshire to return to the table. "I hope so."

***

Cheshire entered the washroom and was relieved to find it empty. *I just need a minute*, he told himself again as he moved to the sink. He tucked his gloves into his pockets and turned on the sink. *Everything has gone so well, after dessert we can go home and it'll just be us.*

He pushed his glasses up to splash some water on his face, letting the coolness refresh his weary eyes. The door opened, but he didn't think anything of it until he heard the click of the lock.

"Herb?" Cheshire guessed, fumbling for a towel. "Don't give me lip about that lobster tail." But as he straightened up, glasses back in place, he startled to see it was Emma leaning back against the door.

"Ms. Peabody?" Cheshire gulped, though he tried not to let his nerves show. "I think you misread the sign."

"I know what you are," Emma said, her gentle demeanor from dinner long gone. She faced him with near defiance that made the chill of her magic frightfully pronounced; Cheshire couldn't help but shudder. "Let me see your brand."

Cheshire's smile contorted with his efforts to keep it in place. "I don't know what you mean...?"

He reached into his pockets for his gloves, but Emma

moved too quickly, with too little space between them; she took his wrists and drew his hands in front of her, forcing his palms up. He was too startled to resist, and given the strength of her grip, he had the uneasy feeling that he wouldn't have been able to.

Emma's shoulders sagged in disappointed recognition. It was inexplicably humbling. "Grace told me about your magic," she said quietly, as if relaying a great tragedy. "And she warned me not to tell anyone. I can see why."

She pressed her thumbs into the center of the sigils branded on each palm; the contact burned, and Cheshire bit back a curse as he jerked both hands out of her grip. It frightened him more than he thought it should, and he was quick to shake out the sting.

"Um, yeah," he said awkwardly. "I'd appreciate it if you kept it to yourself." He chuckled. "Better than Grace did, at least. Are you going to show me yours, now?"

"I don't have brands," said Emma. She rubbed her thumbs into her palms as if also trying to dispel the pain from their encounter. "I'm not a familiar, like you."

Is that what I should be called? "But you *do* have magic," Cheshire pressed. Sweat collected along his spine but he clung to his charm. "I guess Grace has a type after all."

Emma's expression darkened with pity that had his skin crawling. "*Your* magic comes from a demon," she said, and the last of Cheshire's laughter died in his chest. "A powerful one. Humans aren't supposed to have magic like that."

Cheshire stared back at her, speechless. He remembered being on the other end of Detective Alice's cold glare and felt just as small as he had then. *Magic like that*, Alice had said, *shouldn't exist in the world.* He gulped. "What does that make you, then?"

Emma folded her arms. It took a few moments of lip chewing and downward eyes before she straightened up again, and above her head a length of soft white light began to form. Cheshire's eyes widened as he watched the glow shape into a circlet. A *halo.*

"You're..." Cheshire leaned back, dumbfounded. "You're an *angel?*"

Emma tightened her arms self-consciously. "Yes."

Cheshire blinked over and over; the light from the halo

was making him ill, and thankfully it vanished only moments later. He had always known that demons were alive in the world, yet somehow it had never occurred to him that their opposites might be, too. "D...Does Grace know?" he stammered.

"No." Emma looked away. "I'm not supposed to be here, either. But I *will* tell her," she added quickly. "When it's the right time."

"Oh. Wow." Cheshire finally tugged his gloves back on. "So I guess you and I will never get along, huh?" he teased weakly. "Not only your girlfriend's ex, but..."

"A demon's familiar?" Emma raised an eyebrow, though she didn't share his levity. "You understand what you've done, don't you?" she asked, and again the hint of sympathy in her tone made Cheshire cringe with shame. "You've used a demon's magic against the living. Your soul doesn't belong to you. If you're not careful, your master will come for you."

Cheshire shoved his hands in his pockets and shrugged. "I'll just have to be really careful then. It's not like..." He couldn't hide a wince. "Not like I can do anything about it now. Right?"

"No," said Emma, with an immediacy that gut-punched him. "I'm sorry. If I could break a demon's contract, I would have done it the moment I saw you."

Cheshire licked his lips, and with a deep breath he regained his composure. "There you have it, then," he said. "Careful it is." He took a step to her side. "Thanks for the concern, but I think we should get back to the table. Jakub's not comfortable in situations like these."

Emma didn't budge. "Does *he* know?" she pressed.

"He knows enough for now," Cheshire replied, faster and more sharply than he'd intended to, but the thought of Emma taking it upon herself to tell Jakub *anything* spread more cold sweat down his back. "Like you said—when the time is right."

Emma didn't look satisfied, but she nodded. She stood back and let Cheshire unlock the door. "I want to hear more about your story someday," he said as they left the washroom together. "I've never heard of a rogue angel hiding out among humans."

"I'm not a *rogue*," Emma replied quickly. "Heaven is complicated."

"I can only imagine!"

They approached the table, and Cheshire was surprised but pleased to see Grace and Jakub sitting closer together, apparently engaged in an easy conversation. When Jakub noticed them approaching he lifted his head, and the bright, welcoming face he made solidified Cheshire's confidence.

Maybe we won't have as much time as we want, he thought as he crossed the dining room behind Emma. *That just means we have to make the most of it.* By the time he retook his seat, he was smiling easily again.

"So, what did you order me?"

***

Dessert passed with more pleasant conversation. Jakub enjoyed the cake immensely, taking more than his fair share, though he quickly realized that Cheshire wasn't interested in eating it anyway. By the time they had exhausted the reasonable limits of Herb's credit and were ready to leave, Jakub could sense that Cheshire had also reached the limits of his exuberance, and he was eager for them to move on. As they bid their farewells to Grace and Emma, and Herb and Camila, Cheshire hesitated to take Emma's hand.

"Good luck to you," she told him, and Cheshire nodded solemnly, and he wished her the same.

They left the Olivier beneath a sky of roiling clouds. The wind had picked up, and its urgency fueled Jakub with anxious energy as they made their way to the car. "Do you want me to drive?" he offered. "You look tired."

"Do I?" Cheshire rubbed his face. "I'm fine, but you know I trust you with my wheels, if you'd rather."

He wasn't particularly convincing for once, and Jakub held his hand up. "I would," he said, and Cheshire had no qualms handing the keys over. They slipped into the car and sped off back toward Brooklyn.

Jakub tightened his hands on the steering wheel, and watching the metal knuckles of his left hand reminded him of his conversation with Miklos earlier. He took a deep breath. "It's okay, if you're *not* fine," he said. "It's just me."

Cheshire shifted in his seat and surrendered the truth. "I'm a little tired, sure. Even just being in the same room as Herb can be exhausting." He chuckled and cast Jakub an apologetic look. "Sorry about abandoning you with Grace."

"It's fine," Jakub said automatically, only to realize he didn't want to leave it at just that. "We had a good conversation."

"Oh?" Cheshire perked up with great interest. "She didn't give you a hard time?"

"Only a little. I've known her almost as long as you have, after all."

"Yeah, I guess that's true." Cheshire fidgeted some more. "Emma was really something, too, huh? They seemed really happy together."

"They did," Jakub agreed, though his mind was still on his brief conversation with Grace. *Is that what she saw, when she looked at us together?* he wondered, casting peeks at Cheshire's face. *That we're happy together?* It was a dangerous thought—if Grace could see it, there was a chance more people would, too—but he clung to it. *Because we are happy, right? I know him better than anyone.*

Emboldened, Jakub took Cheshire's hand, tugging it closer so he could wind their fingers together. Cheshire tensed at first. If Jakub looked at him, he was sure he would lose his nerve, so he kept his eyes on the road as he squeezed the soft leather of Cheshire's gloves. "Thanks," he said. "For the date."

Cheshire didn't relax; he turned his wrist just enough to grip Jakub back with an urgency that Jakub hadn't expected and which tightened his chest. "Thanks for *being* my date," he said. He kept hold of Jakub's hand almost the entire drive back to Brooklyn.

The sky was heavy and starless by the time they reached Cheshire's building, electricity in the air. Jakub breathed it in; the wind made him restless, and as eager as he was to drag Cheshire beneath cool sheets on a soft mattress, he hesitated. Something about the night felt new to them, and he wanted to hold onto it a while longer.

As they approached the entrance, Cheshire abruptly stopped, and as if having plucked the thoughts straight from his mind, he said, "Do you want to take a walk?"

"You said you were tired," Jakub replied. He felt mysteriously guilty, as if he really had forced his wishes on Cheshire subconsciously.

"Not *that* tired," said Cheshire, and he hooked his arm through Jakub's. "Just down to the water for a little while. I haven't been down there in ages."

"Okay." Blushing, Jakub leaned into Cheshire and let him lead the way down the sidewalk, toward the waterfront.

Cheshire's building was only two blocks from the river. They took their time—hardly anyone was out, and the small park sprawled across the waterfront was dark and empty. The wind throwing waves against the shore served as a perfect backdrop to the flurry of nervous and excited emotion swirling in Jakub's chest. *This is real*, he thought, hugging Cheshire's arm to him, as raw as he had been that first morning waking up in Cheshire's arms. *It's really real*.

"Hey, Chesh." He took a deep breath and leaned his head against Cheshire's shoulder. "You're from Albany, right?"

Cheshire hummed. "Why do you ask?"

Jakub's ears grew hot, and he lifted his head back up; nuzzling was still a little too embarrassing in public, deserted night-time park or not. "You said you were, the first time we met. Remember?"

"Did I?" Cheshire sniffed and rubbed his nose. "Yeah, I was in Albany before I came to Brooklyn. Why?"

There wasn't anything specific in his tone that came across as defensive, but Jakub sensed the hesitation anyway. He understood it so deeply that he ached, and after a long moment of still contemplation, he took another breath. "I'm..." He had to clear his throat and try again. "I'm from Krępiec."

Cheshire turned his head toward him; Jakub ducked again against Cheshire's shoulder, knowing he wouldn't be able to continue beneath eye contact. "It's a village," he said. "We had a little house there, and some animals. But during the war...I had to leave." He clutched Cheshire's arm and forced the rest of the words out. "Soldiers killed my parents, and I had to leave. I just ran and didn't look back... Ran until I met Miklos. We snuck aboard a ship together to come to America."

Jakub stopped. He held his breath, waiting for he didn't know what—as if the history was a spell he had unleashed, that would somehow take form. But nothing happened. Cheshire stayed quiet beside him, waiting to see if he would say more, until eventually offering, "I'm sorry."

Jakub waited a few beats longer, just to be sure. "I've never told anyone that before," he confessed softly.

"You don't have to tell me anything you don't want to,"

Cheshire said quickly.

"No, I wanted to." He hid a smile against Cheshire's shoulder. "I want you to know me better than anyone."

He hoped that Cheshire found that as exhilarating as he did, but the tremor that passed through Cheshire's broad shoulders felt like something else entirely. Before he could put a name to it, Cheshire turned, slipping free of his arm so he could instead draw Jakub's face to his for a kiss. His mouth was heavier than Jakub was accustomed to, more insistent, and he tasted like wine and chocolate.

Jakub gripped Cheshire's jacket and wilted. Cheshire's kisses were strong but his hands were shaking, and he didn't know what to make of it. His knees trembled. But when Cheshire eased back, he was smiling again, his brow slanted with sympathy and understanding.

"You don't make it easy," he teased, and before Jakub could duck back in embarrassment, Cheshire kissed him again. He gave up trying to escape.

I know, Jakub thought, and he slipped his arms beneath Cheshire's jacket to wrap around his back. *But you're still here. Thank you.*

Something struck Jakub lightly in the back of the head, but he ignored it at first, too caught up in Cheshire's uncommonly deep affections. It wasn't until Cheshire pulled back and turned his face upward that he felt droplets against his shoulders and seeping down the back of his neck.

"I guess we should head back," said Cheshire, and a fat raindrop splattered across his glasses, just before the gentle droplets turned to downpour.

They raced back down the sidewalk together, Cheshire laughing as he tried to protect his hat beneath his jacket. By the time they reached the lobby of Cheshire's building, they were both soaked through and panting. Inside the elevator, Cheshire pulled out his hat and laughed some more at the soaked, crumpled state of it.

"Well, I tried," he said. He plunked the hat onto Jakub and then urged his chin up for another kiss. Jakub melted into him happily.

They tumbled into Cheshire's apartment together and immediately stripped off their soaked clothing between long kisses. By the time they reached the bedroom they were naked and shivering from the night air on their rain-dampened skin. Jakub drew Cheshire down to him on the mattress, wanting his broader body draped over him to banish the chill. Cheshire more than obliged; he pinned Jakub down, nibbled and sucked at the tender skin of his throat. His hands were strong and scorching as they groped down Jakub's body to his ass. It wasn't often that he employed so much of his strength, and Jakub groaned in encouragement, arching into his every touch.

"Chesh..." Jakub murmured, and he drew his knees up so Cheshire could squirm between his thighs. Excitement had been simmering just beneath his surface ever since Cheshire's first call; their naked bodies twisting together atop soft sheets, Cheshire's hefty erection stroking his, sent that arousal coursing through him. He clung to Cheshire's shoulders and was happy to let him take the lead. There was something humbling and new in the hunger Cheshire had fixed on him then, and he was ready for it—so ready that he ached, squeezing Cheshire with his thighs.

Cheshire slid two fingers between Jakub's ass cheeks. His breath was heavy and panting. "Do you want me to—"

"Yes." Jakub dug his heels into the backs of Cheshire's thighs and craned his head to cast a meaningful look at the bedside table. "Yes—hurry."

Cheshire laughed breathlessly. Jakub didn't want to let him go for even a moment, forcing Cheshire to drag them both to the edge of the bed. He pawed a jar of lube out of the drawer and held it while Jakub unscrewed the lid—then passed it to Jakub so he could slick his fingers, chuckling all the while. Jakub tingled at the mirth in his voice as much as with anticipation. He bit his lip and spread his knees wider as Cheshire eased two fingers inside him.

"You looked really handsome tonight," Cheshire said huskily as he massaged Jakub's hole. "But I think I like *this* look even better."

Jakub groaned through his teeth. He reached between them to tug Cheshire's wrist; Cheshire took the hint beautifully, stroking and plying him with greater insistence that left him quivering. When he forced himself to meet Cheshire's gaze, it was almost overwhelming—his body throbbed against Cheshire's fingers and already he felt close to release. He swallowed hard. "Come on—I'm ready."

Cheshire drew his hand back, but before going further he crawled back to the center of the bed. He grabbed Jakub by the hips to drag him along; Jakub held his breath at the unexpected show of strength, and was still holding it when Cheshire thrust deftly into him.

Jakub wasn't prepared for how different it felt to be at Cheshire's mercy. So often he had pinned Cheshire down, guided the pace. It felt good to have the man on his terms after so many years of helplessly pining. But Cheshire leaning over him, Cheshire shoving his knees up—Cheshire inside him, pushing in deep with every firm pump of his hips—shook him like nothing he'd felt before. At first he could only moan, startled and intoxicated, as he took Cheshire's cock over and over. He hardly felt in control of his limbs as he gripped the back of Cheshire's neck in desperate need of stability.

Then Cheshire whispered his name, and Jakub shuddered with renewed conviction. He arched against the mattress, angling his hips to better meet his partner; he let go of what remained of his self-conscious inhibitions. And he felt Cheshire respond in kind, each thrust becoming more confident than the last. As they sped up, every ounce of tension from the evening was seared away, leaving only white-hot pleasure streaking along thrilled nerves. Leaving only Cheshire's deep voice, and his powerful body, and the grin tugging at his sweet lips as they rocked, and moaned, and sweated against each other into a blissful, earth-shaking climax.

Jakub collapsed against the bed, skin electric and cock spent, gasping for breath. Long before he had any semblance of composure back he dragged Cheshire down to him for a kiss. Their lips fumbled lazily against each other as he sucked from Cheshire's mouth a low, rumbling chuckle of contentment. It was his lover's signature and he would never tire of it.

"You okay?" Cheshire asked as he helped Jakub stretch his legs back out. "Sorry—I got a little—"

"I'm fine," Jakub said quickly, and he kissed Cheshire again to prove it. His throat burned with sudden emotion and he turned his kisses instead on Cheshire's neck and shoulder to hide whatever his face was doing. "More than fine."

Cheshire relaxed and nuzzled Jakub's ear with his nose. "Good. 'Cause you're incredible." Jakub wriggled with the compliment and kissed little thank yous into his skin.

After only a few minutes to catch their breath, Jakub dragged himself out of bed. "I'm going to borrow your bathroom," he said. "If you don't mind."

"By all means," said Cheshire.

Jakub took his time in the bathroom. Though he wasn't happy about the hot water erasing the warm imprints of Cheshire's hands on his body, it did wonders for banishing the rest of the rain's unwelcome chill. When finished, he toweled off thoroughly—paying close attention to his prosthetic—and hurried back to the bedroom, eager to be under the blankets. But once there, he was given pause.

Cheshire wasn't still in bed; he was standing at the open bedroom window, smoking a cigarette as he watched the rain falling on the river. He hadn't even bothered to put on any clothes. Jakub watched him for a while, and some of his euphoria deflated the longer Cheshire failed to notice his return. When he moved closer, he even thought he detected melancholy in Cheshire's far-away eyes. "Cheshire?"

Cheshire turned over his shoulder, with an ease that suggested he had known Jakub was there after all. "Hey." He rejoined Jakub and offered the cigarette. "My turn?"

"...Sure." Jakub accepted, taking a long drag as he watched Cheshire head into the bathroom. A breeze from the window gave him goosebumps; he closed the pane and hurried back into bed.

Cheshire returned only a few minutes later, without having run the shower. His skin was still cool from the rain. By then Jakub had stripped the top sheet and replaced it with a thicker blanket, and he squirmed in tight against Cheshire's back, determined to warm him up himself if need be. *He must be more tired than he was letting on*, he thought, and he tightened his arm protectively around Cheshire's ribs. *I'll make sure he sleeps in tomorrow.* "Good night, Chesh."

He pressed a kiss to the back of Cheshire's neck; Cheshire covered Jakub's hand with his.

"G'night, Jakub."

***

Cheshire kept still as he felt Jakub gradually relax into slumber. He was exhausted and painfully awake at the same time, the events of the evening playing over in his head. Jakub's warmth against his back was comforting and stifling. He dug his fingernails into his palm, where his brand still itched from Emma touching it.

Jakub knows me better than anyone, he thought. It frightened him—frightened him even more thinking of how much more there was *to* know. What if he knew too much?

He drew his pillow in tighter but couldn't sleep.

***

When Jakub woke up, he slipped out of bed as quietly as he could. Cheshire grumbled in his sleep but didn't stir, so he tucked him in, borrowed a bathrobe, and headed into the next room. Their shed clothing he hung up around the room to better dry, and he started heating water for coffee. The storm had moved on during the night, leaving only a spattering of clouds and a cool breeze from the river. Jakub smiled to himself as he dug through Cheshire's pantry in search of suitable breakfast ingredients.

Cheshire emerged half an hour later. "You had eggs," said Jakub as he prodded them around a sizzling pan. "And there's some cheese, if you want."

"Sure," said Cheshire as he took a seat at the kitchen table.

He smothered a harsh cough against his fist, and Jakub turned to get a better look at him; he had dressed in long underwear and was leaning against the table, his chin in his palm. His eyes were half lidded with sleep and his brow was heavily creased as he stared blearily around the kitchen. Frowning, Jakub poured him some coffee and set the mug in front of him.

"Thanks," said Cheshire, and that time Jakub could clearly hear a roughness in his voice.

"You all right?" Jakub asked, watching as Cheshire took a ginger sip. "You look like you should still be in bed."

"'m just tired," Cheshire replied, but after having to cover another cough and enduring Jakub's intense frown, he surrendered the truth. "I might be coming down with a cold."

Jakub smoothed Cheshire's hair back to palm his forehead. "You don't feel warm. Let's get you some breakfast and then back to bed."

He carded his fingers back through Cheshire's hair; Cheshire's lazy smile at the affection made his heart flutter. "Thanks," said Cheshire. "Smells good."

Jakub returned to the stove, giving the eggs only another minute before sliding them onto plates. "You should have dried off better last night," he scolded gently as he set Cheshire's breakfast in front of him. "That rain couldn't have helped."

"Yeah, probably." Cheshire managed a smirk as he cut the eggs with his fork. "What a night, though."

Jakub blushed, hiding behind a gulp from his coffee. "What a night," he agreed.

"Not only a great time," Cheshire continued, "but I think we can call it the first successful evening we've spent with Herb. Maybe things are looking up."

Jakub frowned around a bite of his eggs. It had been such a whirlwind evening he'd forgotten Hannah's marching orders from back in his apartment. "Maybe because we didn't spend the time *with* Herb," he said carefully. "I'll have to think of something to tell Hannah."

Cheshire's brow rose. "Hannah?"

"She stopped by right after I got your call," Jakub explained. "It...would have been hard to explain how I was dressed without telling her *something.*"

"Very true." Though Cheshire was smiling, he seemed too tired to disguise his trepidation. "So? What did she say?"

Jakub stalled with a mouthful of food; he suddenly wished he hadn't brought it up at all. "She was hoping I could use this dinner to get some dirt on Masterson," he admitted. "She's...concerned. She thinks we should be trying to *beat* Manhattan rather than playing nice with them."

"If she has a plan for that, I'm all ears," said Cheshire. "Unless you mean, she's still mad I didn't just let Herb die when I had the chance."

"She didn't say that." Jakub frowned, realizing that she had probably been *thinking* it all the same. "You did the right thing," he said firmly. "And it's not fair that they put so much on you. I tried to tell her that."

Cheshire snorted quietly, which then prompted another round of coughing. "Thanks, but at this point I don't know what it's going to take to prove myself to any of them."

This isn't the morning I wanted, Jakub thought, his shoulders sinking. *Last night was so incredible.* He took one more gulp of coffee and then set his mug down loudly enough that Cheshire blinked at him in surprise. With a deep breath he scooted his chair closer.

"Don't worry about them," Jakub said, and he took Cheshire's hand for a squeeze. "*I* trust your judgment. Just keep doing what you think is right."

Cheshire smiled, still weary but sincere. He turned his wrist so he could grip Jakub back more easily. "Thank you." He kissed the back of Jakub's palm and then tried to slip free. "You should take off, though," he said. "I don't want to get you sick, too."

Jakub scoffed and pushed to his feet. "I'm not going anywhere," he said. "Who would take care of you?" He kissed the top of Cheshire's head to prove it. "Finish your breakfast and go back to bed. I'll clean up, and if Burke shows up about work I'll scare him off."

That provoked a chuckle out of Cheshire, and he drew his plate closer. "Yes, sir."

Cheshire followed orders, finishing his eggs and coffee before retreating back to bed. Jakub, still enjoying the oversized bathrobe, cleaned their dishes and a few more things around the apartment. He still kept a set of tools at Cheshire's place, so he even felt bold enough to take the forearm plate off his prosthetic, just to make sure the interior hadn't taken too much moisture from the rain. Then he slipped back in the bedroom to check on Cheshire.

He was asleep again, though fitfully so. Jakub watched him for a while, and then at last he crawled back into bed with him. *It doesn't matter what anyone else thinks*, he thought, sidling in close against Cheshire's back. *Or what they know, or what they do. He has me.* He unbuttoned Cheshire's long johns at the chest so he could sneak his hand inside, and was relieved when Cheshire instinctively reached for him back. *And I'm going to protect him.*

Good for You, Barney

Jakub took a deep breath, wrapped his finger around the trigger, and squeezed.

The butt of the rifle rocked against his shoulder with the brunt of the shot. A dozen meters away, the right rear wheel exploded off the axle of a racing armored car, sending it careening wildly back and forth across the northbound I-87. It rocked against the stony embankment, and as the driver overcorrected, it turned into the oncoming lane, spun, and at last crashed onto its side in the middle of the street.

Barney clapped him on the back. "Nice shot," he said, and then he waved to the rest of their crew, leading them away from the tree line.

Jakub shouldered his rifle and followed him down the slope to the road. The intel had been good: two armored cars from the same bank taking different routes to Albany, passing through a relatively empty stretch of interstate just after dark. It hadn't been difficult to pick a spot along the road outside Tillson to wait, with trees on either side to disguise any commotion from the attack. Jakub stood back, watching Barney and the rest of Kozlow swarm over the downed vehicle. Two men Jakub didn't recognize held the guards at gunpoint while the rest opened up the rear. There were *several* he didn't recognize, he realized, helping drag sacks over to their trucks.

"Don't move!" one of the men shouted in Polish. He

pointed his revolver at the guards through the partially shattered windshield. "I said don't fucking move!"

He was young and inexperienced—his finger was already curling over the trigger. Jakub hurried over, his stomach clenched in warning. "Hey," he called, and when he got close enough he grabbed the man's wrist with his metal hand to urge his aim away. "Calm down."

"Don't fucking touch—" the man started to say, but when he looked at Jakub's hand, and then his face, he went quiet. "Sorry, sir."

Jakub let him go. "We don't kill cops," he told him. "It's too much trouble. Stay cool."

"Yes, sir."

Jakub backed away so he could keep an eye on the scene as they continued. The guards inside the car were bruised, one still trapped by his seatbelt and the other pressed back against his seat, watching them grimly. Jakub hefted his rifle and trusted that was enough to keep them docile until the rest of the bags were loaded.

Barney joined him, gun in his hand and looking entirely too pleased with himself. "Problem?" he asked.

"Who are these boys?" asked Jakub in English. "I haven't seen them before."

"They're from Chicago. O'Shea sent them out." Barney pulled a cigarette out of his jacket. "They're a little rough, but they're motivated, and we can use the extra manpower. And firepower." He eyed Jakub's rifle as he lit his cigarette. "You made that, right?"

Jakub shifted the weight against his shoulder. "Yeah."

"Can you make me one?"

"No."

Barney scoffed. "C'mon, Jake, why not?"

Jakub motioned for him to hand over the cigarette, which he did. "Why do you want one?" he asked, and he took a drag.

"Because it's really fucking useful, that's why." Barney gestured for his cig back. "A few of those and we won't even need Bloom anymore."

Jakub frowned as he handed it over. "He's not just a stick of dynamite," he said. "He's smart and we can't handle Manhattan without him. We wouldn't have this intel if not for him."

"Yeah, I know." Barney rolled his eyes as he took a long drag. "Come on, let's get out of here."

They climbed into the trucks and sped off, back toward the city.

***

Miles away and across the river, Cheshire's palms itched as all four wheels burst off the second armored car with roars of fire.

"Whoo!" Herb cheered, and he slapped Cheshire on the back hard enough that he nearly lost his footing. "Jesus, Mary and Joseph, if that's not the damnedest thing. Well done."

The armored car skidded to a grinding, sparking halt. "It's all in the wrist," Cheshire bragged as the pair of them stepped out of the treeline. "And *you* thought I was a liar, didn't you?"

"I did," Herb said, laughing. "I really did. Never seen *real* magic before." He motioned to his Manhattan crew members, who surrounded the armored car with guns drawn. "Knew an old woman who could sing out her ears. She was a walking quartet."

"Quartet is *four*," said Cheshire, keeping to the back of the truck. There were plenty of Manhattanites wearing handkerchiefs over their mouths to anonymously threaten the drivers; no point in him getting identified. "Unless she had three ears?"

"Don't get smart with me, Chesh, you know what I mean." Herb slapped the back of the car. "If you please."

Cheshire blew the lock and only then realized that Herb was watching his face very closely. *Lucky must have told him about what she saw in the car,* he thought, trying not to let any trepidation into his expression. *Sorry to disappoint.* He tucked his hands into his pockets, even though his usual gloves were snug in place to cover his brands.

"Beautiful," said Herb, but there was a slyness to his tone that Cheshire didn't like, either. He flung the rear door open and then stepped back so his crew could begin unloading the bags. "You can blow up anything you want?"

"Just about," Cheshire replied, shrugging

- 183 -

noncommittally.

"How about the side mirror?" Herb gestured back toward the front of the car. "Blow it up."

Cheshire pulled a face. "What for?"

Herb rolled his eyes. "Because I said so," he retorted, but when Cheshire shot him another look, he took another stab at it. "Because I'm *daring* you to. I dare you to blow up the side mirror." He gestured again, and a few of the men doing the unloading hesitated, eager to see.

"No, I'm not blowing up the mirror," Cheshire scolded, and with disappointment the men got back to work. "Herb, it's not a party trick."

"Oh. Well." Herb gave a great shrug. "If you *can't*, I understand."

Cheshire laughed, hoping to dispel the honest tension that was beginning to tighten his chest. "You don't really think I'm going to fall for that, do you?"

"Fucking spoil sport is what you are," Herb grumbled. He grabbed two bags from the back of the car and hoisted one to each shoulder, showing off more than was necessary as he carried them back to the truck. "Go on—make yourself useful." Cheshire rolled his eyes, but he joined in, following Herb's example of carrying two at time even if his back wasn't as up to it as his bravado.

Once the bags were loaded and the guards lashed to the steering wheel of the armored car, Cheshire piled into Herb's Model A with him, and they sped back toward the city. Herb apparently couldn't help but raise the topic again. "What's the biggest thing you've ever blown up?" he asked. "C'mon, tell me."

"Um..." *Shane Foley*, Cheshire thought unwittingly, and he swallowed back a taste of bile. "An oil drum, maybe?"

"Not the Foleys?" said Herb, and Cheshire went cold. "I was under the impression you were responsible for the steel plant back in the day."

Cheshire relaxed with a nervous chuckle. "Oh! Yeah, I guess so." He rubbed the back of his neck. "But that wasn't the whole building at once—I just started the fire by blowing a few little things at a time."

"But *could* you have blown the whole building at once?" Herb continued to press, way too eager for Cheshire's liking.

"You could have, right?"

Cheshire tugged his glasses off to clean them with his necktie. "That would be a waste of a building."

"Fuck you, dodgey Danny, I want to know if you *could*." Herb smacked his shoulder with the back of his palm. "I'd pay to see it, I'll tell you that."

"You can't afford me," Cheshire retorted, but that only made Herb laugh uproariously.

"I can buy you twelve times over," Herb said, and he flashed Cheshire a grin with teeth. "Don't forget it."

Cheshire laughed, even though it wasn't funny. He slid his glasses back on. "Sure, Herb. Sure."

He endured Herb's teasing all the way back to Manhattan.

***

The two gangs reconnected in the basement of the Four Thrones hotel that served as Lucky's base. Jakub stayed with Gertie and the money while Barney and Hannah headed straight upstairs. Though he didn't like the idea of Barney set loose with Herb and Cheshire, he liked the idea of brand new help counting the money even less. Herb's grim-faced enforcer Nicole was overseeing the operation, and he worried how she might respond to a trigger-happy kid from Chicago sneaking bills into his pocket. So he prowled the lines, no longer needing the rifle at his shoulder as deterrent as he kept everyone on task.

With the take evenly divided fifty-fifty and Kozlow's half loaded, Jakub finally ventured upstairs. He didn't know what to expect, and he couldn't help but cringe when the first thing he heard was Herb and Cheshire each laughing uproariously. He followed the sound to the hotel's first floor bar, and there paused: they were both seated at the bar as he expected, but they had Barney between them, and they were pounding the bar with their palms. As Jakub watched, Barney made a mighty face of disgust, and then leaned back to down whatever shot had been in front of him in one breath. His enablers hooted and cheered.

"That's more like it!" crowed Herb, and he slapped Barney on the back so hard he had to clap a hand over his mouth to keep from spitting his drink up. That only made them laugh harder, and to Jakub's amazement, when Barney straightened up, he laughed, too.

What the hell? Jakub thought, and when he spotted Hannah seated with Camila at a nearby table, he shot her a look to convey the same. She had a drink in front of her as well, though untouched, and she motioned him over.

"Hannah," Jakub greeted, hoping his full concern didn't show through given the company. "Ms. Reynoso. The take is all set."

"Thank you," Camila said, spinning a cherry around in her drink. "Is it very good?"

"Best in a while," Jakub admitted. He couldn't help looking back to the three at the bar, and what appeared to be a very animated discussion of pretzels.

"Plenty of reason to celebrate, then," said Hannah, and she cast a significant glance at the bar as well. Jakub got the impression she wasn't sure how much to say in front of Camila. "I'm glad both sides went down without a hitch."

"So am I," said Camila. If she was aware of their concern, she didn't show it. She continued to stir her drink. "Sounds like Kozlow's share will be enough for whatever it is you plan on using it for."

Hannah took a diplomatic sip of her brandy. "I'm sure it will be."

"No, no, you're fucking dumb," Barney said loudly from the bar, and Jakub tensed. "It's *supposed* to be round!" He was waving a pretzel around animatedly while Herb and Cheshire laughed. "Look! Look! I'll fucking show you."

"I'm going to find out what they're talking about," said Jakub, and Hannah nodded, grateful. Camila smiled a little as she finally plucked her cherry off the stem.

By the time Jakub reached the trio at the bar, Barney had torn off pieces of the pretzel to make it into an empty ring, as much as he could given its twisted shape. "Like *this*," he said emphatically.

"That's not round, you dumb fuck," said Herb jovially as he stole the shredded pieces. "It's more like a bean."

"It's just an example, asshole," Barney shot back. "It's *supposed* to be round. Polish pretzels are *round*."

Cheshire leaned his jaw against his palm. Jakub wasn't sure what to make of his expression—there was definitely tension beneath his usual smile, a struggle against the effects of the alcohol. "How would you know?" he prodded Barney. "You've never *been* to Poland, you're as much a yank as either of us."

He noticed Jakub then, and his face lit up with a grin. "Jakub! Come here!" As happy as it made Jakub, he couldn't help the clammy feeling that crept up his back as Cheshire grabbed him by the belt to reel him in. Herb and Barney were too close, watching too carefully; fearful of their attention, Jakub pushed Cheshire's hand off him. The momentary flash of confusion and hurt that creased Cheshire's brow made his stomach squirm.

"What are you arguing about?" Jakub asked, and he was relieved when Cheshire sat up a little straighter, as if having realized at last how intoxicated he was.

"Your boss here is a liar and a fake," said Herb through mouthfuls of pretzel, and Jakub tensed again, expecting a surge of temper from Barney.

But Barney only rolled his eyes and tore off another chunk to throw at him. It bounced off Herb's chest and into his lap. "It's not my fault you don't know anything about anything, fucking Americans."

"Jakub can tell us, then," said Cheshire. "He's more Polish than you."

He snuck a hand up to pinch Jakub's ass; Jakub managed not to startle, and he smacked Cheshire's hand away as discreetly as possible. Maybe Cheshire *thought* he was being more covert, but Hannah and Camila were certainly still watching. "If you're talking about *obwarzanek*, yeah, it's round."

"See?" Barney said triumphantly. He shook the rest of his pretzel at Cheshire. "What do you know? You can't even say his name right."

Cheshire glanced between them in confusion. "That's not important," Jakub said quickly.

"It's not *Jakub*, it's pronounced *Yakoop*," Barney said, as if he were imparting grave knowledge. "You do it wrong."

"*You* do it wrong," Cheshire shot back, though his face was red. "You called him 'Jake' five minutes ago!"

"Does that mean it's *Yake*?" asked Herb, hunting for the pretzel that had fallen to his lap.

"It's *Jakub*," Jakub insisted firmly, so much so that

Barney flinched. "Like everyone has always called me, including you. It's what I prefer."

Barney flushed. "Fine, whatever, I was just saying," he grumbled.

"Ha! He sure showed you." Herb laughed and then tossed the reclaimed pretzel chunk in his direction. "Like I said—"

The piece landed in Cheshire's glass, which apparently was hilarious, because Herb burst out laughing. Even Barney choked on a snort. Cheshire made a face at them before rallying his better humor. "What? Like I'm gonna let it go to waste?" he said, and he grabbed the glass up. Before Jakub could voice a word of warning, he downed its contents, pretzel and all.

"Ew, fuck, that was in his *lap*," Barney whined.

Herb chortled drunkenly. "Pretzels need cheese," he said, and he and Barney burst out laughing again as Cheshire snorted and choked.

"Hell, did you *have* to say that?" Cheshire said while mopping his face with a napkin. But by then Herb had already leaned closer to Barney and was whispering something in his ear. Whatever it was almost had Barney in stitches, and they rocked on the bar stools, cackling like children.

Jakub seethed. Even though Cheshire laughed along with them, something in their tones had changed, and he couldn't stand the thought that Cheshire was being made fun of. "The truck is loaded," he said, struggling to be heard. "We can head back whenever you're ready, Barney."

"Sure, sure." He slumped off his stool and had to brace both hands to the bar to get fully upright. He cast Herb a crooked smirk. "You know that's true, though, right?" he said, with a nod toward Cheshire that had Jakub's blood boiling again.

"Oh, I believe it," said Herb lazily. "Thanks for the education."

Barney moved away from the bar, and thankfully Hannah was soon there to collect him. Jakub hesitated; he didn't want to leave Cheshire alone with Herb. "You coming, Bloom? We can drop you off, if you can't drive."

"Oh." Cheshire glanced between him and Barney and frowned. "Naw. Eggy will take me."

"Burke's not here," Jakub reminded him. He took Cheshire's elbow. "It's on the way, so—"

"It's fine," said Cheshire, and he tugged his arm free. His expression then drooped guiltily. "Really? Have I been saying it wrong all this time?"

"No," Jakub said immediately. He glanced to Herb, who licked his thumb and then pressed it to the bar, collecting pretzel salt. He pulled a face. "No, don't worry about it."

"But was he right?" Cheshire pressed, with greater seriousness. "That I—"

"No. Just...come here." Jakub took Cheshire's arm again and pulled him off his stool. Despite previous appearances Cheshire had no trouble standing or following him a few steps away. Maybe he hadn't had *that* much to drink after all. "I've gone by *Jakub* since I came here," Jakub explained, the words much easier without an audience. "It was...easier. I wanted to fit in. Even Hannah pronounces it that way—you've heard her."

"Yeah, I know, which is why..." Cheshire rubbed his face with both hands. "But Barney said—"

"Don't listen to Barney—I'm telling you, it's fine." Jakub noticed Barney glancing their way at the sound of his name, so he took a breath and tried again in a more even tone. "It's fine. It's just a name—Jay, Jake, whatever. Okay?"

"Okay." Cheshire shrugged and put his hands in his pockets. "Sure. Sorry."

Jakub frowned and started to tell him not to apologize, but he was interrupted by a wide hand clamping down on his shoulder. He tensed and had to remind himself not to elbow Herb in the gut as he leaned over him.

"Don't worry, Freckles," he said, breath smelling of booze. "One'a my boys will see him safely home. He doesn't need a bodyguard here."

Jakub clenched his fists, but he was at a loss to get Cheshire away from Herb in a way that didn't seem too desperate or too paranoid. What if Herb had seen Cheshire being handsy— what if he thought too much of it, after the dinner they'd had at the Olivier? It was too hard to puzzle through when Cheshire wasn't any help. "Fine," he said, wanting to be out from under Herb's grip as soon as he could. "Call me tomorrow," he told Cheshire. "We can talk about where the take is going."

"Sure," replied Cheshire, and he did seem to perk up a bit. "Have a good night, Jake."

He frowned then, as if chewing over the name, so Jakub

nodded to reassure him. "Good night," he said, but it wasn't until he had taken a step and a half that Herb finally let him go. He resisted the temptation to straighten his jacket as he joined Hannah and Barney heading for the exit.

"Bunch of assholes, aren't they?" Barney said as they stepped out into the night air. He pushed his cap up so he could smooth his hair back. "Masterson thinks he's real fucking funny."

"You *were* laughing," Jakub replied. "I didn't think I'd ever see the three of you sharing a drink."

"Hannah and I talked about it," said Barney, but the expression on Hannah's face suggested otherwise. "If I want Masterson to see me as a threat, he's gotta see me as a friend first."

"That's not what we talked about," Hannah confirmed.

"Well, close enough, whatever." Barney waved dismissively as they approached the waiting trucks. A few of the crew had already left in cars to prepare the Kozlow building for the incoming take, and the three of them climbed up into the cab of one truck while Gertie and Stas took the other. "The point is, we didn't need his help tonight," Barney continued as Hannah took the wheel. "And I know that, and he knows that, and that's how it should be."

"It was still their intel and their turf," Jakub reminded him, but then he paused. *If this is ever going to work, maybe...a new tactic.* "I'm glad you were getting along with Masterson, though. You're the boss's son, you should be involved in everything."

"Right? Right!" Barney nodded vigorously. "Exactly. 'Cause I'll be boss someday."

"Right," said Hannah. She still looked uneasy as she started the truck, but she seemed to understand Jakub's direction. "You need to be at that table, whatever the discussion is. Celebrating together is a good start. It shows you contributed just as much."

"Right! Right?" Barney nodded some more, but then he seemed to regret it, as he gave his eyes a rub and then leaned back in the seat. "They'll learn," he mumbled, and he tugged his hat down over his face. "Lemme know when we're back."

Barney settled in. Hannah fell quiet, but she did look to Jakub and mouthed *thank you.* He nodded back, even if he

- 190 -

wanted nothing more than to turn the truck around and throw Cheshire into the back to drag home with them.

He can't cozy up with Masterson at Chesh's expense, he thought determinedly. *That won't work, either.*

***

Herb didn't have his boys drive Cheshire home. After another drink, he insisted Cheshire spend the night at the hotel.

"I convinced your friend to sing for us," Herb said as he let them into a cozy room on the second floor. "Her and her band—they're gonna come to a little party we're throwing come October. You'll be there."

"Oh?" Cheshire followed him in. It wasn't one of the nicer rooms he was sure Herb had at his disposal, but it wasn't the cheapest, either. "Maybe I have plans."

"It's like two months from now—you don't have plans." Herb gestured to the room. "It's a peach, ain't it?"

"Peachy." Cheshire thumped down on the bed and kicked his shoes off. "Thanks, Herb."

"It'll be a masquerade," Herb carried on. Apparently he wasn't leaving yet. "That's fun, right? Weird rich folk shit. Right up your alley."

Cheshire couldn't help his prickle of interest. "Costumes?"

"Yeah—Halloween stuff." Herb gave a great, huffing snort of laughter. "Perfect for a witch like you, right?"

"Uh-huh." Cheshire unbuttoned his jacket, but he suddenly didn't like the way Herb was still hanging around, and he didn't go any further. "I'll dust off my pointy hat and broom."

"That's the spirit." Herb continued to stare at him. "Hey. What's the biggest thing you ever blew up?"

"Oil barrel—no, the—didn't we have this conversation already?" Cheshire looked up, and he *definitely* didn't like the way Herb was eyeing him then. "What?"

"What about the *nastiest?*" Herb pressured him, and though he hadn't moved a step closer, Cheshire felt as if the man were looming over him. "You *have* to have used that on a human at some point."

Cheshire's skin crawled. "It doesn't work on people," he

- 191 -

said, letting a note of seriousness into his voice. "So don't ask."

"So this wasn't you?" Herb challenged, pointing to the inside of his bicep. "I don't get to thank you for this very manly scar?"

"That was different."

"You're sure?" Herb did move closer then, and Cheshire stood up just to avoid being completely boxed in. He was still smirking, but with all the affability of a cocked hammer. "Come on, Cheshire Bloom. Camila told me about your little light show." He waved his hand in Cheshire's face; Cheshire leaned back, his shoulders inching up. "Let me see."

"You asking me to turn you into powder, Herb?" Cheshire retorted. He tried to match Herb's twisted grin. "'Cause you're really tempting me here."

"Oh, wow, sounds like you really mean it." Herb laughed. "Come *on*, I'm serious, I want to see." He gestured to the room around them. "Pick something—blow it up. I'll pay for it." He scoffed. "There's even a bible in the bedside, if you want to give a fuck you to the man upstairs, huh?"

He reached around Cheshire as if to open the drawer next to the bed. The close quarters unnerved him, but not nearly so much as the words; after meeting Emma, Cheshire couldn't help but fear that "the man upstairs" wasn't nearly as far away as he'd once seemed. In a moment of thoughtless anxiety he braced his palm to Herb's chest and shoved him back, with enough force that both had to struggle to keep their balance.

"Drop it already," Cheshire snapped. "I'm not your dancing monkey."

"Fuck, hell, calm down." Herb reared back and laughed scornfully. "I'm just joking, jeez. Don't take it so personally." He shoved back; Cheshire wasn't as prepared as usual, and he fell back against the nightstand, rattling the lamp there. "Go to sleep, kid, it's been a busy day," Herb said, still laughing, as he headed for the door.

Cheshire forced a weak chuckle. "G'night, asshole," he called after him. He waited until Herb had closed the door behind him to move.

What am I even doing here? Cheshire thought as he flopped onto the bed. He dragged the pillow to his chest and buried his face in it. *This is so stupid.*

Cheshire reached out blindly for the phone and managed

to drag it closer, knocking the bedside lamp to the floor in the process. He cringed at the noise but didn't bother checking to see if the bulb had broken. It wasn't until he was halfway through dialing Jakub's number that he remembered he was probably still driving with Hannah and Barney. He considered calling Burke, but he honestly didn't know what time it was, or if Burke would be at his apartment or working at the Morey. The thought of having to explain that he needed a ride home because Herb was a big meanie wasn't all that appealing, anyway.

Just go to sleep, Cheshire thought, squirming deeper into his pillow. *And leave early.* But he couldn't bring himself to stay any longer, so with grumbled curses he dragged himself out of bed, scooped up his shoes, and left.

***

Jakub was exhausted by the time they reached the Kozlow building, but he still helped to unload their take. Burke joined them, eager to know the totals for the books. He didn't carry any bags, but he took notes, chatting all the while.

"Coppers were here not ten minutes ago," he said as he scribbled numbers into his notebook. "I told them to fuck off, a'course. Sure they paid Bloom a visit, too, or tried to."

"Bloom's still in Manhattan," Jakub said, as frustrating as that was.

Barney scoffed as if agreeing with him somehow. "Maybe that marshal will pay them a visit, catch them together."

"You'd better hope they don't," Burke shot back, saving Jakub from saying too much. "'Cause Masterson would roll over on you in a heartbeat. He's one helluva sore loser."

"Masterson and I..." Barney smothered a yawn against the back of his hand as he dragged the corner of a tarp over the boxes they'd hidden the take in. "Fuck. Masterson and I are very chummy now. He says one word and he's a bastard."

Jakub finished stapling up another box and dragged a tarp over it. Though the smarter move would have been to retreat to his apartment, he couldn't stop himself from asking, "What were you two whispering about back at the bar?"

"Huh? Oh!" Barney laughed as they all headed for the stairs. "The way Bloom slammed that shot," he said, sniggering. "Herb, that asshole, he said, 'he sure knows how to...'"

Barney paused then, and he stared Jakub hard in the face as if realizing for the first time who he was talking to. A look of guilt twisted his brow and he waved Jakub off. "Nothing. Sorry, it was stupid."

"Tell me," Jakub said, but Barney only winced harder, and suddenly Hannah appeared behind them. She began pushing Barney faster up the stairs.

"It can wait until morning," she said, and Jakub leaned out of the way so she and Barney could continue on ahead. "Good work tonight, Jakub."

"Sure," muttered Jakub. "Goodnight." He waited until they were a few steps ahead and then continued, Burke close behind.

"Missed something, didn't I?" asked Burke. "What did Masterson say?"

"Nothing." Jakub raked his fingers through his hair. "Forget it."

Jakub grabbed his rifle from the car and marched up to his apartment. Too tired for much more effort than that, he kicked off his boots and went straight to his bed. *Next time I see Masterson, I'll knock his teeth in*, he thought, and he was very pleased with the visual as he drifted off to sleep.

Minutes later, something tapped Jakub's window. He grumbled and turned away, thinking it was a pigeon or a stray cat, but then the tapping became insistent. He rolled over, and a glance at the window sent his exhaustion scattering: Cheshire was crouched on the fire escape.

Jakub clawed out of bed and hurried over. "What—" He bit his tongue as he unlocked the window and shoved it open. "What the hell are you doing out there?" he hissed, though his heart was pounding and his cheeks already flushed.

"Hey." Cheshire smiled crookedly. "Can I come in?"

Jakub huffed and helped him through. "How did you get here?" he demanded as quietly as he could manage. "Did you drive yourself? You shouldn't have after how drunk—"

"I'm not drunk." Cheshire was all smiles as he pulled himself upright in Jakub's apartment. "Ahh, still smells like you in here."

Jakub flushed darker and closed the window behind him. "Chesh," he tried again, but then he noticed that Cheshire had his shoes in his hand as he headed for the bed. "Why aren't you wearing your shoes?"

"Hm?" Cheshire glanced down as if only then realizing. "Oh. 'Cause it's more sneaky?" He dropped the shoes to the floor and winked.

Jakub sighed, but he was so pleased that Cheshire was there that the hows and whys ceased mattering very quickly. He rejoined Cheshire and helped him out of his jacket. "Okay, well, keep being sneaky then," he said. He dropped Cheshire's jacket and then loosened his tie while Cheshire unbuttoned his cuffs, quickly putting their arms in a tangle. "It'll be hard to explain if someone finds you here."

"I know, I know." Cheshire finished with the buttons but then gave up on the shirt and instead cupped Jakub's face in his palms. "I wanted to be here, though."

Jakub stopped, his heart fluttering all over again as he stared up into Cheshire's weary eyes. "Are you okay?"

"Of course," Cheshire lied. His smile dug deeper into his cheeks. "You're really okay with *Jakub*, right?"

Jakub sighed again. "*Yes*," he said firmly, taking Cheshire's wrists to squeeze the seriousness into him. "I don't..." He chewed on the words a while before he could get them out. *He knows you better than anyone, so just say it.* "No one's pronounced it the Polish way since I left Europe. And I like it that way, it feels...new. I needed to feel new when I got here." He squeezed Cheshire's wrists again, for his own sake that time. "So don't change anything."

"Okay," said Cheshire, and his expression relaxed with understanding, more so than Jakub expected. "Good. I was worried." He glanced away. "I was just thinking on the way over...I wouldn't want anyone to call *me* something else. You know?"

"I would have told you the first time we met," Jakub insisted. "I almost told you to fuck off as it was."

Cheshire chuckled at that. "Yeah, you weren't shy. Gosh, that was a long time ago now, huh?" He moved his thumbs against Jakub's cheeks. "Look at all the freckles you've gotten since then."

Jakub gulped, and without thinking he rose up on his toes to steal a kiss. Cheshire was caught off guard at first, but he soon rallied himself, leaning into it. Jakub shivered. *Has it really been that long?* he thought. *It feels like it was just yesterday that he* first *made me feel this way...*

Cheshire pulled back, and suddenly he seemed hesitant. "Okay," he said, shifting his weight back and forth. "Sorry I woke you up—I just wanted to be sure." He let Jakub go and started to turn toward the window. "I'll let you get back—"

Jakub snatched his arm to stop him. "You're leaving?"

Cheshire shrugged. It wasn't like him to look so uncertain. "I don't want to get you in trouble," he said. "Or, you know. Bother you."

"Bother me?" Jakub scoffed. "When have you ever?"

Cheshire replied with a quiet chuckle, but his humor still seemed muted. "I dunno," he admitted. "Have I?" Jakub was tempted to scoff again, but it began to sink in that beneath Cheshire's half smile, he was being serious. There had been a handful of times since their date at the Olivier that he'd seen that doubt creep into Cheshire's face. Whatever had caused it, it made his insides squirm.

"Stay," said Jakub, figuring that was the most direct way to reassure him. He tugged Cheshire toward the bed. "I want you to."

Cheshire resisted a beat longer, but one more tug from Jakub convinced him. With a relieved smile he allowed Jakub to drag him down to the bed. Tired as they were, they didn't make it all the way out of their clothes, but they curled up together and were soon asleep.

***

Just before dawn, Cheshire beat a hasty retreat back out the window. He seemed to take entirely too much enjoyment out of it, threatening to call Jakub "Juliet" from then on. Jakub's exasperated glare put a quick end to that.

Once the rest of the building had roused, Jakub joined Burke and Barney in the diner across the street for breakfast. Despite his behavior the night before, Barney was full of energy. "I'm gonna take a chunk of that money from last night and *invest*," he said while pouring sugar into his coffee. "Invest in *intel*. That's what we really need, right? We need to know *where* to hit, and we gotta have the *manpower* to do it."

"Sorry, I'm glad ye're feeling mighty motivated," said Burke, "but these grand stage coach robberies ye're so keen on aren't all that necessary, are they? Kozlow has plenty of funds coming in these days."

"Yeah, and after this next one, we can set our sights on better things," Barney insisted. "You'll see."

"Better things like train robbery?" Burke pressed. "Didn't that go *really* well the last time?"

Barney scowled at him, but then he walked himself back. "*Yes*, it *did*. That mail gave you your whole operation, didn't it?"

"You know what he means," Jakub cut in. "What exactly are you planning? Whatever it is, we need to go over every detail, so we're not overstepping or missing anything."

"We will, we will," Barney reassured him. "Don't worry." He smirked into his mug. "You'll see."

***

The next two months passed in relative quiet. With the extra funds and muscle Kozlow had no problems keeping up the demand for liquor in the weakening grip of dry laws, and being an election year, they even funneled cash into the right pockets in hope of "reasonable" representatives landing the right offices. Jakub kept his head down for the most part, following Kasper's orders when given and finding plenty of excuses to spend time across town.

"Is everything all right back home?" Cheshire asked one afternoon in mid October. They were perusing the shelves of a small costume shop, with racks of strange and ghoulish masks laid out for the upcoming holiday. "You've been spending a lot of time away from Kozlow."

"You've been spending a lot of time in Manhattan," Jakub replied. He grimaced at a saggy-faced clown mask and discreetly turned it away from him. "You're getting along with Masterson?"

"Oh, sure. He thinks he's gonna have me performing at birthday parties any day now." Cheshire set a jester's cap on his head and flashed Jakub a sarcastic grin. "Just like this."

Jakub sighed and plucked the cap off to toss back on the shelf. "I know you know this, but he's just using you."

"I *know* you know that I know," Cheshire retorted as he turned to continue on. "I'm being careful, believe me. He's exhausting and kind of a ratfink, but he knows a good time."

He picked up a small, black mask, dotted with fake gemstones and accented with a swoop of feathers. "Well?" he said, and he held the mask up to Jakub's face. The backs of his knuckles brushed Jakub's cheek. "This is more like you."

Jakub peered back at him through the holes in the mask. He had the sudden thought of how relieving it could be to slip on better masks than this, to be anonymous for a while in the face of Kozlow, and Manhattan, and everything else. He could almost *hear* Cheshire thinking the same thing, and he reached up to take Cheshire's wrist as if that would solidify the desire between them. But the moment his fingers made contact, Cheshire instead pulled back. He handed Jakub the mask and quickly turned to continue perusing. "Let's see if we can find something to go with it," he said.

Jakub frowned, but he followed. "Sure."

***

The night of the "masquerade" Jakub prepared alone in his apartment. Thanks to Cheshire's influence he was getting the hang of playing dress up, even if he still didn't quite see the appeal. He donned his go-to black jacket over a white shirt, slicked his hair back, and pulled on a pair of gifted white gloves. Cheshire's eye for fashion meant the fit was impeccable, but it still felt a little strange to cover the prosthetic. He poked at it through the glove and wondered if it would actually fool a stranger.

With his mask sticking out of his jacket pocket, and his revolver tucked discreetly in its shoulder holster, Jakub headed down to the lobby to meet the others. Hannah and Burke were already waiting in their outfits: Hannah in a simple gray suit as usual, but with her hair styled up in a bun, and a rabbit mask pushed back from her face; Burke in a garish, orange-striped suit coat and olive green pants. He was already wearing his mask, which looked like tree roots twisted into glasses, and tall antlers poking up from either side.

Jakub snorted quietly to himself as he joined them. "Cheshire's going to have something to say about what you're wearing," he said.

"Has he ever not?" Burke retorted, hands going to his

hips. "Well he can shut his trap, 'cause it's Halloween and I can be a pumpkin if I damn well want to."

"Is that it?" Hannah asked, teasing him. "Why the antlers then?"

"No one would sell me a stem!" Burke retorted as if it were obvious. "It's the best I could find—what of it?"

"It works," Hannah reassured him, and it was a relief to see her smile. "No one will be able to say you copied them, that's for sure."

Burke eyed her as if he suspected sarcasm, but she didn't crack, so he nodded. "Damn right."

They were interrupted by a laugh from the direction of the stairs; Barney headed their way with a half dozen of Kozlow's crew, old and new, bringing up the rear. All of them were dressed in simple, dark suits with some kind of mask, Barney himself carrying a droopy-eyed clown mask. It looked like the same one Jakub had passed in the costume shop earlier in the month, and he eyed it distastefully.

"Fuck, Burke, you've outdone yourself," Barney said, giving Burke a pat on the shoulder as he passed. "Careful where you point those things."

Burke brushed the shoulder of his coat off vigorously. "Make fun and every prong is going straight up your ass, one by one," he shot back. "Mind yer manners."

Barney scoffed, but he wasn't quick enough to supply a comeback. The rest of the Kozlow crew exchanged looks, uncertain if they were meant to defend him, particularly Leon. Hannah rolled her eyes and motioned them all outside. "Just get in the cars," she said, and everyone, even Barney and Burke, hurried to follow her.

Once they were out on the sidewalk, Hannah snagged hold of Jakub's sleeve. "Ride with me," she said. Though reluctant, Jakub nodded.

They climbed into Hannah's car, and Burke, likely eager not to be alone with Barney and the others, helped himself to the back seat. "You tell him yet?" Burke asked as they pulled away from the curb, and Jakub prickled with apprehension.

Hannah took a deep breath before explaining. "Barney has a job lined up for tonight," she said. "And it's a good plan. There's a small cargo ship docked at Pier 17—smugglers picking up a load headed down south was the intel we got."

Jakub frowned as he recalled what he knew of the pier. "That's barely ten minutes from the Thrones."

"It's good cover, right?" said Burke, leaning forward between the seats. "We show at the party, a few of us slip out, come back. Everyone in masks—what can the coppers do?"

"Does Lucky know? That's her back yard." Jakub turned toward him and almost took an antler to the eye.

Burke sheepishly pushed his mask and antlers back. "Boss says she does."

Jakub looked to Hannah expectantly, who didn't look much more confident than he felt in that answer. "Barney said he got the okay," she confirmed. "It'll be a short trip and only a few boxes. That pier hardly sees ships anymore, so it should be clean."

"Should be," Jakub echoed. "What about Bloom?"

"He sits out," said Hannah.

"Better that way," Burke added. "He's *Cheshire Bloom*, if he leaves that party, people will notice. It won't just be us hoodlums there, you know."

Jakub fingered the mask sticking out of his pocket. "I don't like it," he said. "And when we get there, I'm going to make sure Masterson knows about it." Hannah and Burke exchanged a look, so he added, "We're not going behind his back. We can't afford to, you both know that—Barney *needs* to know that."

"No, you're right," Hannah admitted, however unhappy about it she seemed. Her brow hardened. "And if he lied to us about them knowing, *we* need to know that."

They arrived at the Four Thrones hotel just after nine in the evening. The streets were already congested with cars as guests disembarked on the sidewalks, dressed in their masquerade wear. Hannah drove past and parked a block over, where there was less visibility. As they walked back to the hotel, Jakub spotted Big Mitts and their crew entering ahead of them, and right behind them, Thea Hallorran and her date.

Following an impulse, Jakub picked up his pace and reached Hallorran just inside the hotel doors. "Oh, Mr. Danowicz!" she greeted happily, tipping up the brim of an oversized top hat to get a better look at him. She was dressed in a handsome, embroidered topcoat, her date in a dress fit for royalty. "It's good to see you again. But where's your charming friend?"

"Cheshire's probably inside already," said Jakub.

"Then it's sure to be a lively party." Hallorran smirked and tipped her hat back down. "You're doing well with my merchandise, aren't you?"

"Yes, ma'am." He gave his fingers a wiggle to prove it. Though maybe she wouldn't be much impressed by his efforts to maintain her company's brilliant work, he wanted to share his newfound confidence with someone who might understand. "I tuned it up this morning."

Hallorran's smile deepened with sincerity. "I'm glad to hear it," she said. "You come back in if you need any work done, though. Tully is always glad to have you."

"Thank you." They exchanged nods, and Hallorran's date smiled politely before the two women moved on.

"It looks like they've managed to pull in quite a crowd," said Hannah as she and Burke caught up. They moved deeper into the hotel, following the casual flow of Manhattan's elite and its underbelly heading for the main ballroom.

"They had better," replied Burke. "We've been greasing a lot of palms lately." He nodded ahead of them to where the city treasurer was leading his wife into the ballroom.

Would Masterson have invited all of them here, knowing Barney plans on using them as cover for a robbery? Jakub wondered as they continued toward the open doors. He frowned. *Actually, he probably would.*

They stepped inside, and despite the many *real* concerns swirling his brain, Jakub found himself put on edge by the spectacle itself. The ballroom wasn't Manhattan's largest by far, but it was packed, with people milling about around every tall table and hob-nobbing in every available space. The decorations were gothic and almost overbearing, the lighting lower than Jakub would have preferred. Hundreds of masked faces seemed to spin in candlelight glinting off champagne glasses. Against the far wall stood a stage for a band, and Jakub wasn't surprised to see Grace at the head, dressed in sparkling white with a feathered headpiece and train setting her apart as a beacon in the ominous setting.

Jakub slipped his mask on and stayed close to Hannah as they made their way through the throngs. The crowd was already exhausting him and he suddenly looked forward to the prospect of a break during the middle of the evening, even if it was to engage in a felony. Foolishly, he felt a little better thanks to having a mask; none of these strangers would have recognized him anyway, but he could pretend it was like armor.

He listened for Cheshire's voice to rise above the drone of the other partygoers, and when that failed, he braced his hand to a column and rose up on his toes. The first thing he spotted was Herb, who was gesturing broadly so that his long black cape spread out in all directions. He and Camila were near the bar with a collection of men and women dressed with card suits as themes.

"I'm going to talk to Masterson," he said. "Wait here."

"Good luck," chirped Burke, already plucking a champagne flute off the tray of a passing waiter. Hannah nodded; neither of them, it seemed, were any more eager to converse with the man than he was.

Jakub pushed his way through the crowds, taking note of which prominent faces he recognized. He wondered what it said about the city, that so many of the wealthy and elite were willing to heed the invitation of Manhattan's newest and most dangerous crime bosses. Maybe they thought they could expect a moment of excitement, a fireworks display like the *Chicago Smoke* film premiere that had started their Manhattan push in the first place? He cast those thoughts aside as he came up to Herb and Camila.

"And they told me, I lost four whole pints of blood," Herb was saying, flexing in his dark suit, to the laughter of his audience. "Even one more drop and I'd be *haunting* you right now instead of giving you my liquor."

"Lucky for us, then," said one of the men, and Herb laughed, placing his broad palm on Camila's back.

"*Lucky,*" he said pointedly, "for everyone! Maybe someday, Lucky for *mayor!*" He and his audience laughed approvingly while Camila ducked shyly into the fur collar of her gown.

Jakub hung back, uncertain how to proceed. Though he caught Herb's eye, Herb didn't seem to recognize him, as he went right back to amusing his guests. Camila noticed him, but either didn't see or wasn't inclined to acknowledge his subtle attempts to urge her away from the group. Without another option, Jakub gulped and stepped into their circle. "Mr.

Masterson?"

"Hm?" Herb turned toward him with a grin, and Jakub was instantly reminded of his oath to punch the man's teeth in at some point. "Oh, Freckles! It's you!" He poked the lip of the mask that covered Jakub's cheek. "Perfect disguise for you."

Jakub stared flatly back at him. "Can I talk to you?"

"In a minute—I'm getting to the good part." Herb turned back toward his card-suit friends. "Where was I?"

"Four pints of blood," said the Queen of Hearts excitedly.

"That's right! So I lost almost five pints..."

Jakub leaned back as Herb carried on, glancing between the faces of his audience. *Bloodthirsty after all*, he thought as he fought back a scowl. *It's just fairy tales for them.* As he considered what to do, Camila touched his elbow, and the two of them took a few steps away from the small gathering.

"You look very serious tonight," said Camila, watching his face. "Are you concerned about the job?"

Jakub's shoulders drooped with relief. "I hadn't heard if any of yours would be joining us," he said, hoping to confirm without giving away his uncertainty and paranoia. "Wasn't our deal fifty-fifty?"

"All of mine are more interested in enjoying the party." Camila fussed with her immaculate curls. "And it's so close to home. We don't mind leaving it to Mr. Kozlow." She tucked one of the unruly strands behind her ear. "Though we still expect our share of the take for providing your alibi."

"Of course," Jakub said quickly. "That's not a problem."

Camila nodded. "Of course it isn't." She eyed Jakub over the rim of her glasses. "I do want our partnership to work," she said. "I know how valuable your efforts are."

"We feel the same way," Jakub replied carefully, wondering if there was some hidden message beneath the words.

Herb slung his arm over Jakub's shoulders and laughed in his ear. The stifling weight against his back reminded Jakub too much of their first meeting on the mail car, and he had to clench his jaw to keep from yanking away from him. "What's going on?" Herb demanded. "You two sharing secrets over here?"

"Preparing for tonight," said Camila, gathering herself up.

"Oh! Of course." Herb leaned closer to Jakub's face; Jakub stared at a point over Camila's head as he endured. "Don't be nervous, kid, you'll do fine without us. Your boss Barney has it *all* figured out."

"I'm not nervous," Jakub said.

"That's the spirit." He gave Jakub a dull smack on the cheek and then let him go. "Have a drink before you leave— loosen up. It's a party after all."

Herb offered his arm to Camila, which she accepted, and the two of them moved on. Jakub stayed still for a while; *nervous* might not have been the word for it, but he was still drawn tight, the swirl of the masked party-goers around him making it hard to feel grounded. *If everyone knows, there's no reason to worry*, he told himself. *We've done jobs like this a dozen times. It's only—*

Someone pinched his right ass cheek, and Jakub spun around, keyed up and unwilling to take a teasing from *anyone* else. He recognized the rumble of Cheshire's laughter before the rest of him, and all his anxiety unfurled into butterflies. Cheshire was decked out in a white tuxedo with gold buttons and cufflinks, long tails, and a feathered, pointy-brimmed felt hat. The mask resting on his face bore cat ears and whiskers, and a cat-head brooch clasped the ascot taking the place of his usual silk necktie. He of course was grinning ear to ear, and Jakub couldn't help but envy the way he seemed fueled by the lavish commotion around them, whereas Jakub was more than eager to let them all fall away.

"Did I startle you?" Cheshire asked, and he chuckled. "Sorry; I couldn't help myself."

Jakub blushed. If only they were in private he would have given Cheshire more than a pinch in return; even *with* the audience it was hard to deny the impulse to move closer, to let Cheshire's grinning confidence bolster him through the unpleasant social obligations. As important as he knew their secrecy to be, he was beginning to loathe it.

This should be getting easier, not harder, he thought, itching to reach for him. He swallowed. "I like your whiskers."

Cheshire's blushing cheeks went unseen thanks to the mask, but his red ears gave him away. "I like your...*everything*," he said, and Jakub turned even redder. "What did Masterson want?"

Jakub's spirits dampened at the mention, but it was probably for the best. "I wanted to make sure we're still on for tonight," he said, only to be struck by a sudden, new concern. "You heard, didn't you?"

"About half an hour ago," said Cheshire with a dry twist of his lip. "Did they tell you who we're shaking down this time? Herb wouldn't say."

"Smugglers, I heard." Jakub took a quick glance around to confirm that even with so many people around, each was deeply engrossed in some other conversation and not trying to overhear. "We own the liquor here, so maybe drugs? Tech?"

"You'll have to let me know." Cheshire heaved an overly dramatic sigh that Jakub could tell was only half for show. "It's hard being so popular that you have to play decoy."

"I'll tell you all about it later," Jakub reassured him. "In private."

Cheshire's eyes glinted behind his mask. "Ooh, I'd like that."

Jakub licked his lips, wishing that privacy could already be theirs. He took a deep breath, and with the masks between them granting him extra courage, he said, "Maybe we can go on a trip sometime. To Boston, or...Chicago or something." His fingers curled within his gloves. "Somewhere no one knows us."

Cheshire leaned back, surprised. It was hard to tell but there might have been some of that same hesitation biting his tongue. "Y-Yeah," he said, and he let out a quiet chuckle. "You're right—we should." He got a bit more of his breath beneath him and laughed. "Tonight?"

Jakub snorted. He was surprised by his own boldness and happy to let Cheshire drown the moment in humor. "Of course not."

"Good—you know I love seeing you dress up, I want to make the most of it." Cheshire threw his arm around Jakub's shoulders; how different the same gesture felt when it was so much more welcome. "Speaking of, you did real good on the outfit," he said as he steered them toward the bar. "You'll be the best looking thief Manhattan's ever seen."

It was then that Jakub noticed Hannah and Burke were heading for the bar as well, along with Barney and his crew, from another direction closer to the stage. *This is it*, Jakub thought, and he took in a deep breath, glad for Cheshire's strength against his back. "They're not supposed to see me," he retorted. "That's how you get caught."

"Haven't caught *me* yet," Cheshire said, laughing. "But there are a few cops in here, so maybe they'll press their luck tonight."

Jakub stiffened and tried to turn to better see the room. "Really?"

"Chief of Police himself," Cheshire confirmed, sing-song. "But don't worry, I'm pretty sure he's on payroll." He exchanged a nod with Herb as they passed. "That's part of the reason Masterson agreed to this. If it goes over quietly, no one will know it happened. But if anything *does* happen, hard to argue with Manhattan's top cop as an alibi."

Jakub frowned but allowed Cheshire to continue guiding them onward. *Some people in here won't like being used like that,* he thought. *But they might not be able to do anything about it.* "Another dangerous power play," he muttered.

"It's in his blood, sorry to say. Incurable."

Cheshire let him go once they reached the bar. There were already a few guests crowded around, getting their drinks. As Barney approached, the bartender leaned against the counter and said, loudly, "We're running out of Scotch."

"We'll bring up some cases from the cellar," said Barney. He motioned to his comrades. "C'mon, boys."

Barney, Hannah, Leon, and the rest moved around behind the bar, to where a service door led out the back. Jakub glanced to Cheshire, who mouthed *good luck*. He nodded and then followed the rest of them out.

They moved swiftly through the employee back area, to the rear of the hotel where deliveries were typically dropped off. A truck awaited them there, and in the back of it, two burlap sacks that Barney pawed through. "Put on one of these instead of what you're wearing," he said, handing out new masks. They were all the same: white faces with black, round mouse ears, pointy noses and cartoonish whiskers. As everyone changed out their masks, Jakub hesitated before tossing his into the sack, thinking there was a chance the feathers would get bent.

It's just a stupid mask you'll never wear again, he told himself, feeling ridiculous. Even so he managed to tuck it into Hannah's mask as support before climbing into the back of the truck. He pulled the door shut behind him, and with Barney and

Hannah in the front, they were off.

***

Back at the bar, Burke downed a quick shot of whiskey. "Well, there they go," he said. He raised an eyebrow at Cheshire. "If ye're hoping to give yourself an iron alibi, now's the time."

"Oh, I'm on it," said Cheshire, tearing his gaze away from the door Jakub had disappeared through. He made a show of tightening his pony tail and adjusting his mask and ascot. "Believe me." He cast Burke a wink and then headed through the crowd, straight for the stage.

This should be getting easier, not harder, he thought, his mind lingering on the image of Jakub's face upturned, watching him with such close scrutiny. As accustomed as he was to Jakub staring at him, something was different now—a *want* that hadn't been there before, as if he were always on the verge of asking a question. It was exhilarating but mostly terrifying, and Cheshire barely knew what to do with himself anymore when Jakub fixed those piercing brown eyes on him.

By the time Cheshire reached the front of the ballroom, Grace and her band were just finishing their last number. He managed to catch her eye and fixed her with a *look* he knew she'd interpret. Though she tried to be put out, there was no hiding the grin threatening to draw her lips wider. She may have been dating an angel, but he *knew* she enjoyed being at the edge of their high-stakes, criminal antics.

"Enough with that slow stuff," she said to the crowd. "We need something with some *kick*." She motioned for Cheshire to join her. "Care to help me with that, Mr. Cheshire Bloom?"

Cheshire feigned bashfulness as the partygoers turned either toward him, or to each other to whisper. He waited until a few hands patted him on the back to encourage him before climbing onto the stage. The sea of masked faces staring back at him sent his heart thumping with excitement: everyone there knew who he was, would definitely be telling their families and co-workers the next day, *I saw Cheshire Bloom at the Thrones last night*. Thugs, politicians, actresses and businessmen—their rapt attention represented the notoriety he had always dreamed of having, since long before throwing his lot in with a small-time bootlegger in Brooklyn.

"Well, gee," he said close enough for the microphone to pick him up. "I sure hope you play one I know."

"Try to keep up," Grace shot back, and she made what must have been a specific hand gesture to the band behind them. The drummer came in on a quick beat, and as the rest followed suit, Cheshire couldn't help but look to Emma raising the saxophone to her lips. She shot him a cool look before joining into the intro.

Cheshire gulped, but by the time his cue came he was all grins again, facing the crowd with his full enthusiasm.

***

The pier had long since been emptied by the time Jakub and the rest of the Kozlow crew arrived. Its use had declined greatly over the years, thanks to the shallow bank that couldn't accommodate newer, larger ships, as well as the decline of the accompanying fish market and competition from other piers— including Kozlow's own. But it did have one particular use well suited to its circumstances: a landing point for smaller, private boats not looking for neighbors.

Barney drove them straight off from the street out onto the pier itself, past the empty buildings that had once been storefronts, avoiding as much as possible any line of sight from the guard station. They were lucky, with a new moon and plenty of cloud cover keeping most of the pier in shadow. "It'll be fast," Leon explained to the rest of the group as they disembarked from the truck. He reached into the second sack and began distributing baseball bats. "Knock them out, take what you can back to the truck, and we're gone. No shooting if you can help it."

Jakub accepted his bat last. He watched Leon scrape his sweaty palms across his pants. "Are you up for this?" he asked.

"Of course I am," said Leon, and he jerked his thumb behind him. "I'm staying to guard the truck."

"Right..." Jakub fell into step next to Hannah as they headed for the waterfront. *What's he so nervous about then?*

It took Jakub a moment to spot the boat: a small, wood yacht with a power motor and a raised deck. All it's lights were off, leaving it a dark silhouette on equally dark water. A few figures were visible moving about the deck, but no more than that, other than the dull light of a match being struck. Apparently the merchandise hadn't arrived yet.

They followed the wall of a storehouse as far down the pier as they could, but there was still a good distance between the ending corner and the boat. As they reached the edge, Barney turned back and motioned for Jakub to move up.

"Truck should be here any minute," he whispered. "Looks like we can nab whoever's on the boat before they even show up."

Jakub eyed the boat warily. Watching it sway on the water made his stomach turn. "Didn't I tell you we should have all the details worked out ahead of time?"

"What?" Barney shrugged. "We outnumber them—it'll be easy."

"Since they're not here yet, we could bring our truck right up to the edge," Hannah suggested. "They wouldn't know the difference."

"Maybe if Bloom was here," Jakub said before he could think better of it. "I'm not an actor."

"We don't need to act," Barney said quickly. "We just need an element of surprise." He nodded to Hannah. "Take half the boys and come around in the truck. We'll cover you."

Hannah nodded, and she tapped two of the others to take with her. As they scurried off back toward the truck, Barney pulled a revolver out of his jacket. Jakub eyed it as he adjusted his mask. His own breath was suddenly stifling. "Try not to use that," he said.

"I can't cover them from here with a bat," Barney retorted. He nodded toward the boat. "How many do you see?"

Jakub peered into the dark and finally just lifted his mask for a breath of fresh air. "Two: one on the dock and one on the deck. But I thought there were three earlier."

"Yeah, me too." Barney tugged his mask up for a better look, and then they both resettled their disguises. "When Hannah pulls up, they can take the one on the dock. Keep an eye on the cabin for Mystery Man number three."

The truck rumbled down the pier, drawing the smugglers' attention. There wasn't time to argue; Jakub chewed his lip as he drew his own gun. *As few shots as possible*, he told himself, watching the rough outline of a figure emerging from the ship's cabin. *Everyone on the river is going to hear this.*

The truck drew to a halt, and the man on the pier tossed his cigarette into the water as he moved to the rear door. He didn't seem to suspect a thing, up until the back door clattered upward, and a baseball bat cracked against his temple. Jakub darted out of hiding as the rest of the gang poured out of the truck and followed him down the line of the dock. The smuggler on the deck pulled a gun while the other retreated back into the cabin. But Hannah and the boys already had three guns trained on the armed man, shouting at him to surrender, and he didn't get off a shot.

"I've got the third," said Jakub before Barney could get any ideas. As soon as he was close enough he leaped down to the stern of the ship. His stomach lurched at his shoes squealing against the slick wood, but he kept his balance. After shooting a brief, warning look at the second smuggler—who by then was lifting both hands over his head, his face twisted with frustration—he moved toward the cabin, gun raised.

"We're here for the goods!" Jakub called. He could see someone moving about inside. "Don't try anything and I won't kill you!"

Someone was talking inside, and Jakub heard a crackle of radio static. Hurrying, Jakub dropped his bat and kicked the cabin door in. The inside was lit only with a few blinking lights from various pieces of equipment he didn't recognize, but he could see the figure was a woman, stocky with a short bob of hair. She spun about as he marched inside.

"Put your hands up," Jakub ordered, "or I'll—"

The woman flung something at him, and he dodged to the side; glass shattered against the cabin door. In the next moment the woman launched herself at him, fearless, leaving Jakub no time to fire the gun. They grappled roughly in the confined space, until Jakub managed to wrestle his gun hand free. He swung the grip down, hoping a blow to the temple would knock her out and spare them both a bullet. But then her right hand shot out to grab him by the wrist in a startling, *metallic* grip.

Jakub froze. There was only just enough light that he could see pinpoints of red and green glinting off the prosthetic hand, just like his—eerily like his. In his hesitation the woman punched him in the stomach, winding him, but he managed to keep his senses. Forgetting the gun, he instead grabbed the woman by the front of her coveralls and twisted, sending them both tumbling through the cabin door and onto the deck.

The woman still had a grip on Jakub's wrist, but she was caught enough off guard that he was able to twist against the metal and press the revolver's muzzle into the side of her head. "Stop," he barked, breathing hard from the struggle. "Or I'll kill you right now."

"I know," the woman snarled in reply, and the sound of her voice sent a chill up Jakub's spine before he could consciously place it. "I know it's *you* under there." Half sprawled on the deck, she turned her head to glare at him, and Jakub leaned back, stunned to find himself staring down at Millie Tighe.

It had been two years since Jakub last saw Millie Tighe, one of the late Foleys' most loyal members, disappearing into a cloud of smoke from Cheshire's magic. After having cleared out the rest of her family and gang, it hadn't even occurred to him to wonder what might have become of her. As she finally let go of his wrist, he couldn't help but stare at her metallic fingers stretching and then relaxing. There was no mistaking the craftsmanship.

"Where did you get that?" he demanded, pushing to his feet to get some distance between them. His mind was suddenly reeling. "Did you steal it from Hallorran?"

Millie scoffed loudly. "Fuck you—I worked hard for this, after what that devil friend of yours did to me!" Though she was defiant, her grimace twisted with pain that reminded Jakub of smoke stinging his nostrils, and a phantom pain tingled along his missing arm. "Why can't you just leave me alone!"

Jakub tensed, unsure what to do, until they were interrupted by gunshots from up on the pier—then gunshots much closer, as the second of the smugglers that *had* been held at gunpoint turned and fired. His first shot pulled wide and Jakub dove for cover behind the cabin door just in time to avoid those that followed. Cursing and disoriented, he reached around the door to return fire. He only managed to clip the man's knee, but it was enough that he stumbled backwards, and with a shout he tumbled off the side of the boat. The splash followed a moment later, and by the time Jakub came out of cover, Millie was running for the edge. She cast him one more long, hateful look before leaping into the water after her companion.

Jakub held his breath. The commotion up top had subsided, and he waited, gun still drawn, for some indication of which side had prevailed. Then a pair of mouse faces peered down at him from the pier, and Hannah called, "Are you all right?"

Jakub released his sigh and holstered his gun. After grabbing the bat, he moved to the side of the boat and let Hannah and Leon help hoist him back up onto the dock. The fight, such as it was, had ended: one smuggler bleeding from the head remained at the edge of the dock, while a second truck stood a dozen meters away, its tires shot out. Two more figures were stretched out on the ground on either side, but Jakub couldn't tell if they were breathing.

"Phew!" exclaimed Barney as he adjusted the eyeholes on his mask. "That was louder than I wanted. Let's hurry up!"

He and the rest hurried to the back of the second truck—Jakub rushed forward, wanting to be among the first. Barney yanked open the back of the truck to reveal a collection of unmarked wooden crates, no more than half a dozen and none larger than a suitcase. As Hannah began directing them to carry the crates to their own truck, Jakub pulled himself up into the hold next to Barney and ripped his mask off.

"Did you know who we're stealing from?" he demanded, keyed up on gunsmoke and the snarl of Millie Tighe he had never expected to hear again.

"It's their own fault," Barney said, and he snatched a pry bar off the inside of the truck to pop open the smallest of the crates. "Illegal goods going in and out of this city have to go through us—I don't care *who* made them."

The lid opened with a crack, revealing a bundle of straw packing. Without hesitation Barney reached inside, and Jakub leaned in close to see as he drew out a small sack and a gun: a handsome revolver with filigree embellishments, and engraved into the underside of the grip, the round Hallorran logo.

***

Cheshire sang three songs with Grace before he had to beg her, laughing, for a break. After lavishing her with praise for her professional stamina, the two of them abandoned the stage, leaving her pianist to occupy the guests for a while.

"You sure you don't want to join the band?" Grace teased him. "We could use another hand to carry the drums."

Cheshire laughed, though there wasn't anything funny about Emma hooking her arm around Grace's elbow. "I'm not fit enough for the stage," he assured them both. "Besides, I'd rather be a guest star—better billing that way." Grace laughed and gave him a shove, and she and Emma moved on to greet more of their fans.

Cheshire was talking himself out of a pause at the bar when someone tapped his shoulder. "Care to dance?"

"Of course!" he chirped, and he turned to find a woman in a very plain blue suit and a very simple white mask staring at him intently. The bounce of her brown curls was familiar, but in the swirl of the ballroom it wasn't until she latched onto his hand with much greater strength than necessary that he realized who it was.

"Ah, Marshal Adalet," Cheshire greeted, and his courage rose to the forefront. *If she's here, she's not wherever Jakub is,* he thought, and he boldly pressed his other hand to the small of her back as he swept her onto the dance floor. "I'm delighted to see you!"

Hazel scowled, but she kept up with him, her hand a vice on his as they roughly followed the slow pace of the piano. "I can't say the same," she told him bluntly. "Because if you're out here making a fool of yourself, I'm sure it's because you're trying to distract from something else."

"Ha! You've caught me!" Cheshire didn't let her attempts to intimidate him crack one millimeter of his smile. "I did my best, but not even I was able to prevent you from noticing that there is, in fact, alcohol being served at the bar. You'd better clap irons on all of us."

"If I wanted you for booze, I could have had you a long time ago," Hazel retorted, which Cheshire didn't believe for a moment. "Prohibition is not my department."

Cheshire spun them about, wincing a little when Hazel dug her nails into him. "What *is* your department?" he asked.

"You," Hazel said immediately.

Cheshire laughed. "I'm flattered."

"I've figured you out," Hazel continued with determination. "It's the smell."

Cheshire finally began to feel pricklings of true ill

ease, but he refused to let them show. "There may be a hint of lavender in my aftershave," he confessed, feigning guilt.

But Hazel wasn't deterred in the slightest. "You and your crew robbed two armored cars two months ago. You were there for one, but not the other—the car on the *east* side of the river." Her grip on his hand and shoulder tightened again. "And I know because I could smell *you* on the wreckage, just like the first car outside the theater."

Cheshire continued to smile calmly back at her, though internally he was cycling back through their recent jobs, especially the ones where he had deployed his magic. *Don't panic*, he told himself. *She already suspects you for all of them, but can't do anything without proof. So who cares?*

"Oh?" Cheshire raised an eyebrow at her, drawing out his answer. "And what do I smell like?"

"Fire and brimstone," Hazel answered, with utter seriousness.

Cheshire had the fleeting thought that maybe she had been talking to Emma somehow, which he covered with another chuckle. "The smell of something burning at the scene of an explosion," he teased. "I'm sure your superiors are *very* impressed."

Hazel let go of him with a shove. "You're laughing now," she said, her fists clenching at her sides. "But I've got your tail now, Bloom, and I *will* be the one that brings you in. You and your whole crew."

Cheshire thought of Jakub disappearing behind the staff door and couldn't help the edge that crept into his smirk. *Like hell you are.* "But I'm not wearing the tail tonight," he retorted, and he plucked at his mask. "Just the whiskers."

Hazel's face screwed up with fury. "You're fucking insufferable," she spat, and she started to turn away, only to force herself back. "Is this really just a joke to you?" she continued. "Some game you can win at? While the people you hurt mean *nothing?*"

"Marshal, please," Cheshire said, placating. He offered his hand again, and reluctantly Hazel took it up. "You really are barking up the wrong tree. Look around." He nodded toward the dozens of well-known faces surrounding them. "*Everyone* here is playing the game. Cops and robbers, workers and politicians. All of us have our roles. I'm just a little cog in this machine."

Hazel glared back at him, but her temper had quieted. It wasn't reassuring. "I know," she said, surprising him. "And I'm sure that makes it *real* easy to do what you do, when you can tell yourself that. All you 'little cogs' do." Her fingers dug into his shoulder like lamprey teeth. "But *this* little cog matters, Bloom," she continued icily. "What I *do* matters. And what I'm going to do is bring you in. A witch like you is a *much* bigger cog than you think."

Cheshire offered a crooked smile. "Thanks...?"

Hazel narrowed her eyes at him, but she seemed to have said her piece, and she let him go again. "Next time you so much as light a cigarette, I'll be waiting," she said, and with a final glare she marched off into the crowd.

Cheshire watched her go, shrugging to himself to placate the few curious eyes that had turned his way. Strangely enough, having an audience made it that much easier for him to hide any concern he felt over Hazel's declarations. He believed what he'd said—he belonged in settings like this.

Don't I? Cheshire frowned into the sea of guests, all strangers he recognized but didn't know. They seemed to all blend together. When he spotted Burke headed his way, he was all too eager to welcome him over. "They back yet?" he asked.

"Not yet." Burke cast a glance behind him and then back. "What'd the marshal want?"

"Just to let off some steam, I guess." Cheshire grabbed Burke up and swept him onto the floor. "Let's dance."

"What!?" Burke stumbled, fighting to keep up with Cheshire's larger frame. "Fucking—cut it out!"

"C'mon, Burke, have some fun!" Cheshire laughed as he spun Burke around and then had to catch him to keep him from falling over. "Just to pass the time."

"'Insufferable' was right," Burke muttered, blushing hotly, but he played along. Dodging his antlers made it easier for Cheshire not to stare at the far door as they waited for news.

***

"Don't you realize who it is we're stealing from?" Jakub said as he followed Barney out of the truck. His entire body broiled in anger and confusion. "These aren't normal smugglers, it's Hallorran—Manhattan's Hallorran!"

"Yeah, of course I know that," Barney replied, unconcerned. He waved to Hannah. "Get everyone back in the truck."

Hannah removed her mask and passed the orders along while keeping an eye on them, as Barney wasn't headed for the truck—he was moving toward the edge of the dock. Jakub pursued. "Hallorran is an *ally* for us," he insisted. "Why the hell cross them over *this*? There's barely six crates here."

"Yeah, I know." Barney's mouth twisted in a sick grin. "Check this out, though."

Barney pulled a speed loader out of the sack that had been with the revolver and loaded the cylinder. He thumbed back the hammer with a heavier *clink* than Jakub was used to and took aim at the Hallorran boat Millie and her companion had abandoned.

"Wait—" said Jakub, but Barney had already pulled the trigger.

The cabin exploded in a fireball as if having been hit with a grenade. Wood splintered in all directions, smoke roaring into the night air. The river glowed with points of fire licking the ragged edges of the ruined cabin. As accustomed as he was to a fiery blast, Jakub flinched and couldn't help but stare.

Barney cackled with glee as he tugged his mask up. "Ho-ly-shit, did you see that?" He slapped Jakub on the back and then turned to head back to the truck. "Hey—did you see that!"

A shudder ran the length of Jakub's spine, and he whipped around to follow. He grabbed Barney by the shoulder and shoved his back to the side of the truck with a clatter that had even Hannah wincing. "Why didn't you tell me?" Jakub demanded, ignoring the other Kozlow boys drawing closer from the commotion. "You *know* I have ties to Hallorran."

"What's the matter with you?" Barney stared back at him, so startled that it pissed Jakub off even more. "This is a great haul!" He gestured to the flaming boat that was beginning to take on water as the cabin collapsed in on itself. "Yeah it's Hallorran, but so what? You already made that rifle to be like theirs—I thought you'd be thrilled to have the real thing."

"Jakub," said Hannah, edging over to them. "Before you—"

But Jakub's mouth was already twisting in a scowl. A

hundred furious accusations bubbled in his chest. *Like hell this has anything to do with me*, he thought, and he couldn't stop himself from striking Barney across the jaw with his left hand. It made a terrible *thud*. Barney stumbled and caught himself against the side of the truck. "What the fu—"

"*This* is the real thing," said Jakub, yanking the glove off so he could wave his metal fingers in Barney's face. "Only Hallorran has this, don't you understand? I *owe* her for this!"

Barney straightened up, trying to rub his face while appearing unhurt at the same time. "We paid her off for that," he retorted. "If you need another one I'll just steal it for you. You should be glad—no more Bloom firing off that magic of his everywhere now that we have these." His brow furrowed as he gestured to the arm. "No more *accidents*."

Fresh heat coursed up and down Jakub's already wire-taut limbs, and he would have struck Barney again, harder— *much* harder—if not for the sound of gun hammers being drawn back. He barely had time to realize that Barney's hired thugs had muzzles pointed at him before Leon and Hannah both intervened. "Calm down," Hannah was saying, one hand on Jakub's chest as she tried to steer him toward the front of the truck. "All of you! We have to get out of here before the cops show up."

Jakub allowed Hannah to draw him back; he felt hot and sick all over, and he knew he couldn't trust himself in the situation any longer. Hannah steered him toward the passenger side door while continuing to pass on orders. "Leon, stay in the back—calm everyone down. We got what we came for and we're going back to the hotel."

"Y-Yes, ma'am," Leon stuttered, and he urged everyone toward the rear.

Barney dodged away from Leon's prodding, and as Hannah moved around the truck to take the wheel, he climbed up into the cabin next to Jakub. "I don't know what's got you so worked up, but sorry," he said, though he still sounded more baffled than apologetic. "Hallorran won't even know this was us—why would she take it personally?"

"Enough," Jakub grumbled, dragging his glove back on. "You should have told me."

"All right, fine. I should have." Barney folded his arms, but once Hannah was behind the wheel and pulling away from the pier, he squirmed and carried on. "I thought you'd be on board. It was *your* idea to use more firepower on these jobs so that fucking marshal wouldn't be able to pin them all together on Bloom. With these we won't have to use his magic at all."

"Barney," Hannah said, though it was clear she was warning them both. "Enough."

Jakub ignored her. "All you've done is try to ice Bloom out," he said, his temper rising again despite his better judgment. "When are you going to admit we wouldn't have half of what we do if not for him?"

"I admit it!" Barney snapped, though then he seemed to regret it. He growled in frustration and rubbed at his jaw. "I admit it, and I'm sick of it—I don't want it to be like that anymore! I'm playing nice with Manhattan, aren't I?"

Jakub clenched his fists, but he knew the words gnawing at his throat wouldn't help matters any, so he turned instead to Hannah. "Did *you* know it was Hallorran?"

Hannah stared straight ahead. "I knew it was guns," she admitted. "I didn't know it was *Hallorran*."

"You knew it was them or Diamondback," said Barney. "Who else makes guns in this town?"

Hannah grimaced, which said enough—she had at least suspected, but she hadn't said anything. The thought hardened Jakub's anger into bitterness. *I thought she at least would know better*, he thought, but he stopped himself before he could get any accusations out. *I'm not telling her everything either, but… this is different. Isn't it?*

"Whatever," Jakub muttered, too exhausted to argue. He swallowed hard thinking about how Cheshire would react. "I get it."

"It's not that I didn't trust you with it," Barney carried on. "I just thought—"

"No, fine, I get it." Jakub rubbed his eyes, wishing he had his mask back to hide behind. "We'll talk about it later."

They passed several police cars on their way back to the hotel. Once they arrived the boys began carrying the crates in through the back and transferred the contents into empty crates that had once held liquor. "Don't forget to grab some scotch on your way in," Barney said, back to his usual temperament. "And blend in."

Leon tapped Jakub on the shoulder. He was holding the

sack with their masks in one hand, Jakub's black mask in the other. His eyebrows were drawn with concern.

"Thanks," Jakub muttered, and he slipped it on as he headed back into the hotel proper.

The party was still in full swing, and a few guests near the bar cheered when Jakub and the others dropped off cases of booze for the bartender. Jakub moved on as quickly as he could, his gaze darting from one man to the next. Fortunately, Cheshire wasn't hard to spot in his white jacket and hat: he was chatting with a group of young men opposite the stage.

Jakub headed toward him before knowing what he intended to say. Every step only made it harder; Cheshire was fully in his element, laughing and conspiring, practically aglow. He didn't want to be the one to ruin that for him, but Cheshire *had* to know about the job and all it entailed, and he wanted Barney or Hannah to be the one to break the news to him even less.

Cheshire spotted him, and his face lit up with that mess of excitement and dread that Jakub had hoped they'd gotten over by now. But there was no turning back. With a deep breath Jakub planted his feet and motioned for Cheshire to come to him.

Cheshire's smile faltered, but after bidding his audience a charming farewell, he strode over to Jakub. "Hey," he said, his eyes darting up and down Jakub's figure. "You're back, good. How did it go?"

Jakub grimaced. *I hate this.* "It went fine," he said. "The take is in the storeroom. No one got hurt."

Cheshire started to relax, but he could see there was more. "You don't *look* fine," he said carefully.

"I'm not," Jakub admitted, startling himself, and then he couldn't help it; he took Cheshire by the arm and led him a bit further away from the rest of the assembly so he could lower his voice.

"I saw Millie Tighe tonight," he said. "She was one of the smugglers."

"Millie!" Cheshire blinked at Jakub in amazement. "Wow, I really thought I'd killed her," he said, and then he shook himself. "It was really Millie Tighe? Was she...okay?"

"Yeah, but listen..." Jakub rallied himself again. "Chesh, she was working for *Hallorran*," he said, and Cheshire leaned back with the same look of confusion and anger that Jakub had felt. "They were the smugglers we were after. They were loading some illegal prototypes or something onto a boat. Hallorran-made weapons."

Cheshire glanced to the crowd of guests, doubtlessly looking for Hallorran herself. A guilty wince twisted his features that reignited a great deal of Jakub's righteous frustration. "Did Barney know?" he asked. "That it was them specifically?"

"Yeah. I think he was just trying to get his hands on a fancy weapon." Jakub squirmed on his feet. "I'm sorry."

"What? No—no, it's not your fault." Cheshire scanned the room again, scowling. "Why would he do that? He knows what we went through for them! For *you!*"

"I know," said Jakub, wishing there had been a way for him to not say anything at all. When he looked beyond Cheshire he finally spotted Hallorran; she was moving toward the exit with her date, a third woman talking close to her ear. She glanced back into the ballroom just as she reached the doors, and Jakub could have sworn her eyes landed on the pair of them, harried and cold.

Cheshire tried to follow his gaze; Jakub tugged at his suit to interrupt him. He couldn't think of anything good that could come out of Cheshire following her out. "It's too late to do anything about it," he said. "But now Barney *and* Manhattan have their hands on some serious weapons. I'm worried about what they'll do next."

"Shit, of all the..." Cheshire turned in place, and having spotted someone, his eyes narrowed behind his mask. "Come on," he said, and he took Jakub's arm to pull him along. "Barney!"

Jakub kept up, and he gulped when he realized that Barney, Herb, and Camila were all chatting together in the heart of the assembly. Barney glanced up, and his face quickly transitioned from a scowl to a fake grin. "Bloom. I hear you put on a show."

Jakub tugged out of Cheshire's grip. "Maybe we shouldn't do this now," he whispered.

"I just want to talk," said Cheshire, though the hard set of his jaw said otherwise.

Cheshire stopped in front of Barney, though once there he seemed to realize just as Jakub had that the timing couldn't be worse. Herb and Camila were watching them with raised eyebrows, as were a few other lookee-loo guests. He, too, pasted a fake grin into place. "I heard the same about you," he said. "I sure wish you would have told me."

"Told you what?" Barney retorted with a shrug. "Your job was here, and you did it, and I did mine."

Cheshire hesitated, his jaw clenching; Jakub's ached with empathy. "You know we have a relationship," he said at last, and his pretense of humor slipped. "Probably broken now, thanks to you. I deserved to know."

Barney shrugged again; he was clearly beginning to take some enjoyment from Cheshire's obligation of restraint. "If you'd been there that would have just made it harder, right?"

"That's not what he's talking about and you know it," said Jakub. "We're supposed to be all on the same side."

"He's right," said Cheshire. "If you have so much of a problem with me, then let's settle it face to face, without you sneaking around my back, hurting our own allies while you're at it."

"You're just jealous," Barney shot back, but he stepped to the side, clearly looking for a way to disengage. "I did this job all by myself and now I've got a bigger gun than you." He poked Cheshire in the chest. "So just keep doing what you're told."

Cheshire gathered himself up; Barney quickly took another step away from him, and from there he retreated back into the crowd. Jakub had half a mind to follow after him and demand further answers, but he was drawn back by Herb's raucous laughter.

"Rough night, huh?" Herb teased. He raised his glass of brandy as if to toast. "You Kozlows never fail to entertain."

Cheshire turned toward him, conflict clear in his face. "Herb," he said. "Buddy. Did *you* know?"

"'Course I knew," replied Herb, utterly unconcerned. "It's *our* town, ain't it? Where do you think intel comes from?"

He took a sip from his glass as Camila nodded. "Hallorran has never been willing to do business with us," she said. "This was a good opportunity."

"*We've* done business with Hallorran," said Jakub, lifting his left hand. "Did Barney not tell you that?"

Herb shrugged. "Oh, I knew. But Barney wanted his big gun. He was so gung-ho about it, how could—"

"Because you're such good friends with Barney now?" Cheshire interrupted.

"He's your boss, right?" Herb snorted. "Why shouldn't I be?"

Jakub clenched his fists; he could feel Cheshire winding tight beside him. "Because *I'm* the one that saved your life," Cheshire said, with an effort to lower his voice. "When I had every reason not to." Strain twisted his mouth into a grimace. "You don't know what that cost me."

"And I appreciate it, really!" Herb threw his arm around Cheshire's shoulders, despite body language warning him not to. "C'mon, Chesh, don't be sore. It's just business." He gave Cheshire a shake. "I'm sure it twists your knickers not to be the only one who can blow shit up now, but did you really think that was fair anyway?"

Cheshire pushed Herb's arm off him. "*You* think I'm jealous, too?" He scoffed uneasily. "*You're* just mad I won't light sparklers for you on command. I keep telling you it's not some parlour trick, Herb."

"Yeah, I know," said Herb, and though he was still smiling, his eyes narrowed. "It's the real deal."

Jakub stood up straighter; something in Herb's tone clicked for him then, and he watched more closely as the man carried on, and Camila tugged at her fur beside him. "Some *real* witchy shit," Herb said, every word gaining teeth. "You can't help but wonder about someone like that."

Cheshire snorted, offering a shark's grin in return. "It's *you* who's jealous. You're just as bad as Barney."

"He's not jealous," said Jakub, and the dart of Herb's eyes toward him convinced him further that he was right. "He's afraid of you."

"Afraid?" Herb repeated too quickly. He gave a great bark of laughter as Camila looked away. "Of what, a lit match and a few puffs of smoke?" When Cheshire arched an eyebrow at him, seeming to relish the idea, Herb's face contorted briefly before he could wrangle his careless grin back into place. "This pansy peacock fucker has nothing on me," he declared, and with a flick of his wrist he splashed his drink directly into Cheshire's face.

Cheshire reeled back, hissing and swiping at his eyes. Watching the amber liquid splatter across his pristine white tuxedo sent Jakub's blood boiling. After all he'd watched Cheshire endure, from Kozlow and Manhattan and everyone else, he couldn't bring himself to let another insult go unchallenged. He grabbed Herb by the collar of his cape, fully intending to plant his metal fist directly in his smug face.

He didn't get that far. Cheshire grabbed him by the elbow and around the waist to drag him back. The unexpected strength of his arm took Jakub's breath away. Herb didn't even have time to fully register that he had been seconds away from a broken nose or worse; he guffawed as Cheshire pulled Jakub away.

"Jealous was right!" Herb crowed. "Wish I had an attack dog like that!" He continued to laugh as Cheshire drew Jakub, still quaking with anger, toward the wall of the ballroom.

"Fucking *asshole*," Jakub growled, and he finally managed to shake free from Cheshire's grip. "After everything you've done for him, to side with *Barney?* Who's only pretending to play nice so he can put a knife in his back?"

"I know." Cheshire stripped off his hat and mask. "Can you hold these?"

Jakub accepted, and his fury shifted to concern as he watched Cheshire mop his face with a handkerchief. "Are you all right?"

"Yeah—just—stings." Cheshire grimaced as he cleaned up as much as he could. "Son of a bitch. I really like this jacket."

He patted down his stained lapels; Jakub's shoulders drooped and his throat ached. He knew very well it wasn't the ruined jacket drawing Cheshire's brow tight with disappointment and frustration. "Let's leave," Jakub said. "We don't belong here."

Cheshire's wince deepened, and he straightened up to look around the room. "Yeah," he said distractedly. "We don't." He shook himself and motioned for Jakub to hand his mask back. "But we can't leave yet," he said as he wiped off the mask and then fit it back to his face. "If the cops are just now hearing about the robbery, they'll be on the streets. Better they find us here than trying to cross the bridge."

He nodded toward the exit, where Marshal Adalet had her ear cocked to an officer in uniform. She scowled as she scanned the room and spotted Cheshire. She held his gaze, tapped her nose, and then followed the officer out.

Jakub took a deep breath to force the rest of his hackles down. "I'm sorry," he said. "If you hadn't stopped me—"

"Don't worry about it," Cheshire hurried to reassure him. He gave the back of Jakub's neck a squeeze and offered a grin. "Someday I'll let you do it and hold *him*."

Jakub nodded, taking him more seriously than he was maybe meant to. "However you want to handle this, I'm with you," he said. *Even if it means killing Masterson*, he thought, and it must have shown in his face, because Cheshire's smile melted away.

"Let's just try to enjoy the rest of the party for now," Cheshire said, and he put a hand on Jakub's back to urge him toward the bar. "Until the cops break it up."

Jakub allowed Cheshire to lead him. They swiftly met up with Burke, who insisted he had no knowledge of the target of their raid. Jakub believed him, though he wondered how much that even mattered now.

Cheshire stayed close to him for the rest of the night, until the police inevitably did arrive to question the attendees. Naturally, no one had heard or suspected anything, and the caliber of the clientele prevented anyone from noticing the alcohol being swiftly vacated from the bar. Late in the night, everyone was finally dismissed to begin the trek across the city. As much as he hated to do it, Jakub bid Cheshire goodnight and climbed back into Hannah's car with her and Burke.

"Jakub," Hannah said seriously as she pulled them away from the curb. "If this is going to be a problem for you, I'll help you make it right. Whatever parts you need. We can maybe even sell one or two of the guns to Diamondback—they're in the same business, after all."

"It's not about that," Jakub replied, leaning against the passenger side door. He watched for as long as he could as Cheshire strolled down the sidewalk toward his own car. "Don't worry about me—I can take care of myself."

"I know, but..." Hannah sighed, and she and Burke exchanged a look. "I'm sorry," she finished.

"Don't worry about it," Jakub repeated. He believed her. But it didn't matter.

BUSTED

Burke started his Monday early. He woke before dawn, dressed and drew a comb through his hair, and joined Hannah for breakfast at the diner across the street just as it opened.

"All our investments are paying out," he reported to her while piling scrambled eggs onto his toast. "The deputy of city planning we paid to get elected has pushed through the rest of the building permits. Within the next few years we'll be able to overhaul the entire waterfront."

"Uh-huh," said Hannah, and she took a long sip of her coffee.

Burke raised an eyebrow, waiting to see if more would follow. Sometimes she had plenty to say, sometimes hardly anything. Today, not so much, it seemed. "The Morey rented out its last unit yesterday, then," he continued. "Building's full up. Hardy any complaints from tenants. The penthouse operation has slowed down but we're making up for it in other ways."

Hannah took another long sip. "So. Business is good?"

"Going real steady." Burke took a few bites of his breakfast, still thinking she might offer more than that. At last he had little choice but to broach the subject. "How's the boss?"

"He's satisfied with the growth we've had," said Hannah, and at last she began to poke at her own breakfast. "But Barney's getting restless again, and they're both still fixated on Manhattan." She sighed. "Barney's eager to try out that revolver."

Burke snorted. "Did he figure out that if he keeps testing it out in the quarry, he'll run out of bullets before getting to use it on a job?" Hannah didn't have anything to say about that, either, so he pressed his luck a little. "Wasn't it a mistake, letting him keep it?"

"What's the use of telling *me* that?" Hannah retorted. "You think I can just walk up and take it from him?" She drowned a mouthful of eggs with her coffee. "I know we fucked up, but I can't do anything about that now. I don't need to hear it from you, too."

Burke pulled a face. "Danowicz still pissed?"

"He's avoiding me," Hannah admitted. "I know I should have told him what I knew up front, but..." She sighed and shook her head, then went back to eating. "It's over now. If only we could deal with Manhattan once and for all, things could go back to normal."

"'Normal' being relative," muttered Burke. "But I know what you mean."

The bell over the door jingled, and both glanced up to see Jakub heading in their direction, dressed in his jacket. Hannah straightened up. "Jakub."

"Hannah," Jakub greeted, and though he was never much for charisma, even Burke noted the lack of warmth in his tone. He quickly shifted focus to Burke. "If you're headed for the Morey, I'll ride with you."

"Oh, sure." Burke managed not to pull another face. "You gonna have some breakfast first, then?"

"I'll wait for you at the car," said Jakub, and with a curt nod to them he strode back out of the diner.

"I see what you mean," said Burke, and he herded the rest of his eggs together for quicker eating. "Downright surly, isn't he?"

Hannah leaned back in her seat. Burke wasn't typically one for sympathy, but watching her struggle quickly squashed the rest of his appetite. "Guess I shouldn't keep him waiting," he said, and he gulped down the remaining eggs, toast, and coffee. He set out cash for the meal, but as he climbed out of the booth, he hesitated.

"Hey, Zak," he said. "I know ye're doing yer best." He

tipped his chin up, refusing to allow any mushy sentiment into the words. "It's a crime, isn't it? The way they treat you. And I'm a Grade A criminal—I'd know."

Hannah blinked up at him, seemingly uncertain how she was meant to react. At last she decided on a quiet snort of amusement. "Thanks, Burke." Burke smiled back and headed outside.

Jakub was waiting for him, cigarette between his lips. Burke jogged over. "Ready, Danno?"

Jakub shot him a cool glare. "Danowicz," Burke corrected himself, gulping. The pair of them climbed into the Model A and headed across town.

"Hey," Burke ventured, even though he was well convinced it wouldn't lead to much. "Can I ask you something?"

Jakub puffed on his cigarette. "What?"

"Where's yer head at?" Burke asked bluntly, and he told himself not to back down even when Jakub turned his steel gaze on him. "I know ye're right pissed at Barney with every reason to be. But it ain't Zak's fault. Makes the kids restless when mama and papa are fighting."

"I'm not fighting with Hannah," said Jakub, though his tone failed to reassure.

"Might want to let her know that, then." Burke chewed his lip as he turned onto Kent. "Everyone's on edge and they wanna know ye're still on board. Kozlow won't run like it has without you."

Jakub frowned as he flicked ash out the window. "I'm still here, aren't I?"

Burke pulled a doubtful face. "Yeah. Good."

When they arrived at the Morey, Jakub followed Burke up to the penthouse. They had scaled back on their fraud operations in the past weeks, and it was a little early for Gertie and her sisters to have started, but Cheshire was there, dividing up rent payments like a proper landlord. His usually cheerful manners had been subdued somewhat ever since the masquerade heist, visible to everyone despite his efforts to hide it.

"Eggy! Jakub." Cheshire motioned them into the office, his full, fake grin on display as he showed off his ledger. "Did you hear? The whole building is full up. We have *a waiting list*. Exciting, isn't it?"

"That's great news," said Jakub, though with his usual

deadpan inflection. "The new building permits went through, so the boss says they'll start clearing the new land by summer."

"Oh! Great." Cheshire moved around the desk, flattening wrinkles out of his striped shirt and tie. Unusual not to see him in a vest or jacket. "We'll be needing more book-keepers, then. You'd better train them up good, Eggy."

"The hell do you think I've been doing all this time?" Burke retorted, hoping to goad Cheshire into better spirits, by force if necessary. "I'm not here just to be charming, y'know."

That got a laugh out of Cheshire, at least. "A lucky bonus, that," he replied, and he mussed Burke's hair.

"Bloom," said Jakub, and both men flinched at the sudden gravity in his voice. He cleared his throat. "I need to talk to you."

"In private?" Cheshire asked, and when Jakub nodded, he bobbed his head in reply, flustered. "Yeah, sure. Let's head back to my place. I've, uh. There's something I've got to show you, too."

"All right."

Jakub headed for the door. Cheshire lingered a moment to cast Burke a helpless look and a shrug. Burke raised an eyebrow at him and asked, "You need a chaperone?"

Cheshire laughed nervously. "We'll be fine," he said, and he hurried after Jakub, out of the penthouse.

Burke shook his head. "Good luck, kid," he muttered, and he sank behind the desk to make sure Cheshire hadn't made a mess of his ledger.

He hadn't been at it for more than half an hour when the phone rang. He tucked his pen behind his ear and answered. "Burke here."

"It's Hannah," she said, and Burke straightened up in his seat. "Is Jakub still there with you?"

"Somewhere." Burke leaned forward to see out the office door. Gertie and the rest had shown up and he could hear them throughout the penthouse, but he hadn't heard Jakub or Cheshire return from...wherever they'd run off to. *Maybe I should check the ditches for Bloom,* he thought. *Or the alley below his balcony. Danowicz being in a mood and all.* "What's the matter?"

"Barney's calling in the boys for a meeting," said Hannah, with suitable apprehension. "I think he's decided on the next job, and I wanted him to know as soon as I did."

"Not making that mistake again, huh?" Burke replied, though he then immediately regretted it. "Sorry. What I mean is, I'll grab Danowicz. Where is it?"

"In Maspeth, the usual spot. But come here first." Hannah sighed. "I want to be able to talk to him before then."

"Sure." Burke drummed his fingers on the desk. "Bloom, too?"

"...Bloom, too."

"Roger that. We'll see you soon."

Burke hung up and headed into the living room to let Gertie know she was in charge. *Better get on it straight away,* he thought as he rode the elevator down to the ground floor. *Don't want to give Danowicz any reason to think we're keeping things from him, after the last time.*

Burke crossed the street to Cheshire's building and hopped up the steps to his floor. He was still debating on how to best relay the information as he reached Cheshire's door and rapped with his knuckles. "Bloom? Been murdered yet?"

He heard voices inside the apartment, but nothing that was meant for him. It sounded like an argument, and when pressing his ear to the wood didn't make it any clearer, he tried the knob and found it unlocked. *Burke to the rescue,* he thought, twisting the door open. "Bloom?"

"Just *stop,*" Jakub was saying angrily. Burke followed his voice toward the bedroom. "Stop it, you're making it worse!"

"Then *you* stop!" Cheshire retorted. "I can't see what you're doing!"

The hell? Burke frowned as he pushed at the partially open bedroom door. "Hey, Bloom?"

Burke got a good look at the room and stopped dead. Of all the things he had expected to find, he never would have predicted *that.*

They were in bed together, Cheshire on his back and Jakub leaning over him, *naked*—one hundred percent *buck naked*, sweat in their hair, limbs tangled, dicks out. Jakub whipped toward him, eyes bulging in shock; the movement yanked Cheshire's head along, and he cursed loudly. Burke was so overcome with surprise that it took him a while to realize what they had been arguing about: Cheshire's long hair was clogged up in the wrist of Jakub's prosthetic.

"Who's there?" Cheshire called, squinting and panicked. The sound of his voice startled Burke out of his stupor; he retreated, slamming the door shut behind him.

They're fucking. Burke steepled both hands over his mouth and nose as the realization flooded over him. *Oh fuck, they're fucking.* And of all the crazy extrapolations and unwanted images that fact could have inspired, the first thought to dominate his whirling mind was, *Kozlow is fucked.*

It suddenly made a lot of sense, despite the utter insanity of it. All those times Jakub left the building "to keep an eye on Bloom." The overly exuberant grins Cheshire plastered all over his face that Burke had been attributing to nerves around the perpetually murder-ready Jakub. Finding them *drunkenly spooning* in the penthouse after the Manhattan dinner party— Burke could have boxed his own ears for being so *stupid*, how had he ever missed it? Who knew? Not Barney, certainly, or there would have been blood by then, or would be if he ever found out.

Why didn't that piece of shit tell me? Burke thought, and his chest grew tight and hot.

He could hear hissing voices and a series of clumsy thumps within the bedroom. *Bloody hell*, he thought, rubbing his face. He took three steps forward, turned around, and faced the door with his arms crossed.

The door opened and Cheshire appeared. He looked utterly ridiculous: dressed in a robe and his glasses at least, sheepish and concerned, and disturbingly enough carrying Jakub's disconnected arm still attached to a lock of his hair. His thin, bashful smile which used to be so charming filled Burke with irritation. "H...Hey, Eggy."

Arms still crossed, Burke gave a sharp shrug. "What the fuck, Bloom?"

"Don't..." Cheshire stepped out of the room and tugged the door quickly shut behind him. Burke caught only a glimpse of Jakub shoving his arm into a shirt further inside. "Now, don't blow a valve," Cheshire said, gesturing for calm with his free hand. He maneuvered around Burke and motioned toward the kitchen. "Come sit down."

"Seriously, though," Burke insisted, though he followed Cheshire to the table. "What the *fuck*, Bloom! What did I just walk in on?"

"Uh...birds and bees?" Cheshire herded Burke into a chair and then moved around the kitchen, searching his drawers. "I know what you're thinking: Barney would kill me."

"Ye're damn right that's what I'm thinking!" Burke exclaimed, throwing his hands up. "What would possess you to—" He screwed his face up and he gave it a rub before trying again. "Let me guess: that night at the Morey? All that booze?"

"Uh..." Cheshire gathered a collection of tools—a screwdriver, a pair of scissors, a knife—and joined Burke at the kitchen table. "Actually...longer than that," he confessed, and he had the decency to let some of his false humor peel off.

Burke eyed him. "*How* long?"

"Well..." Cheshire gulped and hesitantly met his gaze. "Since his accident."

Burke blinked at him, and that tightness returned, hard and angry and...hurt. "You...you *asshole*, that was more than *two years ago!*"

The bedroom door opened, and both men startled. Jakub emerged, dressed in an undershirt and slacks, suspenders hanging loose. His face was devil-red and eyes dark as he moved stiffly to the kitchen table and sat down next to Cheshire.

Burke held still, watching Jakub like a hawk. Half of him really believed Jakub might cut his throat like a stray witness, and he gulped. "So," he said, gaze darting between them. "Who knows?"

"Just you, now," said Cheshire as he tried to get the prosthetic to lay flat. He had to lean forward and looked ridiculous for it. "Well, no, Grace knows."

"Miklos," Jakub muttered, and he turned the arm so the inside of its forearm was straight up.

"Right! Grace and Miklos. That's...pretty much it."

Burke waited a few beats, convinced that more names would pour out of them. "So," he said slowly. "Not Hannah."

Jakub tensed, but he refused to look in Burke's direction. He devoted himself only to holding the arm steady as Cheshire unscrewed the arm plate. "Not Hannah," Cheshire said, worry overtaking the rest of his embarrassment. "I guess it's too much to ask that you won't tell her, huh?"

Burke glared at him in exasperation. "Tell her?" he repeated, temper rising again. "Tell her what? That you're fooling around behind everyone's back, willing to risk busting up this entire operation for some quick fucks?"

Jakub sank deeper into his shoulders as he began the slow process of trying to untangle Cheshire's hair from the gears in his wrist one-handed. His jaws were clenched so hard Burke wouldn't have been surprised to see cracks form in his cheeks. More disturbing than that was how quiet Cheshire fell.

"It's not about that," Cheshire said, and God help them, he looked sincere. "This is serious."

Burke leaned back and glared at the both of them together. Cheshire stared back, imploring, but Jakub still wouldn't lift his head; though focused entirely on the tedious work in front of him, he was all but bristling.

His hand is shaking, Burke realized, and he suddenly had no idea what to think or even who to trust. Watching Cheshire's concerned, affectionate gaze slide to Jakub made everything fall out of sense. *How did I not know?* he thought, gulping. *No—how could anyone have guessed?* His eyes narrowed on Cheshire. "Why didn't you tell me?"

"I didn't think it would do anyone any good," replied Cheshire. "And I didn't want you to have to lie for me."

"But lying *to* me, that's all fine and dandy, is it?"

Cheshire sighed. "Eggy—"

"No—no more 'but Eggy.'" Burke pushed out of his chair. "How long were you planning on keeping it a secret, then? Until Barney himself walked in on ya? He thinks Danowicz is his right hand and that *ye're* in cahoots with Masterson trying to oust him."

"That's ridiculous," said Cheshire, frustrated. "If I wanted that, I would have done it by now—you know that."

"So I'll just tell him that, yeah?" Burke shot back. "He'll listen to me? I'm telling you, if he finds out the two of ye're bacon'n eggs, Brooklyn is gonna *explode*."

"Then he *won't* find out," Cheshire insisted. He put his hand to the table as if ready to stand, only to remember Jakub's arm was still dangling from his scalp. "We'll be more careful."

"You *ought* to just end it. There's no telling—"

"No," said Jakub, and Cheshire and Burke both stopped to stare. He was gripping the lock of Cheshire's hair tight, his fist trembling.

Burke swallowed again, and his stomach clenched. "Fuck this," he muttered at last, and he rubbed his face with both hands. "Fuck *me*." He turned away.

"Eggy—Burke—wait!" Cheshire tried to follow, only to stop short at the yank on his hair. "Wait—I'm sorry, all right? I'm sorry I didn't tell you."

Burke shook his head, but he did pause to look over his shoulder. "Barney's called a meeting in Maspeth. He wants you both there. It's probably a job."

"Any idea what?" asked Cheshire.

"No." Burke ran his hand through his hair and then continued on. "I'll see you there."

"Eggy—" Cheshire tried again, but Burke didn't stop that time. He left the apartment and slammed the door behind him harder than he'd meant to. The sound of it startled him, and he rushed to the elevator, not allowing himself even one meaningful thought until he had retreated back to his office in the Morey penthouse.

They're really fucking, Burke thought, leaning over his desk as he tried to scratch the image out of his skull. *Are they really steady? Have been all this time?* He glared at the papers in front of him in confusion. *Since the accident? When Bloom almost killed him? Christ, how does that even make sense?*

Burke glanced away, and his attention sharpened on the phone. *If Barney thinks Bloom is trying to jump ship to Manhattan and taking Danowicz with him, that won't be the end of it. He'll be looking my way next.* He licked his lips. *My neck is on the line here, too. He should have told me.*

Burke snatched up the receiver and dialed before he could talk himself out of it. He thumped his fingers on the desk while he waited for Hannah to pick up. Finally, she did. "Zak here."

"It's Burke," he said, and he squeezed his eyes shut. "I'm heading back there. There's something you should know."

***

Jakub pulled his hand back; it was shaking too hard for him to make much progress, and he had no choice but to abandon the rest of the untangling to Cheshire. "He's going to tell everyone," he said.

"He's not going to tell everyone," replied Cheshire immediately. He followed each remaining strand down to the springs and unwound them as quickly but carefully as possible. "Try to calm down."

Jakub scraped the back of his palm across his mouth. *He's going to tell everyone*, he thought, shuddering. *He's right; Barney will have a fit.* "Chesh—"

"It's all right," Cheshire reassured him. He diverted one hand from his work to give Jakub's a quick squeeze. "He's not going to tell. I'm almost done here and then I'll go talk to him some more."

Jakub shook his head, but he didn't know what else to say. Having been caught in such a compromising position was already mortifying enough that he was light-headed—knowing that he might soon have to go over the same conversation with Hannah or worse was nauseating. All the questions they would ask—all the assumptions and accusations—

"I shouldn't have come here today," Jakub mumbled, still shaking as he drew his suspenders up. "This was stupid."

"Calm down," Cheshire said again. He reached for the scissors and then decided against them, continuing with his fingers instead. "You don't have to jump to conclusions."

"But what if Barney finds out?" Jakub pressed. "What about the boss—what about *Masterson*? What do you think they'll do, knowing we're..."

"I have no idea!" Cheshire gave his face a rub, getting grease on his chin, and then chuckled in a desperate attempt to cover up his own anxiety. "Never let us hear the end of it, probably. Stop worrying so much."

He freed the last of his hair and sat back with a long, relieved sigh. "Ow, shit." He rubbed his neck and combed his hair back with his fingers. "Careful with that thing next time."

Jakub tensed defensively as he dragged the arm over to him. "*You* should be *more* worried," he retorted. "Things are bad enough right now, and they're about to get worse."

"I don't see how." Cheshire laughed again as he pushed to his feet, but it was less and less convincing. For the first time, Jakub couldn't stand the sound of it. "I'm already as far out of the loop as it gets."

He headed toward the bedroom; Jakub hastily reattached his prosthetic and gave chase. "It *can* get worse," Jakub insisted. "Now that Barney's got that fancy revolver of his, he thinks you're replaceable. And Masterson doesn't like the idea of anything he can't control."

"I know!" Cheshire hurried ahead as if trying to escape, not that Jakub would allow it. He tossed his robe on the bed and began picking up his discarded clothing. "I know, I get it—Barney hates me. But he's *always* hated me! And nothing I've done has helped, so I really don't know what I'm supposed to do about it."

Jakub stood back as he watched Cheshire yank his shirt and pants on. *I don't know, either*, he realized, and it frightened him enough that he wished he was wearing a gun. "What if there *isn't* anything you can do?"

"Then, hell, I don't know that either, Jake." He tossed Jakub's turtleneck to him. "What am I supposed to say?"

Jakub caught it and put it on, but the stall didn't help as much as he'd hoped. As he bent down to lace his boots, he found himself saying, "Burke said we should just stop."

Cheshire stopped midway through knotting his tie. After a pause he continued. "Is that what you want?"

"No." Jakub straightened back up, but he was afraid to look at whatever face Cheshire might have been making. "Unless, you...?"

"No," Cheshire said quickly, but then he sighed. "I'll talk to him. We can worry about the rest later."

That's what you always say, Jakub thought, but he kept it to himself, too ill to risk an argument. He waited for Cheshire to finish dressing and then followed him out of the apartment without another word.

Burke wasn't in the penthouse. According to Gertie he had been in the office only a few minutes before rushing out again. Cheshire had no more words of reassurance and encouragement as he and Jakub made their way out of the building.

"Should I take you home?" he offered, at a loss. "If he's gone back to tell Hannah..."

"I don't want to talk to her," Jakub said quickly. "Either she'll tell Barney or she won't." He shifted back and forth on the sidewalk. "Let's just go to Maspeth."

"All right."

They took Cheshire's car and drove the way in near silence. Jakub spent the time stretching his imagination: he tried to envision the different possible scenarios, from dreadful to disastrous, and the many ways he might be called upon to defend himself and Cheshire. *If they had accepted Cheshire, from the start, I wouldn't have needed to lie,* he told himself, not that he could imagine ever confessing the truth of his feelings to the rest of Kozlow under any circumstances. *If they accuse us of siding with Manhattan, I'll kill Masterson if I have to. Whatever it takes.* He glanced to Cheshire as they sped across town. *No one hurts him.*

Cheshire was equally lost in thought, but his gaze was so blank and distant, Jakub felt his confidence waver. *What if he's thinking about what Burke said?* he wondered. *What if we just...stopped?* But the thought left him cold and distraught and he couldn't follow that line of logic to any useful conclusion.

They reached Barney's building in Maspeth and found a trio of his new "henchmen," courtesy of O'Shea in Chicago, rolling dice on the stoop. They looked up and fixed the approaching pair with looks of distrust; a harder glare from Jakub convinced them to gather up their dice and winnings.

"Where's the boss?" asked Jakub, and one of them gave him a thumb's down. He and Cheshire stepped past them into the building and descended the stairs into the basement.

Barney was already in the cellar beneath a collection of bare bulbs, chatting excitedly with Leon. "Of course it's going to work," he was saying as the pair of them leaned over a map spread out on the table at the room's center. "What do you think I did all that testing for?" He glanced up as Jakub and Cheshire entered. "Jakub! Bloom! Get over here and tell me what you think."

He doesn't know yet, Jakub thought, and a quick glance around the cellar showed that they had beaten Hannah and Burke. He couldn't bring himself to relax even an inch knowing they could arrive at any minute, but he heeded Barney's gesturing and approached the table.

"Déjà vu," Cheshire teased as he followed a step behind. "What's the great plan this time, Barney?"

Barney wrangled in a bitter scowl. "Don't be a dick, Bloom, you're gonna love this." He pointed to the map.

Jakub leaned over the map and followed Barney's finger to a building in Staten Island, which had dollar signs scrawled over top it.

Cheshire started laughing. He sounded a little manic

and it made Jakub's skin crawl. "A bank," said Cheshire, all out of incredulity. "You're gonna rob a bank."

"*We* are gonna rob a bank," Barney declared, so absurdly proud of himself that Jakub wanted to slap the smug off his face. "I want you there for this one, Bloom. No more sidelines."

Cheshire shoved his hands in his pockets. Whatever he might have been thinking, he was still smiling. "Well, sure," he said. "What's a bank vault if not a very big safe? Makes perfect sense."

"Isn't that a little much, even for us?" asked Jakub. "You'll bring down every cop in New York on us."

"We have a plan," Leon chipped in, which drew another chuckle from Cheshire. He made a face at him. "We do! When everyone gets here, we'll tell you."

"What does Manhattan say about it?" Jakub pressed, and just as he'd feared, Barney smirked.

"Why should they have anything to say about it?" replied Barney. "We won't go anywhere near their turf."

Here it comes. Jakub heard the door at the top of the stairs creak open and gulped. *We go to war.*

Before he could voice further concerns, Cheshire started laughing again, and Jakub cast him a glare. *What the hell is the matter with him?* "It's not funny," he said. "The deal was 'anything outside Brooklyn' they get a say in. If we go through with this Lucky won't stay quiet."

"So what if she doesn't?" said Barney. "I'm not scared of them. I know for a fact they still have their share of the Hallorran take at the Thrones." He puffed himself up. "If they try anything, I'll just sneak a tip to that marshal and have her take care of it."

"Did you forget that they already have leverage over the marshal?" Jakub turned on Cheshire, who was still entirely too amused for his liking. "Cheshire, say something."

Cheshire shrugged. "I wouldn't call it 'leverage'," he said. "All they did was pay off a witness and then paid them more to recant." Jakub glared, but by then there were footsteps reaching the bottom stairs, and he couldn't help but divert his attention.

Hannah entered. Her face was already hard as if she were bracing herself, and she immediately sought Jakub's eye. He turned back toward the map. *This isn't the time for that,* he thought determinedly. *She wouldn't really tell him in these circumstances, would she?*

Burke entered a step behind. He stayed close to Hannah as they joined Barney at the table, followed by the rest of their best Kozlow and Szpliman men, and a few of the new recruits. Barney gathered himself up as everyone's attention turned on him. "This is going to be our most ambitious job yet," he declared. "Real outlaws, like those assholes down south, or the cowboys out west. *No one* will question what we're capable of after this."

Hannah cast another long look at Jakub before wrangling her attention to Barney. "What's the plan?"

"The job is the Staten Island branch of the First National Bank." Barney pointed it out on the map, and the newcomers leaned in for a closer look. A mix of excited and wary expressions watched Barney continue. "We'll hit it before closing, before they've had time to move all the money from the tellers to the vault. Take the truck and two cars. The truck will be a decoy—we'll load it up with vegetable crates, and drive it across the bridge into Jersey once we have the money. If the cops try to road block us, we'll have them busy for an hour opening them up."

Jakub glanced to Cheshire, who was listening with a flat smile in place. *Is that what Barney wants him for?* he wondered. *Cheshire Bloom leaving the site of a robbery with a truck full of sealed crates would be too much of a temptation for any cop.*

"As for the actual money," Barney continued, "we'll split it up between the cars and take two routes to the river. There'll be a boat there that can take the goods up the river—slowly. It'll be dark by the time it arrives in Brooklyn and we can unload without anyone the wiser."

Barney straightened up and looked over the assembly. "Unless someone has a better idea?" he challenged. His eyes narrowed. "Burke?"

Burke, showing uncharacteristic restraint, shrugged. "All seems straightforward to me."

Barney waited a moment as if suspecting an actual complaint would follow, and when none did, he shifted focus. "Bloom?"

"No, it sounds good," said Cheshire. "Honestly, I'm impressed."

"...Good." Barney cleared his throat and carried on. "Since this is a bigger job than usual, in a new place, we'll be masked up. The last thing we need is someone being identified. That goes double for Bloom."

"I can be subtle, don't worry."

Jakub frowned at the rest of the room. Everyone seemed far too all right with the plan, and following Barney into their most dangerous job to date. The lack of any meaningful critique from Hannah, Cheshire, or especially Burke, set him on edge. He took a deep breath. "The plan is sound but I don't see how this is necessary in the first place. What do we need the money for?"

"For our new buildings, of course," Barney replied. "But it's not just about the money." His brow furrowed with determination. "Everyone has to know they can't fuck with us."

Jakub leaned back. He looked to the map, then to each attentive face; though he couldn't point to any particular aspect of Barney's intended plan as a fatal flaw, he couldn't quell his ill ease. *Am I just worried about Burke and Hannah?* he thought, forcing himself to look at them. Both seemed determined not to meet his gaze. *If they tell Barney about us, what will he do?*

"When do we hit?" asked Hannah.

"Tomorrow." Realizing that no one was going to question him after all, Barney regained his earlier bravado. "Stas and I have already timed the route by boat, but we'll take it out again tonight to be sure."

"Who's going to be where?" asked Jakub, thinking there might be one more detail he was missing that would illuminate Barney's motives.

Barney nodded. "Bloom will drive the truck," he said. "Leon will go with him." He pointed to two of the Szpilman boys. "Stas will stay with the boat, while Nowak and Gorski will drive the getaway cars. Hannah, Jakub, Bloom and I will handle the heist itself." He eyed Burke across the table. "Burke, too."

Burke stiffened, but then Barney laughed shortly. "Lighten up—I'm kidding. Edith's daughters will man our pier for when the boat comes in. Burke can stay here and count the money." He snorted. "That's what you do best, right?"

"...Sure." Burke thumbed his nose, but it was clear his usual bite was lacking. Barney almost looked disappointed.

"Then we'll meet tomorrow to prepare," said Hannah,

pushing the meeting past it. "Unless anyone has questions, we should all get back to work for now."

No one had anything else to offer, so Barney dismissed them. Cheshire took the chance to head out first, chatting to no one in particular about how disappointing it would be to have to hide his identity. Jakub quickly followed, goosebumps on his skin. He felt Hannah fall into step behind him, but it wasn't until they reached the upper floor that she caught up and took him by the elbow.

"Jakub," she said, her tone unmistakably serious. "Can I talk—"

Jakub yanked his arm free and kept walking without looking back. "Not now."

But she wouldn't be deterred that easily; she continued after him, catching up again just inside the door leading out. Jakub didn't mean to stop, but Cheshire did, leaving the three of them to cluster awkwardly. "Let me give you a ride home," she said. "We need to talk."

"We don't need to talk," Jakub insisted, though he couldn't bring himself to look her in the face. "And I have things to do."

"I can drop him off later," said Cheshire, trying so hard to sound casual that it came out *extra* guilty.

Hannah shot him a glare so hard he flinched. "I need to talk to you, too."

"No, you don't," said Jakub. He took a step closer to Cheshire and rallied his courage enough to meet Hannah's stare. "Either you need to talk to Barney, or we don't talk about it at all."

Hannah leaned back, her severity easing down in favor of hurt. Behind her, Burke and the rest of the boys started to emerge, and she cast them a quick, anxious look. "Later, then," she said, meaning it for both of them, and then she stepped back.

Jakub pushed past Cheshire and out of the building. The rush of morning sunlight wasn't as much of a comfort as he'd hoped. His hands were shaking. With a deep breath he headed straight for Cheshire's car and let himself into the passenger seat, determined not to say another word to anyone.

***

Cheshire followed Jakub out, but at a much slower pace. He made it out of the building but not much further; Hannah and Burke were lingering just behind, and unlike Jakub, he couldn't just walk away. Out on the sidewalk he turned to face them.

"Hey, Hannah," he said. He looked pointedly at Burke. "Thanks, Eggy."

Burke puffed up indignantly. "Ye've got something to say to me now, have you?" he shot back, though he was squirming. "We tell each other things?"

"Bloom," Hannah interrupted them, and as much as Cheshire tried not to be affected by her disapproval, her hard stare had his stomach in knots. "Please. Do you have any idea what you're doing?"

"I dunno," Cheshire admitted. "I kinda did until this morning."

"I'm being serious." With the rest of Barney's men making their way outside, she moved right up to him so she could lower her voice. "Please don't make everything worse. You know what would happen if everyone else knew."

"So don't tell anyone," said Cheshire. "It's that easy."

Hannah sighed. "It's not, and you of all people should know that."

"I don't know what that means, but it really is." If they lingered any longer they were going to start drawing attention, so Cheshire took a step back and shrugged. "If you tell him and he shoots me for it, I'll be back to haunt you."

"*Bloom*," Hannah said crossly, but Cheshire turned and headed quickly to his car. By the time Barney himself had emerged from the building, Cheshire and Jakub were speeding away.

Jakub hunkered down in the passenger side and was very still, as if attempting to make himself disappear. "What did Hannah say?"

"Nothing important." Cheshire pushed down the accelerator and then had to warn himself not to get carried away, however quickly his heart was pounding for escape. "Try to relax—she's not going to tell anyone."

"What if she doesn't have to?" Jakub asked, though Cheshire wasn't sure what he meant until he continued. "I'm worried about this job. Why is Barney suddenly so interested in you being there?"

Cheshire shrugged. He still wasn't entirely sure what to make of it himself. "It's a bank vault. Even he has to admit he'll need the extra firepower if he wants in."

"I don't like it."

"Me, neither, but it's not as if..." Cheshire pushed his bangs back. The stresses of the morning were already piling up and he couldn't lose his cool, not in front of Jakub. "You worry too much. We've had a lot of jobs go sideways but they always right themselves in the end. It'll be fine."

"And Manhattan?" Jakub pressed. "You've always said we can't go behind Lucky's back."

"And I still believe that, but it's not really our call. I'm not about to run out and tattle on Barney *now*." Cheshire snorted. "If he wants a war, maybe it's time he got one. I won't shed any tears over Herb if he catches one of Barney's fancy bullets."

Jakub went quiet for a moment, and as usual, Cheshire had a hard time interpreting his steady expression. "What?"

"You saved Masterson's life," Jakub reminded him. He sounded like he was waiting for something; it dug under Cheshire's skin. "You could have had a place in their gang at one point."

"Yeah, and it turns out he's a dirtbag, so what?" Cheshire scrubbed at his mouth, reminded of the heat of the sigil flashing across his face. "He's a back-stabber, Barney's a jerk who hates me—it's almost like I can't win!" He laughed, though he stopped when he caught a glimpse of the suddenly easy-to-translate concern on Jakub's face. "Well, what does it matter? I'm just going to keep my head down and follow orders from now on. A good little soldier."

"Right..." Jakub sighed and shook his head. "How did you ever end up with Kozlow in the first place?"

Cheshire hummed. "Is that rhetorical?" he asked. "Honestly, I just kind of fell into it, same as you. It's been pretty rough at times, but...that's the business, right? We're criminals." He shrugged. "It's, you know, it keeps me on my toes. They wouldn't be making talkies about us if everything went right all the time."

"This isn't *Chicago Smoke*," Jakub retorted. "I'm really worried that..." He trailed off, his eye having caught on the name of the cross streets they had stopped at. "Are you taking me back to the Kozlow building?"

"Yes? I said I would."

Jakub shifted in his seat. "Let's just go to your place," he said. "I'd rather avoid everyone if I can."

For once, the idea made Cheshire anxious rather than excited. "Is that really a good idea? If they go looking for you and you're with me? Seems kind of like...throwing salt on a wound." He didn't like the look Jakub was fixing on him, so he added, "There's something I have to do today."

Jakub didn't blink. "What?"

Cheshire came close to lying; guilt course corrected him to a half truth. "It's in Manhattan."

"Oh." At last Jakub faced forward again. "Fine."

Shit. Cheshire rubbed the back of his neck, but they were nearly at the building anyway. *Coward,* he thought as he pulled up to the curb. *You just don't want to have to face Hannah again if she comes looking for him.*

Jakub climbed out of the car; he shut the door behind him and didn't look back as he marched up to the steps. "I'll call you later!" Cheshire called after him, but Jakub spared only a short glance before continuing inside.

Cheshire sighed and put the car back in drive. *Coward,* he chided himself again, and he headed west.

The Manhattan streets were fairly quiet that morning; it was late enough that the *reputable* businesses were up and running, not late enough for lunches to be served. Cheshire parked in a side street and walked to a small café he had visited several times over the last three years. He was early, so he ordered a coffee and picked a table in the corner that offered the most amount of privacy. After about an hour of chatting up the waitress, the door jingled with an incoming guest.

Grace entered the café in a bright, spring sundress, and with her came another pair of women: Thea Hallorran in a lighter version of her usual pants suit, along with red-haired, stony-faced Millie Tighe.

Cheshire stood. Even after hearing Jakub's account of the masquerade heist, he hadn't been able to wrap his mind around the thought of seeing Millie Tighe again: stocky, angry Millie, who he had last seen swallowed up by a fireball of his own making. She was wearing a long sleeved, collared shirt, gloves on her hands, but he had spent enough time with Jakub to recognize the prosthetic replacing her right arm.

The three women approached, and Cheshire kept his expression as humble and neutral as possible. None of them looked particularly happy to see him, even if Grace displayed some sympathy. She reached the table first and allowed Cheshire to kiss her cheek in greeting. "Hi, Cheshire. I got them here for you."

"Thanks." He frowned when he realized. "You're not gonna stay?"

"No, not this time," said Grace apologetically. "I have a *real* date."

More like, Emma doesn't want her near me, Cheshire assumed, not that he could blame her. "All right. See you later."

He suddenly didn't feel like he would, and Grace must have felt it, too, because her smile became a wince. "Good luck," she said, and she showed herself off.

Cheshire took a deep breath as he faced his remaining guests. "Ms. Hallorran," he said, and he held her chair for her. "Thank you for coming even after hearing it was *me*."

Hallorran snorted quietly as she took her seat. "It's a little late for apologies," she said, "but I'll hear what you have to say."

"I appreciate it." Cheshire glanced to Millie, but she sat down before he could consider offering her the same courtesy. Gulping, he took his seat. "Ms. Tighe."

"Bloom," Millie replied icily. She settled in with her arms crossed.

"When Millie heard who I was meeting, she insisted on coming," Hallorran explained. "She's been with us for a few years now, working to pay off the operation we performed for her. I knew a few of the particulars about her accident, but not the most important one." She raised an eyebrow at Cheshire. "I understand you haven't seen each other in a long time."

"About five years," Cheshire confirmed. It might not have been wise, but he added, "You probably won't believe me, but I'm glad to see you, Millie. I didn't know you were still alive."

Millie scoffed mightily. "Because I was weighing on your conscience, huh? You're right—I don't believe that." She fixed him with a hateful glare. "I'm sure you didn't feel bad about killing my brother, either."

Cheshire grimaced as the waitress headed their way with a coffee pot. "If it makes you feel any better, he gave me this," he said, tracing the scar that ran up his left cheek to his ear.

"It doesn't," said Millie. "But good."

The waitress poured coffee for each of them, eyebrows raised at the tense atmosphere. Cheshire tried to reassure her with a smile that lasted only until her back was turned. "You were right, Thea," he said, and though she made a face at him, he continued. "It's a little late for apologies. I know you've got no good reason to trust a word out of my mouth, but I wanted you to know." He faced them seriously. "That robbery on the docks wasn't our idea. Jakub and I didn't know you were involved at all until the middle of it."

"Danowicz was *there*," Millie insisted while Hallorran watched him, thoughtful. "He almost shot me."

"I know! I know, but it wasn't *us*." Cheshire turned his full focus to Hallorran herself. "You know how much we value our cooperation. Neither of us would have taken part if we'd known who we were stealing from."

"I want to believe that," Hallorran said, and her anger seemed more and more like a strained front she was putting on. "But it doesn't change the fact that you and your gang *did* steal from me. And you're not the first one to try and pass off responsibility."

Cheshire leaned back, baffled. "What?"

"I met with Camila Reynoso not long after that night," said Hallorran, and Cheshire felt himself grow pale. "She returned three of our stolen items and insisted they had no idea that we were the target of Kozlow's robbery."

"That's..." Cheshire stared back at her, too flabbergasted even to be angry at first. "Masterson knew from the beginning— he told me so himself."

Hallorran and Millie both were quiet for a long moment, watching and judging him—long enough that Cheshire felt the color return to his cheeks with a rush of heat. But it wouldn't do him any good to let his temper show in front of them; he took a breath to force calm. "I understand how it must look," he said carefully. "But I hope you're not going to take their word over mine. We have a history."

"We do," said Hallorran, and her brow knit with what seemed like sincere regret. "We did."

"But you're not here to return our stolen merchandise, are you?" challenged Millie.

"...No." Cheshire couldn't help but cringe at the thought of Barney packing up his new guns for the promised heist. "That's not my call to make."

Hallorran nodded, disappointed but unsurprised. "I can't say we don't deserve it," she admitted, and when Millie started to protest, she set a hand on her shoulder to quiet her. "We were smuggling those guns instead of selling them for a reason, after all. You could say we played with fire and got burned."

Millie snorted loudly, but then she doused further complaints in a long gulp of coffee. "However," Hallorran continued, and Cheshire's shoulders fell, "if that's the case, I'm sure you can understand why I can't risk continuing any kind of relationship with you and your friends. You obviously have no protection to offer. If your own people don't trust you enough to keep you informed, how can *I* trust you?"

"I understand, but..." Cheshire licked his lips. "I'm sorry to lose that, I truly am," he tried again. "But it's Jakub that matters to me more. If something happens to his arm, you're the only one he can go to."

"If he breaks it, he's welcome to purchase a replacement like anyone else," said Hallorran. "With cash."

Cheshire relaxed with a bittersweet smile. "Thank you," he said, meaning it so completely that Hallorran seemed taken aback. "That's all I ask."

Hallorran cleared her throat. "Then I suppose that's all there is to discuss," she said, and she pushed to her feet with Millie close behind. "Take care of yourself, Mr. Bloom." She allowed a bit of levity back into her tone. "And if you can possibly help it, stay out of my business from now on?"

"If I possibly can," Cheshire agreed, and when they shook hands, he gave hers a gentle squeeze. "And you be careful, too. If Camila really said she didn't know about the river, she lied."

Hallorran's eyes narrowed, but she nodded. "You don't have to worry about us," she reassured him. "We're not as green as we seem."

She turned to go, but Millie wasn't so easily dismissed;

she glared at Cheshire down her nose. "If I ever see you again, I'm gonna pay you back for Charlie," she said. "So watch yourself."

Cheshire held his hands up in surrender. "I get it. I really don't want any more trouble for you, Millie." Millie eyed him a moment longer, and with one final snort she turned on her heel and left.

Cheshire sank back in his chair with a sigh. *I guess that went as well as it could have,* he thought. He drank the rest of his coffee, then Hallorran's untouched mug, and left a generous tip before finally showing himself out.

By the time Cheshire returned to the car, he had lost all inkling of where he intended to go. He sat behind the wheel for a while, sick from too much coffee and wishing he hadn't dismissed Jakub so quickly.

Burke's pissed now, but he'll get over it, Cheshire told himself as he sank deeper and deeper into his seat. *He'll realize why we had to keep it secret. Grace... Maybe Emma will keep her away, but I can't blame either of them for that. Most people aren't friends with their ex-lovers anyway. Hallorran will still take care of Jakub if he needs it, that's all that matters. Herb and Lucky are both sellouts trying to drive a wedge between me and Barney, but...I knew that. I knew that was how this would go from the start. Right? Maybe if I was better at this, I'd be trying to do the same thing. Barney has to see that, too. Right?*

Cheshire took his glasses off so he could rub his eyes. He was tired, bone tired, small and sorry for himself. *Coward,* he thought. With a deep breath he forced himself to put the car in drive. *You're a famous outlaw, just like you always wanted. People know and fear you enough to be your enemy. Isn't that what infamy is?* He pulled out of the side street and started driving without any particular destination in mind. *Even if they don't like you, they'll remember you.*

At long last, Cheshire turned down the next street that would take him back toward the bridge to Brooklyn. *This job will settle it,* he thought with determination. *I'll just play ball and everything will work out.*

***

Jakub managed to avoid Hannah and Burke for the rest

of the day. He stopped in his apartment only long enough to call Miklos, giving him a brief summary of the events of the morning. He then promptly ignored Miklos' advice of talking to Hannah and wandered the sidewalks, smoking down what remained of his cigarettes, ducking into small shops and diners when paranoia got the better of him.

Outside himself, he knew there were smarter and likely necessary ways to deal with the revelations of the morning. He didn't return home until after sunset and went straight to bed without knowing if Cheshire had tried to call him.

In the morning, Jakub roused early and left out the fire escape. Afterward he felt like a fool, so he went to the diner across the street for breakfast. If a conversation was meant to happen, someone would find him, he told himself. He would leave it to fate.

The bell over the door jingled when Jakub was nearing the end of his breakfast. He held his breath but didn't look up. *They have until the coffee is gone,* he thought, but when someone did slide into the booth opposite him, he was startled to see a gnarled hand gripping the end of a cane. At last he lifted his head.

Kasper Kozlow sat across from him. Jakub glanced to the door and out the window, expecting to see Hannah or even Barney hovering nearby, but other than a pair of sleepy customers and the diner staff, they were alone. Jakub took a long sip of his coffee. *Even if Hannah wouldn't have told Barney, would she have told the boss?* he thought, aching and anxious. Kasper didn't look disappointed or cross enough for that, but Jakub was hard-pressed to keep from retreating out of the diner entirely.

"Jakub," said Kasper by way of greeting, and he lifted a hand toward the waitress. She headed over with a fresh mug and the coffee pot. "I trust you have a moment?"

Jakub nudged his mug toward the edge of the table in hopes of a refill as well. "Yes, sir. Can I help you?"

"I wanted to talk to you about the job tonight," said Kasper, seemingly unconcerned about the waitress overhearing as she poured their drinks. "This is an important step for us, and one not likely to be repeated anytime soon. It needs to go smoothly."

The waitress moved on, and Jakub took another long

sip of the fresh coffee. "Everything Barney described sounds on the level," he said diplomatically. "If we can follow the route down to the river once or twice before the job, that should be fine." He watched Kasper over the lip of his mug, judging. *He can't know. This can't be about Cheshire and I.* "Though if you'll excuse me for saying so...I'm surprised you gave your consent for this job at all. We don't need this payout."

"It's about the statement as much as the reward," Kasper admitted. "With this job, we'll have the clout necessary to take a final stand against Manhattan. Then things can go back to normal for a while."

"Normal," Jakub repeated doubtfully. "If Barney is able to rob a bank, I can't imagine he'll stop at one."

"He will if I tell him to," Kasper replied, leaving no room for argument. "And I say we stop after this one."

"...Of course." Rather than risk betraying more of his concern, Jakub cleared his throat. "I'm relieved to hear that."

Kasper nodded as if they had reached an understanding. "I wanted to talk to you specifically," he admitted, and Jakub grew tense again. "I heard you had some disagreement with Barney after the Hallorran robbery."

"I did," Jakub admitted, though he was still deeply uncertain of how much was safe to share with Kasper. "He didn't tell me who we were stealing from. I want to know the whole score before going into something, that's all."

Kasper nodded again. Was he so willing to forgive all slights? Though Jakub had only ever shown and felt as much respect for the man as was absolutely necessary, what little he held decreased. "That won't be a problem going forward," Kasper reassured him. "I've spoken to Hannah about it as well. I don't want to hear any more about infighting or insecurity."

"I understand, sir," said Jakub, and he was surprised and disappointed by how oblivious Kasper was to his contempt. *As if his leadership has ever amounted to anything*, he thought bitterly. *He has no idea what goes on in Kozlow.*

"You know," Kasper carried on thoughtfully, "I especially don't want to see any tension between you and Hannah." Jakub hid behind another sip of coffee. "I always hoped that the two of you might get closer with time. It would give me a lot of comfort to have you as family *officially.*"

Jakub choked and had to set his mug down. "You want

me to *marry* Hannah?"

"Don't look so embarrassed," Kasper scolded him. "It would be a good match, if for no other reason than the convenience of it." He paused a beat, waiting to read Jakub's reaction. For once his feelings must have come through, as Kasper then sighed quietly through his nose. "But not all of this old man's dreams can come true. As long as you can provide a good example to the rest of the family, that will do."

Jakub leaned back; the rest of his appetite was finished. "I'll do my best, sir."

"Good, good." Kasper tugged out his wallet and counted out a few bills, enough to cover both of them. "Go on, then," he said, motioning for Jakub to leave. "You'd better start getting ready for tonight."

"...Yes, sir. Thank you."

Jakub hurried out. It wasn't until he was crossing the street that he finally spotted Hannah in the entranceway of the Kozlow building, waiting for him. As much as he wanted to ask what *exactly* she had told Kasper for him to feel his minor lecture necessary, he didn't want to open the door to any further conversations.

"Good morning," he greeted succinctly.

Hannah got the hint. "Good morning," she said, and she motioned for them to move away from the building again. "I'm heading over to Staten Island to case the bank. We should go over the route."

"All right," said Jakub, and he followed her to her car.

They talked a bit about the job on the way over, but only that. The route Barney had laid out for the heist made sense; from the bank there were only a few turns to get onto the boulevard that would take them to a small, waterfront park. A few upscale homes had a more than decent view along the boulevard, but it would take a very dedicated river-watcher to glean any details of a troupe of robbers, given the distance, if anyone even cared to look. Jakub tucked a cigarette in his mouth and moved to the shore to look out over the water. The breeze from the northwest nudged him toward the bank and cooled the back of his neck. It was an eerie sensation.

"I haven't been on a boat since I came over," said Hannah. "Have you?"

"Not really." Jakub struck a match and cupped his hand

around it as he lit his cigarette. "I'd rather just drive one of the cars back."

"That's fine." Hannah stepped closer, and Jakub braced himself. There was nowhere to run this time. "I remember when you first joined up," she said. "Skin and bones, barely spoke, practically feral." She smiled at him, but Jakub was too wary of the point she was going to make to think it sincere. "You haven't changed a whole lot, but you *have* changed."

"And?" asked Jakub. "You're not going to propose, are you?"

Hannah sighed and rolled her eyes. "I can't believe he said something. I want you to know I have *nothing* to do with that."

"You're sure?" Jakub pressed. He had the sudden thought that he couldn't be sure of anything; he'd kept his torch for Cheshire hidden against all odds for nearly a decade, and he had no idea if anyone was capable of hiding the same.

"I'm very sure," Hannah said, still trying to be serious and light at the same time. "Please, Jakub, you're like a brother to me." Some of the humor melted off. "You know I want you to have someone who makes you happy."

Jakub tensed all over again, but before he could get any words out, Hannah continued. "I had a feeling you liked him, back when you were kids. I just thought...you grew out of it."

Grew out of it? Jakub thought, sucking hard on his cigarette. The words gnawed at him more than he ever would have expected: grew out of it, as if Cheshire were a childish fantasy, or a bad habit that needed to be overcome. An inconvenient right of passage to take part in and then discard, like Leon had.

"I didn't," Jakub said coldly.

"I didn't mean anything by it," Hannah said quickly. Her shoes scraped on the sidewalk. "I'm sorry I didn't realize, but I really wish you would have just told me."

Jakub frowned as he was forced to remember the many times Miklos had advised him of the same. "I'm...sorry," he said, uncertain if he really meant it. Even then he couldn't imagine having ever told her by choice. "But it's not like it would have made a difference. Barney's never going to accept him."

Hannah started to answer. Jakub could see the words in the pinch of her eyebrows, something like, *he might have, if he'd known about you sooner.* Or maybe, *he would if Bloom wasn't the way he is.* Some kind of instinctual defense of her family she'd been using as armor for too long. Then she closed her mouth, let that go, and tried again. "Probably not," she admitted. "Maybe it *would* be better if he just went over to Manhattan."

Jakub flinched. "Burke told you that, too?"

"It's not that I'm out to get him," Hannah continued, taking a step closer. "I don't want to see him get hurt any more than you do. Hell, he's doing a fine job of managing the Downs; maybe he can just focus on *that* from now on. But he's never really been one of us—if that hasn't changed by now, I'm not sure it ever will." She took Jakub's shoulder; he held very still. "He'll be fine on his own whatever he does, but *we* are family. We need to always remember what's really important."

Jakub stared straight ahead, once again taking in the Brooklyn skyline. Despite many trips across the river, he hardly ever spared a moment on the view of his home of many years. From this distance he couldn't hear the *clunk, clunk, clunk* of machinery, the cars blaring and muffled gunshots, but each was so familiar he could taste them in his throat. Fourteen years he'd lived there, longer than he'd lived back in Krepieç, and in that moment all he wanted to do was turn and run. Run and not look back, because nothing there really mattered anyway: not old man Kozlow skulking around the dingy apartment that he pretended was his fortress; not Barney and his back-alley soldiers who had more loyalty than sense; not even poor Hannah, the only bucket on a sinking ship.

In fact there was really only one thing that mattered, and Hannah was right: Cheshire would never belong there. Jakub took one last, long breath on his cigarette and tossed it into the water.

"You're right, Hannah," he said. "I know what's important."

Hannah eyed him as she let him go. Maybe she realized they meant different things, or maybe she didn't; Jakub didn't give her the chance to ask. "Let's drive the route one more time and then find somewhere to hole up until tonight," he said. "It's a long drive back, so no use making it now when we'll just be turning around."

"Sure," said Hannah. They started back up the bank

toward the car.

***

By the time Cheshire arrived at the Kozlow building that morning, it was only to learn that Jakub had already left for the job. He didn't have much choice but to catch a ride with Leon in the truck.

God was it awkward. Cheshire spent the entire hour-long drive fussing with his jacket; he had chosen a bulky workman's coat for the heist, uninspired as far as disguises went and not a great fit. His hair he had swept up under a cap and he was even wearing a cheaper pair of spare glasses. At a glance anyone would have mistaken him for a blue collar warehouse worker, his physique earned after years of heavy labor. He didn't like the thought much, but at least it distracted him from Leon.

"I know it seems like this came out of nowhere, but Barney's been working on this for weeks," Leon rattled on as they took the bridge out of Brooklyn. "He's thought it through, he's cased the bank. It's going to work."

"Oh, no, I believe it," said Cheshire, at a loss as to how else he could respond. "It would have been nice if he filled in *all* of us on this plan of his, but no, I'm excited. It's gonna be quite a headline!"

"Well," said Leon, and Cheshire cringed at his diplomatic tone which promised nothing he wanted to hear, "to be fair, the more people *know* about a plan, the higher chance there is of it *leaking*. Which has happened before."

Cheshire's first instinct was to rush to Burke's defense, but the reminder that they hadn't properly spoken since the day before held him back. "Yeah, I get it." He rolled down his passenger side window for some fresh air. "As long as it goes well, it's fine."

Leon squirmed behind the wheel. "Barney *is* the boss, you know," he carried on. "Everything will go smoothly if we stay in line."

"No, yeah, I understand that." Cheshire hunkered down, uninterested in any further conversation. "I'm a good little soldier."

"Bloom," Leon started, but then he sighed and shook his head. "You never change."

Cheshire pulled a face, but he wasn't in the mood to pass barbs. "How's Wanda?"

"Huh? Oh. She's good." Leon then filled the rest of the drive rambling on about his sister and nephew, allowing Cheshire to supply the bare minimum of interested responses. The thought that he would at least get to blow up a bank vault was a welcome one.

The entire crew met up at the parking lot of a local community center. Jakub and Hannah were waiting for them, leaning against the side of her car. She was talking and Jakub nodding along, which might have been a good sign, but it made Cheshire nervous all over again anyway. He climbed down from the truck and needed a bit more effort than usual to call up a grin.

"Jakub! Hannah." He tugged on his lapels. "What do you think? Will the locals recognize me?"

Hannah looked unamused, and Jakub looked...well, like he usually did, stoic and unreadable. As Cheshire drew closer, though, he thought he detected an extra intensity to Jakub's usual stare, one he was at a loss to interpret. He could only assume it was some kind of warning to keep his mouth shut.

"You look fine," said Jakub, and he definitely looked then like there was more on his mind he was holding back. "Have you been over the plan?"

"Of course." It wasn't his first robbery by a long shot after all—how hard could it be? Cheshire shrugged and tried not to make a face when Barney joined them with two of his new boys. "The boss has got the whole thing figured out, right? We're just following his lead."

"Damn right," Barney said sharply, as if trying to correct him for sarcasm. He pulled a folded paper out of his work jacket. "Now come have a look."

He spread out over the hood of Hannah's car a crude, hand-drawn map of the bank's interior, showing the positions of the exits, the tellers, and the way back to the vault. Everyone else nodded along as if they'd seen it already, so Cheshire committed as much as he could to memory and nodded, too. They each accepted a large, dark handkerchief from Barney without question, but when he offered Cheshire a revolver, that prompted some doubt.

"You know I don't need that," Cheshire said, eyeing it.

"You don't have to use it," Barney said, pushing it at him insistently. "But you're supposed to be in disguise, so you need to wave *something* at the tellers." Cheshire frowned at the image, but he accepted the gun and tucked it into his belt.

After killing a bit more of the time until dusk—which was spent mostly listening to Barney brag about how bewildered Manhattan would be—they split up to their vehicles again, steeled and ready for the heist.

"Chesh," said Jakub, catching him just as he was about to climb back up into the truck with Leon. His eyebrows were drawn tight and he lowered his voice ominously. "You're bringing the truck back to the Kozlow building after we're done, right?"

"Yeah?" Cheshire turned toward him, one hand still on the open door and his pulse suddenly in his ears. "That's the plan."

"Stick around after, okay?" Jakub held his gaze gravely. "We should talk."

"Oh." Cheshire managed to smile instead of gulp, barely. "Sure thing." He tipped his chin past him. "But you'd better get back before Hannah hears that."

Jakub snorted, but he took the warning seriously; Hannah really was still watching them as she tugged open her own car door. "Good luck in there," Jakub said, and he turned to jog back to her. Cheshire breathed a sigh and continued into the truck.

THE HEIST

Leon drove them the few blocks to the bank and parked in a nearby alley. As per the plan, he opened the back bay door to reveal nailed vegetable crates. He then sat himself down in the back to smoke a cigarette as if just a regular driver on a break while Barney parked on the sidewalk nearby, leaving his Chicago muscle to take the wheel. There was a sharp, determined energy to Barney's posture as he disembarked, too immature for it to be mistaken for confidence. It set Cheshire on edge as he fell into step alongside him. A real bank heist—it should have been a thrill, but with Barney leading the charge and him not being allowed to make a show of it, he was finding it hard to work up his usual enthusiasm. There wasn't anything clever or artful in waving a gun at frightened civilians.

"Don't forget, these people aren't like back in Brooklyn," Barney warned as they approached the entrance to the bank. "They don't know you well enough not to sell you out, so don't give yourself away."

"I remember," Cheshire reassured him, and they each donned their handkerchief masks. *I just have to stay in line for now, and everything will get better.*

The second car pulled up to the sidewalk directly in front of the bank entrance, and Jakub and Hannah climbed out with their faces already covered. Jakub hefted his rifle to his shoulder, and his solid, unhurried gait as he headed for the door put Barney to shame. As much as Cheshire had seen him in action, he couldn't help a little shiver of awe: *this* was certainly the hardened, skillful criminal he had spent his childhood foolishly idolizing, so easy in his role that Cheshire wished he could have committed it to film.

Jakub entered the bank first and immediately sprayed a line of bullets across the far wall—much too high to risk hitting anyone, but enough to blast the wooden molding off the tops of the line of tellers, casting splinters and one shattered clock onto the terrified employees. Barney shouldered his way in right after, bellowing, "Nobody move! This is a robbery!"

"We're regular cowboys now, huh?" Cheshire remarked to Hannah as they entered right behind, but she didn't spare him a glance let alone a response.

"Hands up!" Jakub ordered, making an adorable effort to hide his accent as he herded the bank's only three customers into a corner next to an overpaid and underprepared security guard. "Don't try anything. Lie down—keep your heads down and I won't shoot you."

Hannah shot her way into the teller booths, and amidst the whimpers and shrieks she cornered the workers back below the countertops. So far so smooth, at least. Cheshire drew his gun just so he would fit in and swept his gaze across the lobby. Just as they'd hoped the number of patrons and staff numbered under a dozen, and the neighborhood was well-off enough that none of them had ever suspected a bank robbery to reach them. No one was inclined to fight back or make a scene.

None except for the security guard, apparently; as Cheshire passed by Jakub and his hostages on his way toward the back, he noticed the aging man in a security uniform reaching for the weapon on his belt. Cheshire leveled his revolver at the man and thumbed back the hammer, though he kept his finger far from the trigger.

"Ah, ah, old-timer," Cheshire scolded. He crouched down and held out his other hand. "These look like fine people; let's not make things harder for them, hm?"

The security guard went pale, and without any further hint of resistance he allowed Cheshire to take his gun. His hands shook, and Cheshire felt rotten for it as he straightened up and followed Barney into the back.

By then Barney had cornered the bank manager and

what might have been her assistant in a side office. Cheshire could just about see him grinning full through his mask. "Like candy, huh?" he bragged, and he waved Cheshire over. "Keep an eye on these two while I handle the vault."

Cheshire scrunched his nose as he took Barney's place opposite the manager and assistant, his gun only loosely aimed in their direction. "Don't you mean the other way around?" he asked. "Or did our friend here tell you the combination?"

Barney gave a bark of laughter that Cheshire *definitely* didn't like as he headed toward the vault. "Oh, don't worry," he said. "I've got it."

The bank vault door was an immense steel square, crouched up against the far wall like a guardian sentinel. Cheshire looked from the turn-handle to the hinges, assessing each for the easiest point to blow, just in case whatever combination the manager had given up didn't pan out. It took him a few moments to realize that when Barney reached for the dial, it wasn't to put in any numbers; instead he wedged something into the mechanism, then moved to the other side to do the same at the hinges. Satisfied with whatever he was up to, he then jogged back past Cheshire and pulled out his gun.

It wasn't a weapon Cheshire had ever seen before, though he recognized the intricate engraving on the revolver's barrel and grip enough that he didn't need to guess. Barney thumbed back the hammer with a loud, distinct *clink*. "Hey," said Cheshire, turning away from the manager. "You don't really think that's—"

Barney fired. In an instant, the short hall leading to the vault became a fireball. Cheshire reared back as several explosions detonated nearly at once, sending a wave of blistering heat and choking smoke screaming at them. He crashed into the manager and her assistant, ears ringing painfully and balance reeling, the revolver falling forgotten from his grip. For several seconds he couldn't properly see or hear, but he felt the shuddering impact of the vault door against the marble floor, and soon after, scorching heat along his arm and hand.

His glove and jacket sleeve were on fire. Too stunned even to curse, Cheshire frantically patted himself out and finally resorted to ripping both gloves off. His palms burned with a heat they—for once—weren't the cause of, and his heart pounded against his ribs.

"Shit!" Barney tore his singed cap off and slapped it against his thigh to rid it of embers. He smelled like burnt hair but there was glee in the part of his face Cheshire could see, and together they looked to the vault.

Hallorran's revolver—or rather, it's ammunition—had done the job admirably: the vault door had had its lock and hinges blasted apart and lay face down on the ground with its insides embarrassingly exposed. The walls and ceiling were badly charred but the building itself hadn't caught, leaving only plumes of smoke between the robbers and their prize. Barney let out a triumphant shout at the sight. "Did you fucking see that?" he gloated, and he opened his jacket to reveal two large sacks tied around his midsection. "C'mon, let's grab the loot and go!"

Cheshire followed dumbly. He blinked at the twisted, jagged hinges as he climbed with Barney over the safe door into the vault. The smoke stung his throat even through his facemask, acrid and unfamiliar to him, and he felt as if his teeth were still rattling from the blast. Were explosions always so jarring when someone else set them off? When Barney tossed one of the sacks to him he followed his lead, shoveling bags of cash and a few heavy-seeming safety deposit boxes inside.

"Hey," he said as they sinched their full sacks tight. "So I guess that's the Hallorran revolver I've heard so much about? Was that really the right way to do this?"

Barney laughed as he dragged his sack over his shoulder. "What's the matter?" he taunted, eyes gleaming wickedly. "You didn't think I'd need *you* for this, did you?"

The words struck Cheshire hard, and he couldn't react even when Barney laughed and shouldered past him. His stomach clenched with nausea as he struggled to keep up. *Not needed?* he thought, and his heart raced all over again. By the time they charged out of the back room, he was sweating. *He brought me here just to show me I'm not needed.* He clenched his jaw until it ached.

***

Jakub didn't have any trouble keeping the bank patrons in line. Most of them were either rather young or very old, and after watching the security guard give up so easily, they kept their heads down and their mouths shut. His rifle was intimidating enough even that Hannah was able to take her eyes off the tellers and fill a sack from each of the stations.

The explosion from the back had everyone ducking beneath their hands. Jakub quieted them back down with only a few words, despite a ripple of apprehension up his spine. The explosion sounded different—it *smelled* different. Cheshire's magic was so familiar to him that even the vibrations echoing up through the floor felt wrong against the soles of his feet. He wanted to head into the vault to check, but by then Hannah was finishing with her sack and she motioned for him to clear a path to the door. They would have to get a move on if they were going to outrun cops to the waterfront.

Barney and Cheshire dashed out from the back moments later. Though they were still masked, even just a glimpse of Cheshire's pinched, harried eyes convinced Jakub that he had been right, and something had gone wrong. With Barney hollering for retreat there wasn't anything he could do about it, though, so after firing one more spray down the line of registers, Jakub followed the rest of them out onto the street.

A few people had gathered in the general store opposite them to watch, drawn by the commotion. Police sirens wailed from somewhere down the street, their cars not yet visible but still too close for Jakub's liking. There wasn't time to ask Cheshire about the explosion, as he and Barney were already dashing toward the corner, and Hannah was dragging her loot into the back seat of their getaway car. Jakub leapt into the passenger seat and Barney's goon hit the gas; they tore away from the curb almost before Jakub could get his door closed.

In the back seat, Hannah twisted to watch behind them. "So far, so good," she said with cautious optimism. "I think we made good time."

"That explosion didn't sound right," said Jakub, "but at least they got the vault open."

Beside him, their driver laughed. He was one of Barney's new Chicago friends that Jakub had never bothered introducing himself to, stocky with thick biceps. "You just haven't been down to the quarry," he said. "You'd've recognized it, if you had."

Jakub frowned at him; it took him a beat to catch his meaning. "The Hallorran?" His ears rang with the memory of that night on the pier, and the heavy, distinctive *clink* of the revolver's unique hammer.

"Of course. How else would you open a vault like that, without an expert cracker?"

Jakub ground his teeth, and he turned to cast Hannah a look. She spared only a brief wince before turning her attention to the street behind them. Jakub settled in his seat once more. *This isn't just a message to Manhattan, then,* he thought, gripping the stock of the rifle crammed in with him. *He's going to sideline Cheshire for good.*

Maybe that was what Hannah had been getting at, back at the riverside: maybe she was hoping he'd convince Cheshire to lay low for good, worry about tenants and bureaucracy and leave the real gang work to the family that *mattered.* The thought made him sick to his stomach.

Luckily, he didn't have time to dwell on it; as soon as they turned right onto Richmond Terrace, a black and white blew through the light coming from the west and fell in behind them. A moment later its sirens blared to life, and Hannah cursed.

"I said too much," she muttered, and then she leaned forward to talk to their driver. "Can you lose him?"

"Hold on," he replied, and they braced themselves as he jerked the wheel suddenly, barely making the turn onto a side street.

Jakub leaned his head out the window to watch the police car screeching past the turn, its front wheels bouncing on the sidewalk. By the time it had backed up and righted its course, their driver had turned again; Jakub had to jerk back inside as they nearly clipped the side of a parked car. "That car wasn't coming from the bank," he said as he kept an eye out through the side mirror instead. "That must have been bad luck."

"We have to lose it before we get to the water," Hannah cautioned.

The driver grunted. "Don't worry; I know what I'm doing."

He made another dangerous left on the narrow, residential streets; Jakub heard a few startled shrieks from bystanders on the sidewalks. The route took them straight back to the waterfront drive they had left, and they continued on at a more leisurely pace, fitting into the flow of traffic for a few minutes before ducking again through the side streets.

"The boss had me learn this area good," the driver bragged, and though Jakub frowned, he couldn't dispute it.

They reached the rendezvous point in just under twenty minutes, as planned. Stas was waiting with the boat pulled up close to the shore, its engine running: it was an old fishing boat, twenty footer, with low sides and made from sturdy wood. The second car was already parked on the street; Barney and his driver were wrestling two sacks out of the back.

Jakub climbed out of the car and hefted the rifle to his shoulder. He could still hear police sirens much closer than they should have been, and watching Barney laugh breathlessly as he carried his loot down to the boat made him wonder if they'd had a close call with the coppers, too. *If they see us get on this boat, Chesh's truck decoy won't be worth much*, he thought, turning away from them to watch the street.

The sirens wailed louder than ever, and from around the nearest corner a cop car swerved onto their isolated side street. There was far too little time to think: the cop in the passenger side already had his window down, and he immediately opened fire, the first two bullets shattering glass while another three buried in the head and shoulders of the stocky driver. He was dead before he could draw his gun. Too far to make a run for the shore, Jakub threw himself down next to the car's wheels and crawled to put as much metal and rubber between him and the gunfire as possible.

Don't kill cops, Jakub reminded himself as he put his back to the front bumper. Even when a second black and white pulled [NEW YORK!]Bang!Bang!BOOM! in behind the first, guns blazing, he carefully lowered himself to the ground and took aim at the cruisers themselves, aiming for their tires and bumpers. If he could just hold them off long enough to make a run for the boat—

The first of the two cruisers erupted in a fireball. Even crouched behind another car Jakub felt the rush of hot air and licking flames, and he had to cover his face with his sleeve. Smoke and ash stuck in his hair and set him coughing. His body ached with the unfamiliarity of the blast, and for several seconds he couldn't get his bearings while officers hollered for retreat. Then Hannah had him by the arm, dragging him up. He barely managed to keep a tight enough grip on his rifle as he let her drag him down the slope to the river. His feet striking water jolted him fully aware, and with Barney yanking at him from above, he dragged himself into the boat with Hannah close behind.

"Go!" Barney shouted, and the boat lurched clumsily away from the shore. As Stas turned the bow around, the cops on the shore collected themselves; everyone flinched and ducked for cover as several rounds struck the hull. But the boat kept going, and as soon as Barney had his balance he was aiming his revolver again at the shore.

"Wait!" Jakub shouted, snagging hold of his jacket. "You'll kill them!"

Barney fired anyway, and this time it was his own car that exploded in a plume of fire. The remaining cops on the waterfront dove to the ground as they were showered with red-hot debris. The pause in their gunfire was all that was needed, and with the boat engine roaring, the Kozlow gang made their retreat across the water.

"They're not getting my car," said Barney, and then he tugged his handkerchief off and laughed, sharp and a little manic. "Shit. Is anyone hit?"

"They killed Nowak," said Hannah, sounding largely unconcerned; she was focused on Jakub, patting him down for injuries. "Are you all right?"

Jakub tugged his mask down and was grateful for the fresh breeze off the water as he took in a great gulp of air. "I'm fine," he said, combing the ashes out of his hair. He turned toward Barney. "Did you kill any cops?"

"I dunno. Maybe." Barney holstered his revolver and sat down on the side wall of the boat. "Shit, Nowak, huh? In that case I hope I got one or two at least."

"You should be hoping you didn't," Jakub shot back. "This was supposed to be about making a statement, not drawing a whole new burrough down on our heads."

Barney pulled a face. "What's a bunch of sleepy Staten Island pigs gonna do to *us*?"

"They just killed Nowak!" the second driver protested, and Barney at least had the decency to look guilty. He stood and took the man by the shoulders.

"And I got them back for it, did you see?" Barney said,

and Jakub had to move toward the rear to get further away from him, for his temper's sake. "They're gonna think twice before messing with us again, that's for sure."

Jakub leaned his rifle against the side and sat down at the stern of the boat, letting the churning of the engine block out whatever else Barney was saying to the others. *Manhattan was always going to retaliate for this*, he thought, watching the thick, tarry smoke rising up from the two destroyed cars on the shore. They were already far enough away that the officers moving around them were tiny and hard to make out. *But now cops looking to avenge their own?* He glanced back to Barney, who was leaning close to Stas as he steered the ship and clapping him on the back. *All for Barney's ego. This is never going to get any better.* Hannah tried to meet his gaze, so he ducked his head and began searching his jacket for a cigarette. *It's only going to get worse, and I never belonged here to begin with.*

Jakub tucked the cigarette between his lips, but as he resumed his search this time for matches, he felt something wet lap against his ankle. He glanced down, thinking that his soaked pants had just shifted uncomfortably, only to realize there was a puddle a few inches deep at the stern of the boat. And it was growing.

"Hey!" he called, cigarette falling from his mouth. "Hannah!"

***

Cheshire and Leon didn't have any trouble crossing the bridge into New Jersey. It was nearly a straight shot from the bank across the river, and there was just no way the cops had time to prepare a defense on either side of the bridge so quickly. Halfway across Cheshire had thrown his jacket and cap off the side, taking his only pleasure of the evening so far in watching them flutter off to get ruined on the shore somewhere. Good riddance.

Now dressed in a purple vest, his hair down and combed, he felt as if the weight of anonymity had been lifted, even if he wished he'd thought to bring an extra pair of gloves. But he still didn't feel *right*, not by a long shot.

"That big gun of Barney's is really something, huh?" he rambled, leaning back in his seat as Leon drove them onto the boulevard. "Makes a great big *boom*, and I know a thing or two about *booms*, believe me. You ever see that thing go off?"

"Yeah, plenty," replied Leon guardedly. "He's been practicing."

He looked just as uncomfortable as Cheshire felt, but that didn't stop the stream of nonsense coming out of Cheshire's mouth. "Hallorran really outdid herself," he continued. "Big ol' fireball like that. Nearly singed my eyebrows off! I could'a done it just as easily, mind, and with a bit more finesse. Would have spared my gloves!" He laughed, even though Leon giving him a side-eye made his humor curdle in his stomach. "But yeah, he sure is proud of the damn thing. And it did the job, can't argue with that."

"You sound jealous," said Leon, and if only he had managed to inject some teasing into his voice, Cheshire could have easily laughed it off. As it was, it sounded like a warning, and it made Cheshire's already anxious stomach clench and harden.

"It's not like that," Cheshire insisted. He knew that saying more would only make things worse, but he couldn't help himself. "I don't care if he wants to use his fancy gun to blow things up—I can do that on my own time whenever I want! What difference does it make who pulls the trigger as long as it works? And it did."

"Uh-huh."

"Just seems like a waste, is all. He's gonna run out of those fancy bullets eventually, but *this* well never runs dry."

He waved his hand at Leon, only to remember a beat too late that he wasn't wearing his gloves. Leon glanced over, and his brow furrowed. Had he seen the brand carved into Cheshire's palm? Whether he had or not, Cheshire had only one method of recourse: he just kept talking. "Unless he thinks he can just rob Hallorran *again*, but she's on to him now, and Jake and I won't help him a second time."

Leon continued to eye him warily. "You speak for Jakub, now?"

"Huh?" There wasn't any reason to panic over a question like that; everyone knew that Jakub had every reason to leave Hallorran the hell alone. Explaining that should have been a few simple words, but after the confrontations that morning, and the sudden thought that Leon of all people would be extra eager to rat him out to Barney, Cheshire couldn't put his thoughts in proper order. "Uh, no. Of course not. But Jakub, you know, he has history with Hallorran. He was real mad about the last one—I'm sure he's not keen on a round two. I mean, I really think."

"Right," Leon said slowly, and Cheshire could just *feel* Jakub's icy stare from across the distance between them, and he finally stopped talking.

Their trip through Jersey was surprisingly uneventful, to the point that Cheshire started to worry. A heavy truck speeding through the city, across bridges and countryside, should have drawn some concern. He wasn't much of a decoy if no one took notice. It was even a relief when they entered Jersey City and began to see black and whites throughout the downtown, but they still didn't encounter any real resistance until falling in line for the tunnel to Manhattan. By then Cheshire had his window rolled down and was leaning against the door, eager to be spotted by *someone*, and he was rewarded with several officers parked alongside the toll booths pointing to him as they shared furious whispers.

"It's about time," Cheshire muttered as one of the police cars started flashing their lights. The officers motioned for Leon to pull over, which he did.

"You didn't put anything in the van, right?" Leon asked, looking a little pale as four police officers headed toward them, and one of the patrol cars maneuvered in front of them to prevent them from speeding off. "You're sure it all went in the cars?"

"I'm sure, Leon," said Cheshire, cracking his knuckles. "It's just veggies back there. Let me do the talking."

The officers spread out, two on each side, and the highest ranking of them—a middle-aged woman Cheshire had no hope of charming with good humor—stopped just beyond the passenger side door. She was already unsnapping her gun holster. "Good evening, sir. Heading into Manhattan?"

"Ma'am," Cheshire greeted in return. Now that the game was on he felt much more like himself, and he settled on a restrained but definitely cheeky smirk. "Just passing through. We're on our way to Brooklyn."

"Are you." She had a suspicious gleam in her eyes that made it clear she didn't need any extra hints to know exactly who he was. Without any loot on him, Cheshire found it easy to enjoy the infamy free of worry. "What's in the truck?"

"Vegetables! Potatoes and onions mostly. There's a little diner down on Bedford that makes a mean vegetable soup." Cheshire gestured as he spoke out of habit, though he forced himself to stop when her sharp gaze reminded him again about his bare palms. "I'm a friend of Edith, the owner. Got her a deal on produce from out in Long Valley."

The officer did not look one inch convinced. "Do you mind if I have a look?"

"Not at all!"

Cheshire swung his door open, and the officers each stepped back, eyeing him warily as he climbed down from the cab. Leon disembarked as well, hands half raised as if unsure what to do with them. Cheshire tried to make up for his lack of confidence by doing a little turn to show off his lack of weapon. "You can search me, too, while you're at it," he invited. "I've got nothing on me."

The woman stayed back, a hand on her gun, while one of the other officers took him up on it. Finding nothing, they herded him toward the second police car parked at the back of the truck. He stayed still and obedient, smiling pleasantly at his apparent guard dog while the others opened up the rear.

As promised, only wooden crates labeled for produce lay inside. It was only then that Cheshire realized he had no idea where Barney had gotten the goods from to begin with, and he couldn't help but hold his breath as the first was pried open. An officer reached inside and pulled out a large cabbage.

"You said potatoes and onions," the woman officer said, eyeing Cheshire.

"Mostly," he corrected her.

"Long Valley, hm?" the woman prodded as her compatriots continued to root through the truck's contents. "Dreary out there, isn't it?"

Cheshire shrugged. "It's all right."

"Which farm did you say you picked up from?"

You think you're gonna catch me like this? Cheshire thought, unable to help a smirk. "If you have to ask, you haven't been out there," he said breezily. "You could just read the label on the crates."

She returned his humor with icy irritation. "Excuse me.

I just didn't expect to finally meet the famous Cheshire Bloom hauling turnips like a common workhorse."

Cheshire shrugged again. "Potatoes and onions. Mostly."

The woman glared at him, but she was interrupted by one of the toll booth operators jogging toward them. He tipped his cap and offered the officer a slip of paper. "Excuse me, ma'am, but we heard back from the Staten—"

The woman cut him off with a hard look as she accepted the paper. After a quick scan her eyebrows rose; Cheshire pretended only polite curiosity when she looked to him.

"Well, Mr. Bloom?" she asked. "Would you like to hear the latest from Staten Island Police?"

Cheshire's natural instincts guided his mouth into a barely interested half smile. "Why? Is there competition out there I haven't heard about yet?"

"See for yourself," she replied, and she handed over the paper.

Whatever this says, don't you dare make a face, Cheshire told himself firmly as he accepted. The toll booth agent's handwriting was barely legible in the fading light, and he held it close to his face, hoping that by squinting he could help cover up any reaction to the hastily scrawled words: *Robbers running by boat, 1 killed, 2 cops, boat hit.*

Cheshire handed it back. He was pretty confident the officer wouldn't be able to glean any panic in his expression; he was less sure she wouldn't hear his pulse thumping out of his ears. "By boat!" he declared. "That's a new one—wish I'd thought of it. Do they think it's Lucky?"

"No," the officer retorted, losing some of her patience. "No, they don't." She glared at him a moment longer, waiting for a proper reaction, only to scowl. "You're a real piece of work, Mr. Bloom."

"I get that all the time," Cheshire replied automatically, though his mind was spinning. *If the boat's been made already, there's no point in us wasting our time here.* He swallowed. *It can't be Jakub. He's fine.* "Well then, if you're done rifling through our cabbages, we'll be on our way."

"No." The woman waved to the officers in the back of the truck, who were each keeping one eye on the goings on outside. "Keep opening up those crates—I want to see inside each one."

"You don't have a warrant for that," said Cheshire, and though his smile remained in place, the humor behind it sloughed off. He raised his voice so the rest of her officers would be sure to hear. "So unless you have a real good reason for having pulled us over, we'd like to go now."

"There's been a robbery," the officer insisted, "and *you*, in your entirety, are probable cause enough." She poked him in the chest while still keeping one hand on her gun. "And you're going to stand right there until every one of these crates has been checked."

Cheshire held up his hands in surrender and promised to do just that. He glanced to Leon, who could only stare back, confused and anxious. *Even if we could break through the tolls, we can't do them any good if we get trapped in the tunnel. We just have to wait.* He leaned back against the patrol car and tried to look passably casual. *Jakub can handle it.*

***

Jakub heaved another bucketful of water overboard, but it didn't seem to be doing much good. They'd already tossed as much weight as they could bear, save for the heist loot and a few life preservers, which Stas had insisted on seeing as he couldn't swim. Jakub didn't say anything on that but he wasn't all that confident about his chances, either—he hadn't been in water over his head since he was a young boy.

I was supposed to be driving the car back, he thought, emptying yet another bucket. The water kept leaking in, every inch submerged allowing for more of the bullet holes in their hull to take on the river. It wouldn't be long before the engine flooded completely. "Barney! We have to make for land!"

"We are!" Barney snapped back. He'd finally lost that smug grin of his at least, and he turned to Stas. "Why aren't you heading east? We need land!"

Stas, already wearing one of the preservers around his neck, wiped sweat from his brow. "You said not to! If we get too close to Governors Island there could be military—you said so!"

Barney cursed and looked to the island—they all did. The lines of soldiers barracks were only barely visible from the water, but there definitely were lights flicking on along the pier, and it didn't take much imagination to paint figures on the shore as war-deprived soldiers willing to take up vengeance for murdered cops. Lights on the water to the west and southwest proved there were plenty of police themselves on their tail, and way too much distance between them and their port. Even if they were able to continue up the river as planned, too many people knew how they'd made their escape, and soon every pier along the shore would be occupied.

"Then the closet land is Manhattan," said Hannah, voicing the conclusion each of them had hoped to avoid. "We make for Battery Park and risk the rest on foot."

The jagged Manhattan skyline had never looked quite so foreboding. *Lucky will have heard about the heist by now,* Jakub thought. *She'll know it's us.* He ached for a cigarette. "She's right. We won't make it if we have to circle Governor's Island."

Barney scrubbed his fist across his mouth. "Fuck, you're right." He slapped Stas on the back. "Get to the park. We can land where the ferry does."

"O-Okay!"

The rest of them went back to bailing out the boat as best they could, using buckets and oars and hands. The boat continued to sink. Stas pushed it as fast as it would go, but they were still almost thirty feet from shore when the motor gave out with a pathetic sputter. By then Barney had at least had the good idea to tie as many of the life jackets together as he could, making a decent raft for them to load the bank loot along with Jakub's rifle. Stas refused to give up his.

"You'll be fine," Barney reassured him impatiently as they floated the makeshift raft out over the back end of the boat, which was almost completely submerged by then. "Just hold on to the money and keep kicking. It's not hard."

Jakub shuddered as the water sloshed up to his thighs. There was nothing to do but continue forward, and he tried to keep his prosthetic gripped to his rifle and out of the water as the boat fell away beneath his feet. *I wonder if Cheshire can swim,* he thought, focusing on that idle curiosity to hold back the panic that threatened to bite its way up his spine the higher the water climbed. *Probably. He can do whatever he sets his mind to.*

"You okay?" asked Hannah, staying close at his side as they began the slow kick to shore. Jakub nodded but didn't want to open his mouth so close to the river surface. *If we get out of this, I'm taking Cheshire's bathrobe,* he promised himself.

By the time they reached the shore a small crowd had gathered, drawn by the spectacle of their boat gurgling beneath the water. Two men had even jumped the railing along the park shore and were waiting with arms outstretched to "rescue" them from the river. Stas reached them first, thanking the strangers over and over as they pulled him onto the concrete promenade, then Hannah and the driver of the second car. As Jakub reached the shore, however, he didn't have much choice but to pass his rifle up to Hannah, which their savoirs took clear notice of.

"Getting late for a swim," a middle aged man teased, but cautiously, as he offered Jakub his hand. "What happened to your boat?"

"None of your business," Barney retorted, though he then had to shove the revolver between his teeth to keep it dry as he passed up one of the money bags.

Jakub allowed the man to haul him up onto solid ground. Once his feet were planted he felt steadier, though not any less anxious; the strangers were looking to each other, and the telltale whine of approaching police sirens seemed to alert them to the situation they'd stumbled into. He could feel his nerves beginning to unravel, and determined not to be caught off guard again, he grabbed his rifle from Hannah and leveled it at the small group of bystanders.

"Up against the railing, *now,*" he ordered, prodding the older man who had helped him up with the barrel. "Get down on your knees and keep your hands on the top rung."

"What the hell is going on?" the man protested, but another, harder poke shut him up, and he and the others nervously complied.

Barney and his two men continued pulling up the money while Hannah moved deeper into the park. "We have to go," she called back to them, the blaring of sirens drawing ever closer. "If we have to leave one—"

"No!" Barney insisted, and he finally dragged the last sack over the rail. "We've got it—let's go."

They made a run for the parking lot. It was still early enough that several cars were about, their owners spread out across the park. They bolted to the nearest, an older Ford with a push ignition that couldn't have been easier to steal. Jakub wondered if it belonged to one of the men they'd accosted as they piled inside and tore out onto the street.

As soon as they had turned a corner and were out of sight on the park, Hannah slowed to a much more leisurely pace. "We can't keep going like this," she said, slapping long strands of wet hair out of her face. "There's no way they won't shut down the bridge before we can get there."

"There's nowhere safe for us in Manhattan," said Jakub, crammed in the back seat with Stas and the Chicago driver. He had to struggle to position his rifle in the tight space. "If the cops don't find us, Lucky will."

"But we *can't* go to the bridge," Hannah insisted. "Cops are dead—they'll shoot us on sight."

But Masterson won't? Jakub thought. He honestly wasn't sure. "Then let's go north, as far as we can. We'll stay away from the rivers and find somewhere to hole up."

"Harlem," said Barney, snapping his fingers as if it were a brilliant idea. "We'll head north into Harlem. Cops won't think of that!"

Jakub started to protest, though again he couldn't immediately think of whether it was a decent idea or a terrible one. "That's Big Mitt's territory, and they've thrown in with Lucky. What if they rat us out?"

"They'll have to find us first," replied Barney. "And if that fucker Masterson comes sniffing around, we'll play it like Mitts let us in. Shake them up."

That would only work if we had Cheshire, Jakub thought, biting down hard on the impulse to say as much. *He can talk his way out of anything.*

His doubt must have been radiating, though, as Hannah cleared her throat. "I don't see we have much other choice, rather than break into some building at random. Cops will be watching the shores—we need to get off the streets, and no one will expect us north."

"Fine," said Jakub, and he and the others hunkered down in their seats as best they could, hoping not to attract any attention.

It was slow going through the city. Hannah was an excellent driver, her ears ever vigilant for the sound of distant or approaching sirens, and she maneuvered the streets with perfect caution that was nevertheless agonizing. Crammed down in his seat with his rifle wedged in beside him, Jakub was sore and buzzing with anxiety by the time they reached Harlem. Hannah drew them to a halt along the side of the street and twisted her door open. "Everyone stay quiet," she hissed, and they piled out.

She had brought them to a large public park, its entrance bordered by tall trees, a short, wrought-iron fence separating the street from a squat municipal building. By then it was late enough in the evening for the facility to be closed, but not so late that it would seem unusual for employees to be working, or for park visitors to be lingering inside the grounds. The five of them crept up to the municipal building; Jakub made sure to reach the door first before anyone could suggest blowing through the lock. After working his metal fingers a few times to get an idea of the necessary force, he closed his fist around the door knob until the metal contorted, and he was able to shear the assembly off.

"Beats having to pick it, huh?" Barney whispered, patting Jakub on the back. "Good work."

Jakub pursed his lips. "Sure," he said, and he led the way inside.

The interior was dark. Everyone breathed a sigh of relief as they moved down the entry hall. There were only a few offices in the building, two large supply closets, and at the far end an activities room that doubled as a cafeteria. After making sure all the curtains were drawn, they all sprawled out on the floor of the large room to catch their breath and let their nerves unwind.

"As long as no one saw us come in, we should be safe for a while," said Hannah. She pulled a chair close to the double door entrance and sat down with a long sigh. "Fuck."

"Fuck," Barney agreed, but now that they were in relative safety, he couldn't keep from grinning. "We made it, though."

"We haven't 'made it' until we're back in Brooklyn," Jakub scolded him. He shrugged out of his soaked jacket and was tempted to take off his shoes, but that seemed like tempting fate one step too far. "This was really stupid."

"It wouldn't have been stupid if it had worked," Barney retorted. "And it would have worked if the fucking pigs hadn't shot through the boat."

"We're not going to argue over what went wrong," Hannah interrupted. "It doesn't matter, because we're not doing anything like it again, ever." She fixed Barney with a hard eye. "Boss's orders."

Barney rolled his eyes, but his hand shook as he slicked his hair back. Maybe he had some inkling of how close the call had been after all. "Yeah, I know, but at least we got the loot. There's got to be a million dollars in here!"

"A million?" Stas repeated, perking up. "Honest?"

"Honest! You can help count it when we get back." Barney grinned wickedly. "And we did it all ourselves."

We're not back yet, Jakub wanted to say again, but he busied himself with spying through one of the windows outward. It seemed quiet, but there was a building full of apartments across the street, and there was no telling who might have been looking out of the dozens of windows there. *We're not home free by a long shot.*

There wasn't anything to do but wait, so Jakub checked his rifle to make sure it hadn't been water damaged and settled in.

***

"This is a bad idea," said Leon, yet again, as he buckled himself into the truck's passenger seat. "We should be at the bridge."

"If they made it to the east shore, they're home free," reasoned Cheshire, his tone level despite all ten fingers drumming the steering wheel. "If they didn't, we can't help them until we figure out where they are, and we're not going to do that driving around aimlessly in a vegetable truck."

"Then shouldn't we be following the cops?" Leon persisted. "They were the ones tailing the boat in the first place."

Cheshire shook his head, though he kept his attention locked on the hotel they were parked across from. "We won't know if the coppers we choose to follow are heading toward the others or toward another roadblock until it's too late." He stopped fidgeting to instead grip the wheel tight. "But Masterson isn't going anywhere until he knows where. If he steps out of that building, we'll know Barney and the others have been made."

Leon continued to squirm. "And if he spots *us?*"

"Then I guess I'll just blow him up!" Cheshire replied, and he laughed. "Leon, calm down. You're safer with me than anyone else, and you know that." He glared up at the Four Thrones; his palms already felt hot and itchy, and he wasn't sure if it was dread or anticipation hopping him up. "I can handle Masterson."

"Okay..."

They waited unspeaking for another fifteen minutes, watching as traffic gradually thinned into a sparser than usual night time crowd. A few cars pulled up to the Four Thrones that emptied familiar-looking thugs, though Cheshire couldn't be sure if they were moving any faster than usual. *Jakub's fine,* he told himself over and over as he went back to drumming his fingers. *He's fine, he's always fine. You'd know by now if he wasn't. Somehow.* He swallowed. *He said we should talk, and it seemed important, so no way he's letting himself get killed before then.*

At last the main doors opened, and out strolled Herb himself, Camilla on his arm and a posse at his back. As they split up to their vehicles Cheshire started the truck up. "Don't worry," Cheshire told Leon preemptively. "I'll only follow close enough that we don't lose them." His lips quirked. "I'm sure even if he does spot us, he'll let us tag along. He'll want to give me an earful for this."

"That's not encouraging," said Leon, but he had no choice other than to hold on as Cheshire pulled onto the street behind the Manhattan entourage.

***

Jakub and his compatriots waited in the municipal building for over an hour, watching the occasional car drive by. A police car made a pass at one point, and Jakub held his breath, but it moved on without raising any alarm. Still, his tension never unwound, and even as the others took a few minutes of sleep where they could, he remained strictly vigilant.

"I think they've made us," he said, taking up his rifle.

Hannah joined him cautiously at the window and peered out. He pointed her toward two tall men leaning against the wall of the apartment building opposite them, next to an open window. Both were standing close together and chatting inaudibly as they passed a cigarette back and forth. It didn't seem that either was paying much attention to the park, but that only made Jakub more concerned. It would have been more natural if they *did* look over occasionally.

"How long have they been there?" Hannah asked.

"One came out not long after we got here. The other almost half an hour ago." Jakub chewed his lip. "I don't like it."

As they watched, a third figure climbed out of the open window to join them: a burly woman wearing a holster. The man currently holding the cigarette offered her a puff, and they continued to cluster together. She cast only one look at their car parked across the street and then turned her back.

"I don't know," Hannah said, squinting at them. "It's hard to tell."

"They know we're here," Jakub insisted. "We should go."

Without waiting for Hannah to agree, Jakub began moving around the room, urging the rest of their companions up. "Barney, we have to go," he said, pushing the money bags toward him. "We'll come out the other side of the park—there has to be a closed business we can break into or something."

"You're sure?" Barney asked, screwing his cap into place.

Jakub was spared from having to answer when Hannah cursed, and she hurried to help Jakub rouse the others. As Jakub struggled into his still-wet coat, he risked a glance across the street: a car had pulled up to the curb behind theirs, and the three figures from across the street were headed toward it. One held open the rear door and out climbed Big Mitts.

With his own curses Jakub made for the kitchen, everyone quickly following. As he'd hoped there was an outside door, and they all rushed through it, keeping as close to the building as possible to avoid being seen as they circled around back. What sounded like a shout of recognition spurred Jakub faster, and before anyone could consider standing their ground he charged ahead deeper into the park.

"Don't even *think* about firing on Mitts," he demanded of Barney as he led the group off the normal path. There were very few trees or other obstacles to provide cover—they could only hope to reach the other side and find another building as shelter. "We'll never survive a shootout."

"I got it, I got it," Barney wheezed, all out of bravado and gripping one of the loot bags tight.

More shouts chased them down the length of the park. "We know it's you, Kozlow!" Mitts themself hollered, but Jakub didn't stop running, so no one else did, either. At the very least Harlem would demand a portion of their take, and he hated to think of how Barney would respond with the Hallorran still at his hip.

The other end of the park came into view: a parking lot, a fence, and open streets beyond. There was a chance they could split up among the buildings, lose Mitts' gang long enough to each find their own hole-up for the rest of the night; Jakub felt that chance immediately crumble as he watched three cars pull into the lot. Each had barely parked before a collection of familiar Manhattan thugs piled out brandishing guns, Herb and Camila among them.

Jakub headed for the nearest tree and pressed himself against its trunk. *We're fucked*, he thought, holding his rifle at the ready with no idea who to aim at, if anyone. Barney stumbled into him a moment later, and his wild eyes said the same. There was no hope of them staying hidden and they were outgunned on both sides. "Barney," Jakub hissed, "you've got to give them the money."

Barney shook his head, so preemptively Jakub snatched his wrist, just in case he was thinking of drawing the Hallorran. "Don't."

"I know." Barney huddled closer as the rest of them took cover along the path, both enemy gangs closing in on either side.

"Hey, Barney!" shouted Herb as he strolled up to the cobblestone sidewalk at the edge of the park. Camila hung on his elbow, dolled up in a fur coat as usual, both of them confident in their surveyal of the situation. Their loyal soldiers stopped, fanned out to prevent their quarry from sneaking past. With Mitts and their crew handling the rear, Kozlow was trapped. "The fuck are you doing hiding in the bushes like that? You're breaking my heart, here."

"You're the ones with guns out!" Barney retorted, and Jakub couldn't help but hold his breath, fearful of every word out of his mouth. "We're supposed to be allies!"

"Well, yeah, I thought so, too!" Herb waved impatiently

for them to come forward. "Quit skulking around back there and let me see that ugly mug of yours, we've got—"

He was interrupted by a *crunch* of metal, and he turned about, just as baffled as all of them to see the tail lights of a tall delivery truck. It had backed into the lot and kept going, straight into the rear of Herb's car and rocking its front wheels onto the curb. Everyone stared in blank confusion and a few guns went up.

"Sorry!" a voice called from the open driver's side window, and a hand reached out to wave. Jakub thought he might faint at the familiar, sing-song apology. "Sorry, that was my mistake!"

"Wha..." Herb turned fully to stare as Cheshire roared the truck forward again; the car rocked back with a heavy rattle. He was so caught off guard it took him a while to settle on a reaction, and he gestured angrily. "Bloom! What the fuck are you doing?"

"Sorry!" Cheshire called again, and with the truck a safe distance and finally stopped—blocking the entrance to the lot from the street—he stepped down from the cab. He left his door open as he headed toward the group with hands raised in surrender. "Sorry, I didn't mean that—I got distracted."

"What the fuck is he doing?" Barney hissed, but Jakub had no idea and could only gape.

"You owe me for that," Herb said. "Do you know how much that car cost?" He didn't seem to know what to make of Cheshire, either, and he visibly struggled to bring himself back on script.

Cheshire laughed, not a care in the world as he strolled up to the line of Manhattan thugs. Each gave him a wary look, and even Herb was on guard, but no one tried to stop him. "Of course!" he said. "I'll buy you a whole new one if you want. You know I'm good for it, Pal.

He stopped right among the line, and everyone stared at him as if he'd lost his mind. Jakub was half convinced of the same, but he had no idea what to do, palm sweating around the grip of his rifle. He leaned out from around the tree just enough to hopefully gain Cheshire's attention.

"Right now you're a good-for-*nothing*," Herb retorted, swiftly regaining his characteristically grating charm. "Look at this mess you're in!" He waved his arm at the standoff. "Are we staging a reenactment or something? Because I could have sworn you and I have done this dance before."

Cheshire glanced into the park, unperturbed. When he spotted Jakub, a relieved smile showed briefly in his face before he could settle back into unconcerned amusement. He gave Jakub a wink and turned back to Herb.

"What can I say?" he teased. "It's hard to find a better partner."

Jakub settled himself with a deep breath. When he looked again, he realized that Leon had slipped out the other side of the truck and was leaning close to the rear door, waiting. "He has a plan," Jakub whispered to Barney. "Whatever happens, just follow his lead."

"Like hell," Barney muttered, but he didn't move a muscle.

"Mr. Bloom," said Camila, and the park was so quiet even her gentle voice carried perfectly. "Please call your people into the open. They're being rude."

"Yeah!" Herb motioned for him to continue to the inside of their circle. "Get out there too—I want you where I can see you."

Cheshire moved to the fore, putting a good twenty feet between them though still maddeningly calm. "How about here?" he goaded. "Can you see me? 'Cause if so we should get started with the negotiation, I suppose."

"Call your people into the open," Camila repeated.

Jakub readied himself, but before he could even begin to move Cheshire shook his head. "Naw," Cheshire said easily. "They're fine there, and this is between you and me, anyway. Right?"

Herb gave a loud scoff, and when Cheshire held his ground, he started to laugh. "Yeah." His smirk grew vicious and Jakub's skin crawled. "Yeah, of course it is. *You're* the one who broke his word, after all."

Jakub held his breath as he lowered himself onto one knee. He had no idea how well Herb's or Mitts' people could see him, but he didn't care; he put Herb squarely in his rifle sights. Cheshire had left him a clear shot and he knew he could sweep half their line in a matter of seconds if he had to. If Mitts shot him in the back...at least Cheshire might have time to make a run for it. He was so busy focusing, a hundred scenarios in his head, that he didn't notice Barney moving until the sack of cash dropped next to him.

"This is fucking stupid," Barney muttered, and he shoved the Hallorran into the back of his belt as he stomped out of hiding.

"Barney—" Jakub was far too late to grab him; he had no choice but to reposition his shot, curses in his throat. *If we get out of this*, he thought, teeth grinding, *I might just kill them both.*

***

Maybe I should just let Herb kill him, Cheshire thought, sweating through his good shirt as Barney stalked up beside him. Flying by the seat of one's pants was hard enough *without* a passenger, let alone one as volatile as Barney.

"Enough of the bullshit, Masterson," Barney snarled, looking rather ridiculous in his soaked clothing and a bandana still hanging off his neck. "We all know you're not going to shoot us dead, so get to *the point*."

"Oh, we know that, do we?" Herb said, eyebrows raised. Barney's arrival had all the guns back up; even if Herb didn't give the order himself, it wouldn't take much to start a nasty shootout with them smack in the middle. "You just decided that, huh?"

Cheshire shrugged. *His attention isn't on Barney, it's on you,* he thought. "He's an ass, but he's right," he said. "Everyone knows we didn't want to be here. It's bad luck, that's all. Nothing to go to war over."

"War?" Herb repeated, and he scoffed some more. "My friends here putting a few bullets in Kozlow's boss and their biggest gun isn't 'going to' war, that's 'finishing' one. And you've given us every reason to do it."

"And a vault's worth of reasons not to," Cheshire insisted. "Don't be—"

"You're not getting this take," Barney talked over him. "We worked hard for it and it's *ours*, so give us some terms we can agree on before the cops find us here."

Cheshire tried not to wince; if Barney was determined to call Herb's bluff, there wasn't much he could do but put up a confident front, too. It even seemed like it might work, for a moment: Herb looked to Camila, and though he said a few joking words about "the gall" of it all, he was clearly seeking her authority. Camila considered for a long moment, staring at them from over the collar of her thick fur coat, and finally she motioned for her soldiers to lower their weapons. That they complied was reassuring until she spoke.

"I want Bloom," she said.

Cheshire felt the air rush out of the park. All eyes had been on him all along and he'd welcomed them, but suddenly each was a knifepoint, none more so than Barney's beside him. Instinct wrung a laugh out of him, but panic crushed it thin. "Oh. My. I'm flattered, but—"

"Like we talked about," Camila went on, and Herb's smug grin had him burning all over. "You'll come over to Manhattan and work for me from now on. Then we take fifty percent of tonight's take and everyone goes home."

"We didn't talk about anything," Cheshire tried to protest, but he hadn't prepared for this and the humor leaving his tone was far too obvious. He turned to Barney. "Barney, I didn't—"

"Were you in on this?" Barney demanded, glaring at him with every ounce of the bitter distrust he'd distilled over the years. "Did you fucking tip them off?"

"Of course not! She's messing with you." Cheshire looked back to Camila, but she was deadpan and Herb triumphant. "Lucky, come on, what I *told you* was that I'm *not* interested. Just take your fifty percent like we agreed at the Thrones and get this nonsense over with."

"You don't speak for us," Barney snapped, "and they're not getting *any* of this take!" He gestured angrily at the truck. "You show up right behind them and expect me to believe you're *not* on their side?"

"I had to follow them to find you at all! I'm not—" Cheshire shook his head, nearly at a loss. All the Manhattan goons were watching him with snarling amusement now, Herb most of all. "Herb, friend, *tell him.*"

Herb shrugged, insufferable. "You've been my good buddy since day one and everyone knows it."

Is this the play? Cheshire thought, his pulse frantic and downright jittering as he tried to make sense of the situation. *Play along until Jakub is safe and then turn on them?* He could feel Barney glaring holes into his face and knew, with nauseating certainty, that even if he pretended to turncoat he could never go back. Everything he had built with Kozlow would be over. They didn't need him and he would lose *everything*.

No, Cheshire thought as the full consequences of that pounded through his chest. *No, Barney's wrong—they need me. Jakub needs me.* "Oh yeah?" he said, desperate and downright manic as he lifted his hands. "If I was really working for Lucky, would I do *this?*"

It wasn't difficult to imagine the fire. Cheshire turned his focus on the parking lot and all three of the cars Manhattan had arrived in exploded in a trio of brilliant orange and coiling black. The blast echoed like canonfire, shocking the line of goons so badly that some dropped to their hands and knees while others whirled in panic. Even Herb stumbled, buffeted by the rush of hot wind and shielding Camila from the debris. His face was blank with shock.

Don't stop. Cheshire shoved Barney to the ground and spun. With the light from the burning cars he could easily make out Mitts and their crew, struggling to regain their wits and their weapons. *Don't let any of them shoot.* His stomach lurched, and at the last second he turned his focus away from the figures and to the iron fencing that stretched down the path: one by one the rods shattered, chasing the Harlem gangsters away from the fiery scene. A trashcan showering them in blazing garbage sent them scattering.

"Manhattan does not own Brooklyn!" Cheshire shouted as he turned back to Lucky's crew, and a frightened laugh rippled out of him at the blazing, unholy spectacle. "And it sure as hell doesn't own Cheshire Bloom!"

Well you can't fucking stop now, said his conscience. He zeroed in a few off-color bricks making up the park's stone path—they cast gravel and dust into the air when they burst like land mines, a rough smoke screen shielding him from the still struggling gangsters. He could feel tiny, edged pebbles pelt his legs like shrapnel, and Barney cursed as he covered his face. With that reminder Cheshire hauled him up again.

"Get to the truck!" he ordered, pushing Barney on. He turned back to look for Jakub and spotted him rounding the same tree he'd been at earlier, but his rifle was raised and his finger squeezing the trigger.

Even then, Cheshire startled at the report of the gun. He turned and was stunned to see Herb reeling back, a gun in his hand and blood soaking his chest. Camila reached for him, stricken, but she had no hope of supporting his weight and they tumbled to the ground.

For almost a full minute, Cheshire stood frozen. He blinked around the glowing park at the chaos he'd raised and couldn't for the life of him remember why it had seemed like a good idea seconds ago—or if it had at all. Black smoke billowed from flaming wreckage in all directions like a vision of Hell, and the air burned to breathe. Most of their enemies were in full, terrified retreat, while Jakub and Hannah fled from hiding with Kozlow boys in tow. He should have been running, right? Instead he stared at Herb, who was gripping the gunshot wound in his chest as Camila tried to staunch the bleeding. Maybe he was always meant to die by a bullet and Cheshire should have let him bleed out in his car a year ago.

But it was too hard to think about that then, when Herb stared up at him with all his arrogance and childish humor gone. He'd learned his lesson too late and he deserved a witty taunt into the grave, a *"you wanted to see my magic"* remark, but the hollow fear in his eyes replaced any satisfaction Cheshire might have felt with a cold and piercing shame.

"You'll burn in hell," Camilla told him, shaking but fierce, and Cheshire gulped, believing her.

"Cheshire!" Jakub called, and at last Cheshire fought back to his senses. As he turned to run he caught glimpses of metal barrels reflecting the firelight, and he blew up the first revolver he was able to make out; the holder let out a terrible scream that rattled Cheshire's nerves, and thankfully it was enough to discourage any others from taking aim against him as he dashed for the truck.

Jakub was standing in the open back of the truck; it lurched forward, and he had to grab at the door to keep from being thrown. Even so he kept his eyes on Cheshire and waved him on; Cheshire reached the vehicle just before it turned out onto the street, and Jakub helped to haul him in so they could close the doors behind him.

"Holy moly," said Cheshire, still gripping Jakub's arm as they tried to settle among the vegetable crates. The police hadn't bothered to re-cover all those they'd opened, leaving box lids and even a few cabbages strewn about. The interior reeked of smoke and without any light it was difficult to get his bearings. "Did everyone make it?"

He was met with only a shift of boxes as the truck rumbled on. He squinted into the dark, trying to determine just how many of them had crowded in, but having gone from painfully-bright to no light at all, he couldn't get his eyes to adjust. All he could be sure of was Jakub's metal hand clenched tightly in his vest. "Is everyone all right?" he tried again. "Leon?"

Leon coughed, closer than Cheshire had expected due to the tight confines. "I'm okay."

"Oh, phew." Cheshire relaxed and even let out a quiet chuckle. "Sorry if I singed you there; I really didn't mean for it to get that hot. What about the others?"

"Hannah's driving the truck," said Jakub, and even just the sound of his voice helped loosen Cheshire's wound-up guts. "I think she has Stas with her up there."

Cheshire was almost afraid to ask. "Barney...?"

"I'm right fucking here," Barney muttered, and Cheshire couldn't help but startle. "Gorski, too."

"Not sure I know who that is, but good." Sitting seemed like too much trouble given the circumstances, so Cheshire braced his free hand to the truck's side and welcomed Jakub closer for stability. "Hell, though, cops said they got one of us...?"

"Nowak," said Jakub. "That was at the river, though."

"Cops said?" Barney prompted.

He didn't sound like his usual, berating self—in fact he was uncommonly quiet, and it put Cheshire on edge again. "It's a long story," Cheshire said, and when that didn't ease any tension, he added, "Ask Leon."

Whether Leon was about to back him up didn't end up mattering. "It's fine," Barney said.

He didn't offer more than that. No one did, and as the silence dragged out Cheshire began to sweat all over again. With the rush of the standoff in the past, his thinning adrenaline made everything a little clearer, and a little frightening. He wound his fingers in Jakub's coat. "Thanks for covering me. I didn't even see that asshole had a gun until he went down! You're a lifesaver, literally!"

"I had a good shot," said Jakub.

Silence again. Cheshire gulped. *Barney's never this quiet*, he thought, bracing himself for whenever the angry shouting and accusations would begin. *That was...probably too much, even for me. So why isn't he all over my ass?* "Uh, sorry it got a little out of hand, there," he tried yet again. "I knew you guys needed some backup but we didn't really have a plan for... well, any of this? But we made it out and they didn't, so that's a win, right?"

Cheshire laughed, hoping to provoke at least *some* kind of reaction, but all he could make out were uneasy figures in the dark. "No one's going to mess with Kozlow after all *that*, right?" he carried on. "Pow, pow! A bank vault in the bag *and* Masterson is probably out of the picture. That's not bad at all. As long as—"

"Bloom," Jakub interrupted, and Cheshire shut up. "Let's talk about it later."

"Oh, sure." Cheshire couldn't make out Jakub's face in the dark, and the steel in his tone wasn't much help. *How mad is he?* he thought unhelpfully. He forced his fingers to unwind and instinctively smoothed out the fabric he had wrinkled by clinging to it. "Sorry."

Jakub scratched lightly against Cheshire's back, which he hoped was a good sign. But he kept his mouth shut.

***

No one spoke the rest of the trip, until Hannah stopped the truck almost thirty minutes later. They could hear bells and sirens in the distance, and Jakub held his breath as someone opened the back of the truck. It was only Hannah, thankfully, and she only cracked the door enough to see in.

"Everyone all right?" she whispered.

"We're fine," Jakub spoke for the group. "Where are we?"

"Grocery store." Hannah opened the door a bit more so Jakub could get a look at the darkened building she'd parked behind. "Least conspicuous place I could think of for a delivery truck."

"Ahh, good thinking!" said Cheshire, but he buttoned up when Jakub gave him a nudge. Hannah already looked worn thin and nothing out of Cheshire's mouth was about to help.

"Is the coast clear?" Jakub asked.

"No." Hannah cast a quick glance behind her. "Still a few hours before dawn, but there are police everywhere. I think we should hole up for as long as we can before making a plan to get home."

"Keep that door open for a minute," said Barney. "Can't fucking see in here."

They rearranged the crates in the back as best they could, so that at least no nails were exposed and each had some kind of lid. Though it was still stifling and crammed, each picked their spot to hunker down for the remainder of the night. Everyone looked exhausted and Jakub was faring no better; he still felt as if he were vibrating in his skin, alert for every squeal of tires or police siren. His hair smelled like smoke and magic and it kept his heart pounding. Even if he couldn't get any sleep, he welcomed the opportunity to try.

Once the others were settled, however, Cheshire suddenly pushed Hannah out of the way and climbed out of the back of the truck. "I need some air," he said, ignoring Hannah's attempts to draw him back.

"I've got it," Jakub said quickly, hopping out of the truck. "Just stay in the cab and we'll get out of here at dawn." Hannah didn't look convinced, but she headed to the front of the truck.

Thankfully, Cheshire didn't go far; only a few paces from the truck was an employee entrance, and he paused there to catch his breath. It wasn't like him to show his discomfort so openly, and Jakub continued to buzz with frustration as he hurried over. "Chesh? You okay?"

"Hm? Oh, yeah." Cheshire winced and rubbed his face. "I mean, not really, but yeah. Are you okay?" He reached for Jakub and then hesitated. "I really am sorry, I didn't—"

"Shh," Jakub hushed him quickly, paranoid that they were still very much in the open; any passing car could see them, and Barney in the truck would hear every word if they weren't careful. Seeing Cheshire's mouth clap shut again made him feel rotten, though, so he rushed to reassure him.

"It's okay," he whispered. "You're fine—just keep it down, okay?"

"Yeah. Sorry." Cheshire took his glasses off so he could rake his hair back. "I know that was bad, I just didn't know what else to do. Barney was never going to believe me unless I did something to prove it."

"It's not your fault, that..." Jakub stopped as Cheshire's words fully registered, and he stared hard into his face. "Wait, what?"

"I thought about going along with it," Cheshire continued to whisper, his expression so earnest that Jakub didn't know whether he wanted to slap it off his face or drag him into his arms. "I could play nice with Herb but it's not like Kozlow would ever take me back after that, right? I had to do *something*." He replaced his glasses and scratched the back of his neck. "Maybe my head's just full'a smoke, I couldn't think of anything else."

Jakub stared, a tremor in his chest and at a loss. "You had a dozen guns on you," he said, emotion forcing his voice out louder than he meant for. "They could have shot you full of holes and you're worried about *that?*"

"Well...yeah!" Cheshire checked himself before he could get swept up in Jakub's volume. "Of course I am—what do you think I've been doing all this time? I'm tired of putting you in the middle of this." He scraped the back of his palm across his mouth anxiously. "I have to make it work somehow," he said. "I *have* to—I know what Kozlow means to you and I don't want to lose you over all this."

Jakub's stomach dropped, and for a long moment he could only stare. *Have I really never told him?* he thought. Barely an hour ago he had watched Cheshire stand up to Manhattan's worst and raise hell, almost getting himself killed in the process—he couldn't quite shake the thrill of panic he'd felt, watching Herb level his gun. All for *his* sake, so he wouldn't have to choose between his "family" and his lover. Jakub's guilt and outrage collided with hours of anxiety, and without thinking he gave Cheshire a push that shoved his back to the door.

"You won't," he hissed, furious with himself for never managing to say it sooner. "You can't—I'm not going anywhere."

Cheshire blinked at him in confusion. "What?"

"Stop worrying about what Barney thinks," Jakub tried again, shaking with the effort of keeping his voice down when the words were so important. "He doesn't matter—none of them do." He gripped Cheshire's soot-stained vest and couldn't stop the rest from tumbling out. "*You're* the only one who matters to me, understand? You're more important to me than anything else. So don't do anything that stupid for *them* ever again."

"Oh." Cheshire continued to stare back at him as gradually the words seemed to sink in. A slow, hopeful smile crept across his face. "I am?"

Jakub gulped. "Yeah," he said, and the relief that beamed through Cheshire's grin had his stomach back in knots. "Of course you are—what do you think *I've* been doing all this time?"

"I have no idea," Cheshire admitted, and Jakub desperately wished they had more privacy to prove it to him.

The truck's back door creaked, but for once Jakub didn't pull away immediately. "We'll get out of this together, all right?" he said quietly, and he waited until Cheshire nodded to finally let him go.

"Jakub?" Barney called as quietly as he could manage. "You all right?"

Jakub led the pair of them back to the truck, but he let Cheshire climb in first. Barney watched, and with the streetlights on him, Jakub could finally make out the genuine fear buried in his suspicion. "Thanks," Barney whispered to him, but Jakub just shook his head as he climbed in after Cheshire. Whatever Barney *thought* they had been talking about, it didn't matter.

None of them mattered and he and Cheshire would be free of them soon enough.

Bang! Bang! BOOM!

Just before dawn, Jakub snuck out of the truck again and broke into the grocery store. He returned with a tarp: he, Barney, Hannah, Stas, and Gorski crowded beneath it as close to the truck cab as they could while Cheshire and Leon assembled a floor-to-ceiling wall of vegetable crates behind them. It was only three boxes deep, and anyone who inspected the truck too carefully was bound to notice the unusual usage of space, but Cheshire assured everyone he could pull it off and no one had a better idea.

They set out for the bridge at first light. Crammed into the back Jakub had no idea of how long it took or what traffic looked like. All he or any of them could do was stay as low as possible and hope.

The truck stopped, and everyone held their breath. Jakub could hear Cheshire chatting with someone but not any of the words, then the driver's side door opening. "They're going to open the back," he whispered. "Not one sound." His four companions went dead still.

The back of the truck opened, and despite the circumstances, Cheshire's sing-song voice, perfectly at ease, helped calm Jakub's pounding heart somewhat. "Potatoes and onions, mostly," he was saying. "The tunnel crew sure had a great time opening them all up! I pounded the nails back in, figured you'd want the same experience."

"Maybe I do," said a man. "Every last one'a them."

"Be my guest," replied Cheshire smugly. "I've got all the time in the world."

Everyone in the truck tensed in the short silence that followed. With no view outside the truck Jakub had no idea what state the bridge was in, how many cops were around or what they could possibly do if discovered. But then another voice joined the pair, a very familiar woman's voice, and Jakub wilted with relief.

"Sir, this could be a trick," said Gertie. "The tunnel said they didn't find anything in the truck and Bloom was just trying to pull attention away from the river. This could be the same thing."

"You think I'm that unoriginal?" Cheshire retorted. "Not that I have any idea what you're talking about, naturally. What happened at the river?"

The policeman heaved a deep sigh. "Christ, you're probably right." His voice began moving away. "Hey, Perkins! Get on the horn and let our guys on the river know to keep an eye out! Bridges too!"

"Hey wait!" Cheshire called after him. "You really don't want to look? I could have anything in here, you know?"

Barney muttered a curse under his breath; Jakub elbowed him. As Cheshire continued to badger the officer, they could hear the van doors creaking shut. "I'll follow him back to Brooklyn, sir," Gertie volunteered. "If he is trying to meet up with the others, I'll get Alice on it."

"Yes, good thinking, officer. You said you're with Precinct 49...?"

The doors closed, and the rest of the conversation carried on beyond their ears. No one relaxed until the van started back up, and at long last they were underway again, across the bridge.

"That was too damn close," said Hannah, "but it sounds like we're okay."

"We're not okay until we're back," Jakub insisted, preventing anyone from lowering the tarp just yet. "But yeah, seems like it."

Half an hour later, the van stopped and shut off its engine. Once again everyone held their breath as the back doors opened, and they could hear the boxes being unloaded. "All'a you fools are under arrest," declared Burke's familiar accent.

"What in the name of all Hells ever imagined was that unholy mess? Some real American cowboys."

Barney shoved the tarp down and scowled at him. "You weren't fucking there, all right?"

Burke glared at him from over the top of the boxes that Gertie and her sisters were still dragging out of the truck. "And thank God for that, then. Did you at least get any money while you were at it, or is it at the bottom of the river?"

"Christ, shut up," Barney muttered, and he shoved a few of the crates out of his way so he could climb down from the truck. "Yeah, we got the fucking money, all right?" He shoved his sack into Burke's chest. "Start counting."

Burke stumbled but managed to keep a grip on it. "Yes, sir," he said, and he backed away so the rest could disembark.

Jakub stretched his aching shoulders and knees once he was out in the fresh air again. They were outside the Kozlow building—it felt as if weeks had passed since he saw it last—with a decent crowd around them, some faces familiar and others not. Gertie was dressed in her police uniform from their daring armored car heist, looking mighty proud of herself. As soon as Hannah was out of the truck she embraced her.

"Thank God for you," she said, and Gertie laughed, agreeing with her.

"It was pretty damn close, to be honest," Cheshire was saying, and Jakub finally spotted him up on the sidewalk, chatting with some of the newer Kozlow boys Jakub barely recognized. They were listening to Cheshire prattle on but without the gleam of fascination that the new recruits used to fix him with. Their attention was somehow...cold, their eyes pinched with suspicion. Barney and the others that had been on the disastrous mission said very little as they pulled their take from the truck and then helped shove the crates back in. The air was tense, and it put an itch between Jakub's shoulders.

"Then *boom*, right in the heart!" Cheshire carried on as if oblivious to the silent, furtive glances being cast his way. "Jakub's the best shot there is—he saved my bacon for sure. We never would have pulled it off without him."

"Uh-huh," said one of the members of his audience, but he didn't look at Jakub. He only watched Cheshire.

"Hey, Bloom," said Jakub, and he could feel the entire assembly draw in a breath as Cheshire turned his head. "Why don't you bring the truck over to Edith's? She could use the produce."

"Oh! Good thinking." Cheshire was all grins as he offered his small audience a salute and stepped off the curb. "Only if Gertie tags along. I'm so jealous of her uniform."

"Fine, fine," said Gertie. "We can pass by the precinct on the way, make it look good."

"That's the spirit!"

Gertie headed back to her "borrowed" black and white, but before Cheshire could get too far, Jakub snagged him by the elbow. "When you're done, come back here and see me," he said, firmly enough that the others would easily interpret his intentions as a reprimand. "We need to have a conversation."

Cheshire gulped, and Jakub wished he was smooth like him, to know how to deliver some kind of silent reassurance that his temper was only for show. "Sure thing," Cheshire said, and his grin struggled back into place as he resumed his path to the truck's driver side door. "Will you still be my shotgun, Leon?"

"I'll pass," said Leon, and with a shrug Cheshire pulled himself up into the cab.

Only after Cheshire and Gertie had driven away did the tension begin to unfurl, though even then Jakub could clearly see some of that uncertainty shifting. Burke must have sensed it, too, as he hefted the sack Barney had passed him and swiftly headed inside. "Okay, well, I'll be taking this to the basement, then," he declared. "Lots of counting to do."

Hannah followed after him with the other bags while the rest of Kozlow milled about. Jakub felt Barney move to his side and his skin crawled, but he held still. Once Burke was out of sight, Barney gave a sharp huff. "Thanks, Jakub," he said, and he patted him on the back. Jakub held very still. "You did really good last night."

"Sure," said Jakub as everyone around them began to mutter and whisper. Gorski headed to the three Cheshire had been regaling and started speaking fast under his breath, while Leon and Stas leaned close together.

"You saw, didn't you?" Leon was saying in Polish, and Jakub strained his ears to catch every word. "His hands? Lit up all red?"

"Yeah," said Stas, still raking soot out of his hair. "I've

never seen him without his gloves, so I never—"

"He *never* takes them off—now we know why." Leon turned toward Barney and switched to English. "You saw too, didn't you? Bloom's hands?"

Barney took his cap off so he could smooth his mussed hair back. "Yeah, I fucking saw," he said as he headed up to the front door. Jakub followed just so he'd be sure to catch all the conversation. "I'm going to go talk to the boss."

Leon turned back to Stas as they passed. "I got a pretty good look when we were in the truck," he carried on. "That's not just magic, that's *evil*."

"Keep it to yourself," Jakub snapped, and both men startled. "The boss will decide what to do."

"Yeah—okay," Leon chirped, though when he gulped Jakub knew better than to think he would actually keep his mouth shut. There were too many hungry ears around.

We can't stay here, Jakub thought, a slow burning panic thrumming through his joints as he entered the building behind Barney. *They were never going to really accept him, and thanks to last night it's not even safe.* The thought of having to tell Cheshire so threatened him with nausea, and he had to force himself to stop and take a breath. *It's not his fault—I don't want him to think that it is.*

Barney paused at the elevator to look back. "You okay?"

"Yeah." Jakub headed instead for the stairwell. "I need a minute to make sure my arm is all right," he said. "I'll check in with you and the boss later."

"Sure thing," said Barney, and something hard slid into his face as he boarded the elevator. There was no question what he was about to pass on to Kasper.

Jakub hurried up to his apartment. He left his rifle out on the table, in easy reach, just in case. *Masterson couldn't have survived that, but that doesn't mean Lucky is finished*, he thought as he sat himself down and unscrewed the cover plate on his forearm. *The cops will start watching the building if they haven't been already. Barney can't be trusted—or Hannah, for that matter.* He dragged his kit out from under the sofa. *There's no reason to stay here any longer—it has to be now.*

Thankfully, Halloran's well-made prosthetic hadn't suffered too greatly in the ordeals of the night previous. Jakub made sure to scrub dry any moisture and tighten every screw, then wound the mainspring. He felt the key turning in his chest too, filling him with determination and adrenaline. Yet somehow, he was also strangely calm. He knew very well what it felt like to *run*, and those memories of panic and escape hummed beneath his surface, but this was different. For the first time it didn't feel like running *away* and that gave him all the focus and energy he needed.

Once his arm was closed and secure again, he began moving about the apartment. There wasn't much that he owned, and he wasn't sure he even had a decent suitcase to put it in, but he gathered what belongings were worth keeping in a corner of his bedroom, out of sight from casual eyes. He had the feeling Hannah might come check on him, and after everything he couldn't be certain of what she would do, if she had any inkling of what was driving him now.

As Jakub dug through his drawers, his hand came across soft wool. Swallowing, he drew out from the most hidden corner of his wardrobe a burgundy suit coat of worsted wool: Cheshire's Christmas jacket, which he had in a fit of drunken childishness spirited into his collection years ago. He pressed it to his face and was convinced that even after so long, it still smelled like Cheshire and his magic. The thought that Cheshire would catch him with it and require an explanation was a mortifying one, but it was even more unconscionable that he could leave it behind.

I'll give it back to him, Jakub resolved as he carefully folded the jacket and hid it among his luggage, along with...a few other articles of clothing he had been bold enough to swipe over the years. *When we get to wherever we go, I really will give it all back*.

With his most basic preparations complete, Jakub took a quick shower to rid himself of the stink of river and smoke, then changed into fresh clothes. He didn't like the idea of too much going on inside the building without him knowing, so he made his way downstairs floor by floor, ears open for gossip. Everyone was talking about the heist, of course, though those with forward-facing windows also had plenty to say about the police car parked outside. It had to have arrived pretty soon after Gertie left in hers, an unbelievable stroke of luck for a family that didn't deserve it.

Burke wasn't in his apartment, and Jakub didn't catch

him hanging around, so he headed down to the basement. What he thought he'd say to him, he had no idea, but he was eager to know what version of the night's events had made it to his ears. As far as he knew there were only two people who would ever suspect what Jakub had planned, and he was determined to be a step ahead.

He opened the door to the basement, and a figure already halfway down the stairs turned to look up at him. It was Barney. "Oh, Jakub," he said, pausing to let Jakub catch up. "Good. I gotta talk to you."

Jakub was relieved that he'd remembered to bring some cigarettes; he pulled one from the pack and lit up as he followed Barney down the stairs. "What did the boss have to say?"

Barney shook his head. "I'll tell you in a minute." Jakub didn't like the sound of that, but he didn't question as they continued down.

Hannah and Burke were talking in hushed tones in the cellar, though they silenced too quickly for Jakub to catch any of the words. As he and Barney emerged Burke perked up in the most earnest "I didn't hear you coming" approximation he could manage and said, "Hey, boss. Here for the numbers, aren't you?"

"Why else?" Barney retorted, watching as Hannah pushed one of the satchels onto one of the wall shelves. "So? What's the take?"

Burke opened a notebook on the table in front of him. "Fifty-seven thousand, four hundred ninety-five dollars. And twelve cents."

Jakub strode forward to steal a look at the notebook while Barney sighed in disappointment. "Fuck," said Barney. "Really thought we'd get a hundred thousand at least."

"It's better than we planned," Hannah said as she set another bag into an unmarked crate and forced it shut. "And that total doesn't take into account the items from the safety deposit boxes."

"Right, right," said Burke, paging through his book. "Some jewelry, a few small antiques." He pulled a face. "Pretty sure you nabbed evidence of someone's cooked books, too. Could be some blackmail potential. Hannah and I were just talking about that."

Jakub cast Burke a look that had him gulping.

"Anyway," Burke prattled on, "I amn't no appraiser; we'll sit on that part of the loot for a while and then get it pawned when things quiet down."

"Yeah, that's fine." Barney waved dismissively. "Thanks."

Burke's face screwed up while Barney wasn't looking, and he quickly began gathering his notebooks up. "Sorry but I'm gonna take five now if that's all right. I could use breakfast."

"Me, too," said Hannah, and the two of them started toward the stairs. "And a damn nap."

Barney waved again, and as the pair of them left he turned to face Jakub. He looked a little too proud of himself considering everything that had taken place, and Jakub leaned back, holding his cigarette to his mouth to help keep the disdain out of his face.

"So," said Jakub, watching Barney closely. "What a night."

"Yeah. Shit." Barney gave an incredulous chuckle; how dare he sound so nonchalant. "What a score, but it shouldn't have gone that far. That asshole could have gotten any one of us killed." He fixed Jakub with a more serious look. "Thanks for standing up to him."

Jakub didn't blink. *He must mean when we talked outside the truck? How much did he actually hear?* "Sure," he said.

"The boss says Bloom's grown too powerful too fast," Barney carried on, and Jakub continued to hold very still, his anger crushed deep beneath his diaphragm. "He's becoming *dangerous*. Whoever survived that shoot out is gonna be scared of *him*, not Kozlow." He shook his head. "He was already throwing in with Masterson. If he ever got in his head that he didn't need us, it'd be a real problem for us."

For a moment it might have looked as if Barney had some idea what he was talking about. Could it be it had finally occurred to him just how lucky Kozlow had been all this time, that Cheshire *hadn't* pushed his weight around or jumped sides? If it was clarity, though, it didn't last long. That dangerous, too-eager gleam was already creeping back into his eyes.

"So?" said Jakub. "What does the boss want me to do about it?"

Barney smirked. "You always know what's up, don't

you, Jake?"

"I'm the only one who can get close enough to him. He trusts me." Jakub stared hard into Barney's face. His heart was pounding and some part of him dared Barney to look a little closer, to figure it out. Part of him wanted the excuse to hurt him. "What do you want me to do?"

"Take one of his hands," said Barney, insufferably pleased with himself, and it took all Jakub's strength to stay composed. "You saw it last night, didn't you? His palms lit up all red? *That's* where the magic comes from." He lifted one hand and drew on his palm with his finger. "Lose one and he won't be as strong. That ought'a put him back in line."

It doesn't work that way, Jakub thought, not that he really knew. His anger clawed about in his chest as Barney kept talking. "It's not like we need him for that anymore anyway," Barney said, looking ever more convinced as he went. "He needs a fucking wake-up call." His mouth twisted into a sneer as he wiggled his fingers at Jakub. "He owes you one anyway. Right?"

Jakub felt the fingers of his left hand sting with ghostlike heat at the mention. He remembered waking up in a hospital bed and the hellish week that followed, buried under pain and weakness and uncertainty—but more than any of that the weight of Cheshire's guilt crushing the breath out of him every time their eyes met. Day after day he had woken up furious and sick with the fear that a stupid accident had taken something precious from him when he needed it most. Barney would never understand. Jakub wasn't even sure that Cheshire did. But anyone who thought they could wield that memory as a weapon in their favor was dead wrong.

Jakub took a long breath on his cigarette. Let it out. "I'll take care of it."

***

The drive to Edith's was longer and more fraught than Cheshire thought it ever could or should be. Despite his exhaustion his mind wouldn't stop spinning with images of the night before, and he found it difficult putting them all into place. Like his head was full of smoke after all.

Jakub said we'd figure it out together, so that's what'll happen, he told himself, over and over, as his fingers drummed against the steering wheel. *He wanted to talk even before everything went to shit. But it'll be okay.* His stomach twisted into nausea as he thought of Jakub's face upturned with that seeking expression he had yet to fully suss out: that heavy, piercing stare that seemed to expect something from him. No one had ever looked at him like that before, and he didn't know what to do or if he should be excited or terrified of it.

As if anyone can fix a stare like Jakub anyway, Cheshire thought, trying to amuse himself. *Nothing I can do but...wait and see.*

Edith was just opening her diner when they arrived, and she made a fuss about the number of vegetables she was expected to hold onto. Cheshire and Gertie unloaded everything anyway, promising to bring all the boys back to help peel potatoes.

"What the hell really happened out there?" Gertie asked as she passed Cheshire a crate full of cabbages. "Some folks at the upper floors of the Morey said they could see smoke."

"It's, uh, a whopper of a story," Cheshire replied, smiling around a wince. "You won't believe me."

"I never do," she retorted, and though she was obviously teasing, it still stung a little. "Give me the *real* story later, okay?"

"I only ever tell the *real* story."

"Sure, Bloom." Gertie laughed and carried the crate inside, leaving Cheshire to pick up the rear.

Gertie ditched her stolen patrol car in a church parking lot as soon as they were finished with the vegetables, and it was a good thing, too: as they made their way back to the Kozlow building they passed several police cars on patrol, and even one recently parked across from the building itself. Cheshire slowed the truck long enough for Gertie to jam her uniform jacket under the seat and then they pulled up nice and easy, not a care in the world.

"We've been real lucky so far," said Gertie as they each twisted their door open. "Let's not cock it up."

"Would I ever?" Cheshire retorted, and he climbed out.

The cops watched closely, but Cheshire pretended not to notice. He moved around behind the truck and opened the back door, just enough that anyone passing by would be able to see the carriage was empty. Leaving it that way, he headed back to the front and strolled into the building easy as you please.

Burke was waiting in the lobby, reading a newspaper. He looked up as Cheshire entered, and his wary expression didn't help the state of Cheshire's stomach any. "Bloom."

"Hey Egg...ah." Cheshire shrugged, but Burke rolling his eyes seemed like a good enough sign, so he came closer. "Did we make the news already?"

"Special edition." Burke offered him the paper. "You gonna let me know how much is true?"

Cheshire accepted, gulping at the headline *HELL IN HARLEM* printed across the top of the insert. "I'll, uh, let you know in a bit," he said. "Jakub asked me to come straight up. Probably has an earful for me."

"Probably," said Burke, though his tone disagreed. "Keep me posted, won't you?"

"Yeah! Of course." Cheshire saluted with the newspaper and then headed to the elevator. "And when I do, I'll tell you exactly what happened without one single exaggeration."

"Don't you always?" Burke shot back, and at least that felt a bit more like normal. He shooed Cheshire on.

The fourth floor was quiet. Cheshire found Jakub's apartment unlocked but empty, and he helped himself to the sofa. Despite the anxiety buzzing through his chest he stretched out across the cushion to read the newspaper. Maybe if he forced himself into the appearance of ease, he would feel it?

The paper was mostly speculation, having been rushed through in a few hours since the late evening heist: it had only the bare details of the bank heist, the sinking boat, the fire in the park. Hints at those responsible but no names. Cheshire winced at the mention of police officers killed at the riverside, their names withheld until the families could be notified. They had already planned to lay real low after this job was done, but he didn't have much faith that they'd have the chance to.

Cops will be all over us for as long as it takes, Cheshire thought, *and who can blame them? Barney always takes things too far.* He sighed. *Not that I'm one to talk, I guess. What will Jakub say?*

The door opened a few minutes later, and Jakub came in. Cheshire's stomach went tight, but he pasted a smile in place. "Hey," he greeted, and he gave the newspaper a shake. "Everyone's talking about us already."

Jakub already had a lit cigarette in hand, and he took in a

long drag as he crossed the room. His face was hard and Cheshire ducked instinctively behind the newspaper. "'Armed hooligans make off with over fifty Gs! Dramatic river showdown!'" He chuckled. "At least Barney got the message he was looking for."

Jakub sat down on the sofa close to Cheshire's hip. His body felt hot and coiled tight, like a heated spring, and when he took a breath Cheshire hurried to intercept, not ready to hear whatever was about to come out.

"Not sure what he thinks we'll do about the cops," Cheshire said. "We can probably expect a call from that marshal sometime soon. But Manhattan has to be out of our hair this time, right? I mean...they *have* to." He licked his lips and tried not to think of Herb and Camila staring up at him among the smoke. "Feels like...things are gonna be different, now. One way or the other." He chuckled nervously. "I gotta admit, I'm not really sure what comes next."

Jakub hummed distractedly, which didn't help Cheshire's nerves any, and it prompted him to continue rambling. "I'm sure it'll be fine," Cheshire carried on. "It's like you said, we'll be...together, right? So stop worrying; it'll work out somehow."

"Yeah," said Jakub, his voice still rough and distant. "Right." He was quiet for a moment, and Cheshire began to sweat, before he finally said, "Hey. Let's leave town."

Cheshire blinked. He wasn't sure that he had heard right at first and was afraid to respond in case he'd gotten it wrong, but then Jakub kept going. "Barney's brought down way too much heat—there's no reason we have to stick around for that. So let's just go. We can start over somewhere else. Build something for ourselves."

Cheshire peeked over the top of his newspaper. He didn't know what he expected to see, but Jakub's profile was calm and focused. "Maybe even go clean," Jakub suggested, and before Cheshire could even boggle at the suggestion, their gazes met. Jakub stared at him with as much confidence as he'd ever seen him display. He meant it, and Cheshire tensed as if the sofa might flip out from under them at any moment.

"Just you and me," said Jakub, and for once Cheshire could perfectly read the hopeful emotion in his voice. "What do you think?"

All the tension unfurled; all the weight sloughed off. Cheshire stared back at Jakub, shocked at the suggestion that it could be just that easy—and then shocked with the realization that it *was*. All those years spent climbing Kozlow's ladder, each success that fell a little short of real victory, the money and the suits and the building...suddenly none of it mattered. What should have been a sobering thought was unexpectedly liberating, and Cheshire let the newspaper fall to the floor. "Okay."

Jakub straightened up. "Yeah?"

"Yeah," said Cheshire, and he barely had time to form a smile before Jakub pounced for a kiss. Cheshire welcomed him, wrapped him up, exhilarated and overwhelmed. *He was right—this is all that matters*, he thought. Jakub shivered in his arms, so he held him tighter. Even when the kiss ran out and they could only stare at each other in amazement, he didn't want to let go.

I really would give up everything for him. Cheshire at last managed a breathless grin as that revelation sent his heart pounding, and he couldn't help a quiet, "Wow."

"You mean it, right?" Jakub said, his expression taking on a familiar, steely intensity. "You're serious?"

"Yeah," Cheshire said again, unfazed. He laughed and darted in for one peck on the lips. "Let's get out of here."

Jakub wasn't satisfied with just that: he pounced again, with such enthusiasm that Cheshire's shoulders were pushed back to the arm of the sofa. But Cheshire couldn't stop laughing, making a mess of Jakub's passionate kisses. When Jakub finally gave up it was abruptly and all at once; he struggled out of Cheshire's arms and all but vaulted to his feet.

"I'm already packed," he said, and he kept talking as he headed into the bedroom. "I'm sure you need to go back to your apartment, but we should leave as soon as we can. We're only going to see more cops show up here."

Cheshire blinked stupidly and had to grip the sofa back to drag himself up. "Okay." He chuckled some more, still mostly incredulous, as he leaned forward to try and see into the bedroom. "But we probably shouldn't be seen leaving here together."

Jakub returned dragging a packed duffle bag and the case for his rifle. "You're right," he said as he shoved both next to the door. "After you go I'll wait half an hour. There's no leaving through Manhattan now but if we go north we can take a ferry to the Bronx and head for the rail station up past Crotonville..." When he realized that Cheshire was still just staring at him blankly, he stopped. "What?"

Cheshire shook himself. "Nothing!" He pushed to his feet and moved closer, licking his lips. "Just seems like...how long have you been planning this, exactly?"

"Yesterday," said Jakub. "I started thinking about it after Burke caught us, and after last night, I'm not sure we have a choice."

Cheshire's heart sank guiltily; Jakub shifted his weight and hurriedly added, "It's not your fault. Barney's plan was always going to go sideways."

"Yeah, but, I *am* sorry," Cheshire said, and he took Jakub's shoulders, as much for want of that comfort as to convey his sincerity. "You've been with Kozlow a long time, and because of me—"

"Don't," Jakub snapped, though he then quickly softened his tone. "Chesh...listen." He covered Cheshire's hands with his, and though the press of his metal fingers was as always a sobering reminder, the earnest emotion in his face left Cheshire breathless. "I joined up with Kozlow in the first place just to keep myself alive. I *stayed* because of *you*. As long as we leave together I don't regret anything. Okay?"

"Okay." Cheshire grinned even though his throat was suddenly tight with emotion. "I stayed because of you, too," he said, and he laughed. "Fuck Barney. Let's just go."

"Fuck Barney," Jakub agreed, and he stole one more kiss before urging Cheshire back. "Go on—I'll meet you at your place."

"Right-O," Cheshire agreed, light as air as he slipped out of the apartment.

Fuck Barney, Cheshire thought, trying to temper his pace as he skipped down the stairs. *Fuck all of Kozlow. What haven't I done for them, huh? Worked my tail off for them. And when has any of them shown me an inch of gratitude? Never!* His already tight chest began to clamp down further as the euphoria of Jakub's confidence in him gave way to more sobering revelations. *A lot of them have been hoping to see me gone for a long time. They're not gonna miss me. Barney said himself he was gonna replace me anyway.*

Cheshire reached the ground floor and there paused, a

hand on the wall to keep him steady. His mind swirled with all the jobs they'd pulled together thanks to him, the late nights he'd spent with the crew drinking and laughing...and he suddenly couldn't think of a single one of them that would stand up for him if asked. Even before his fiery display the night before he'd begun to sense that distance widening between him and the rest of the gang, and especially him and Hannah. There wasn't any chance of ever winning their approval now.

All those years spent living exactly the kind of life he'd always fantasized about...and so little to show for it. Cheshire scrubbed his sleeve across his face as he struggled to not let that thought drown him. *They only have half of what they have because of me, and they'll never admit it*, he thought, an uncomfortable bitterness stewing in his gut. *They'll all be glad I'm gone.* He took a deep breath. *They'll miss Jakub, though. Good—they can blame me for that, at least. That's one thing I'll have done that matters to them.*

Cheshire reached for the door to the lobby but then paused, glancing down the further stairs that led into the basement. A wicked, defiant little thought crept into his brain, and before he could entertain any wiser ones, he hurried downward. *That, and maybe one other thing.*

They couldn't have made it easier for him: Cheshire opened a satchel on one of the nearby shelves and discovered stacks of bills, bound and counted. All those little presidents at least sure seemed happy to see him. Cheshire grabbed the bag off the shelf and headed back upstairs. *Severance pay*, he thought to himself, his mood improving by leaps and bounds as he vaulted out of the stairwell. *This will be plenty to set up me and Jake somewhere. After last night, we earned it.*

He came out into the lobby and found Burke was still there, though less welcome of a sight was Leon sitting with him. They were sharing a cigarette and talking in low tones, though as Cheshire approached he heard Burke say, "That's a load of horseshit, and you know it."

"But I saw—" Leon started to reply, but he clapped his mouth shut when he finally took notice of Cheshire. "Bloom."

"Hey there." Cheshire managed to keep his manners light as he offered the pair of them a smirk. "Ten bucks says you were talking about me just now."

Leon went a little pale, but Burke didn't miss a beat,

shooting back with, "Ye're the only horseshit around here worth yammering about, aren't you?"

"Can't argue that," said Cheshire, and he gestured for Burke to join him. "I'm heading back to the Morey. Care to join me?"

Burke raised an eyebrow, but he bobbed his head and hopped to his feet. "Sure. Might as well make sure the cops haven't raided the place. If you think the pigs out front won't hassle us?"

"They can try," replied Cheshire, but as they started to leave, Leon called him back.

"What's in the bag?" he asked, and he wasn't a good enough liar to make it sound like he didn't already suspect.

"Breakfast," Cheshire shot back. "I'm starved!" He waved to Leon without looking back and continued outside.

Another cop car was parked out front—or at least, Cheshire had to assume it was. A man and a woman were seated inside, and they watched closely as Cheshire led the way to his car and tossed his bag in the back seat. As he and Burke pulled away from the building, the second car even started up to follow. Burke hunkered down in his seat nervously.

"Must've been some show," Burke muttered. "Been a while since the cops paid us this much mind."

Cheshire spared the following vehicle a glance before focusing on the road. "Don't worry about them. If they were going to arrest us they would have done it by now."

"Not sure that's true, but what do I know?" Burke squirmed a bit more and finally faced Cheshire. "So? Ye're gonna fill me in on yer version now?"

Cheshire frowned; he desperately wanted to know what Hannah and Barney had told him, but he caught himself before he could ask. "Not sure it really matters now," he said instead. "I'm sure you heard the most important parts already. Masterson's dead—I blew a bunch of stuff up. We got the money."

Burke cast a wary look toward the back seat where Cheshire had stashed the satchel. "Uh-huh."

"Burke...listen." Cheshire took a deep breath, stalling to get his proper thoughts in order. "I just wanted to say...I'm sorry." Burke gave him his full attention, and he started talking faster to keep from being interrupted. "Sorry I lied to you about me and Jakub. Sorry I've been, well...me. All the time." He rubbed the back of his neck self-consciously. "You've always been on my side and I've just made things harder on you."

"Kozlow's the one making things harder," Burke said with a jerky shrug. "Don't have to apologize for that part."

"Yeah, well..." Cheshire offered him a wince of a smirk. "I still should for what I'm about to do."

Burke sank deeper into his seat. "Fuck."

"Jakub and I are leaving town," Cheshire continued. He needed to get it all out before Burke started *really* swearing. "Tonight. We're not waiting around for Barney to find out about us, or for the cops to come down on Kozlow for their own getting killed." Despite his best efforts, some of his bitterness soaked into his tone. "It's not like Barney's ever gonna soften on me, so I'm through pretending he will. I'm out."

"You get what that means, right?" Burke asked, his voice hard. "The two of you take off outta here with a piece of the take, you know what'll happen."

"Yeah, and I'm saying, I'm sorry." Cheshire stopped at a red light, giving him the chance to face Burke seriously. "However this shakes out, he's going to be looking at you, next. That's why I wanted to give you the head's up as soon as I could."

"Fuck." Burke rubbed his face as it went through several different frustrated expressions. "Ye're really screwing me here, you—" He cut himself off, glaring intensely into his lap; Cheshire held his breath as he waited for him to continue. And he did, louder and harder than before. "No—fuck him— fuck *all* of them. I'm out too."

Cheshire's heart skipped. "It might not come to that," he said apologetically. "But you—"

"No, seriously, fuck them. Fuck Kozlow!" Burke gestured sharply as he carried on. "Ye're not the only one they've been dicking over all this time, y'know that, right? Stuck my neck out for them—backstabbed my own for them, and what's it gotten me? *We're* the ones that ended Foley. *We're* the ones that put Kozlow in the papers and on the map. Where's their gratitude, huh? Tossed out in the gutter, that's where!"

"You've been a team player for them the whole time," Cheshire encouraged him, continuing through the intersection. "That penthouse operation never would have gotten its legs if not for you."

"Ye're damn right it wouldn't!" Burke retorted. "Put my goddamn blood into that building!" He looked up through the windshield and grimaced as the Morey came into view. "Guess that's over, then. But whatever, fuck'm. They're never going to get their act together, and with Manhattan going down in flames the city's a lost cause for people like me. Time to cut my losses and move on."

"Burke..." Cheshire sighed. "I really am sorry."

Burke shook his head. "Naw, I know it ain't you. We both just backed the wrong horse." He sighed and pushed his hair back. "And I mean them—not me backing you."

Cheshire smirked even though his throat was suddenly tight. "Thanks, Burke."

They reached the two buildings, and Cheshire pulled the satchel full of cash out of the back as they climbed out. "You can come with us," he offered, determined not to think too far ahead to what that meant. "Depending on how this goes down..."

Burke was already shaking his head. "And be your third wheel? Not unless ye're giving me everything in that bag."

"Will five grand do?" Cheshire offered, already opening the satchel.

"No, shit, it's a joke, wiseass." Burke waved him off. "I don't need yer handouts. I've got a stash of my own up in the penthouse anyway."

Cheshire laughed, but as he closed the bag back up, his humor sobered. He offered his hand. "I'm gonna miss you, Eggy."

Burke eyed the hand for a moment as if there was a chance he might not accept. A pained look twisted his features but he wrangled it down before finally accepting. "Yeah, I know you will," he said, with an ease that didn't match the strength he put into his handshake.

Cheshire smiled, understanding, and he let Burke think for a minute that he was going to let the farewell pass with all manly pride intact. As soon as each let go and started to part, however, he added, "It's okay to cry, just don't let the girls see you."

"I'm not crying!" Burke shot back, casting Cheshire a glare before turning to hurry away. "Fucking blind, you are."

"You can dry your tears on that god-awful tie you're wearing," Cheshire continued to taunt, raising his voice the further Burke got from him. "Good excuse to buy something with taste!"

"Well you can—" Burke made a sound of frustrated exasperation and flipped him off. "Just get outta here!" he shouted, voice rougher than a moment ago, and he walked as fast as he could to the door. Cheshire grinned, warm with bittersweet relief, but when he headed for his building his attention was drawn by the unmarked police car parked across the street.

Forgot about them for a minute there, Cheshire thought, and despite the temptation he didn't acknowledge them as he continued inside. *We'll have to lose them before we head for the station, but we will. Nothing can stop us now.*

***

Jakub had told Cheshire he would wait half an hour before leaving himself. It was unquestionably the longest thirty minutes of his life.

After calling to arrange for a cab, he spent most of the wait pacing his apartment. He visited the window several times even though it didn't give him a view of anything except the alley below, he checked and rechecked his packed bags. He stopped himself again and again from lighting up a fresh cigarette after his last burned down, knowing that the pack would be empty by the time he left if he didn't. His chest buzzed with energy he couldn't use yet, and he couldn't stop thinking about Cheshire's slow, hopeful smile.

Just the two of us, he thought, anxious and ecstatic, his heart in his throat. *A whole new life.*

At some point he managed to calm down long enough to pick up the phone receiver. A portion of his enthusiasm turned sour as he dialed Miklos' number.

"Hello?" greeted a sleepy-sounded Miklos. "Miklos Horvay."

"It's Jakub. Sorry if I woke you."

"It's fine." Miklos yawned. "What is it?"

Jakub shook his head. After everything that had happened overnight, he'd forgotten that barely twelve hours had passed. If Miklos had gone straight home after work he probably hadn't heard one word about the heist and all that had followed. "I need to tell you something," Jakub said, determined to be clear with every word. "There was a job last night, and it went bad. I'm sure you'll be able to read all about it in the paper, even though not all of it is true. I think Jersey will be fine but you should stay away from here or Manhattan for a while, if you can help it. I don't know what happens now."

"Wow," said Mikos, waking up more and more. "That bad, huh? Are you all right?"

"I'm fine," Jakub said automatically, but then he had to pause a moment. "I'm all right, and so is Chesh, but it's bad enough that we can't stay." He took a deep breath. "We're leaving town, tonight."

"Oh." Jakub could hear him sigh on the other end amidst a rustle of fabric. "Well, damn. If it's as bad as that I'm sure you're right." His tone lightened with his familiar good humor. "Be careful out there, Kuba."

Jakub grimaced. In his excitement to have gained Cheshire's agreement he'd forgotten there were things he'd be leaving behind after all. "I'll write," he promised, twisting the phone cord in his fingers. "Plenty."

"I have the feeling I'll just have to keep reading the papers," Miklos teased. "But I'd like that."

He still sounded too well-resigned, and it made Jakub's palms itch. "We'll see each other again," Jakub insisted. "You found me after six years when I wasn't looking to be found. I'll write you an invitation this time."

Miklos was quiet for a moment, but Jakub could sense his gentle smile. "Okay," he said. "I'll look forward to it." He chuckled. "In the meantime, take care of that big ham of yours."

"I will. See you later, Miksa."

"You, too."

Jakub hung up. He had promised to wait a little longer, but the goodbye had him keyed up and a little anxious despite their promises, and he couldn't bear to stay put any longer. He swept through the apartment one last time even knowing there was nothing left worth taking, and finally he donned his coat, hefted his luggage and left.

He was just about to step into the elevator when Hannah came out of the stairwell, and their eyes met.

She caught on immediately. Jakub didn't even bother to keep the truth out of his face, or to try to come up with a passable lie or justification. He didn't even retreat into the elevator to escape. As Hannah's expression twisted with a pained look, Jakub kept still. It for some reason felt important to him that she know he wasn't running away; for the first time, he was running *toward*.

"Jakub," Hannah said. She took a hesitant step forward. "Please, don't."

"I'm sorry," Jakub said, though not as an apology for leaving.

Hannah took another step. "Let's talk about it. If it's—"

"This isn't about Bloom," Jakub interrupted her, not wanting to hear one more word about Cheshire from her mouth. "I don't belong here." Though he knew how much it would hurt for her to hear, he couldn't pretend anymore that the truth wasn't obvious. "Kozlow isn't family to me; it never has been. It's time for me to go."

Hannah's shoulders sagged with defeat, and as much as he meant the words, they still felt rotten in his stomach. "Take care of yourself," Jakub said, and he finally stepped into the elevator. She didn't try to stop him.

A couple of Barney's new boys were milling about in the lobby, having taken up positions by various street-facing windows to keep an eye out for cops. Jakub crossing to the entrance with luggage in tow turned a few eyes his way; it might have been smarter to sneak out the fire escape, even if that meant exciting the police's attention, but Jakub couldn't bring himself to care about them. He strode directly out of the building without acknowledging anyone.

Thankfully, his cab had arrived a few minutes early. Even before the driver could get out to offer help, he loaded his bags into the back seat and climbed in. He gave the driver Cheshire's address along with a wad of bills. "Make it quick."

"Yes, sir!" the man chirped, perhaps with some inkling of just who he was ferrying. He quickly put the car in gear.

As they pulled away from the curb, Jakub gazed up one last time at the old brick Kozlow building that had been home for so many years—longer than he'd called any other place home. He didn't like that thought much, and he tried to busy his imagination with the places he might call home next: another cramped city apartment, his guns wedged in among Cheshire's suits; maybe a fancy house in the suburbs with tall hedges a lawn full of soft, green grass for Cheshire to lord over their unsuspecting neighbors. It still almost didn't seem possible, but Jakub clung to each open path, letting that dusty old fortress slip away behind him.

***

It wasn't that Barney didn't believe it, or that he didn't *want* to believe it. He'd always known that it was only a matter of time before Cheshire Bloom showed his true colors and fucked them over. But believing it meant having to act on it, and *that* part, after what he'd seen the night before...was a little harder.

There was no denying it, though. He stood with Leon in the basement, poring over the collection of different bags and boxes they'd separated the bank vault take out into. One was missing.

"I told you," Leon said, trying to sound insistent and apologetic at the same time. "I saw him walk right out the front door with it."

"You watched him walk right out with it," Barney repeated, fixing him with a cold look.

Leon flinched back. "What was I supposed to do? I asked him about it, but he just kept going." He leaned back, carding his fingers through his hair. "You don't really think *I* stand a chance against him, do you? After last night?"

Barney scowled to hide his gulp. A few of the boys were starting to gather at the base of the stairs, and their expectant looks had him sweating. He pulled his cap off to smooth his hair back as he stalled. *It's not like he'd ever use that on us, but...* "Fuck. Who the hell does he think he is? He doesn't get to decide his share."

A murmur spread through the men gathered at the base of the stairs, and Hannah emerged. Her eyes were tired and red with emotion Barney had rarely seen on her, and it put him immediately on edge. He didn't want to ask what was the matter with so many people watching, so he offered only a shrug. "What?"

"What's going on?" Hannah asked, her voice as rough

- 310 -

as her expression.

"Bloom swiped part of the loot and took off with his little weasel," Leon blurted out. He cringed back when Barney shot him a glare, but it was too late.

Hannah's shoulders fell, though she didn't look surprised. "Does the boss know yet?"

"No." Barney folded his arms; the thought of having to climb the building and explain the truth to his father already had his stomach knotting. "It's fine," he said, shrugging again. "Jakub will handle it."

Hannah's weary eyes immediately turned hard. "What?"

"He and I talked about it already," Barney explained, though he didn't like the disdain creeping into the faces of his men. They didn't really expect him to chase after a witch himself, did they? As the boss's son? His palms grew clammy. "Bloom knows I'm on to him, so it'll be easier for Danowicz to get closer to him. He's going to teach him a lesson."

Hannah rubbed her face. What the hell was the matter with her anyway? Barney smacked Leon in the ribs. "Run up and call one of the boys over at Bloom's building on Kent. They can keep tabs on him until Danowicz catches up with him."

Hannah let out a sharp sigh as she straightened up. "Jakub's gone."

Barney stared at her in blank confusion. The words just didn't penetrate. "What?"

"Jakub's gone," Hannah repeated, not that it made any more sense the second time. The more she talked, though, the more Barney felt cold and heat scuttle over his skin like a feverish sensation. "He packed up his apartment and left. He and Bloom are leaving together."

"He wouldn't," Leon said, baffled. "He's one of the best we've got!"

His disbelief shook Barney open. "That's fucking stupid," Barney snapped. "He *just* told me he'd handle it—he *hates* that asshole!"

Hannah's face contorted into a strange, frustrated grin. "What?" Barney carried on loudly. "He does! We've all seen it!"

"Barney, the two of them have been in bed together, literally, for *years*," Hannah said, and Barney recoiled as if struck. "He's the last one that's going to do anything to Bloom now. They're *gone*."

Barney's head spun with confusion as everyone exchanged stunned looks. "I only just found out about it from Burke," Hannah continued in a gentler tone. "And it doesn't matter now, because they're not coming back. Whatever they took, just let them go."

Even in his shocked stupor, those final words carved into Barney's chest. "No," he said immediately, propelled by sheer instinct. Everyone was staring at him, and though he could barely get his eyes to focus he just *knew* what each of them looked like: they all thought he was a fool. A weak, cowardly fool who couldn't see what was right in front of him. The thought that Cheshire was speeding off with the money he'd bled for, that god-awful smirk on his smug face, was sickening enough. That Jakub, his brother-in-arms, had lied to his face for that traitor buffon's sake, was like a red-hot iron in his gut.

What would his father say? The suffocating dread of that explanation crowded out even the memory of the fire and brimstone from Harlem, and Barney gathered himself up.

"No, we go after them," he demanded. He gave Leon a shove. "Call the boys on Kent and tell them to stay on Bloom no matter what."

Hannah blinked at him in disbelief. "What? No. Barney, just let—"

"Call *everyone*," Barney told the rest of the gang, and they each nodded and gathered themselves up; everyone who hadn't been in on the heist was eager for a fight, and seeing them rise to his orders filled in any gaps in Barney's confidence. "There are only so many ways they can skip town; we'll chase them down and ambush them. We're not scared of a few fireworks, are we?"

The boys all grunted their agreement and started back up the stairs. Even Leon, already pale, bobbed his head and hurried after to make the calls. Barney squared his shoulders and followed after, a hard coil of anger winding tight in his chest.

"Barney, this is stupid," Hannah said as she followed him up the stairs. "You saw what Bloom can do."

"I don't care if he's a witch or the devil himself," Barney shot back. "I've got *this*." He patted the revolver tucked into his belt. "All I need is one shot at him." He ground his teeth as he fixed his gaze ahead. "One for *both* of them. Get your gun and come on."

He stormed ahead, and just like he knew she would, Hannah sighed and fell into line.

***

When Jakub arrived at the building on Kent, he spotted Cheshire's car but not Cheshire himself. The doors were unlocked, so he shoved his luggage into the back seat and went inside. The lobby was empty, but when he reached the elevator the door opened, and a man inside flinched at the sight of him. Jakub recognized him as one of Leon's cousins who had moved into the building alongside Cheshire, and the wary look in his eye told Jakub everything he was afraid of: Hannah had already spread the news.

"Excuse me," Jakub said coldly, and the man bobbed his head as he darted out of the elevator, sweat on his brow. As the doors closed Jakub in, he could see the man heading straight for the payphone next to the front desk.

Shit, Jakub thought, and he checked the revolver in his holster to make sure it was fully loaded. *This could get ugly.*

He knocked on Cheshire's door, and it took long enough for Cheshire to answer that he started to get nervous. When the door opened and Cheshire grinned at him, dressed in a fresh, green suit and positively effervescent, his worries briefly washed away. He tugged Cheshire into a quick, urgent kiss.

Cheshire chuckled against his mouth. "I'll take that to mean you're ready to go," he said. "Let me just grab my stuff."

Cheshire moved deeper into the apartment. As Jakub peered inside, he realized that not much had been disturbed, and the only bags Cheshire had prepared were two large garment bags and a satchel. He frowned. "Are you only bringing clothes?"

"What else is there?" Cheshire replied earnestly, and Jakub had to admit he didn't have retort for that. He ducked into the bedroom, and when he emerged it was with a paper bag. He grinned hopefully as he offered it up. "For you."

Jakub blinked at it in confusion. "What for?"

"Just because!" Cheshire pushed it toward him, so Jakub finally accepted and reached inside. "Honestly, I bought it as a birthday present, but in all these years you never did tell me what the actual day was. But I know it's in April, and it's still April now, so..." He gestured for Jakub to continue.

Jakub pulled out the gift: a cap of brown wool, bearing a short bill and a buttoned strap on the side. Though much simpler than anything he would have expected Cheshire to pick out, even Jakub's untrained eye could see that it was hand stitched, and expertly so.

"I didn't know we'd be going anywhere when I bought it," Cheshire prattled on, and he watched, hawklike, as Jakub donned the cap. "But you could use a travel cap now, right? What do you think?"

"It fits," Jakub said. He held still as Cheshire reached forward to smooth his bangs back, under the hem, but he didn't care for that and immediately combed them down again. "How does it look?"

Cheshire laughed. "It looks perfect on you. Do you like it?"

"Yeah." Jakub felt his cheeks grow hot; it was a ridiculous thing to get emotional over, considering the position they were in and what they might soon face, but he wished he knew better how to express to Cheshire just how happy the gesture made him. "Thank you."

Despite those shy shortcomings, when Cheshire's smile widened it seemed he understood after all. "You're welcome," he said, and he kissed Jakub on the cheek. Jakub swayed forward, looking for something more, but then Cheshire turned sheepish as he returned to his luggage. "There's, uh, one more thing. And before you say anything, I'm sorry."

"Sorry?" Jakub frowned, but when he got a better look at the satchel Cheshire was scooping up, recognition sent his heart pounding. "Is that—"

"I know, I know," said Cheshire, though he didn't really sound *that* apologetic. He motioned for Jakub to head out and followed right after; he didn't bother to lock the door behind him. "And I'm pretty sure Leon knows I have it, so we should probably get a move on."

Jakub pursed his lips, but any irritation he might have felt over Cheshire's impulsiveness crumbled before it could form. "Hannah knows something's up, too," he admitted as they headed for the elevator. "She saw me leaving with my things."

"Then we should *absolutely* get a move on."

They came out of the elevator into the lobby, and

immediately Jakub spotted Leon's cousin again, talking into the payphone. He eyed them as they passed, voice too low to hear. Jakub watched his free hand hesitating at his belt.

"Hey, Bloom," the man called. "Where are you—"

"Fuck off, Szpilman," Jakub snapped, one hand on his revolver, and the man quickly ducked back, even the phone monetarily forgotten. They continued out uninterrupted again.

Cheshire shot Jakub a high-browed look as he stowed his garment bags in the back seat of the car, alongside Jakub's things. Jakub frowned at him in return. "What?"

"Nothing!" Cheshire smirked. "I love it when you're bossy." Jakub blushed, but before he could think of a retort, Cheshire handed him the money satchel. "Take a peek while we drive. I'm not even sure how much I took."

Jakub took the satchel with him to the passenger side, and as Cheshire pulled them away from the curb, he began thumbing through the bands of bills. His eyes grew wider as he went, and he glanced behind them with renewed paranoia as if expecting Barney to already be on their tail. He couldn't tell if the cars behind them were following or not. "There's twenty thousand in here," he said. "That's a third of the take, not counting the deposit boxes."

Cheshire whistled. "Just try and say we didn't contribute more than one third of the effort into getting us out of that mess alive last night, I dare you."

Jakub closed the bag back up, his mind whirling again with the possibilities of the life they might now have. "This is good. It'll last us for a long while."

Cheshire hummed a few bars of an aimless melody, staring forward with such fixed attention that something *had* to be on his mind. Jakub gave him a while to get the words out; normally his patience would have worn out, but he instead prodded at his new hat, enjoying the stiff shape of the wool.

"Did you really mean all that up in the apartment?" Cheshire said at last. "The part about going clean, I mean."

"Yeah. Kinda." Jakub frowned. "We could. We can do almost anything."

Cheshire cast him a surprised glance, and it wasn't until then that Jakub realized how childish he must have sounded. He scrubbed the back of his palm across his mouth. "I didn't think that far ahead yet."

Cheshire's disbelief softened into fondness that didn't help Jakub's embarrassment any. "Almost anything," he echoed, and he grinned. "Lots of places that could use a tough guy and his charming partner," he said.

"You weren't bad as a landlord," Jakub volunteered. "You filled the Morey up." He paused, grimacing. "I'm sorry you have to leave it."

Cheshire waved off his concern. "It's a'right. I was more a pretty face than a landlord anyway. I know a thing or two about selling a con." He laughed. "Maybe I'll go into politics!"

In other circumstances, Jakub might have immediately voiced his concerns; driving through the city toward freedom, a new life theirs for the taking, he couldn't consider anything from Cheshire a bad idea. "Whatever you want," he said. "Wherever we want."

"Yeah," said Cheshire, and he grinned openly as they continued their race north.

They made good time to the ferry station, though once there they didn't have any choice but to abandon the car. Cheshire sold it to a woman in the parking lot for ten dollars, and then they were off again, chugging across the river on a rickety old boat. Given his recent misadventures, Jakub stayed as far away from the railing as he could, his stomach anxiously knotting with every subtle lurch. Cheshire kept his arm around his shoulders the entire way across.

On the opposite bank they caught a taxi, and the escape continued. It was a long drive north, at first through bustling morning city streets, then past suburbs and into rural roads and flowering trees. The relative tranquility of the countryside tricked Jakub into forgetting for a while just how many people might have known about their plans, and what danger could be waiting for them. With the cabbie's ears open they couldn't have discussed it anyway, so Cheshire filled the time with idle chatter.

"Y'know, I don't think I've ever been on a train," he said. "I even missed the last one *you* were on. Sure wish I'd been there for it; things might have worked out very differently."

"There's no point wondering about that now," Jakub told him. "We're okay." Cheshire gave his hand a squeeze that helped to fuel him the rest of the trip.

It was approaching noon by the time they reached the

train station. It was a small yard, with only two platforms and a charming old building that sold lunches as well as tickets. The next train out of town wouldn't be leaving for another hour, so Cheshire bought them each a ticket, and they sat outside with their luggage, eating sandwiches.

"Did the ticket clerk give us a strange look?" Jakub asked, not looking back at the building. "He seemed tense."

He was hoping Cheshire would tell him he was imagining things, but no such luck. "He did," said Cheshire. "The taxi driver and the ferryman did, too." He shrugged. "Guess we're just that famous now."

It's not me that everyone recognizes, Jakub thought, without blame; he was more concerned about Cheshire's safety than anything else. The thought that they could come so far only to be stopped by an over-eager cop or *especially* some Kozlow ally was a sickening one. "After we're out of here, we should switch trains as soon as we can. There's too many people on our trail."

Cheshire nodded along and gulped down the rest of his sandwich. "There's an outfit up in Boston that might be willing to put us up for a while. Or we could head out west. I never did get to meet Herb's fancy Chicago guests. Or further west than that!" He chuckled to himself, grinning with each possibility. "They've got legal gambling out in Nevada now. Or say we hit up sunny California? A heist in every state from here to the coast!"

He laughed some more, and Jakub leaned in closer, glad to see him in good spirits.

An hour later, their train pulled into the station as promised. Its passengers disembarked, and as the staff began making preparations for the next board, Jakub felt his nerves creeping up on him again. It didn't seem real that they were only a few steps away from their escape. He continued to stay close to Cheshire as they each pushed to their feet, willing his unending optimism to rub off on him. Those hopes were dashed when a squeal of tires drew his attention to the station's parking lot, where three cars were jerking to a halt. All their doors started opening at once, and without waiting to make out any faces, Jakub reached for his gun. "Chesh, the bags—"

Cheshire turned, but before he could reach down a man leaned out of the nearest of the cars and opened fire. The platform erupted in pandemonium. Departing and would-be passengers screamed and ran in all directions, those that were close enough fleeing to the station building, while others scattered up and down the tracks. Jakub returned fire and thought he clipped the man, but by then the rest of the cars were turning out their goons as well. There were too many guns already firing, and even when Cheshire's magic exploded the front bumper off one of the cars, the men didn't retreat. Without any other cover on hand, Jakub and Cheshire abandoned their suitcases and made a dash for the nearest train car. As soon as they were through the doors several of the windows were shattered by gunfire, and they ducked to the floor beneath a hail of glass.

"Spread out!" Barney shouted to his men, and Jakub clenched his jaw. All the anger he'd felt staring Barney down in the cellar rushed forward once more, and part of him was grossly relieved he had the chance to channel that now. But that thinking was also dangerous, and instinctively he reached into his jacket for a cigarette. As satisfying as it might be to risk everything for one shot at Barney, they needed to keep a cooler head to get out of there alive.

Thankfully, Cheshire seemed to have gotten that memo in advance. He crouched down beneath the windows of the train car, his expression as calm and attentive as Jakub had ever seen on him. "Figures," he muttered.

"Bloom! Danowicz!" Barney shouted as the screams from the bystanders thinned out and faded away. "Come on out! The longer you draw this out, the worse I wanna hurt you."

Jakub snorted as he lit his cigarette. Rich, to hear Barney talk like that. It boosted his confidence more than it probably should have. *No matter how many of his borrowed goons he has out there, between Cheshire's magic and my gun, they don't stand a chance. I'll put a bullet in anyone who tries to stop us.*

"Can you see the bags?" he asked, lifting his head.

Cheshire was already peeking through the half-shattered window, distracted. "I guess we should have known they wouldn't let us skip town that easily."

Jakub worked his metallic fingers to make sure they were up to the incoming task. "It might have gone over better if you hadn't taken their twenty large," he retorted.

But he was only teasing, and Cheshire must have seen

as much, because he flashed Jakub a smirk. "Why, Jakub," he taunted back, "I thought you *liked* money."

They were interrupted by a sharp *clink* from out on the platform: a metallic percussion so pronounced, so recognizable, that Jakub knew immediately what would happen next. He snatched Cheshire by his tie as the closest handhold and yanked him down, further away from the door. Seconds later the Hallorran bullet hit, and the traincar rocked with a bone-rattling explosion and searing heat. The stinging, noxious smoke that plumed out from the blast was so unlike Cheshire's magic it made Jakub sick. Then it cleared, and the pair of them sat up and stared at the charred hole Barney's revolver had punched clear through the train.

Jakub turned quickly to look his partner over, and was relieved to find him unharmed—startled, a half-panicked grin tugging at his lips, but unharmed. "Cheshire," he said. "The bags."

"Right." Cheshire blinked off the remaining shell-shock from the blast. "They're right where we left them. "

A good twenty feet from here, then, Jakub thought, and just to be on the safe side, he fished out the winding key for his arm. A few turns of the mainspring and he was confident it would hold up for however long the conflict dragged on. "Do you think you can cover me long enough to reach my suitcase?" he asked.

"Oh, I think I can do that and then some," Cheshire replied, his voice already sharp and eager for it.

Jakub thought to caution him—they didn't need a repeat of the night before—but he closed his teeth around the words before they made it out. If after everything Barney had seen, he had still chosen to come after them for money they were owed, he deserved a firestorm and then some.

So much for cooler heads, Jakub thought, and he flinched as Cheshire plucked the cigarette out of his mouth.

"Let me borrow this," said Cheshire, and he smirked as he tossed the cig out the window.

It exploded the moment it touched the ground, louder and flashier than Cheshire would have normally pulled from something so small. The familiar, tangy smell of his magic was a strange comfort, even when overlayed with the cursing and shouting from Barney's unprepared goons. *We can do this,*

Jakub thought, his body coiling tight as he watched Cheshire also tensing in preparation. *As long as we're together, we can do anything.*

"Jakub," Cheshire said, "whatever happens—"

He didn't need to finish; Jakub already understood. He surged forward and pressed a kiss to Cheshire's mouth, a solid affirmation that sent his heart thudding. *We can do anything,* he thought again, and as he leaned back he locked eyes with Cheshire to convey exactly that. *"Go."*

Cheshire grinned. "Aye, aye," he said, and he pulled himself out of the train, Jakub just behind.

***

Barney and his men were just pulling themselves together again as Cheshire emerged. He had brought a dozen of them—mostly over-eager nobodies that had no idea what their gang owed to sweet-talking, safe-cracking Cheshire Bloom. But there was no time for pageantry this time; determined to provide the cover Jakub needed, Cheshire immediately turned the empty platform into smokey chaos. His gaze snapped from discarded luggage to public trash cans, exploding each into fire and ash. The blasts sent grown men scattering and blinded those who stood their ground, trying to return fire.

They really thought they could count on Barney and his one little gun? Cheshire thought, brimming with satisfaction as Barney threw himself behind a pillar to escape an exploding purse. *We'll teach'm, won't we, Jake?*

Jakub was only a few steps away from the bags. Cheshire recognized the Szpilman from his building nearby, gun up and aimed, and without a second thought he focused his magic on the trash can beside him. The metal drum exploded, shrapnel splintering in all directions. The Szpilman cried out and was quickly swallowed up by the smoke. It gave Jakub the last few seconds he needed to reach his rifle case, and out came the big gun. He was a sight to behold, and Cheshire hurried toward him as he leveled the rifle at their remaining adversaries.

If ever there was a scene fit for the papers. Cheshire continued to blow up everything he could get in his sights, disrupting their would-be assassins long enough for Jakub to take them out. Any advantage Barney thought he had with numbers evaporated as those that could turned and fled, blistered from the magic, while others fell to Jakub's gun. Cheshire thought he might have even seen Leon limping into cover behind the station. His palms radiated heat, but it was Jakub's warmth against his back that heightened his every sense. *This* was why he had stayed. He and his partner, back to back against the world, ready at last to claim their freedom. *This* was why he'd welcomed his magic in the first place. He looked for Barney among the chaos, eager to settle their long feud once and for all.

A bullet raked across Cheshire's right ear with a stinging pain, and he lurched back as his glasses were sent tumbling off his face. The fiery battleground he had been in such control of was suddenly a blurry mess. He tried to hastily reassemble a map of the landscape in his mind's eye, but Jakub calling his name, turning toward him, only made it harder to focus. They didn't have time for Jakub to worry about him.

"Traitors!" Barney shouted from further down the platform, and there it was again: the heavy *clink* of the Hallorran revolver. Cheshire knew that even if he could visualize Barney well enough to destroy him, the gun was already firing and it would be too late.

No, Cheshire thought, even greater heat flooding into his open palm. He could picture far too easily the bullet leaving the barrel, Jakub standing directly in its path. *No—why do I have magic at all if not for this?*

He felt the seal on his palm sting like a white-hot brand—felt the rush of wind and smoke a moment later. He couldn't see but he could *see* the bullet shatter apart from the fire he'd lit inside it. The blast reversed all momentum, like a shockwave knocking down whoever had until then remained standing. He heard Barney scream, heard bodies thumping onto the platform, and then...quiet. The smoke began to thin and the station at last fell still.

***

Jakub held his breath. His gaze swept over the destroyed platform, a fire or two still burning in places, Barney's dozen goons either collapsed or fled. Barney himself lay motionless several yards away, blood on his face and shirt from the explosion that had gone off so close to his face. The layer of biting smoke over Cheshire's magic was proof enough that the Hallorran had gone off, but it had all happened so fast Jakub wasn't sure what to make of it.

Did he explode the bullet in mid-air? he thought, looking to Cheshire in stunned awe. "I didn't know you could do that," he said.

"Me, neither," Cheshire admitted, looking to his open palm in similar amazement. He drew it closer, squinting. "What *did* I do? I can't see a damn thing."

Jakub continued to stare at him, speechless. Cheshire had done the impossible but he was far more concerned with poking at his bleeding right ear. "Crap," he muttered, "I can't believe they shot my *other* ear. It must be some kind of rite of passage." He pressed his hand flush to the ear to staunch the bleeding. "It's not even properly symmetrical."

Jakub sighed; leave it to Cheshire to be more concerned about the scar than anything. He didn't seem to have any idea yet what they'd finally accomplished and what it meant for them. But that was fine. If Cheshire could go straight back to being himself after all that, they would be just fine.

Jakub let the gun slip from his hands. "Well," Cheshire started to say, "I guess we survi—"

Jakub drew them together for a kiss. Any moment now time would start back up, and they'd be off and running again, into new dangers—into a new life. But first he wanted his kiss. Light as air and overflowing with relief and affection, Jakub leaned into Cheshire's warm and charming mouth. By the time they pulled back, he was sure he could have grown wings.

Cheshire squinted at him. "Are you *smiling?*"

Jakub's cheeks went hot. "I thought you couldn't see," he retorted, but when Cheshire's quiet laughter tickled his ears, he couldn't deny it; he *was* smiling.

Voices picked up in the distance, along with the bells from fire trucks and police sirens. Jakub took a deep breath to refill his composure and then stooped down for Cheshire's glasses. One of the arms was broken but he helped Cheshire fit the frame to his face enough to see for the moment. "We have to get out of here," he said hurriedly. "Should we steal a car?"

"They'll be on us by then," said Cheshire, and suddenly a wolfish grin spread across his face. "Grab the bags—I've got an idea."

He headed for the front of the train, and though Jakub understood at once, he didn't have it in him to tell Cheshire that stealing a locomotive was probably a *terrible* idea. He stashed his rifle back in its case and drew Cheshire's garment bags over his shoulder, but as he rose, ready to make a run for it, his attention was drawn by a shift of movement.

Hannah was kneeling next to Barney. The sight of the blood slicking his face gave Jakub a chill, though he realized soon afterward that he was still breathing after all. The thought that he would finally wake up to cops and handcuffs was a fitting one, and it kept him from drawing his gun. Instead he watched Hannah take off her suit coat and press it over him to try to stop the bleeding. Her face was hard-set with frustration he'd seen on her plenty of times, and despite the finality with which they had parted earlier, deep down he did hope that she would at least realize she had her own chance to escape.

Hannah raised her head. There was a twisted kind of apology in her face, something in her grimace that said *I told him so*. But what she said was, "Good luck, Jakub." Jakub nodded, and he hurried toward the front of the train.

Something exploded, and Jakub's pulse picked up all over again as he hurried to the engine car. Once he got closer, the trail of smoke leading to the destroyed coupler explained plenty. "This is going to be a lot easier to track than a car," he said as he climbed aboard.

Cheshire helped him set everything down and then directed him toward the front. "We won't take it far," he assured Jakub as he showed off the engineer's manual. "Just to get us away from here. We can dump it somewhere more scenic and *then* steal a car."

They didn't have much other choice. With the engine already prepped for their *scheduled* departure, manual in hand and a few lucky guesses, one last pull of a lever had the train lurching forward. With a *chug, chug, chug* the engine began to pull away from the station, leaving its passenger cars and the devastated Kozlow gang behind. Jakub leaned out the back, and as they began to truly pick up speed he spotted a half dozen cops flooding onto the platform.

"We'll have to stop before the next station," Jakub said as he returned to Cheshire's side at the front. "As soon as they realize what happened, they'll call ahead and—"

Cheshire wrapped his arm around Jakub's waist and tugged him closer. How ridiculous, he thought, that after everything even a simple gesture like that could take his breath away. "We will," Cheshire promised him, his face alight with hopeful exuberance as the train sped them onward. "Don't worry, Jakub. We made it." He grinned. "We're going to be just fine."

Jakub relaxed into his arms. "Yeah," he said, believing it. "I know we will."

They leaned close together as the train carried them on, toward their next adventures and a new life.

THE END...

...OR IS IT!?

The prequel series has ended, but Jakub and Cheshire's adventures continue in Bang! Bang! BOOM! the graphic novel, written by Melanie Schoen with art by Del Borovic. Please visit our website to purchase in print or digital, and follow us on social media for updates!

www.bangbangboomcomic.com
🐦 @BBBOOMComic
📷 @BangBangBoomComic
𝐭 @BangBangBoomComic

CPSIA information can be obtained
at www.ICGtesting.com
Printed in the USA
FSHW011404160820